"Smith's talent for characterization and creating convincing aliens is remarkable."
—*Aboriginal Science Fiction*

To the Phneri, every spot of blood, every crumb of dirt, every wound and scar and broken bone, tells a story. By dissecting each sinew and bone of Ekkikka's body, Akktri and his warren had reconstructed his death and life. Somewhere inside himself, my partner remembered a bullet, fired from my pistol, smashing into *his* body. "You feel it, don't you?" I asked.

"Yes, Beverlee," said Akktri. "You shoot strong but artless." He jerked his chest the way Ekkikka had cartwheeled and fell to a chilling imitative death.

I shuddered.

"David Alexander Smith's worlds are solid and well realized places where the reader can slam the doors and not have the chrome fall off . . . he writes science fiction meant to be read by grownups."
—Alexander Jablokov, author of CARVE THE SKY

"A fascinating tour through the author's imagination."
—*SF Chronicle*

Tor books by David Alexander Smith

Future Boston
In the Cube

DAVID ALEXANDER SMITH
IN THE CUBE

TOR®

A TOM DOHERTY ASSOCIATES BOOK
NEW YORK

This is a work of fiction. All the characters and events portrayed in this book are fictitious, and any resemblance to real people or events is purely coincidental.

IN THE CUBE

Cover art by Wayne Barlowe

A Tor Book
Published by Tom Doherty Associates, Inc.
175 Fifth Avenue
New York, N.Y. 10010

Tor® is a registered trademark of Tom Doherty Associates, Inc.

ISBN: 0-812-52374-1
Library of Congress Catalog Card Number: 93-7997

First edition: August 1993
First mass market edition: August 1994

Printed in the United States of America

0 9 8 7 6 5 4 3 2 1

To the old maestro
John Dickson Carr
who turned me on to mysteries

Acknowledgments

My eternal thanks and special praise go to three people for their unflagging efforts. *Alexander Jablokov* relentlessly shot holes in the mystery and then helped me patch them up. *Dee Morrison Meaney* restrained my similes and played matchmaker for Bev. *Sarah W. R. Smith* kept the Phneri truly alien.

Four other individuals also worked on the manuscript as if it were their own. *Rene Bane* defended Bev against sexism. *Barb Hendee* helped Bev's character evolve and change. *Jim Kenney* taught Bev the tricks of the detective trade. *Steven Popkes* nurtured overall thematic structure like one of his bonsai.

Acknowledgment must also go to the Cambridge Science Fiction Writers Workshop, for it was the incubator of *Future Boston,* the universe in which this novel is set. So I owe gratitude to the FuBos working group: Jon Burrowes, Steve Caine, Pete Chvany, Jr., Alex Jablokov, Geoff Landis, Resa Nelson, Steve Popkes, Sarah Smith, and Terri Windling. All these folks worked hard, chipped in, and cared about the book. Few writers are favored with such good and talented friends as these.

Finally, acknowledgment must go to those whose creations wandered into the story and who allowed them to remain. The popcorn aliens kindly sold me Jon Burrowes; Alex and the Targives contributed the bioengineered menagerie; and Sarah and Resa found the first Phner.

Cambridge, Massachusetts
July 1988–April 1992

1

"MY BEVERLEE, WAKE up quick-k-k!" Sharp claws pricked my throat.

Water spewed under the doorjamb, flooding around the windowsills, lifting furniture. I thrashed toward the door and seized the knob, but the inrush pressure held it shut. The torrent raised me up until my face was squeezed against the ceiling, my nose and mouth closed. I was drowning in a Basement corridor. I tried to scream for my father but my mouth wouldn't open.

Akktri bent over me, his hands on my chest. His buckteeth overhung his small, downturning mouth.

My head buzzed from the blast of a stunner. "What happened?"

"If-f-fraim is k-k-killed, Beverlee," he said in his high Phner voice. "See here!" He tugged the sleeve of my good shoulder. "You end his art."

My eyeballs vibrated as I groped into a sitting position. Ifraim Lemos was a cheapjack parolee, one of the score of grifters I made a few beans monitoring for the City. A few hours ago he'd left his permitted zone, so I'd roused myself to track his beeper signal, a tricky proposition in the Boston Cube, where you have to think in three dimensions *and* remember all the twisty corridors. I had expected to find him drinking, toking, carousing, or engaging in similar harmless peccadilloes. I'd tailed him, caught him, and——then what? Stunners that knock you out jangle short-term memory. I stood and swayed.

Ifraim had fallen on his back onto a pile of discarded light fixtures, arms outflung as if crucified, face twisted in agony. A huge splotch of blood, brown and clotted with dust, filled the cavern where his chest had been, flesh and clothing marooned in it.

Mechanically I bent and lifted his side. Spongy meat fell from a huge ragged hole in his back. I retched, dropped the body, and knelt on the floor. "I did—this?"

Akktri came up next to me in consolation. "Beverlee, he is artful dead." He extended his arm in a half-comforting, touchless gesture reminiscent of my brother Mack.

I squeezed my eyes shut to avoid seeing the gore that soaked my trousers. "I've never made art."

"You soon make more art, just after." Akktri has trouble with verb tenses, time sequences, and causality—*before* and *after* are almost the same word in Phner. He bounced up and scowled in a posture that I'd come to recognize was his perfect imitation of myself when I'm exasperated with Mack. "See! See!"

A golden brown ball of fur that resembled a beaver with a short, stubby tail was crumpled against some black moulded plastic rocks. "Ekkikka Phner dies too."

I staggered over to the little body. Ekkikka's fur, fine and silky, was spiked with crusted blood. "How?"

"You shoot many shoots." Akktri scuttled between my legs to look at his dead fellow. He put his hand into the chest cavity, lifted skin, and stuck his nose in close, the better to see and esfn the splintered ribs. "Tza tza tza!" He fisted air to imitate bullets whizzing. "You hit Ifraim. He falls, boom. You shoot and shoot. You shoots Ekkik-k-ka Phner." He fell limply and his body assumed the exact crumple of the nearby corpse. "As it is."

I turned the dead neck to see the small pinched face with its shoebutton brown eyes, and swallowed. "I didn't mean to. I'm sorry."

"No, no!" Akktri stamped his foot and again I recognized

the gesture, this time as one of my own. "You *want* Ifraim dead, because he stuns you. So you shoots even though he is recently-dead-but-not-worth-esfn'ing." At least that's what I think the word Akktri used means. "Now-soon-future-certain we esfn Ek-k-kikka," my companion added.

Half a dozen more Phneri came up around us. They'd probably heard the shots and recognized one of their own from the crunch pattern of the fracturing bones. They lifted the body. "Rods come," finished Akktri cheerfully. "You go to jail." They bore it away like pallbearers.

I went back to Ifraim Lemos's cooling corpse and settled myself into a broken-seated plastic chair, kicking my feet among peeling wallpaper strips, flaps of loose yellow and pink paint, and gypsum crumbles.

Above me, steel I-beams were thatched with prock infill to support Boston's hundred and eighty interlocking stories. Most of the Basement, the Cube's bottom ten levels, is plain corridors and rooms the same as upfloor, but Ifraim had fled into an area of unfinished urbhole: exposed two-by-fours, terra-cotta tiles, and cemented cinder blocks, all crisscrossed with pipes, wires, ventilation ducts, and abandoned bric-a-brac. Most of it is damp and pungent with stale odors absorbed permanently into the porous surfaces.

The Phneri swear that, after the Siege and Iris Sherwood's great Basement Flood, they scoured all the ocean slime out of Boston, but to anyone who lived through that awful summer of 2061, the Basement always smells like the sea, the sea that lies just outside Boston's prock walls, the sea that invaded our ways and killed Billy O'Meara, my father. The sea air is the breath of death.

Years ago, this theater had been the Elks Hall. Now it was thick with dust and debris. Rugrats and aliens had systematically stripped everything of value, leaving only junk without parentage: a hospital stretcher with tubular metal dropsides, a dented trombone slide piece, and in the corner a deflated basketball.

Boston's Basement is my turf. I make my living in the Basement. I find things and people down here.

But though I'd carried a projectile gun all the years since I got my license, I had no deaths on my conscience. Now I had two.

My cheeks still burned from the stunner. A pissmop emerged from the shadows, snuffling toward Ifraim's body, but his urine was mingled with his blood. Dissatisfied, the Targive-modified miniature dromedary slurped into the darkness, hawking and spitting, looking for another yellow oasis.

Tiny explosions popped——bursting epidermal cells destroyed by the stunner——as I massaged my left thigh to bring life back into it. Ifraim's angry face was white and blue at the lips and eyelids. A fragment of just-recovered memory flickered before my eyes: Ifraim's features registering outrage as my bullet blew his chest apart, his cheeks and eyeballs flaring red from hydrokinetic shock.

You don't need a license to buy a stunner and, if you're clever, you can illegally modify it to crank up its power. Ifraim Lemos was a fool, but he must have found a clever friend. I was a fool too. Underestimating him wasn't the first time I'd been stupid, just the worst. I was lucky to be alive.

Three rods arrived a moment later and took in the scene at a glance. "Was that necessary?" asked the larger of the two women, nudging Ifraim's torso with her foot. Her breast patch read Sergeant Magdalena Ahumada.

"He stunned me." I nodded at Ifraim's weapon, fallen from his hand.

She picked it up, frowned at the modifications, and clucked. "This baby must've hurt bad," she said with a trace of reluctant sympathy. "Your license, please. Who the hell are you?"

"Beverly O'Meara." I fished out my Boston Key. "Investigator. Part-time parole officer."

"Uh huh. Meat eye and cubehunter." Sergeant Ahumada stuffed the key in her reader. "Okay, so that's why you were hunting him. Well, where's the bot eye, dammit?" she demanded of the other two rods. "Where's the blackbird?"

"You can see it was self-defense," I said as we craned our necks, searching for a black occluding circle. "Life-threatening situation, justifying deadly force." I hoped I was telling the truth. "The reads'll verify it."

In fact, reads are often incomplete—even Iris's eyes don't look everywhere at once. A confident demeanor sways both people and eyes.

"Looks like it," she replied with no more commitment or emotion than if she were predicting the weather. She took my arm. Her grip was strong. "Why are your hands shaking?"

"Chula Conrad," said a voice above us.

We turned and looked. A blackbird floated imperiously near the ceiling. "Deputy Assistant Secretary to City Operator Iris Sherwood," it said.

The two other rods snickered at this pomposity, but were careful to do it silently and out of the eye's vision.

"D'you get any of this?" Ahumada asked the hoverer.

"Some." The blackbird lowered itself. "Plug in your reader."

She pulled the small rectangular screen from her belt and keyed it on. Onscreen we saw an overhead shot of the corridor whizzing by, date-time-location displayed in the lower left corner. "The eye is moving toward the incident," Conrad said. Corridors and doors went nova, brightening and expanding as the lenses readjusted from light to darkness.

I watched the fringes of the screen, searching for Ekkikka's image. Was he in the read? Would Ahumada uncover his death and charge me with negligent senticide?

Seen from high above, I tumbled backwards at Ifraim Lemos's first blast, crashing into the metalwork. A wobbled close-up as Ifraim cranked up his stunner, a black baton as long as my forearm with a wide can on the firing end, to maximum. At the edge of the fish-eye view, a crescent-shaped Beverly O'Meara flailed in distant pain.

A bomb went off in Ifraim's abdomen. Red blood sprayed behind him. The stunner, flung free, twirled. Lemos crashed to the ground, his head bouncing, then his body froze as the eye stopped the action.

"Inconclusive," said Chula Conrad.

Ahumada thoughtfully tapped the stunner handle against her palm. "Guess it's all right," she allowed, tugging her long black hair. She sounded disappointed. "You got any better reads, or should we just close this file now?"

Instead of replying, the eye resumed playback. "O'Meara is blinded," Conrad narrated icily. "She is still firing." My arm rose like an addled cobra and bullets shot every which way, the fish-eye lens distorting their paths into hyperbolas as they ricocheted out of sight. The picture cut to a different view, evidently from another blackbird arriving from the opposite direction. "A Phner is hit." My bullet pulverized Ekkikka's body. He splattered through the air, slammed into the wall, fell in a dustrag heap. I looked away.

"Lemos has now expired. O'Meara is unconscious," said Conrad. "You have clear grounds for a charge of reckless sentslaughter. Guard the Phner corpse. Confiscate O'Meara's weapon. They are evidence. A copy of this read is being filed with the Operations Director and the Chief of Police. Conrad out." He finished and I wondered what else was on that read, and why Chula Conrad had shown us only parts.

"You didn't mention the bystander," snapped the sergeant, spinning around at me.

"I was stunned. My memory——"

"Sure, sure." Ahumada reholstered her reader. "Surrender your weapon. Where's the body?"

I handed her the pistol and made a show of looking about. "You mean it's not here?"

Ahumada swore. "No corpus delicti. The child-eaters must have made off with it while you were conked out." I clamped my jaw shut at her slander of my companion's species. She fumed for a moment, then said, "You know, you're damned lucky."

"How so, Sergeant?" I asked softly, though I knew what she meant.

She grunted. "If the Phneri took the body, we'll never see it again."

"But you have the reads," I said, though I thought I knew the answer. "And the Phneri are sents of Boston."

"No body, no case," said Ahumada. "Archaic Bostonian criminal laws. But watch your throat in the night, dearie. The little buggers have race memory and they *all* have sharp claws. Now go home."

"You're not filing charges?"

"Of what?" she growled at me as the blackbird rose and disappeared. "I got no evidence. Nothing to prosecute. Vent." She was frustrated. "Got it, meat?"

"Got it, Sergeant. May I have my gun back?"

Ahumada glowered. "Don't push it, meat eye. Go home and live with yourself."

I cringed and left.

Sometimes I wish Boston were less compact. The seven minutes it took me to get home were too little to calm my shakes. With my hand on the doorplate, I paused and flinched, remembering my stunner nightmare, the cataract of water pouring onto me. Taking a deep breath, I opened the door and closed it behind me, ignoring my parrot's perky synthevoice greeting, and sat in my big chair. My tired eyes drifted over to the holo of Billy and me on my oak rolltop desk.

He has his arm around my nine-year-old shoulder as I hold up my string of Picasso-eyed flounder caught in Boston Harbor. Back in 2050, I was a skinny, bony, round-faced Irish kid with freckles everywhere. Almost thirty years later, I have brick-red wavy hair, worn shoulder-length, a small nose in a round girlish face, and big shoulders that make my breasts seem even smaller than they are. My freckles run down my cheeks, neck, and chest, as well as up my calves and thighs. Only my stomach and abdomen are clear. People say I look much younger than thirty-nine. At the moment, I felt sixty.

After a while Akktri returned from the Phneri funeral and let himself in. To the Phneri, only memory is eternal. A physical object is real only when it ends. Through the dead body and their memory of it, the Phneri see the structure of a life. I don't understand it.

Akktri was filthy, mud and dirt and blood clotted in his fur. I sat motionless in my easy chair, since moving would set off painful skin sparks from the stunner's residual effects, and wished that my ritz would float a cold beer over to me.

"You *know* what happened," I finally said to him. "With Ifraim and Ekkikka, I mean."

"Yes, Beverlee. We esfn his death." He caught a shedfly in his claws and held the thing by its wings. "We have wahoo fish now?" Akktri, like most of his kind, is always hungry.

I had no interest in food. If the Phneri had esfn'ed Ekkikka's death, they knew when I fired, and how. Perhaps they even knew what was in my mind and soul. "Am I a murderer?"

"You shoots first," my assistant replied judiciously. "If not, If-f-fraim k-k-kills you."

"Not him, buddy. Ekkikka."

"Ek-k-kikka?" Akktri looked at the blood in his fur, on his hands. He brought them up to his mouth with happy concentration.

Ekkikka's blood. I surged out of my chair and reached for Akktri. Retreating, my sidekick flattened his head to the floor. "No, k-keep my art longer," he chirped.

"You're soaked."

"Yes, yes! Blood shows art Ekkikka mak-k-kes." The Phneri, savorers of death and finish, feel no more grief for a dead Phner than you would for an old pair of shoes.

"We're getting clean." I scooped him up in my arms, carried him to the shower despite his protestations, and held him under. Akktri's whiskers wiffled and he waggled his hands, turning up the soft pads to be tingled by the needle spray. He looked down his doughy belly between his legs to where a spiral of red and brown waltzed down the drain. "Ek-k-kikka had our esfn," he said with a mixture of sadness and satisfaction. "We remember."

I put him down. "Pick out the shedflies yourself." My clumsiness would have torn their disposable wings off and left the creatures embedded. One by one, Akktri extracted them, intact and buzzing, then crushed them with a giggle and a snap of his strong short fingers.

I got a towel and he rolled around in it. "I can still see Ekkikka die," I said mournfully.

"Good," said Akktri. "We are all dead, Beverlee. You are dead-in-future-but-not-esfn'ed. Ekkikka is dead-and-completed-and-dispersed. We structure-remember the way he dies."

To the Phneri, every spot of blood, every crumb of dirt, every wound and scar and broken bone, tells a story. By dissecting each sinew and bone of Ekkikka's body, Akktri and his warren had reconstructed his death and life. Somewhere inside himself, my partner remembered a bullet, fired from my pistol, smashing into *his* body. "You feel it, don't you?" I asked.

"Yes, Beverlee," said Akktri. "You shoot strong but artless." He jerked his chest the way Ekkikka had cartwheeled, and I shuddered.

Every Phner has a memory of killing. A memory of being killed. A memory of birth and mutilation and ecstasy. And the screaming terror of the Endless Fall. Against this ocean of tragedy and experience, the death of another individual Phner is just another teardrop.

With such melancholy thoughts, I dozed off.

The phone rang.

"Miz O'Meara?" said the no-nonsense woman's voice of Boston's City Operator. "It's Iris Sherwood. May I see you—now?"

2

I HAD NEVER spoken with Iris Sherwood before—a woman that important was unlikely to be calling *me*—so I figured this must be another of Mack's practical jokes. If so, it was in bad taste. That would be typical of him.

"Mack?" I mumbled sleepily, rolling into a seated position and blinking at the screen. "It's too early for this."

"Miz O'Meara?" a woman's gravelly voice demanded, as if confirming a lineup identification. "Miz Beverly O'Meara? The investigator? It's Iris Sherwood."

I blinked and focused. It *was* her—I knew that face from my nightmares—though twenty years older. Back then she had fewer lines, less gray in her hair. Her eyebrows and cheekbones were thick with skin, bunkers protecting her tough gray eyes.

"What do you want?" I asked cautiously, although she was surely calling about Ifraim Lemos. Never reveal a hole card until you have to.

"Did I wake you? My daughter has disappeared somewhere in Boston." She was seated at a huge black desk, the wall behind her dark with tiny points of light. Probably real sky, I thought enviously.

"Gone?" I asked when my throat was under control. "Gone where? Not out of the Cube?"

"I very much doubt it." Her big, active fingers fluttered on her desk's surface and she looked down her long nose at her infomat. "I'd like to see you in my office right away."

Clumsily I shoved the covers aside and walked barefoot to

the screen. Now that my temporary fright was quelled, I wasn't about to work for this harridan, not after her role in the Siege. Besides, she was powerful and ruthless, and I'd do better to stay away from her. "Ma'am," I said carefully, "it's been a long day for me, in case you haven't read your own cit reports. Please hire someone else. Goodnight." I cut the line and put the no-knock on.

A half second later, it reactivated. That settled who she was, all right. "Pardon me, Miz O'Meara," Sherwood resumed. Her tone was both apologetic and grudging, as if two people were fighting for control of her vocal cords. "We were inadvertently disconnected. You must find my daughter Diana. She is missing."

So was Billy O'Meara. We never even had a body to bury.

"Why me?" I asked, sure I could deflect any reason.

She sighed heavily, the wrinkles in her strong face sagging and deepening with worry and fear. "Diana may be in the Basement. And the Basement, I understand, is your specialty."

As if it were my fault. As if Iris Sherwood would never sully her hands with the lower levels. The bottom ten floors of our big block of prock are the oldest, lowest, most dangerous part of Boston. The part below sea level. The part you can drown in if it floods. The part I grew up in.

"Can you come see me now?" she asked.

No one ever saw Iris Sherwood in person. She was as unreachable as the reclusive Targives. Now she wanted to talk to *me*.

Well, I had something to say to her, something I'd been holding for twenty years.

"All right," I said after a moment. I would enjoy seeing her face-to-face, just to tell her off. "Since you think it's urgent, I'll be right up. I'll need to bring my associate along."

"Naturally." She bowed her head deliberately. This woman would wipe her feet on the mat leading to the guillotine. "In ten minutes, shall we say?"

That must have been what we said, because she hung up.

Akktri was asleep, curled into a couple of blankets on my bed that he had shoved into a nest shape. He was mewling and squirming, arms and legs twitching, claws stretched out wide.

I squatted and tugged his left leg. "Wake up."

"We fall!" he shrieked. "We fall from space!"

"Wake up, Akktri." I slapped the bottom of his foot.

"We crash!" His back arched and his limbs windmilled. He twisted frantically as if clawing his way up from underwater. "We crash! We break! We die!"

"Akktri." I put my hands on his chest and massaged it. "Akktri!"

His claws scraped my arms with deep red lines. "Beverlee? Beverlee, we fall forever."

"Not you, buddy." I put my hand against his small head and stroked it. "Your parents and grandparents."

"All of us fall, Beverlee," Akktri said mournfully, pawing his eyes. "All of us fall and die."

"Shh. It happened long ago. Long ago."

"No." As he awoke, his fear dispersed like a corridor smell after the air scrubbers have been through. "No. It happens now. It always happens now." His fingers felt the tension in my forearms. "Beverlee, you are excited. We hunt?" he asked, fully alert now. "We fish?"

"Yes. Someone wants to be our client."

My assistant raised his head and made a noise like a spoon going through a garbage disposal—cheering in Phner. "Austin is here before," he said.

"Austin and I broke up months ago," I said. "You just see his hairs." I'd cleaned the sheets several times but that is pointless with a Phner—the past is so indelible to them that Akktri would be seeing indicia of Austin for years.

"Small partick-kles of skin." Akktri eagerly pushed the ridges of sheets around with his quick claws and sniffed. "Sweat. Spit-tle." Their narrow, toothy mouths have trouble with glottal stops. "And other subs—"

"That's enough," I interrupted hastily, then crossed to my closet, pausing to glance at my nineteenth-century Colton's survey of Boston and South Boston.

Collecting antique maps is my hobby, taught to me by my dad. They're my way of getting closer to Akktri, and of making real Boston's past, so rich with age and events. When I look at maps, I admire the arrogance of their makers, who drew crisp boundary lines as if their pens could hold back the sea. Perfect illusions of control and knowledge, so vain, so human.

I no longer had my gun, so there was no point in strapping that on. But the knife and sheath went around my right ankle as always. Even on a simple locate, you never know when you're coming home, so you go armed at all times.

Iris would want her employee to look both competent and unthreatening, so I pulled on underpants, bra, loose denim jeans, and a long-sleeved blue shirt.

Akktri was sitting on the bedclothes, his small hands held before him like a pious prairie dog. Honest cits, bred on tales of Phneri atrocities in the early years after the Endless Fall, see fangs in his square sharp teeth, claws in his delicate nimble hands. He's worth any three rods on Boston's police force and has saved my ass at least twice. "Come on. We're invited to the penthouse to meet the great Iris Sherwood." I put a Boston-Brahmin nose into my voice.

"You hate her," he said.

"Yes, of course," I answered, disconcerted. "You know what she did."

"In the Siege, we boom Boston," he replied. His head shivered as he reached into Phner race-memory. "Boom. Ka-tcha. Boom. Shrowar." Akktri made the sound of ocean waves. "Shrowar."

"Yeah. Her." His good humor was grating. "Let's go."

He curled himself comfortably into a ball. "We are there later," he murmured, closing his eyes.

"She's in a hurry. Her kid's missing."

"Perhaps finished?" he purred hopefully.

I shivered at that. Though I love Akktri dearly, the Phneri esthetic about death is too alien. In my mind, I saw the bot eye's read of Ifraim Lemos yanked backwards to land in his own blood, sprayed ahead of him out the divot my bullet had ripped through his guts. I saw more bullets spew randomly from my gun. I saw Ekkikka destroyed by one of them.

"Iris doesn't have your perspective, my friend," I said. "We humans are slaves to time."

"Is the mover slave to its tunnels?" he asked, jumping onto the floor.

Visitors to Boston are always impressed at how, in a ten-million-soul Cube a klick on each side and a klick tall, you can apparently go from anywhere to anywhere within seven minutes—assuming no Bostonians elbow you out of the way. But the movers reach only public places. Our City hides its true wealth and power far from view, like a snooty dowager keeping her good sterling in moistureproof containers.

"Destination?" the mover's hidden speaker quacked once Akktri and I were inside.

"Forty." As far as this clunker went. For a cellarbum like me, going upfloor in Boston is like a salmon swimming upstream. We'd have to change movers several times.

Mover gates and security procedures were introduced in 2062, the year after the Siege. In late August 2061, when the drought was killing several hundred a day, several Bostonians who called themselves American patriots climbed a hundred and fifty levels of empty mover shafts—they weren't scoped back then—intending to kill the head of the City's Department of Public Works, Water Division, a woman named Iris Sherwood, whom events had thrust into a position of enormous responsibility and power.

Two of the assassins died en route, one by a fall, one from a slit throat. The third, Lem Snow, made it into her office. Iris shot him.

The end lobby was a spiderweb atrium, each corridor lined with mover ports leading away in every direction, each guarded by an authority checkpoint. Level 40, one of the lower ones, is fully botomated. The arch glowed lime green as Akktri and I approached.

"Namessh?" it asked. Its speaker drum must have been fuzzy: the gruff male voice lisped like a bouncer wearing a throat-warbler.

"Beverly O'Meara and my assistant Akktri Phner. We're on our——"

"You are cleared for door sheven, Mizh O'Meara. Have a pleasshant day."

"She sees far," chirped Akktri.

"You got that, buddy," I said, impressed and intimidated.

We changed again at Level 100, our prompt approval given by an actual human so eager to please she personally showed us to the right door.

"Much structure," Akktri said when we were rising again, this time in a silent and friction-free skymover. He whistled, rapid and staccato, his small bright eyes darting as his claws slid softly along the mover's carpet-over-prock floor. "Order and strength behind smooth surfaces. Power concealed but watchful."

It's part of City lore that a City Operator never resigns, but instead dies in office. People say that City Operators have Targive implants to help them interface better with the bots, eyes, spatiens, and Phneri, and with the half-biological City organism itself.

As we rose, Akktri fell silent except for tiny peeps and whistles, whose almost inaudible echoes calmed him the way touching walls with your fingers might reassure you in pitch darkness.

"Mary, mother of Christ," I muttered in awe when we emerged onto Level 175 a few moments later.

The sexiest man I'd ever seen, dark and matinee-idol handsome, was sitting at an efficient desk, working intently on a format. Those screens, linked into Boston's network, can collect or transmit data from any source they can access. Someone who worked for Iris Sherwood probably could access anything he wanted, from police headquarters to the secretary of the Club Benedictine.

I gaped. Bostonians can afford to buy beautiful bodies, but this man was sculptural: chiseled jaw, broad shoulders, bedroom brown eyes with thick black brows and lashes. His confidence crackled like electricity.

He looked up briefly. "Miz O'Meara, I'm Charles Beaufort. Iris said you'd be coming. She'll see you in a bit. She's engaged."

"Busy?" I blurted. Very urb, Bev. "She hauls me out of bed to make me wait?"

"Happens to everyone," he said sympathetically. "Please have a seat."

Only one chair was available. A Targive-modified jellyfish stiffened with electric reinforcing wire, it moulded itself to my body and adjusted its temperature for maximum comfort.

"Why did Iris send for you?" he asked me, manipulating his infomat.

"Didn't she tell you, Chuck?" Nice try, I thought, but I don't breach confidences, even from people who aren't yet clients.

"I prefer Charles," he said with a touch of frost, glancing down at the infomat.

"I'll remember that," I replied coolly. Prickly, this one. Perhaps a bit too self-assured.

"It has to do with Old North," he went on, unruffled. "I've been researching its configuration for Iris." He gestured at his desk and screen.

"Increase Mather's house?"

"No, it belongs to the City. Part of the Old North Historical District." Incomprehension softened his face in intriguing ways. It made me want to surprise him more often.

"Increase Mather built the first house on that site," I explained. "President of Harvard. It burned in the Great Fire of 1676. A new one was built in 1680. Revere didn't buy it until 1770."

"Ghet-toes," Akktri said happily, waggling his short-clawed fingers. "Surfaces shaped by gravity and decay. Humans stuffed into ghet-toes."

"In the late nineteenth century, the Revere House was a verminous slum," I said. "Akktri likes its thick past."

So did my dad. Billy had taken me there as a child. I still remembered the sandpaper warmth of his big rough hand. "We Irish lived ten to a room," he growled proudly, as if it were an achievement. I think that's why I'd taken Akktri, to let him esfn for himself.

"Would you ask the Phner to sit with you?" asked Charles, paying no attention to my reminiscence.

"He bothering you?"

Charles shifted in his chair with repressed impatience. "Please."

"All right, then." I whistled for my assistant, who bounced into the chair, shoving his hands deep into its sweet-smelling armrests.

"Please ask him not to do that," said Charles.

"Ask him yourself. He's no pet."

"I thought he worked for you." He hit keys on his infomat. "Please remove your knife."

"Come again?"

He gestured at his screen. "On your right ankle. You can keep the sheath, but I must have the knife, or you cannot see the City Operator."

"Hey, I don't *want* to see the City Operator, dammit. *She* called *me.*"

Charles briefly closed his eyes. "The knife, please." He held out his hand.

So his banter had been only to get me to sit in his clever chair. I unbuckled the leather strap and gave it to him. "Take good care of that."

"Naturally." With a gesture he wiped his infoscreen clear, then his brown eyes grew still and distant. "This way." With a gracious sweep of his arm, he accompanied us into a mover, laying his hand on my back with a pleasant firmness. "Up."

Hissing and clicking, Akktri ran his claws gently along the paneling around the doorframe. "Sugar maple wood!" he spun in agitation and chittered at me. "Hand rubbed lemon oil!"

"Thank you for coming," said Sherwood's voice as the mover's doors opened.

If Iris Sherwood had been born a horse, she would have been a Clydesdale: strong, shaggy, and tough. She was almost a full head taller than me and much thicker. Her long brown gray-stranded hair was pulled into a loose knot secured by a gold pin about twice the length of my finger. Akktri was fascinated by it. From this vantage point it looked antique: slightly tarnished, undecorated, and nicked along its length.

"She's scanned. So is the Phner," Charles replied. He withdrew, but his crisp cologne lingered.

Iris Sherwood wore a sweater of mid-gray, a color that did not suit her but instead emphasized the fatigue in her wise, unforgiving face. The sweater's elbows were stressed and near to fraying. For all her frump, she looked like a dangerous ascetic, an intellectual believer. A woman who could conceive of blowing out Boston's bottom floors, and then could do it.

Akktri bounced whistles off Sherwood's body to sense its density and hear its changing shape as she moved. He was also probably reading her heartbeat, respiration, and skin conductivity. He'd know if she'd ever broken any bones, how it happened, and when.

"Ir-riss is very tense, very afraid," he said.

"Miz O'Meara." Sherwood approached, both gnarled hands outstretched. She clasped mine and released them. "Is this your partner?" She leaned over and peered at Akktri, who sat on his hind legs, glancing between us.

"Associate. He's a Phner. You used his kind to place the shape-charges that flooded the Basement and ended the Siege." My voice was ragged with barely controlled anger.

She ignored my jab. "Yes, I did. I'm sure he remembers. Sit on my desk," she said to Akktri, patting a spot. "You can esfn me better up closer."

"Thank-k-k you," Akktri replied, slipping into a chitter in his eagerness. He sprang up without scratching the desk's chinese-lacquer surface. I've seen him catch soap bubbles in those claws and watch the colors swirl, esfn'ing the patterns before the air ends them.

"You're surprised?" Sherwood asked me. "You know that I use aliens. Usually they're superior to humans. As I told you a moment ago, my daughter has disappeared. I'd like you to find her."

"I'd rather not work for you." It was as much as I could manage right then, standing before this woman I hated and feared and blamed.

"No one ever wants to work for me," she said in a matter-of-fact tone that almost fully concealed her bitterness. "But a girl is missing in the Basement. This time the girl is mine. I am coming to you, as the girl's mother, to ask you for the help you can give a mother. Find my child."

She said all this in a dry voice, folded her hands, and looked at me, as if the proposition had just been proven. Q.E.D. "I have downloaded Diana's biography into your home reader, and also transferred funds equal to your most recently published retainer and four days' wages. I trust this will be sufficient to enable you to start." She squared her infomat.

"I'll *never* work for you, lady," I blurted.

"Oh?" Expression vanished into the lines in her face like a fugitive fleeing into a crowd. "Why not?"

"You killed my father." Memories engulfed me of the Siege's aftermath, as I searched through the soggy Basement, trying to find Billy. Crossing City Hall Plaza looking at the corpses, refusing to turn away, holding back my retch and gag in a futile effort to find the bloated body that was William O'Meara's.

"I killed everyone's father," she replied indifferently. "Or sister, or brother, or cousin." She said all this with a trace of boredom, as if she'd had this conversation many times before. "I killed some of *his* warrenmates in the explosion." She nodded at Akktri. "Didn't I, friend?"

Akktri seized in thought. "Yes-s," he said, his thin high voice far away. "Yes. Some of us are trapped. We are crushed into ceilings. Some drown in k-k-corridors. We die." He thumped his short tail against the lacquer. "We destroy Boston. We rebuild Boston. End is beginning."

I was grinding inside at her attempt to deflect the conversation onto Akktri, who she knew wouldn't be ruffled. "Of course a Phner would forgive you. They don't care about individuals and neither do you. I'll leave now."

"Wait," she called abruptly as I rose. "Sit down. There is one person I care about as you cared for your father. I love Diana," she said, using the word in a distant, intellectual manner.

"Iris?" murmured Charles from the ceiling.

"I'm occupied," she said in a warning tone.

"Sraweesi insists."

With a scowl Sherwood glanced at me as if to say, forgive me but this will only take a minute. "Yes?"

A brisk man's voice came over the air. "Vinnie Akibira will be arraigned tomorrow."

"Today," said Sherwood calmly. "It's after midnight."

"Iris, your reads'll crucify him. Suspended and fired for sure, indicted most likely."

"So they will."

"You've got to stop it. He's a good rod."

"He's a disgrace," she snarled. "He took bribes. He entrapped honest cits. He abused his position."

"Vinnie Akibira is a rod who nails perps. And you're going to destroy him for that." Sraweesi's tone was heavy with sarcasm.

"Why, yes," she said with some surprise. "What my eyes

witness, they report." I started but she was intent on her unseen supplicant. "Policy is policy," she added. "That applies to rods as well as cits. Vinnie Akibira's fate is out of my hands. Sherwood out. Charles?" she added in a different tone.

"Yes, Iris?"

"When Deputy Commissioner Ulkudge calls in a few minutes, put her through. No one below that level."

"What about Roderick Petravelli himself?"

Sherwood smiled without opening her lips. "Our esteemed police chief won't humble himself so. My apologies, Miz O'Meara," she said when the connection was broken. "But one should act in a crisis, not wring one's hands."

"You lied to Sraweesi," I said.

"Pardon me?" she asked, her tone a mixture of curiosity and warning.

"Your eyes saw me kill a cit," I went on. "Ifraim Lemos. They didn't report it."

"Really." She called it on her infomat. "Ah. Reviewed by a very minor and overzealous monitor in our department." She leaned over her nose a bit to read more carefully. "Disposed of on the spot by the arresting officer. File countersigned by both Boston Police Department and Office of City Manager. Nothing untoward at all here." She spun the infomat for me to peruse.

"But that wasn't all that happened!" I didn't know whether it was this woman's outrageous self-confidence or her outrageous probity that caused me to press. "Only motivation distinguishes manslaughter from murder. Even your drones can't tell that. You should've hauled me in."

"You overestimate your own importance," she replied coolly. "According to the record, my central bots analyzed your fire pattern and concluded there was no realistic probability of a successful prosecution. So Sergeant Ahumada was empowered to release you. Now, do you wish to incriminate yourself further, or can we return to *my* problem?" She drew a deep breath, clearing her mind, then her fingers stamped an angry tarantella over her desk's surface and the room darkened.

The media wall to our left showed a haphazard cluster of tumbledown slate, brick, and shingle roofs. "Can you recognize it?"

Akktri hopped to the screen, pushing his short brown nose at it, his whiskers flicking like tiny brushes.

"Laser holo." He was bewildered that she would ask such an obvious question.

"No, no. Where is it?"

"In a room with smoke and sawdust," Akktri decided. "It is cold outside."

"Not the hologram," I interjected. Akktri would keep giving her details about its manufacture for hours. "Old North Historic District," I answered for both of us.

Sherwood nodded as if complimenting a studious pupil. "North Square disney. Revere House two days ago, at fifteen-thirty. You see that cluster of people?" She gestured at the screen. "The blond girl? Now see her again."

A young woman stood before a fireplace, languidly resting her delicate right hand on the white marble mantle. Her long hair was thrown carelessly over her left shoulder, framing the pale yellow bouquet of orchids that she wore at the neckline of her pastel summer dress. She might have been painted by John Singer Sargent.

To the girl's left stood Iris Sherwood, stiff and uncomfortable, chin lifted away from the camera, bony face frozen in an overwide smile.

"My daughter," she said with unmistakable pride. "Diana."

Akktri and I stepped forward gingerly, as if the girl were real, rather than simply a three-dimensional hologram.

Daughter bore little resemblance to mother: half a head shorter, Diana Sherwood was svelte where Iris was thick, willowy where Iris was chunky. Her skin was pale, dresden-delicate, her arms and calves lithe and fluid even in repose.

Down at knee-height, my sidekick whistled. "Fine quality

pick-k-ture. Make us closer." I hefted him and he crawled around my shoulder to perch behind my neck. His nose and coppery whiskers were in constant motion as he pored over every line in Diana's face.

"She is emotional," he concluded after a moment. "Unrestrained. Sexual. Undireck-ted."

Sherwood's eyes flickered acknowledgment at each trait. "My opposite in most ways," she said with a trace of sadness.

"She is stubborn," Akktri went on. "Strong-willed."

Sherwood sighed. "Well, my daughter and I are alike in that, I'm afraid."

"Not your daughter!" Akktri squeaked flatly. "Bones and face are too strange."

"Right but wrong," said Sherwood with a hint of a smile. "Diana is not blood of my blood, flesh of my flesh, but she *is* my daughter. She was adopted."

"When?" I asked.

"September 4, 2061."

A Siege baby, I thought. Diana Sherwood was a Siege baby. Thousands died in the three-month Siege that gave us our independence from America. When it was over, Boston had hundreds of new orphans. They were all brought to City Hall Plaza—it was still undivided and unroofed then—and exhibited, like trade-show prototypes or lost luggage, for any relatives who might return to claim them.

I suppose technically I'm a Siege baby too, even if I'd been nineteen when I was orphaned. I felt a surge of affection and pity for this unseen daughter, whoever and wherever she was, sundered from her family by the Siege, only to become the adopted child of the Butcher of Boston.

I looked again at the confident supple girl, her arm so imperially stretched out, standing before her big horse of a mother. If I do it, I'll do it for you, I addressed the image. "Seen enough?" I murmured.

"Yes." Akktri leaped nimbly into the air, landing without a sound in his characteristic attentive hands-up posture.

Sherwood recalled the previous scene and tapped a head standing before the Revere House entrance. "That's Diana. I'll run the record forward."

Sounds invaded as if a window had been flung open on a boisterous party: the loud babble of animated conversation, a jumbled stew of unintelligible but unquestionably Bostonian English. The frozen figures resumed their movement, an orange halo forming around Diana and following her as the figures moved out of range. "That's the last anyone has seen of her," said Sherwood.

"Why'd you call me now? Did something happen?"

"Too many hours had passed." She shrugged. "I decided to start looking for her."

Who is this glacier? I wondered. "How'd you get that holo?" I nodded toward the frozen heads.

Sherwood returned to her desk and seated herself behind it. "We're linking all eyes into one system."

I stuck out my lower lip. "People don't like eyes. What's your casualty rate among blackbirds?"

"People are angry only when the eyes are clumsy. Most areas in Boston have been scoped for years." Sherwood knitted her hands behind her head, her fingers rubbing the hasp of the big gold hairpin. Clenched in a fist, it would make an effective and deadly weapon, especially if wielded with the element of surprise. Did Iris know that? "Elevator monitors," she mused as if listing her grandchildren. "Doorways. Store cameras. Vidphones. Correlating the images is the main problem," she added in a more practical tone.

"Why?" I asked. "Why does anyone need to peep all this?"

Iris Sherwood snorted. "Have you forgotten Lem Snow?"

"A whole system just to be your personal bodyguard? That's excessive, even for you."

"Not for me. For the City."

I blanked. "Come again?"

"Boston eats, drinks, sleeps, vents. The Cube can burn, it

can starve, it can suffocate or lose its mind. Boston is a huge, powerful, changing being. I am its guardian."

"And to guard it, you sacrifice people," I snarled. "Like you sacrificed my father."

"He was warned," she replied stolidly. "Everyone was warned. Warned and warned again." She rubbed her forehead as if at an old headache. "Most people are damn fools." Her voice was bitter with fatigue. "I ought to have it engraved on my doorplate just under my title: MOST PEOPLE ARE DAMN FOOLS. A fitting motto."

"My dad was nobody's fool, and he *still* died. Where were *you?*"

"Being shot at, as you may recall. Besides, if we'd had the Basement wired, we could have located him." Her shoulders slumped a little. "And the hundreds of others. We could have sent people to bring them to safety. *Now* do you see what I want the network for?"

"Your daughter's missing. Why not use all those eyes to find her?"

"Couldn't trace her by read. You see—"

Charles Beaufort's voice interrupted us again. "Putting through Ulkudge."

"Siddy Obberader." The Koltsoi's thick dull tones, usually supercilious, were tight-reined meek. "We ask for dercy for Biddle Akibira."

"What can I do about that?"

"You can decertify de reads," said the police chief of staff. "You can find dem ambiguous."

"Why would I do that, Ulkudge?" Sherwood was curious. "He broke laws."

"You don't judge a rod by what laws he breaks or duddn't break," said Ulkudge. "You judge hib by how maddy crooks he catches, how maddy hoddest cits he brodects."

"You know," mused Sherwood, "that's what's wrong with your whole force. Results merchants, not rulemakers. Principles are a luxury to you. Well, not in Free Boston. Cry your crocodile tears somewhere else. Sherwood out."

"Iris, you should choose your battles with more care," Charles Beaufort said regretfully. "Don't waste energy on small things."

"Principle is no small thing." Her cheeks were winched taut. "Sherwood out."

"You said you couldn't trace Diana," I resumed. "Why not?"

She stood silent, her face framed by the dark night beyond her window, where IPOB's black needle reached from the ocean toward the stars.

The Interstellar Port of Boston is the nexus through which flows all trade into and out of the City. IPOB is headquartered in the world's tallest structure, a single monofilament-reinforced needle three hundred stories high that stands at the entrance to Boston Harbor like a cenotaph. That structure has seen duty as an asylum, a fortress, and a trade center. Within it are offices, holding areas, kitchens, embassies, and at least five different self-contained biospheres.

At its base, IPOB lets out onto Long Wharf, which was extended into the harbor to accommodate it. I take satisfaction in the thought that every visitor, no matter how long or difficult his journey or how important his station, walks into or out of the City along the same avenue used four hundred years ago by disembarking sea voyagers.

More than a hundred stories below us, tiny lights sparkled on the sea. I moved to the window, drawn by the harbor's ebony glitter, wondering at the myriad aliens and humans who worked there, our bridge to unimaginable other worlds. In the blacklit shadow of IPOB, the burnt and drowned remains of South Boston crouched like dirty feet. My father and grandparents grew up there, before the water rose and the aliens came and we had to move to West Roxbury.

"Name a level, a quadrant," Sherwood said, watching the water traffic, "and I can bring out its corpses by the handful.

But to reach into that warren and pluck out a single person—I can't do that. Not and keep her alive and healthy."

Like poker, I thought. The winning strategy is to be uninterpretable and statistically correct. My dad was a terrible poker player, much too flamboyant for his own good.

"All I'm good for is killing," murmured Sherwood as if talking to the stars and the IPOB needle outside. "Find Diana. Find her and bring her back safe."

We stood for a moment, observing the glittering blackness, while Akktri meandered around the floor, stalking unseen demons.

After a moment, Sherwood shook her head. "I can afford you," she murmured with gentle sympathy, as if the need to earn money were a faintly embarrassing condition like elderly incontinence. "Any cit could do as I am now doing. This is not abuse of office."

"I don't care about that."

"*I* do."

I was taken aback. "Where does Diana go to school?" I asked after a moment's uncomfortable silence.

"Louisburg."

Of course, I thought. The most exclusive finishing school in the Cube, far above the hoi polloi like me. Iris's daughter might have been born a rugrat, but she had risen far upfloor. Now her mother needed me, another Basement rat. Payback, I thought. Justice.

"I'll find her."

3

"Now THAT THAT's settled, I have something for you." Sherwood headed around to her desk and handed me a dark brown rectangle as long as my finger.

"A Boston Key? I already have one of these."

"Not like this, you don't," she retorted. "This is a Master."

"Oh?" The key was the same mud color on both sides, devoid of writing or markings. "What will it do?"

"Whatever you need it to." She smiled cryptically and escorted us to the mover door.

I halted. "No more explanation than that?"

"It contains more technology than you can comprehend. Let it suffice that this key lets you do anything I want you to be able to do."

"When do I use it?" I asked warily.

"Whenever you feel the need."

"No, thank you." I dropped the key back into her palm.

"Take it." Her voice held the tone of a leash being tested. She closed her hand around mine, pressing the key back into it, then seemed to realize that her actions were too forceful and lifted her hand to my shoulder, where it lay heavily, unused to camaraderie. "It may help you sometime, if only to get back in touch with me. And one more thing." She paused. "Diana may have acted rashly—in a moment of weakness." She made it sound like a question whose answer I knew.

I stopped and turned. "What are you getting at, Iris? What's eating you?"

She flushed as if caught in an indiscretion, then looked

down at her square hands. "I've said too much," she stated after an awkward silence. Even those words seemed an effort. "Find her." She covered my hand with hers. "Please."

I passed again through the waiting area where dreamboat Charles graciously returned my knife to me—he'd oiled the sheath, I noticed, and thanked him—and then back into the public mover.

The atmosphere of City power seemed to follow me like an aphrodisiac. Master Keys were rare, their use controlled. So Iris wanted me to think I had one. Why? She had no reason to trust me with the real thing—maybe she just wanted me to feel important. Probably this key had only a few expanded features, such as a more powerful locator, limited sending and receiving capabilities, perhaps some modest override control. Was it a tool or a collar? Either way, I decided suddenly, I would decline the trojan horse, and carry the thing but not use it.

We had a couple of hours before Louisburg School would open for business, so I returned to my apt on Level 15 at the fringes of the Basement. A converted office building that's a remnant of terrestrial construction materials from the days when people lived one place and worked another, 15 Fed 70 is built of huge green and yellow concrete pillars that rise through the floors—the Parthenon as rehabbed by Teamsters.

My brother Mack doesn't like my neighborhood, but really, what's the difference between Level 15 and Level 115? One corridor is much like another—rectangular, enclosed, orderly. As long as you're above the high-water mark, an apt is an apt. Who cares how high you are when all your windows are vid sims?

"We hunt now?" asked Akktri as soon as we were inside.

"We eat now," I replied firmly. I gathered him in my arms, then suddenly tossed him at the ceiling.

"Yee-ow!" he chittered excitedly, flinging his arms and legs as wide as he could.

Phneri can accelerate their time-sense for brief periods—

react more quickly, move faster, think more clearly than normal. It's a survival reflex that conjures up terrifying and sad memories of the Endless Fall. At the same time it can be, to judge by Akktri's constant requests, a terrific buzz akin to the rush of a rollercoaster ride.

So my partner yipped like an ecstatic coyote, his fur outstretched, until he landed on the bed in a golden heap, giggling and pawing the air in delight. "Yew-ee-yow!"

"Again?" he piped, scrabbling over the covers to me. A Phner can't create the sensations for himself—surprise or danger are essential elements. "Again?" Akktri repeated, tugging my elbow.

"No. You're already expecting it." I pulled on a shirt. "We hunt, remember?"

"We hunt! Okay! We hunt!"

Phneri syntax sounds like pidgin because their language has no verbs. Instead the Phneri use concepts that concatenate existence and time, words like destruction-imminent-but-necessary or existed-once-now-ended-and-memory-still-influences-events. Putting these into English strips nearly all their content; most Phneri thoughts cannot be translated into any human language. As a result, the Phneri despair of telling humans what they mean and simply use present tense for everything, like sullen tourists in a foreign country, frustrated at their inability to express themselves.

People claim that the Targives have a wetware implant that will let any sentient understand the Phner language, but every Targive gift conceals a scorpion, so only the desperate accept their offer.

Of course Tarmods—Targive-modified creatures designed for a variety of purposes—are omnipresent, although were-wherewear has been illegal ever since a rubbery pseudoshirt seized control of Fess Filomena's skin and inverted it, turning her inside out like a cauliflowered tomato that bled thin juice into the mover shafts.

The Targives are a race of nomadic hermits who travel

throughout known space. Every planet of sentient beings has a Targive citadel. No two are alike; each is a unique bioform from native life.

Their basilica on Hnar is a giant circulating pump modified from a Hnar jellyfish, a vast transparent web of pumps, valves, ducts, sinkholes, ponds, and boiling/evaporation chambers through which the Targives constantly circulate different colored liquids: ammonia, blood, seawater, urea, formaldehyde. On Nenananoo, on the other hand, it is an impenetrable jungle of encrusted stone, lichen, cement, and rock that groans and creaks as its towers and tunnels shift their burdens.

The South Boston Targive cathedral is made of flexing chitin probably extracted from scarab beetles, praying mantises, cockroach backs, and dragonfly wings. It extends and extrudes limbs like an inverted tarantula, its black-brown sides glistening with an oily sheen that is maintained by small multilegged things that emerge from just below sea level, climb its sides like leeches, then die in the sun, crisping and burning in a bright blue flame before falling, like flares, back into the ocean to extinguish themselves with a hiss.

Perhaps their quest to build on each planet from the creatures of that planet is a kind of religion, proselytizing by co-opting and corrupting. Perhaps it is a fun-house mirror, reflecting back to a culture all that it wishes not to see. Perhaps it's simple economy, for the transport of genetic material and information technology is far less massive and thus far cheaper than importing authentic Targive forms. Perhaps the Targives themselves no longer exist, having dissolved and leaving behind only semisentient Tarmod servants who endlessly re-create temples in homage to their vanished creators.

I made coffee and breakfast, then got Mack on the line. "Diana Sherwood," I began when his round hairy face came on. "Student at Louisburg School. Dig up background on her and anyone close to her," I said, my mouth full of microwaved bagel and warm jam. "Here's her bio," I mumbled, shoving the datacube Iris had given me into the reader.

His plump cheeks sagged minutely. "Dangerous?" Mack is balding on top, perhaps because he rubs his head all the time, and he combs his wavy hair ineffectually over the thin spot.

"Just a locate. Girl. Maybe she ran away, maybe she's on an extended one-night stand." I answered in a clipped fashion, slipping into poker mode: deadening the muscles of my face, carefully choosing my words and expression. Mack is too curious, prying almost, and too willing to use his knowledge as chips in our sibling poker game.

Until our father died, Mack and I had never been close. His death drew us reluctantly together, our bond the halves of an oyster shell wrapped around a pearl of sorrow. The differences in our personalities make most of our conversations painful or guarded.

Our relationship is like a sprained ankle—familiar, tender, bruised. Mack and I know one another too well. I loathe his apathy; he's appalled at my recklessness. He seldom leaves his apt. A dilettante, he can shrug off his feelings like an overcoat, hang them in the closet, forget them for weeks on end. Now Mack tries to pretend that Billy's death never happened, or at least not that way. He actively shuns interest in the Siege or the past. I've learned not to put too much stress on our sprained-ankle bond.

He was scanning food from the cube. "Diana Sherwood. Louisburg School," he clucked with mock admiration. "And they hired *you.*"

I stuck my purple tongue out at him. "Dig for me, will you? Where would she go? Who are her friends? What's she into? Find her dirt. Find her gold."

"Sure." Mack nodded and glanced down at his infomat. "Adopted right after the Siege," he said, his eyes jumping. "Oh, *that* Iris Sherwood. Where'd the daughter come from?" He kept reading her history. "Iris refused all citations or promotions afterward, did you know that?" He chuckled. "The mulehead caused no end of consternation. Various politicos wanted to kick her upstairs to something cushy and uncontroversial, but our Iris just planted herself. And she's still there twenty years later." His voice dropped and his tone sobered. "Little sister, you've never had a client like this. I don't like it."

He was voicing my own misgivings, but I reflexively rebelled. "What's wrong with ambition? You think I can't do it? Rich kids get lost just like sloshfeet."

"Sure, but they call urb eyes. Why does this client want you?" asked Mack bluntly. "Why not someone more competent?"

"Thanks for the vote of confidence," I replied with more than a trace of bitterness. "I can find the girl, no sweat."

"This woman is too powerful." He snorted. "You're being used."

"That's what people pay detectives for, or have you forgotten? So long, big guy. Call when you find out something I can use," I finished nastily, cutting the connection.

I hung up, regretting that I'd lost control and vented anger. Hell. The case was barely three hours old and I was already growing my on-duty crust. Moments ago I had been suspicious when Iris Sherwood legitimately held back information from me, a complete stranger, yet here I was, already doing the same thing to my brother.

Akktri was sitting on the table, deboning a freshwater perch and enjoying the phosphor decay patterns on my vid screen.

"Was Iris telling the truth?" I asked.

"Humans never know the truth," he chortled. "Iris is human." He lifted his head and closed his eyes. Phneri have tremendous memories, virtually photographic. My partner took a deep breath and shook his small head—changing mental pictures. "She states hopes as truth."

"We'll have to talk again with Iris, won't we?"

Akktri had returned to his fish and was peeling it farther apart. His attention is like a mosquito, quick but hard to capture. Then he recognized my tone and his eyes widened. "We hunt *her,* too?"

"Maybe." First rule of meat eyes, I reminded myself: Always act as if your client is a crook.

I glanced at Colton's 1855 Survey No. 13 of Boston's Voting Wards. The jewel of my map collection, it's a medley of soft pinks, yellows, and pastel greens crosshatched with the names of ancient, vanished streets: Cornhill, Blackstone, Ann. My eyes were drawn to South Boston, at the time still being laid out and settled, and to the streets where my Irish grandparents had lived before the water drowned them. Was a missing girl easier to find when you only had two or three levels to worry about?

The high-speed main downmover let me out, slightly dazed, on the plaza before the Old North Church. Beside me, Akktri zipped off as I swayed slightly and shifted my feet on the worn brick cobblestones.

After the aliens came, the good people of Boston, in their wisdom and political patronage, kept a few areas like Beacon Hill as historic districts. All property here is maintained exactly as it was on Splashdown Day—August 22, 2014, 5:05 P.M.—when the gray glubs crashed through the sky into the harbor, to destroy and remake our lives.

A few meters away, Akktri scurried up to four Phneri craftsmen who were laying worn bricks and chittered excitedly with them. Ever since the Siege and the flooding of the Basement, the Phneri redo the historic streets monthly—when labor is cheap, service improves—keeping the pavement as it was when first esfn'ed. They even age the mortar.

Though the recreations are flawless to us, Akktri says that to a Phner, no two objects are identical, because they have unique histories. Crumbled-and-unesfn'ed, he once explained, is as far from irradiated-and-embrittled-and-will-end-soon as blue is from yellow for us. The Phneri regard their duplicative ability as merely an illusion of no significance, a parlor trick suitable for entertaining children and humans.

The five little creatures clustered together, hefting bricks. Their heads bobbed and fingers pointed, like elderly book collectors inspecting a rare Dell mapback mystery, clucking over its dog-ears but nevertheless well satisfied to add this curio to their collection.

To settle my stomach, I lurched through the church's varnished oak doors and crawled into one of its authentic white Puritan box pews with crimson felt trim and golden brocaded tassels. Lying flat on my back, I closed my eyes and crossed my arms over my chest, hands on each opposite elbow like an unwrapped mummy, until my internal fluids calmed down. Akktri would find me eventually.

Growing up in Boston, I've always loved history. Billy took me everywhere: to the *Constitution,* reberthed several times; to Bunker Hill and up the Monument tower; to the Castle Island fort, once again an island cut off from South Boston by the rising water. When I think of him, I see myself as a small child, looking up at a thick-bellied, self-educated Irishman explaining about the past.

The Boston Billy grew up in was different, a moated castle rather than a spaceship. In the Fifties we lived on the fringe of the police ghetto near the big three gates, in the forest-floor scrub of shifting shadows made by the upspringing prock towers that reached ever higher, competing for sunlight like redwoods. When they finally roofed and domed the whole place, and layered in prock connecting floors, they took the light from the groundies and made the Basement.

Right to the end, Billy couldn't see it changing. He'd walk home past god-hivers and mover thugs, glaring at them with his jaw thrust forward as if itching for a fight, then slam the door shut, sweep me up in his arms, and tell me how his day went. When I got a little older and rugran with the others, he cut me a bamboo bungee stick and sewed a calf holster for it. "You're a little girl, Bev sweetie," he said, outfitting me with it, "and there's nothing like a fast, sharp stick to even things up. Now get out and don't do anything you're ashamed to report to your old man."

That stick came in handy during the Siege, in the early days when we kids chased leeches and customs out of town, and later on when a half-eaten orange was a thing to kill for.

Now I'm an cubehunter and I uncover recent history, personal history, unwritten history, and concealed history. I carry a knife rather than a bamboo rod, but when I feel it rub against my calf, I think of my father, and his multiply broken nose, and I wish he were alive.

Old North, Boston's oldest church, is one of Akktri's favorite places, as soaked with history as a fruitcake is with rum. From its belfry were hung the two lanterns that told Paul Revere the British were coming by sea—across the Charles River tidal estuary into Cambridge—thence to march on Lexington and Concord.

The tombstones in Copp's Hill Burying Ground behind the church are pitted with musketball dents from when the garrisoning redcoats used them for target practice. Akktri swears he can still smell the powder.

"Beverlee?" my Phner friend called from the entrance to the church. "We hunt?"

Eyes closed, I smiled. "Yes, we hunt." I sat up and we walked across North Square.

"This is where the eye showed the last image," I said when we stood before the Revere House. In the yard on the left, a bronze bell cast by Revere himself was mounted, mottled with green and orange tarnish. "Can you find Diana?"

Akktri blinked. "She is unfinished." He used the Phner word that means unstable-and-vulnerable-to-collapse, a word the Phneri often use to describe living things. "The paths of our lives are distant."

"Never mind," I said. "Be Diana. Walk as if you were her."

"As you say, Beverlee." My assistant flattened his fur and held himself still, composing his mind. Then he straightened up on his legs and . . . *became* Diana Sherwood.

The effect was extraordinary. Akktri suddenly stood among a crowd. Unseen people brushed him fore and aft and he reacted with small haughty motions. He shuffled forward, silently moving his head, face, and hands as if conversing.

"Is the raccoon epileptic?" asked a casual passerby.

Here was a remarkably beautiful and intelligent creature, doing a flawless, muscle-by-muscle simulation of a human whose body architecture was fundamentally different from his, someone he had observed only through a single holo recording, and all this out-of-town thumbhead could see was a wog having a fit.

"You're a fool, gijo," I answered without looking around. A scramble of gaijin and G. I. Joe, it's our term for Americans. Flagwavers. Tax leeches.

"There's no need to be *insulting*. Typical of you beaner snobs." The tourist beetled off, complaining about churlish Bostonians as her guidephone whispered in her ear.

"I await," Akktri said in a haughty voice without ceasing his remembered actions. Uncanny.

I moved around behind my companion as he jiggered slowly toward the entrance. "Hold it." Akktri froze completely rigid.

"He *is* having a fit," said the disgruntled tourist to her husband from a safe distance away. She bent to snap Akktri's picture. Aliens are rare outside Boston.

"Keep going," I called and he moved again, a tiny pied piper.

"Sign!" he shouted with glee a few seconds later. "Clear sign! Look! See!"

I rushed to the spot around which Akktri was furiously circling and sniffing. I craned over, hands on my knees, but saw only uneven bricks. "What is it?"

"There! There!" Akktri gesticulated frantically at a point on the ground. "And here!" He pranced a couple of meters to another spot, dodging particular bricks like a kid playing hopscotch.

"What do you see?" I asked respectfully.

"Diana is here. *I* am here." He jumped to a brick. "I am

waiting and nervous." He pointed to the grout. "I drag my feet—so. I maneuver my weight back and forth. I am pressed by others." He crouched, his nose barely above the pavement, and inched alongside the area.

"Now what?"

"Up come two humans." He rapidly sketched their positions. "I am surprised. They speak and I am not surprised now. I come with them as they go. See? They lead. I follow. One turns—here." His little hands were vibrating. "I am ek-kcited by what he does. Now we must flee. Quick! Quick-k-k! Away!" Akktri squealed, charging through the gate next to the Revere House.

I hustled after him. One side of the empty backyard abutted the house. The North Square side was fenced. The two remaining sides were clapboard and concrete walls.

"This way!" A narrow passage led behind the house. We hurried down it, Akktri in the lead like an oversize chipmunk Sherlock Holmes, I panting behind like Lestrade.

"And there!" Akktri pointed to a door.

"What do you see here?"

"A man slumps against the wall. His body is punched by tiny fists traveling very fast."

I skidded to a halt. "What?"

"Pow, pow!" Akktri screamed, his body shaking. "Pow-pow-pow!" He poked stiffened fingers into himself.

"Bullets?" I hazarded. "Machine-gun bullets?"

"Very fast!" answered Akktri in a staccato voice. "Ba-ba-ba-ba-ba-*bah*! Like that!" His small chest spasmed and jerked around as if slugs were slamming into him. "Brass cylinders land on dirt." He winced and clutched his furry stomach, hunching over and mewling.

"Cartridges? Bullet shells?"

"Bonk, bonk!" my sidekick replied, moving his hands around to indicate where they had landed. "Ping, ping! Rubber is burning!" Akktri cried. "Friction as it spins against brick-k-k! Gasoline exhaust stinks North Square! Noise and screech of grinding iron!"

"Cars? Personal movers without guides?"

"Cars," he repeated, perplexed and preoccupied. "K-k-cars? Maybe cars. Do cars paint steel black-k-k?"

"Yes," I answered gingerly, squatting down beside him. "Cars paint steel black."

"Cars!" He shuddered with exhilaration. "Cars."

"When, Akktri?" I asked. "Weapons haven't used projectile shells for forty years. Automobiles were banned from the Cube thirty years ago. You aren't seeing Diana."

"Blood!" my little companion screamed, again seized with frenzy. "Blood splashes red on the wall!" He leaned against it, sobbing with grief. "Along the concrete!" His hands roamed its clean gray surface. He reached out a finger, gazed at it, then touched its tip to his tiny orange tongue. "Blood. Old blood! I die." He slumped against the wall. "My body is cold and hard in dirt and rain."

"It's okay, my friend." Quickly I gathered him up, cradled his head, and held him. Akktri's reconstructions are strong— as the Phneri say, his sight could lift a river. "It happened long ago," I murmured soothingly.

"It *is* past," he agreed in a weak voice. "I hold its end. But its history is bright. You do not see?"

I stroked his neck and back. "I wish I could see what you do."

"No, you should not ask this." Akktri was solemnly gentle, a parent preventing his child from hurting herself. "Seeing not is better for humans. You would not appreciate this art, but its ending is"—his sparkling eyes widened and his whiskers tingled—*"delicious."*

I took him back to North Square. "Can you find Diana's sign?" I asked.

Akktri searched. "It drowns in many other signs," he reported, crestfallen, after several moments' investigation.

"Don't feel bad," I said. "Too many feet have come and

gone." I had half expected this; merging into a crowd is the best way to disappear in Boston. "Let's trace the trail from the other end, shall we? We'll go see her school."

We hopped a mover, which let us out a few moments later.

I instinctively hold my breath whenever mover doors open. When the Siege came upon us, that hot summer of 2061, I was a tough teenager—a wild rugrat, liberated by the Cube-emptying chaos and the thirst to roam the corridors. For a day the Siege was a lark. For a week it was heroic. For a month it was a struggle. At the end it was simple, grim survival.

Throughout, Billy drank and worried, convinced he was going to die. Since our mother's death a few years before, he had become ever more morbid, seeing in the aliens the cause of everything that had gone wrong in his life, grumbling that the 2016 Uprising had been a good thing, the only way to beat the wogs.

About the third day he quoted W. C. Fields, "It was horrible. I had to subsist on nothing but food and water." The joke rang hollow. Alcohol dehydrates the body, so the heat and thirst got to Billy before Mack and me. We both fled the house and his pathetic whining, coming home only to change clothes or sleep.

After ten days of Siege, I returned home to a scrawled note: "Looking for water. Back by supper. Dad." I thought nothing of it. Truth be told, I was relieved to have the apt to myself.

We never even had a body to bury.

Two days later Iris's Phneri minions blew holes in the seawalls, flooding the Basement to cool the City. The warnings in a dozen languages—PROCEED IMMEDIATELY TO LEVELS 11 AND UP—reverberated through the hot baking halls. Unheeded: by this time, the only people left in the Basement were those too poor or dull to have relocated upward. Or wild kids whose fathers weren't paying attention to their whereabouts or their activities.

When the booms sounded, I ran to an emergency stairwell,

one of the secret places we kids had found and claimed as our own empire within the walls. I charged up it, turning and turning. Below me the City rumbled with the hot breath of a waking dragon. I lost track of levels and just ran, terrified, until I got sick and leaned my head on the mildewed prock and cement, gulping bile. Then I ran some more, farther upward.

Below me sounded a hideous rumble and a huge sighing wind, like a giant coughing, as the ocean invaded our home. The walls shook, rattling my teeth and knees. Drafts of moist sea air shot up the tunnels like diaphanous heralds of death.

Everyone and everything below Level 10 drowned.

When it was over, the Phneri cleared out the corpses, removing teeth and repairing fillings before restoring them to dead vacant skulls. Flushed with joy over their new citizenship—granted by Iris for services rendered during the Siege— the Phneri rebuilt the walls and restored the Golden Dome, clucking and chattering, hugging themselves with satisfaction at this wonderful catastrophic ending.

Now I live on Level 15, above the high-water mark. And the Phneri still sing of that day and Boston's bursting.

We stepped out of the mover and I held my breath, squinting into the cerulean blue sky. White mackerel clouds moved slowly overhead. It's a holographic illusion to cover the prock ceiling a hundred meters up—but a convincing, disorienting one. You get into a mover, drop for a few seconds, and emerge suddenly sixty-six years in the past.

Grass grows in the Boston Common. Seagulls squawk overhead. When the wind blows from the east, it's flavored with low-tide spume and brine. In winter we sometimes have snow flurries. Were the storms Iris's doing? I wondered. As City Operator, were such details beneath her? Did she have a Deputy Assistant Rainmaker?

On impulse I walked over to Government Center, thinking about the Siege babies. Somewhere in Boston, sometime in the Siege, Billy had died. I missed him dreadfully. "Akktri," I said suddenly, my voice catching, "can you see my dad here?"

My sidekick quivered and dropped low to the bricks. "Many many feets," he said after a moment. "Trails in all direck-k-tions. Too many. Not here. Not *here*. Billy is not *here.*"

"Oh." The hand clutching my chest and throat eased.

Although Beacon Hill's exteriors must be preserved untouched, you can scour the insides however you want. Pleasure palaces, smugglers' dens, and religious temples are cheek by jowl with embassies of thrill-seeking aliens and fortified homes of Boston Brahmin families too proud to relocate. And atop the State House, at the crown of the Golden Dome, the Boston Cricket still swings in the synthetic breezes.

Akktri adores Beacon Hill's age and diversity, four hundred years of history preserved in the cracking mortar and uneven cobblestone streets.

Though Louisburg School occupied several adjacent townhouses on the square itself, its only visible sign was a tiny faceplate—brass more than two hundred years old, Akktri informed me—positioned neatly over a lion's head doorknocker.

I extended my hand to rap and the lion growled, "What the dickens is your business?"

I blinked. "We made an appointment with Dean Tolliver a few minutes ago."

The lion considered this. "So you did, Miz O'Meara."

The stairs we climbed leaned precariously, as if depressed. Along the wall were paintings of headmasters past. In high wing collars, with muttonchop whiskers, they stared haughtily through the varnish and soot on their cracking, rippled surfaces.

Akktri bounded up the stairs. The past is his drug: surrounded with authentic human history, he turns into a kid in a candy store.

At the landing before us stood a huge glass bell jar containing a gigantic stuffed osprey, its wings spread wide and its claws closing around a haddock.

"Good kill haddock fish," my partner said, pointing. "Ended at different time than bird ends."

"It's long dead, not worth eating," I replied with a smile.

"I know, I know," hopped Akktri, nettled. "Haddock future fish? Object-not-ended-will-end-soon?"

"When we find Diana, *lobster* future fish." That, of course, thrilled him.

The carpeting beneath our feet was threadbare, its colors bleached into sickly pale pinks and browns. A grandfather clock with a tarnished silver rising-moon dial ticked heavily. The wallpaper was stamped leather—Akktri chattered in enthusiastic detail about how the cows were slaughtered, gutted, and tanned. Silhouette cameos lined the underlit corridor, and the air was musty and still.

Dean Christopher Tolliver's office was dominated by an old-fashioned mahogany partners' desk with a kneehole that went all the way through. Pencils spewed like fireworks from a ceramic toby mug in the image of a glowering Winston Churchill. A wooden swivel chair stood behind the desk, a leather pad tied to its back. On the wall behind the desk hung framed holos of Tolliver with various dignitaries. One that caught my eye showed Tolliver with Chief of Police Roderick Petravelli, presenting a plaque to a handsome, swarthy young man. "Three knows each other," Akktri said, putting his nose up against the holo's magscreen. "Knows each other good."

The bookshelves lining the room were filled with paperbacks in neat shrink-wrap plastic. A serious collector of deservedly obscure science fiction authors, I mused, running my finger along the spines and reading forgotten titles sideways.

Akktri leaped onto the desk and sniffed among Tolliver's papers and holos. My partner made a sound like a radio being tuned as he muttered contentedly to himself. I recognized the Phner word that means copies-of-originals-not-copies-of-copies. His small hands touched and tested, his nose and eyes alert.

A whistled injunction in Phner came from a voice behind us. We jumped and turned.

"Miz O'Meara? I'm Chris Tolliver." A willowy man, tall and boneless, sidled into the room, his limbs moving with slow effortless grace. "You're early."

He was wearing a white linen suit. A silver fob chain looped through the vest buttons into his double-breasted waistcoat pocket. A white straw boater with a red band perched jauntily on his head.

I stepped forward. "Pardon us." My partner whistled hello to Tolliver and leaped onto the floor.

"None needed," he replied disarmingly, barely glancing at my license. His handshake was dry but personal, the soft fingers adjusting deftly to my grip.

He tipped his hat, then frisbeed it toward his coatrack. It struck the stand and bounced aside. "Missing is my norm," he confided, stooping to collect it, "but the panache of impalement makes trying worthwhile." He crossed to his desk, settled himself in his swivel chair, and regarded the two of us over long steepled fingers. Strands of thin, light brown hair snaked up his high-domed forehead like new ivy over a rock. "To come so early in the morning, you must have urgent business." He resettled his black hirohito spectacles—double circles like a cutout bicycle—on his long nose. "How may I help you?"

I sat in the warped antique windsor chair to his left. "I want to find Diana Sherwood."

"Mm." His thin graying eyebrows, sad and downsloping, fluttered like fretful moths. "Where did you lose her?"

"She's been gone thirty-six hours, Dean Tolliver," I replied. "No joking matter."

"Thirty-six hours? Perhaps not," he allowed. "Still, Diana has a life beyond these hallowed halls." His tone mocked himself. "Is there reason to suspect unpleasantness?"

"Not that I know of," I said. "But whenever a child is missing, it's cause for concern."

"She's no child," replied Tolliver. "Diana is a young woman who knows her own mind. And Boston is a safe place. Especially for her, with her interfering mother." A short stout balding man in a black frock coat brought in a lacquered tray with a Prairie-style tea set on it. The cozy was a replica of Fallingwater. "Would you like some lapsang souchong?"

"Thank you. Who might have seen Diana?" I asked as Tolliver poured.

He handed me a cup. "Hu Nyo, her roommate, of course."

"*That* Nyo family?"

"You've spilled tea in your saucer. Have another napkin. Yes, *that* Nyo family." Tolliver blew on his tea to cool it. "Great-granddaughter in straight matriarchal succession of the dowager Mi Nyo herself. Even at eighty, Mi Nyo is commanding, but one would expect that of the chief of Boston's largest mercantile combine."

The woman who single-handedly masterminded the Bar Harbor Compact. The woman who launched the Secession with the line, "We've got to have a revolution before we all go broke." A bank balance whose logarithm was still a bigger number than mine. "Who else might know where Diana is?" I asked carefully.

He tapped the point of his chin, then sipped his tea. "Vladimir Abernathy, Diana's principal tutor. Her friend Tuoali Aleabola, perhaps. Hu, Tuoali, or Guillermo Rey should know where she is. An excellent student, one of our real success stories." He nodded at the holo on the wall.

"Diana is missing. Are you this unconcerned about all your students?"

"Have I stopped beating my wife, you mean? Pfui." I had never heard a person make this sound so naturally, with a breath of air blown through the mustache on a negligently uplifted upper lip like a summer breeze through lace curtains. "We are between class sessions, and neither I nor my staff are chaperones."

He said all this casually, almost condescendingly, but from

the corner of my eye I saw Akktri roll his hand in the movement that meant Deception. To keep the conversation moving and give myself a chance to think, I asked, "What does Diana study?"

"Our core curriculum, of course." He tugged his waistcoat down, then moved to the window. Lifting the damask curtains, he stared onto Louisburg's authentically preserved streets. "Address, etiquette, custom and conversation for the alien races one might encounter here in Boston."

I decided to tap his veneer and see what personality might be revealed through the cracks. "A snooty finishing school."

Tension crept up his shoulder blades as he turned back to me. "Would you have been more impressed if I had described it as a multidisciplinary, interactive tutorial focusing on interspecies sociology, psychology, history, linguistics, and culture?" His sharp gray eyes challenged me. "I thought you clever enough not to need inflated labels."

Akktri was scrambling over the furniture, making small noises to himself, his claws and whiskers twitching as he tested surfaces. He perched like a gargoyle on the smooth pate of a marble bust of Franklin and whistled cheerfully. His hands and feet shifted his weight on Ben's brains.

"He loves your collections," I said as a deflection. "He's a historian. A student of the past."

"We keep much of it here." Tolliver's wistful expression returned to his vertical face. "In this decadent, soulless age overrun with alien influences, we must preserve our human culture. Everything in this room is pre-contact—deliberately out-of-date. Including the schoolmaster." He glanced wryly at me and touched his glasses, then looked distantly out the window as if his childhood lay there. "We live on a jerkwater port, a minor stop off an insignificant galactic loophole. Very deflating."

Tolliver's attitude was uncommon. Bostonians tolerate most aliens the way a dog tolerates its master; what choice does it have? The master is often kind, if thoughtless, so the dog's life could be worse. Being of a practical disposition, the dog conceals its resentments, and even fetches slippers or sits up and performs tricks for dog bones. But, when it and the other dogs gather beyond the hearing of their masters, they dream of a world where they are in the sofas and the masters are in the wooden houses and mildewed musty rugs.

I decided to bring him back to a subject nearer at hand and asked, "What was Iris Sherwood's role in the Siege?"

"How will that help you find Diana?" he asked, a bit sharply.

"It probably won't. I just want to know."

He appraised me. "You were—thirteen or fourteen?—during the Siege."

"Thanks for the compliment. I was nineteen."

"Then you remember the events."

"They made no sense to me, then or now. You're a historian. You teach courses on the Siege. You ought to have perspective."

"History is what happened before one was born. Anything more recent is simply memory, and therefore subjective." Tolliver sighed. "The more I teach my Siege course, the less I know. The curse of education and age. As events recede, they become lifeless and dry." He sat up straighter. "If you want to know about the Siege, ask Mi Nyo. I wonder: did we do anything, or was it all inevitable?" He chuckled sadly. "Of course, this attitude may explain why she created a trading empire while I write pamphlets and grade essays." He took several long swallows of tea. "I will tell you only one thing, though, a thing I know from personal experience. Iris Sherwood's soul is made of petrified wood. And it was the Siege that made it so."

"It changed me too," I said, thinking of dead Billy. Did he die the way Ifraim Lemos had died? Or was he drowned? For a moment I wanted to confess to Tolliver, but then the thought of confiding in this stranger sickened me. He had not earned it. "Thank you." I finished my tea and stood up. "I'll start first with Hu Nyo. If she's not there, may I search Diana's room? I might learn something about where she's gone."

"I'd prefer that you didn't." Tolliver handed me a key that glowed red at one end. "This will guide you."

I nodded. "Thanks for your help." Akktri and I started for the door.

"A final word, Miz O'Meara. If by chance you see her, remind Hu that she is several weeks late with her midterm paper." His voice was sad and distant, as if speaking into a vid he knew was disconnected. "She is always late with her work."

4

"WHY DO YOU lie to Tolliver?" Akktri piped.

The pointerkey was leading us along a dark hallway with sloping floors and brooding lacquered landscape paintings. Now and then a doorway leered from the walls as if drunk, its crooked sides and jamb planed down to accommodate its rickety trapezoid. My assistant scampered cheerfully along, sniffing dust balls along the fringes of the dark blue runner that carpeted the hall.

I let his question pass. "What did you think of him?"

Akktri clambered onto my shoulders. I grunted and staggered to keep my balance as he curled his warm body around my neck. He squeaked in my ear, "Tolliver is wise and beautiful in his past. He burns his past for warmth."

I nodded thoughtfully. "Bitter man. Anyhow, I haven't lied to him yet."

"Your future does." Akktri struggled to find words. "Your future makes your past a lie."

"I didn't agree not to search," I replied defensively.

Akktri barked derisively. "He tells you not to. He think-k-ks you agree."

"I'm not responsible for what Dean Tolliver thinks."

"Words, words." Akktri impatiently waved his small hands and clutched my hair. "You are a trick-k-k-ster with your human lie-language. *I* do not lie, even in your language. Words, words, words," he concluded like a hectoring parrot.

"Well," I drawled, "then I guess *you* can't search either, can you?"

"I search!" he said indignantly. "Tolliver is not talking about me!" He covered his nose with his hands. "Hee hee. Clever Beverlee keeps him from thinking about little Akktri! I search! We hunt!"

"Uh huh." I suppressed a smile. Akktri doesn't know what hypocrisy is. "Anyhow, Tolliver was shading the truth too. Shielding someone or hiding something."

"You are noticing?" my sidekick asked, tugging my ear in surprise.

The key's tip changed from blue to green as we approached a paneled door on our right. "We're here."

"Door of oak-k-k wood," said Akktri. His head darted forward and he licked its varnished surface. "All here of wood. Maple, pine, teak-k-k. Old trees that knew sun and wind but not k-kerosene or fusion."

The door had neither bell nor palmspot. I knocked twice.

The hallway grew quieter somehow, as if unseen people had arrested their movements. I glanced at Akktri out of the corner of my eye. His hands made scurrying motions as he nodded and gestured at the door with his nose. I knocked again, then slowly inserted Iris's Master Key into the slot. Might as well see what it was good for.

We entered a tiny foyer with archways on either side leading into two bedrooms where I could see desks, papers, and datacubes strewn about: a student's junk. Clothing was heaped over lamps like soft sculpture.

Akktri, his hearing better than mine, shot toward the right-hand bedroom. I followed.

Long black hair fell like rain down the creamy beige back of a nude young woman as she knelt on the narrow single bed, her thighs pinning an equally nude young man. She rode him rhythmically, breathing with deep satisfaction. His arms were spread wide, fingers knotting the coverlet as he pushed up against her. Their clothing was tossed in sudden heaps about the room.

As I was retreating swiftly and quietly, intrigued but more

worried that I would be discovered, the girl looked over her shoulder at me. "What do you want?" she panted.

"I—excuse me—I thought the rooms were empty."

"And you always enter locked rooms?" The woman—though very young, she had too much self-possession to be called a girl—relaxed and slapped the man's haunch. "We're done, lover." She rose, dropping him out of her, and stepped with opulent young nudity over to a man's shirt too large for her, slipped into it, and laid its seams together, where they molecularly sealed, leaving no line as it flowed down her stomach and hips to just enough decency. Her throat and legs were moist with fresh sweat.

The man's hands flew to cover his groin, then he angrily rolled sideways off the bed. "Get out of here!" he shouted at me.

"Sorry." I hastily retreated, putting up my hands. "As I said, I thought no one was here."

"And now you realize your error," said the woman as her cuffs slid themselves up her forearms, letting them cool. "Wait outside."

"I'm looking for Diana Sherwood," I said. "I have authorization to be here." I put milquetoast outrage into my voice.

"She's not here." The young woman before me looked Cambodian Brahmin. Her skin, much of which was visible, was a beautiful light tan, the byproduct of both oriental and Yankee lineage. Smooth, soft, and round, it had a flawless even color like vanilla ice cream tinted with the tiniest dash of chocolate. In Boston, skin that color and texture means power and money. I envied her.

"Are you Hu Nyo? May I come in?"

"You *are* in." She languidly seated herself on the bed. Tucking her bare legs under her, she brushed her long straight black hair. Her soft eyes were wary with the placid, judging gaze learned in the cradle by those born to wealth and privilege. Under this calm superiority, I felt gauche.

Akktri was moving on my shoulders, deducing their past.

Breaking in on them was no way to start, so a straightforward explanation would probably fail. I had to pick an identity quickly, one that they could insult, humiliate, and therefore feel superior enough to talk to. "My name is Beverly O'Meara," I said in a prissy voice. "I am a senior assistant administrator in the unincorporated entities department of Dewey, Cheatham & Howe. I'm sure you've heard of our law firm."

She shook her head. "Never."

Not surprising, since I'd just invented it, so I haughtily sniffed. "Yes. Well. We're *very* exclusive. No aliens need apply. I'm looking for"—I pulled an image card out of my pocket, held it at arm's length, and squinted as if at a personal holo—"a Miz Diana Sherwood. Miz Sherwood is a collateral beneficiary of a small testamentary trust. I'm sure you appreciate the delicacy of my position." I glanced at her to make sure she appreciated this delicacy. "Miz Sherwood is entitled, pursuant to the trust documents and related codicils, to a periodic stipend whose amount varies depending upon market fluctuations, investment performance, and the dividend history of certain private holding companies." My voice was developing a natural rhythmic singsong that suggested an infinite capacity to spew out details. "Her great-aunt Beatrice established the trust some time ago and I'm pleased to report that, after taking into consideration inflation, currency conversion, the usual Loophole import losses, and Boston vat—"

"Why do you want her?" Hu interrupted with brisk impatience tinged with condescending tolerance. People always believe you if you act stultifyingly boring.

"Yes. Well. I'm required by the indenture to determine certain aspects of Diana's social status, courses being taken and so on. If you don't mind me telling tales out of school"—I giggled a little—"we in the unincorporated entities division have had a good many heated arguments over the proper interpretations of several pivotal clauses of the bequests. Why just last week—"

"She's not here," the man cut in, returning from the bathroom. Tall and saturnine, he had on a blousy white shirt with a drawstring neck, deliberately pre-contact like Chris Tolliver's straw boater. His muscular brown chest was sprinkled with dark hair. I recognized him from the holo I'd seen on Tolliver's wall.

"Yes. Well. Perhaps you could take a message for me?" I didn't give them a chance to refuse. "You see, I am a senior assistant administrator in the unincorporated entities department of—"

"You told us that already," he snapped, moving over to Hu to run his hands along her neck and massage her shoulders.

"Yes. Well. And who might you be, sir?" A little officious stress often squeezes the truth from people. "Do you have standing in this matter? Are you Tuoali Aleabola or Guillermo Rey?" I pronounced the names with infuriating slow precision, determined to impress these people with my cosmopolitanism.

"It's pronounced Ghee-*zher*-mo, not Ghee-*yer*-mo," he corrected me, scowling in irritation.

"You are he? Does Miz Sherwood know you?" My voice was irritatingly nasal.

He chuckled and glanced suggestively at the bed. "She did, once or twice."

"Yes. Well." He plainly wanted me to ask him about prior sexual exploits—from his perspective, he was short one screw because of me—which meant I'd probably get more out of him if I snubbed him. I turned crisply and dismissively away. "Miz Nyo, as a young lady of some substance, perhaps *you* could help me."

Guillermo Rey didn't like having the spotlight shift away. He moved gracefully in front of me and took my arm, turning me back to face him. "You've got a pretty big pussy there." His tone was both suggestive and scornful.

I blushed and started to titter, then hastily covered my mouth with my hand. I was a senior assistant administrator on duty, after all. "That's my research associate. It's a Phner," I added in a stage whisper, as if we were keeping a dreadful secret from Akktri.

"Furry, too," the man murmured.

"Oh, certainly," I replied, deliberately obtuse. "They are covered with fur everywhere except their hands." I reached up, patted Akktri in our private hand code that meant Scare This Guy, and rolled my left shoulder so that my companion tumbled into my arms, wiggling his torso with glee. "Ask it yourself." I lobbed him at Rey.

"Hey!" yelled the youth.

"Hee yow!" cried my Phner companion gaily, twisting his body instantly so he sailed by Guillermo Rey's suddenly averted face and neck. Akktri twisted again to land silently at the foot of the bed, caught my signal that said Scram And Search, and sped into the empty bedroom across the foyer.

Hu Nyo methodically brushed her lovely hair. Maybe someday I could afford hair that smooth and straight. She glanced at Guillermo Rey, who was badly embarrassed.

"Yes. Well. As I may have mentioned, Miz Nyo, I am a senior assistant administrator in—"

"Come on, Hu." Guillermo turned away from me in disgust. "We've got to get out of here. Where's the bag? Did you get everything we need?"

"Naturally, lover," she replied without interest, rolling her neck so her long hair fell down her back. Putting her brush on the bed, Hu stood, her shirt moulding itself flatteringly to her form, subtly firming to lift her bosom and hourglass her waist, then headed for the bathroom as the tail demurely pulled itself down over her buttocks.

"I have a few more questions for Miz Nyo." I sat, my gaze downcast and far away, and crossed my ankles, tapping my fingertips together, waiting for Guillermo Rey to get impatient.

"I haven't seen Diana in a while," he said abruptly, then crossed to the rumpled bed and stretched himself upon it, resting his head on one hand and grinning at me. I found myself intrigued by the way his trim legs moved. He filled his pants well. He shifted his hips, the adult muscles taut and firm under a youth's soft skin. Age ruins a man's skin by infesting it with coarse hair.

"Where might she be now?"

"Seeing her folks." He cocked his thumb toward the ceiling. "Somewhere upfloor. *Way* upfloor." He looked at me differently, then slipped off the bed with easy grace. Standing, he came over to me. "You smell good, you know." He leaned his nose near my shoulder.

Evidently his missile was omnidirectional. Sexy though he was, I held my ground. He was too close, within hitting distance, but to yield would show weakness and encourage him. Plus I was convinced he wouldn't hit a woman, especially a simp. "Yes. Well."

He leaned forward as if to kiss me.

I blew a puff of air into his right eye.

He blinked and snorted and I slid out of his attempted embrace, patting my hair as I did so.

"Yes. Well. About Diana," I said as if nothing had happened. "What do you know about her?"

"We're in a few classes," he replied, wiping his eye. He crossed to the oak rolltop desk and nonchalantly shuffled through Hu's papers.

"Where might she have gone?" I asked.

Guillermo answered desultorily, his mind apparently elsewhere. No, he hadn't seen her. No, her behavior hadn't seemed unusual. When I asked who she had been close to, he clammed up sharply, and I got the impression of a spurned advance. I also sensed concealment; no one could be as aggressively ignorant as Guillermo was claiming. I wished Akktri could see him—my assistant would read his tension—but he was lost in the other bedroom. I decided to prick Guillermo to break his shield and see what emerged through the cracks of anger.

"Now, then, Guillermo." I pronounced his name wrong again.

"It's Ghee-*zher*-mo," he corrected me absently without turning back.

"Yes. Well." I acted bored again and examined my fingernails. "What does this have to do with Diana's collateral legacy?"

"Legacy?" he snorted. "What legacy do any of us have? Aliens have taken from us all that is human." He pointed a finger at me. "You remember the Uprising?"

Every Bostonian knows the 2016 Uprising. Thousands of people were gassed in the Financial District by unknown terrorists who disappeared in the confusion. Corpses lined Batterymarch Street and Merchants Row, bodies like unbagged garbage waiting for pickup. "Yes," I shivered.

"Those who died were martyrs. A chain of martyrs forms a rope. Anyway, what do you know? You're just a brainless assistant administrator."

"*Senior* assistant administrator, and there's no reason to become personally insulting, sir." We heard Hu returning from the bathroom. "Yes. Well. Much as I'd like to continue this fascinating conversation, young man"——he scowled at the phrase; good——"I really must ask Miz Nyo where——" Seeing Hu, I stopped, speechless.

She wore chameleon trousers that made her lower half effectively transparent so that she seemed to be a torso floating in air. Made from the retinas of an enormous dumb galactic herbivore, Targive-modified to transmit light as well as sense it, they passed photons around their surface and out the other side. Hu's waist, legs, and feet were a ripple in the background, like a pane of glass held underwater.

Her blouse was red-and-blue moire: it shimmered and changed in interference patterns designed to make the observer's eyes ache. Her hair——that beautiful black hair she had so lovingly combed——was coated with yellow glop and sprang from her head in broad bands like banana leaves or a child's drawing of the sun's rays. She had covered her eyes with flat yellow disks the size of coasters and deadened her face so the muscles barely moved.

She looked totally inhuman, unrecognizable: all traces of her meat body converted into stylized geometric forms. An expensive ensemble, impeccably worn. The height of fashion. It scared the living vent out of me.

Hu drifted across to the doorway and rotated her head, smoothly as a bot, at Guillermo. "Come ing love urr," she said in the uninflected metallic sounds made by a throat-warbler. "Bring the bag."

Guillermo nodded, unsettled but decisive. Her balloon head swiveled unhurriedly toward the door.

"Miz Nyo?" I interrupted in genuine agitation. "Miz Nyo! I still have a few questions to——"

Hu cruised on. I stepped into her path. My feet didn't want me to. "Dean Tolliver asked me to remind you that you're late with a midterm paper." Though idiotic, it was the only thing I could think of. "Aren't you doing the work?"

"Why do you per mit your self to be used as Tol live urrs fnurr." It was like listening to chalk. Her mouth was a small red oval in a still, sallow face like a coptic death mask.

"Used?" I shrugged. "It's common courtesy, Miz Nyo."

"All right then if you hap pen to see him tell Tol live urr I see no point in com plea ting his fool ish ven ting pay per. Are you come ing love urr." Her head rotated back toward Guillermo, who had grown quiet.

"Sure, Hu," he muttered, scooping up a dark green sool overnight suitcase into which he stuffed papers from the desk.

"The door please." Hu's hands were immersed in spherical blue deprivers, and now she raised them like basketball pods at the ends of her arms. Better than handcuffs or restraints, they imprison your fingers and make you helpless. I knew a couple of ways to get out of them, but was willing to bet Hu didn't. She wanted the thrill of deliberate helplessness—what will people do when given unexpected power? She was fooling herself, of course—nobody'd touch a Nyo scion. If she wanted real thrills, she could change her face and stroll the Basement.

I squeezed her arm, cold and slick as lard. "I need to speak with you, Miz Nyo. When you're more able to talk."

"Ha ha ha. Ask at Cloud Pal ass. May I go now."

"Yes. Well." I turned the doorknob and she levitated upward and through.

My stomach churned unpleasantly. I licked my lips and glanced at Guillermo.

"Let's get the hell out of here," he said.

"Sure." I too wanted to be rid of Hu's memory. "Akktri!"

"Yo-ee!" My assistant shot into the room, dashing about the foyer as he checked its recent past.

"Come on."

He gestured animatedly back at Diana's room. "K-k-clear sign."

"Hush." I bent down close to his perplexed face. "We have to go now."

His ears drooped but he caught my tone of voice. "Ok-k-kay," he said unhappily. "We hunt later."

Guillermo was waiting at the door. "After you." Akktri and I passed through and he locked it behind us. "Oh, Miz O'Meara?"

As I turned, he slapped my face.

The blow caught me totally by surprise. I stumbled backwards, hand to stinging cheek.

"I don't have to put up with your snide vent," he spat, holding my chin with his hand and moving it from side to side. "You hear me, Beverly? You insulted me. I don't like that. And you pronounced my name wrong." His grin was savage. "Tell your client Iris I've got powerful friends." He shoved my face away, rose, and strode briskly down the hallway after Hu.

Akktri crouched by me, darting his glance to my retreating assailant. "Why do you not signal me to attack-k-k?" He swung his small arm in Guillermo's direction. "I rip his throat out. End his art."

Akktri's loyalty and fearless tough talk always touch me. "Don't you have to wait for the art to be finished?" I asked. "Besides, he might be helpful."

To my surprise, Akktri grew thoughtful. "Yes-s-s," he said. "Guillermo is violent and stup-p-pid and angry. I wait for more of his art."

"He's trickier than he looks. Ouch. I underestimated him and he suckered me." I shook my head.

"The art of his life is fouled," Akktri added.

I breathed deeply, trying to flush Hu's reek out of my lungs. "What did you find in Diana's room? I didn't want you to say anything while Guillermo was there."

"Much confusion. Much disorder." My assistant was troubled. "Human has not words. Things tak-k-ken and things brought. Past-existence-now-removed-will-return. Past and future knotted. Paths twisted and mud-dy." He shook his head as if the truth were a fish whose spine he could break in his jaws. "Deception and lies and pain."

"Work on it. You'll get it."

Akktri hopped in frustration. "Need to show you in the *room.*"

"Why not just tell me?"

"No words, no words!" He shook his fist at the door. "But you are only there then, not now."

"I got a glance at it."

"You listen with mud ears." Akktri's tact tends to disintegrate when he gets excited. "I show your future."

"Right." I collected my Phner bundle in my arms and scratched his ears and chest. "Meanwhile, we've got a few things to do."

"We hunt more?" he asked.

"You bet." I hefted him, remembering Guillermo giving me the Look—anger, impotence, hatred of authority, vindication—a look that signifies danger and revenge at the next encounter. "First, we go see the place of disappearance. Second, we check what Mack's found."

"And third?" Akktri rubbed his small hands together like a hyperactive miser.

I tickled his whiskers. "Third, we come back when the coast is clear and burgle Diana's room."

5

I FOUND A mover and instructed it to take us to the Old North disney. Disneys are Boston's historical playgrounds, carefully choreographed to simulate the City's past in tourist-pleasing ways. Within these protected arenas, contrived pseudoevents are frequent. Pickpockets and con artists flourish here, since marks are much easier to take when they think you're an actor who'll return the goods after the joke is finished.

When the doors shoofed open, I was surprised to find myself staring at the familiar rectangularity of corridors.

"O'Beara?" demanded a gruff, phlegmy voice. "Roderick wants you."

I leaned my head into the corridor, where a two-meter-plus-tall Koltsoi was wiffling idly, her long graceful limbs waving in fussy irritation. "You did this, Ulkudge, didn't you?" I asked. "Redirected me here?"

"Daturally." Ulkudge came effortlessly to a stop, her nose twitching to let me know she thought my gesture maladroit. "We tracked your key and asked the moober to bring you to us." She flowed into the mover and shoved her key into its slot. We accelerated.

Except for the way they move, every aspect of Koltsoi is hideous. Their faces are spotted with about eight lumpy asymmetric light-organs plus, on their gray and brown cheeks, two big heat sensor pads that look like portable audio speakers. A Koltsoi's nose, which droops in yellow tendrils like a tumescent goldenrod flower looking for a horny bee, is the only spot of brightness in a skin the color of chocolate pudding.

The bulbs interfere with their vocal path and make them pronounce English as if they had a perpetual head cold.

Incapable of awkward motion, they walk and drift like angels. A drunken Koltsoi falling facefirst onto the pavement is still more graceful than the best human ballet dancer. But Koltsoi, at least the ones on Earth, enjoy nothing better than officiously interrogating humans. These qualities made Ulkudge useful to Roderick Petravelli. Unlike Phneri, they are rare in Boston, so having one on your staff is a status symbol.

"What does the chief want me for?" It couldn't be Ifraim Lemos, I thought; that was too recent, and probably too small-scale for the chief's personal attention.

Ulkudge tittered. "He wants to ask a fabbor."

"Me? Are you sure?"

"I don't beliebe it myself," sniffed Ulkudge as the mover sighed to a halt, its doors opening. "You first, death-lubber," she snipped to Akktri.

Whistling something nasty in reply, Akktri hopped onto the floor as the Koltsoi elegantly hauled me along. Their great strength, the by-product of a musculature designed on pneumatic extension rather than lever-action contractions, is part of their beautiful movement. Akktri bounded along behind us.

We were in the Boston Gymnasium, Petravelli's favorite off-duty social club. I smelled sweat and cotton; the doughy walls on either side glistened faintly with moisture. In the distance men grunted. Everything was too brightly lit with slightly red-shifted and infrared lamps, to make everyone look ruddy, healthy, and sleek.

"Here she is," said Ulkudge when we arrived. She flung me forward like a dowager disposing of a tissue. Once free of her grip, I stumbled clumsily into the crystalline frame of his workout environment and banged my kneecap painfully against one of its clear-cylinder legs. Knowing Ulkudge, she probably calculated a course that would lurch me into it. That's her kind of humor.

When you've been Boston's Chief of Police for many years,

power becomes as much part of your atmosphere as cologne. Though in his seventies, Roderick Petravelli looked forty-five. Twenty years ago, he had looked only a little younger when, just after the Siege, he had ascended to his current position. His face now was a bit broader, the lines a bit more furrowed, the muscles tighter. His body, clad in a sprayon matte white exersuit, was still muscular with neither potbelly nor lovehandles. Probably had his guts sucked every month. His hair was silvery white, wavy, and combed close to his head.

The environment framed him like an open-walled cage. Inside the cube formed by its bars, the holographic tactile display was manifesting most of the torso of a huge finbacked alligatorlike lizard, whose multitoothed jaws Petravelli was prying apart with his meaty hands. At each end of the enclosure, the carnivore's body ended abruptly as a chopped salami. It writhed, its liquid-black eyeballs rolling toward Petravelli, as he flung its head from side to side, his forearms straining.

"Dimedrodon," said Ulkudge, enjoying the spectacle. "Late Garboniferous protomammal." At least I think that's what she said; with Ulkudge's thick accent it was often hard to tell. "Works deldoids and driceps."

Petravelli often held court at this gym, to remind everyone how fit he was. His routines tended toward swashbuckling and derring-do. "What did Ulkudge tell you?" he grunted without taking his eyes off the creature he was trying to flip over.

"She said you want to ask me a favor. I didn't believe her."

"You should." Petravelli shook his head, flinging sweat off his roman nose. "Ulkudge seldom errs. That's why I use her."

"Ulkudge," I said slowly, "is full of shit. That's why she's brown."

Petravelli smiled thinly, unamused. "You don't like her. She eats from your plate, because she intrudes in your Basement. But that is a ferret's role. Ulkudge goes into the Cube"— he rammed the Dimedrodon's head into the floor and the beast roared with pain—"and finds perps. She brings them to me."

"It's the way they're caught," I murmured, willing my cheeks not to twitch into a smile. Wrestling dinosaurs, for goodness sake.

"Not by me." Petravelli threw aside the animal, which vanished as it fell outcube, and foraged forward. A machete had appeared in his hand and he swung it ferociously, cutting through thigh-thick bamboo shoots, his white hair disarrayed and plastered to his skull with sweat and dew. The scraws and cries of hawks and tree birds echoed above us. "All that Sherlock Holmes sleuthing," Petravelli said, reholstering his machete as he reached a small clearing. "Crawling on hands and knees with your nose pressed against a magnifying glass, digging in the mud for burnt candle stubs." His tone and manner suggested tolerant disapproval, a bloodhound owner watching his dog root through a pile of leaves.

"Really. I suppose you have a better way?"

"To have a crime, you must have a perp," he said, abdominals tensing as he bent to lift a huge fallen log. Petravelli liked to have troopers punch him there. Especially female ones. Hard, but not too hard. I'd heard stories. "Before it manifests itself in the world as an act, every crime exists as an idea in its perp's mind." He levered the log aside with a leonine growl, then held up his cupped hands like parentheses enclosing space. "And it ends as a memory in its perp's mind." Petravelli tapped his skull. "So if I know the minds of all the perps in Boston, I have captured knowledge of all the crimes in Boston. Past and future. Your Phner partner may appreciate this concept better than you do."

"The mind crosses time," Akktri said all too agreeably.

"Your own recent encounter, for instance, with—what was his name?"

"Ifraim Deemos," replied Ulkudge on cue.

"Ifraim Lemos." Petravelli took his time sounding the words. "Was your killing of him murder, manslaughter, or self-defense? Iris, with all her bot eyes, can never know that. But if I know your head, *then* I will know that answer."

So he *had* known, and that was the reason he had brought me here. But for what? "What does any of this have to do with me?" I answered, more shakily than I wanted to.

"There is a mind, in Boston, that you are closer to than I," replied Petravelli, returning to his adventure. He was bicycle-paddling a Hnarfil waterwalker upriver—evidently his routine now wanted him to work his gluteals and quadriceps. "I want you to get inside his head."

"I'm already on a case," I answered stiffly.

"That's *why* I'm asking now, not yesterday or tomorrow," the chief answered with a snap. "You were at Louisburg school this morning. The person who interests me is a student there. Guillermo Rey." Even panting as he forged through the river's turbulence, Petravelli pronounced the name correctly. "You know him?"

I rubbed my cheek, sore from Guillermo's slap. "We met."

"I want you to spy on him."

"Why not Iris Sherwood's bot eyes?"

Savages screamed in the distance. Petravelli leaped from his boat, a broadsword appearing in his right hand, a dagger in his left. He pivoted and his blade sliced through a Zulu's pike, disarming that foe, then spun and caught another warrior in the neck. The first Zulu fled. "Come on, Bev," Petravelli chuckled, turning from his triumph to grin broadly and give me a grand conspiratorial wink. "Aren't there dozens of ways to diddle a bot? Even a clever colleen like you probably knows a few. In your time, you've probably shorted an eye for a little B-and-E. Hmm? Or thrown a prock snowball? Splat, and out it goes. In your youth, in the Siege? Right?"

I nodded noncommittally. "It's been done."

"Naturally," Petravelli continued. A mammoth, overmuscled chieftain now stood before him, a necklace of human jaws slung over his enormous ebony chest. The Nubian laughed loudly, his fists on his hips.

With a rebel yell Boston's Chief of Police roared, ducked his head, and charged, catching the startled Nubian in a bear hug. "And then there's fudging stored records," he gasped as he linked his hands to each other's wrist and, with a groan, lifted the giant so that his splayed black toes no longer touched the floor. "A good juggler can make history run backward or stand on its head. Cut it and splice it. Besides, you put honest cits on camera, they turn mean."

The Nubian's eyes were bulging, the tendons in his neck standing out. He was pummeling Roderick across the shoulder blades, but the chief hung on and the big Nubian was wheezing, his struggles weakening. Suddenly he collapsed, his arms drooping, head lolling as his tongue fell sideways out of his mouth.

Petravelli dropped the unconscious body and stood, his arms loose and curled, panting heavily. "Bev," he said, gulping air, "how many times have you caught honest cits, had them give you the Look?" Ulkudge handed him a towel and he wiped his face, reveling in the sensation.

"Often." I thought of Guillermo bristling beside me after he slapped me. "Recently."

"Real human hatred in the Look." Petravelli nodded as if we were viewing a shared memory. "That fool Iris wants to put eyes everywhere. She'll get the Look a hundred thousand times. She'll turn honest cits into perps, she will. That's no way to grease the wheels of society. No way to run a city."

"Interesting view you have of police procedures."

"It works, smart girl," he said tartly, and I had a glimpse of the wrath that descended on those who displeased him.

"No disrespect intended, Chief," I replied without a trace of irony. "Pardon my tone. You're undoubtedly correct. After all, you've had years on the job."

"I have. And now I'd like this favor from you."

I shrugged a question. "Why me, Chief? I can do it for you, as long as it doesn't interfere with my assignment. But what's in it for you?"

"I can't get anyone close to that rugrat."

"What do you mean?"

Stepping out of the cage, Petravelli twirled his towel into a rope that he laid around his shoulders. "I'm fairly convinced Guillermo Rey has friends on the force. He's shied away from anyone on staff that I've run at him. But he has a roving eye." Petravelli looked me up and down, his big broad nose moving like a paintbrush. "You might catch it." He began drumming his fingers on the workout frame, repetitive yet staccato, glancing at Akktri as he did so.

My partner's head jerked around and his whiskers stiffened. His teeth rattled in his head. He bolted for the door, chittering incoherently.

"Akktri!" I caught him forcefully.

"We fall! We fall from sky! I die!"

I pulled him close and stroked the fur on his neck and back.

"Beverlee?" He whiffled. "Beverlee?" His claws dug my arm. "His noise. Struc-k-k-ture is of us falling, soon-to-end-without-being-complete."

Holding Akktri, I returned. "Please don't drum your fingers in that cadence. It reminds him of the Endless Fall."

"My apologies," he murmured as Ulkudge sniffed. "And my *assistant* apologizes as well," he added with a barb, glancing pointedly at Ulkudge.

"Yes." The Koltsoi's riffling nose tendrils indicated either acquiescence or pique. Possibly both. "Bardon me."

I turned to Akktri. "You all right?"

My sidekick's head wobbled but he was becoming chipper again. "Yes."

"So—will you do my favor?" resumed Petravelli, sliding into the silence. A thought seemed to strike him. "Ulkudge." He snapped his fingers. "Do you have O'Meara's weapon? The one improperly confiscated from her earlier today?"

The big Koltsoi fussed momentarily, and then with glum sinuosity produced it.

"Thank you." Petravelli took the pistol, checked it briskly, and handed it to me handle first. "There."

I accepted the pistol and, notwithstanding Petravelli's inspection, examined it myself. His eyes widened slightly in surprise and, I thought, tacit approval. I bent, rolled up my trouser leg, and slid the gun back into its holster. "All right," I said, rolling down the trouser and straightening up. After all, what he was asking would be small trouble, and he *was* the Chief of Police. "I'll do it. When do you want a report?"

"Good. Two days. Report to me personally. Now I must shower." He nodded briskly at Ulkudge. "Escort Miz O'Meara and the Phner out."

Wordlessly, the tall Koltsoi yanked me by the scruff of my neck and, with a tasteful cant of her brown multisocketed head, hustled me down the corridor.

6

AFTER BEING ESCORTED into a mover by Ulkudge, who finished the action with a graceful pirouette and some delicate finger-wavings that are probably Koltsoi scatology, I peeled myself off the floor and shakily ordered it to 32 Franklin 175.

"Mack O'Meara's apt?" chirped Akktri. He crouched solicitously before my face, his hands held together like a feckless trainee paramedic. "None of your bones are brok-k-ken," he added helpfully.

"Glad to hear the news." My clothes, which Ulkudge's manhandling had bunched, were trying to pull themselves back into order and were squeezing me, so I paused, loosened my waistband, and let them readjust themselves.

"Why see Mack?" Akktri went on. "We will see him earlier."

I laughed. Akktri's malapropisms always cheer me up. "After all the new friends we've made so far, I need to think this through before doing anything further." With my hand I delicately poked and massaged my jaw.

"They didn't seem lik-k-ke our friends," Akktri noted.

"They weren't."

"Oh. You are jok-k-king again. You do this when you are nervous and want me not to know."

"You're getting too perceptive." I rubbed my neck and rolled it, hearing a disconcerting muffled click. "This is a fine kettle of fish, isn't it?"

"Fish?" My watson bounded onto my shoulders. "Mack-k has fish? I love fish!" His claws dug painfully into my neck. "Lots of fish for us? What kind of fish?"

It took the remainder of our mover ride to untangle that one.

My brother Mack lives in the remnants of the old New England Telephone headquarters. Built in the 1940's, it's a granite and reinforced concrete layer cake with a heavy-wood and steel-grating lobby. I call it the Superman building because its architecture resembles what George Reeves could leap in a single bound, after he was through changing the course of mighty rivers.

To get to Mack's apt, we walked along a corridor tiled in a brown-and-tan checkerboard pattern that reminded me of a cheap dentist's waiting room.

"What constipated Tulgut did *you* offend?" Mack said when he saw me.

"Ulkudge," I replied testily, stepping past him into the apt. "Petravelli's muscle."

Half of Mack's apt is in the old building. The other half reaches into the procked spaces created when the City was hived in the 2040's. Prock, a synthesized alien polymer modified from the nasal mucus of a huge silicon-based geovore, squirts out like a liquid and hardens upon contact with oxygen into a ceramic stronger than reinforced concrete. The Targives introduced it when they arrived in the Twenties and it promptly became the building material of choice. The hiving occurred in the Thirties and Forties when, in the largest eminent-domain proceeding in human history, the City of Boston took all the building interstices and had them layered together to form the Cube.

Most Bostonians have windowalls that display the Arnold Arboretum, Nantucket beaches in wintertime, and other post-card shots. My brother lives in a place with real six-panel glass windows that used to overlook Post Office Square (back when Boston needed a post office, back when mail was paper). They rattle, slide vertically, and form a pass-through between his living room and bedroom. I like their incongruity.

"Do you have any fish?" Akktri asked. He stood between

my legs, one hand wrapped around each calf. "Fresh dead fish?"

"Fresh fish? Hmm." Mack thoughtfully tapped his chin.

"If no live ones." Akktri prefers to end them himself. Death is a Phner taste sensation.

"Fresh—fish," Mack said as if my diminutive assistant had just made a brilliant quip. "Fresh—fish." He luxuriated in the sibilant words.

"Fish! Fish!" Akktri was bouncing with excitement like a golden jackhammer.

"Don't tease him," I said softly. "It's been a tough day and it's still morning."

"All right." Mack slapped his hands together. "How about some raw Boston Harbor flounder? By an amazing coincidence, I *think* I picked some up earlier today." He headed into the kitchen.

"You bluffer," I said lovingly. "You sweetie." Following him over to the icebox, I patted him roughly on his warm upper back.

Mack peered over his left shoulder. "The meter's on, huh?" he asked, meaning was I on a case. I nodded, and he reached in and lifted out a long rectangular packet wrapped in white paper. "Here," he said to Akktri, placing the packet on the butcher-block counter.

"Oo-ee-yow!" My little friend jumped lightly onto the counter and sniffed along the folds. The prize within reach, his movements assumed the solemn tender precision of a priest consecrating the host. He would esfn each instant of this as only a Phner can: unfolding the paper, wrinkle by greasy wrinkle. Starchy and fishy smells.

Watching his absorbed pleasure, I smiled. He was transported with delight.

I followed Akktri's every deft movement, thinking about the impossibility of appreciating Phneri perception and intelligence. He was seeing and understanding things that are the thickest fog to us humans—unless you got your brain plowed by a Targive, a price I was unwilling to pay. Tarmods are not mere augments but substitutions; for everything they put in, they remove something else, a different feature each time. I wondered if Iris had been plowed, and if so, what had she conceded? Her humanity? Her emotions? That would fit with the Targive humor, to take attributes the owner found super-fluous. Once her feelings were gone, had Iris convinced her-self that what she had lost was vestigial or unimportant?

Targive biosystems had permeated the whole Cube to the point that when Iris called Boston an organism, she spoke with more truth than metaphor.

Once Boston existed on solely human technology, but no more. Spatiens and Sh'k waldoes tend to Boston's ecology, crawling through sewer pipes to churn up sludge that can be fed to the pissmops and slugs. Without them the City would destroy itself in toxic backup inside of a day. Llonr dataform recorders drive Tulgut ganglia receptors to send images and datafood throughout the City, to be gulped down by Targive-modified iridescent mitochondria and encrypted into secure data storage that reproduces by cellular fission.

But the true penetration was cultural: were Hu Nyo's shim-mershift patterns Navajo, Polynesian, Shaker, or Phner? We can no longer identify, except to say that, in some vast melt-ing-pot alloy, they have merged and now bespeak our Boston. Or even biological; for the right price, the Targives would cram anything you wanted into your cerebellum . . . in return for extracting a hunk of their choice.

Akktri had one corner of the paper gripped between two fingers and was lifting it like a shy virgin on his wedding night. He folded back the skin, his claws running delicately over the flounder's scales, and extracted the skeleton intact.

Phneri make extraordinary surgeons—when they're al-lowed into Mass General, for they can seldom be persuaded to focus on whether the patient lives or dies. So they become morticians and coroners, their reports mishmashes of irrelevancies such as what kind of Q-tip the deceased used to clean her ears.

"While you've been watching him eat, I've done the basic locate for you," Mack murmured, moving over to his console. "Checked her medical history. Blank. Hospitals haven't got her. Rods no record. No transit outside Boston. I'm checking her friends to see if anybody's disappeared with her. Maybe she's just lost?"

"Only children get lost," I said, leaning against the wall. "Adults disappear. Diana's no child." And all the City data was linked together, which meant that she was not merely misplaced. If she'd left Boston, the exits would have recorded it—unless the girl were deliberately trying to vanish. Iris had confidently asserted that this was impossible, but Iris might not know her daughter as well as she thought.

"She's no adult, either," Mack disagreed. "At least not judging from her file. What about kidnapping?"

"Let me think." To what purpose? "Nobody's heard from the abductors," I began. No one would get in touch if Diana was already dead. Perhaps she was; the Revere House had already proven a dead end. I automatically glanced at Akktri, still absorbed in his flounder.

"Possible," I said finally, when it became clear that Mack was waiting for a reply. "The client is an important person. Reserved. Cunning and cautious." I stopped, hoping to be let off the hook, but he was studiously silent. "I don't think I should say any more," I finished reluctantly.

"Have you checked with the mother yet? Iris Sherwood could find her quick enough."

Mentally cursing myself for the oversight, I said smoothly, "The client says I can't ask Iris," and then realized that what I had just claimed was, in fact, not disingenuous. Iris *was* two people, a mother and an administrator, and she'd built a chinese wall between them as thoroughly as if she'd severed her corpus callosum.

"Come on, Beverly," Mack pressed, oblivious to my dilemma. "You can spill it. Who am I going to talk to? What difference does it make?"

"A difference to *me*. I promised the client confidentiality."

"Talking to family doesn't count. You know that."

"I said *no.*"

Mack recoiled. I wiped my mouth and said in a calmer voice, "They're *my* hole cards, Mack. They stay down."

"Okay, okay." Mack put up his hands and eased away, as he always does when met with active resistance, but I could tell he was hurt, almost frightened by my resolution. He settled his butt on a counter stool and made an enormous corned beef sandwich, heavy on the mustard.

Mack never got along with our father. Billy envied Mack's brains and always goaded his son to achieve more, to desire more. The younger child, I tried to please both of them, working hard to live up to Billy, defending Mack whenever Billy's insults had driven my brother from our house.

After Billy's death, Mack refused even to go to City Hall Plaza to search for him. Twenty years later he still avoids the subject. He doesn't want to know where Billy died.

"So you're here just on business," he said, pushing bread down on the meat like a man squeezing shut an overloaded suitcase. "Well, now I've reported. I've performed the service you required. Are you finished with me, or is there something else you can use me for?" His tone mingled anger and irony.

"Take a look at this." I held out the Master Key Iris Sherwood had given me. "How much can I do with this?"

"Mm. A key. Something unusual about it?" Mack took a huge slurpy bite. His tongue scooped a cribble of corned beef off his lower lip. He took the key in his left hand and turned it over. "How'd you acquire this? Whose is it?"

"Can't you tell that from the key itself?"

" 'Course I can." He grinned with yellow teeth. "Since you ask." Sandwich in one hand and key in the other, he shambled into his office. I followed.

Mack's office walls were overgrown with infogrit: faxes,

maps, printouts, photos, diagrams, and endless scribbles. All flat surfaces were indented with tan and brown rings because he used overfull coffee cups as paperweights. The floor was invisible under intellectual dandruff: an exploded tarot deck, self-driving screws, scattered music cubes, miniature lead soldiers from antique war games, and rare collectible dodecahedral dice.

You don't walk in Mack's office, you shuffle through white kudzu. When he once tried to get his landlord cited for undermaintaining his apt, the building inspector ordered him to clean up his room first. With perverse pride, Mack still had the fading report tacked up between a three-year-old poker tournament notice and the latest set of bridge double-dummy puzzles.

"On second thought, I'll wait here at the door," I said warily. "It might eat me."

"Sure." Mack forded his way into the calamity and shoved some tilted stacks of paper books onto the floor. A chair emerged like a dazed rescued cave-in victim. He plopped himself on it and plunged his hand into the forage, extracting a handheld controller.

Hearing our rustle, Akktri charged the mess. I stood, fists on hips, as my buddy burrowed and chortled to himself.

Sometimes I think Mack and Akktri are just two little boys, one masquerading as a balding overweight datasifter, the other as a beaver. I should issue them short pants, suspenders, and bandages for their skinned knees.

"Power on, Lucille." Mack burped. He had wolfed his macfood in eleven bites.

Only one space on the wall was bare. This square now glowed faintly. "Ready and willing," said a sultry woman's voice.

Mack inserted the key. "Whose is this?"

"A Master," replied the computer. "Very strong. Very potent. No name either. It's blanked. Unusual."

"No name?" Mack turned to me. "Where'd you get it?" he

asked me insistently. "From Iris Sherwood, the girl's mother? She could do that. Why'd she give it to you? Why should you need it on so simple an assignment?"

"Lucille," I asked, again deflecting his questions, "what'll it do?"

"Almost no limit on this widget," said the box. "What do you want? I'm itching to try it out."

"Search the last two days' reads for Diana Sherwood."

"Public or locked?"

Mack and I glanced at one another. "You can get into restricted scans?" he asked.

"I can with this joystick," Lucille boasted. "Quite a key you've got, Beverly. We're just warming up. This is abacus stuff so far. Ask me something *hard*."

"When's the most recent record?"

"Piffle. Too easy. Two days ago in the afternoon."

Around the time Iris said Diana had vanished. "Revere House? Old North Historic District? Display it."

The screen showed the image I'd seen earlier in Iris's office: Diana amid a crowd.

"Resuming realtime."

The people milled about and we heard murmuring voices. The figures passed out of range.

"Okay, that's the end of the recording," I said to Mack. "Find more reads of this time and location. Display them."

Mack cocked an eyebrow. "You think it'll do that?"

Before I could answer, the scene shifted to another eye. As Diana headed toward the Revere House's entrance, two humans in black turtlenecks and trousers pinned her on either side. Their faces were shielded by Red Sox baseball caps. They pressed against her and she squirmed.

"Hey, hey." Mack leaned forward and plucked his lower lip. "This is getting interesting."

Iris had not shown me this. I bit my thumbnail. "This shouldn't be here."

Could this part of the read be unknown to Iris? But then

how could *we* be seeing it? Iris, the mistress of all reads, surely must have known about this one. But if she knew, why not tell me?

Diana stiffened as the right-hand figure spoke in her ear. They were wearing smudgers, distortive fields that blur a person's features enough to make the face unidentifiably generic. As she twisted in their grip, the left-hand figure whirled and fired a shot at us. A blob of orange goo expanded, hit our eye, and covered the entire screen with the bright amber you see when you look at the sun with your eyes closed.

Why was this read legible now? The Master Key was Iris's creation—it did only what Iris permitted. Why would she conceal a read from me, yet allow me to access it? What flavor of truth did she want me to taste? How was she trying to manipulate me? And why?

"It's over," Lucille said smugly.

"A prock snowball," commented Mack. "Antisurveillance weapon. Diana was kidnapped. By pros."

Did Iris think me too dumb to uncover the read on my own? But she must have allowed for the possibility, maybe even expected that I would see it. Even if the read could not be destroyed or privacy-locked, it was not public, and Iris could easily have instructed the key to eff-eff anything she didn't want viewed.

Iris had claimed Diana had just disappeared, had hinted at a runaway. Evidently she was denying the evidence of her own bot eyes. I leaned against the door frame, papers crunching under my sneakers.

"Does your client know?" Mack asked, interrupting my thoughts.

"That it's kidnap?" He nodded. "I'm *sure* the client knows," I answered. Anger and frustration flooded through my mind. "But *I* didn't." Iris had withheld an essential piece of the scene. She had no respect for me.

"Your client's using you," Mack concluded.

Why had the lying bitch pretended a kidnapping was a

disappearance? Not wise if you want your ransom money to buy you live bait instead of dead. Did Iris truly care so little for her daughter that she'd treat her like a white chip ante?

"Bev, what's going on?"

I shook my head faintly, my mind far upfloor.

Akktri popped out of the debris and glanced alertly from Mack to me.

I turned away, wrapped my arms around my chest, and shook off the tentative hand he laid on my shoulder. "Not right now."

"I get frightened for you when the meter's on." He put his hand back on my shoulder. "You turn into someone else."

This time I reached up and covered it with mine. It was warm and gentle. "I know."

"Your meter is always on these days," he added. "You're becoming harder, more distant."

I tightened. "I'm growing up. Not like some people."

"I see," Mack bitterly replied, dropping his hands and turning abruptly away. Immaturity and childishness were old insults, ones that Billy had thrown at him. I regretted my choice of words, but to mention the mistake would bruise him further.

After Billy died, Mack tried to take care of me. I have no idea why. Up until then he had shown little interest. Nineteen, cocky, and nubile, I rudely rejected his fumbling efforts.

When he once tried to grab me to prevent me from walking out on a lecture of his, I kicked him in the kneecap. His face paled to the color of death and he clapped his pudgy hand against his leg. With great slow dignity, he gathered his things and left.

We did not speak for more than five years.

One hot lonely August, the anniversary month of the Siege, I sent him a goofy singing birthday homunculus.

He phoned an hour later.

Today Mack still wants to be my big brother, though he has no idea how. He knows that he cares for me. Perhaps he thinks that's all that's required. I don't know, and Billy never taught us. So we coexist, and if we do not love one another, at least we understand one another.

"Let's find out more about this girl, okay?" I asked after we had silently shared memories.

"Sure." Mack straightened and wiped his mouth, recovering his composure. He can escrow pain. I can't. "Sure." He resettled himself before the screen. "Where do you want to start, Bev?"

"Anything in Diana's Louisburg records or transcripts we ought to know?" I asked Lucille.

Mack ran his finger down the screen info. "Her grades are peaks and valleys with no apparent pattern. Courses started and dropped. She doesn't study," he deduced authoritatively.

"You should know. You never did."

He stuck out his tongue. "Takes firsts when she bothers to work. Flunks otherwise."

Academic performance did not concern me. "What about her social life?" I asked the screen. "Any good home movies?"

"Slugloads," Lucille replied.

"Let's see 'em."

For the next twenty minutes, we watched up various domestic dramas. Diana and Hu sharing their room. Diana in history class sitting near Guillermo Rey. "Who's the stud?" asked Mack. "Her guy?"

Diana's hand crept over to stroke Guillermo's forearm. She leaned across the space between them, whispered in his ear. When he laughed, she took the opportunity to touch his neck, shoulder, and hands in the not-quite-believing way young people do when they've just discovered sex. Chris Tolliver, lecturing from the front of the room, scowled.

"Looks that way," commented Lucille with newfound primness.

"What about Guillermo Rey?" I asked. "Do you have any recent scenes of them together?"

"Viewing." The Boston Common, observed from a ceiling

camera. A crowd—all human beings—gathered around the Freedom Steps across from the State House. No Aliens Need Apply: NANA. Some held up NANA signs. Humanity First's shibboleth.

I have little sympathy for the xenophobes who want to expel all aliens, along with their culture and technology. The Pilgrims came to this country four hundred years ago, alien invaders who melded with the local population, and a whole lot less gracefully than our starborne visitors. We Irish arrived two hundred years after that. Immigrants make Boston what it is.

Of course Billy wanted them all gone. "It's our City, dammit," he'd growl, a beer in his fist.

"They have rights just like we do."

"We were here first."

"And the English before us and the Indians before them," I argued, full of high-school civilization-class wisdom. "They were dumped here just like we Irish were, don't you remember that?"

"That's different," he replied. "The Phneri are animals. Baby-eaters who took our homes. Vermin."

"They were lied to, packed like slaves, shoved through the Loophole, spat upon going and coming," I said hotly. "Just like us Irish."

"Watch your mouth, you foul child," he roared, rising from his chair. "They came, all those filthy wogs, and they took Southie from us who sweated and died for it."

And there was no answer to that. In the distance, the bat-winged Targive cathedral squatted like a vulture on the crown of Telegraph Hill, amidst the drowned and burned and blackened wrecks of the triple-deckers.

"Closer," breathed Mack, captivated by this new form of voyeurism. My eyes are never limp, he once said when I questioned him.

A saturnine young man faced the throng from behind a

levitating lectern. As the picture expanded, his face grew and we saw it was Guillermo Rey.

The boy was a fierce, commanding speaker with a swaggart's self-righteous oratory. He used his fiery voice to surge the crowd's emotions up and down, now thundering at them like a Puritan preacher, now softly coaxing them like a nurturing parent. He moved well on the stand, his jeans trim and tight.

"Rey continues in this vein for another thirty-six minutes," Lucille dryly commented. "The remainder is a syntactic null."

"Thanks for the warning," I replied. "Where's Diana?"

Lucille put an orange circle around a blond head in the front row. At Diana's right stood a shorter, rounder woman with shiny black hair. Now and then one of them nudged the other and they tittered.

"Zero on them. Subtract Diana's blather. I want to hear the girls' conversation."

"Lipreads too?" asked Lucille with, I thought, a trace of self-satisfaction that she must have learned from Mack's vocal patterns. He always likes to show off knowledge or new tricks.

I nodded.

"A moment," the computer added. The figures froze and the sound cut off. Jerkily, the image swung around until we were three-quarters flush on Diana and Hu Nyo—I recognized her now. Behind the pair stood a whooping crane with a receding hairline and a bobbing adam's apple—Chris Tolliver. He was gazing raptly at Guillermo over the two young women, who were still talking mainly with each other.

"Add their vocals," Mack instructed.

Guillermo's speech returned as a muffled susurrus, like an argument in another room. "No one else will be as good," we heard Hu Nyo say in a low voice. She put her arm around her roommate. "Tonight."

"I'm not ready," Diana replied. Her voice sounded high,

thin, and apprehensive, but in the flare of her pale eyes, I saw a glimpse of her mother.

"That's all I can extract," Lucille interjected, stopping the movement.

"Is this guy Diana's boyfriend?" asked Mack.

"Guillermo claimed not. Said Diana was hot for him but he wasn't interested."

"He's lying."

"Oh?" I asked skeptically. "What makes you an authority?"

"Little sister, a man is a nymphomaniac with a penis," Mack said with a twinkle in his hazel eyes.

The crowd was dispersing. Guillermo was at the vortex of a small maelstrom of people. He basked in their attention like a lizard in the hot desert sun, warming his ego, as Diana pushed through the crowd. "Great job," she said, kissing his cheek.

"Glad you liked it." Guillermo pulled her close. "You ready?" he murmured softly.

"He's fondling her buttocks," commented Lucille.

"I'll be back when he's finished," I said, annoyed, and headed for the bathroom. While I did my business, the lights brightened as if the power had surged.

"It's copy-blocked," Lucille was saying as I returned.

"Will it stop our sophisticated lock-picker?" Mack teased her.

"What are you doing?" I demanded, crossing to the machine.

"Copying the key."

I strode angrily up to him and grabbed for it. "I didn't give you permission to do that."

"Sorry," said Mack disingenuously. "You weren't here."

His typical gambit. "Don't give me that vent. You waited until I was out and then sneaked it in."

"Do you want me to stop? I'm just trying to link it into the system, is that wrong? Besides, did your client tell you not to?"

"My client didn't expect I'd show the thing to my unethical

big brother," I said, struggling to extract the key from its slot. "Hey, is the screen changing color?" Numbers flickered spasmodically across its featureless surface.

Mack's expression showed concern. "Lucille? Talk to me."

By now the computer was shimmering with irregular rainbows the color of oil slicks. An unpleasant ozone smell like frying plastic wafted toward us.

"Stop copying," Mack ordered in sharp agitation.

With a sudden pa-thoom, the Master Key was fired across the room. It thwacked the far wall, dislodging several decaying faxes, and rebounded into the clutter. Thin gray smoke trickled from the empty slot.

"Christ!" Mack leaped to the screen.

"Akktri!" My sidekick's head surfaced like a jack-in-the-box. "Find the key." He dove back into the debris and rustled through it.

His face gray-white as volcano ash, Mack turned to me. "My core's been wiped. All my special food cuisinarted."

I broke out laughing. "Serves you right for sneaking behind my back like that."

"This can't happen." Mack was shell-shocked. He gaped down at his hands. "There is no way on God's green earth to nuke Lucille's core like that. What are you going to *do* about this?" Mack shouted desperately.

My jaw dropped in outrage. *"Me?* Why is this *my* responsibility?" Just like Billy, to blame someone else, claim helplessness, and complain. "It's your own damn fault."

"It is not! I couldn't predict this. Fix it!"

"How the dump am I supposed to do *that?"* I demanded furiously.

"I don't know!" he yelled. "Make time go backwards!" Mack flung his hands wide. His automatic defense mechanism—pretend tragedy is comedy.

Akktri popped clear of the mess and returned the key to me. It was completely unscathed.

"Will it still work?" I asked my companion.

He ran his whiskers along it. "It is as it is." The Phneri phrase for everything. "Unchanged-and-not-a-copy."

"Jesus." Mack collapsed into an overstuffed armchair in his living room. "You're over your head, little sister."

I folded my arms across my chest. "I'm stirring a pot. I can feel it."

"The pot's going to stir *you*." Almost calm now, he gestured at his fried computer. "I can replace this cow pie. Barely. But I can't replace your thick red head if it gets sizzled. Has anyone told you the truth yet? I need a drink." In the kitchen, Mack uncorked a bottle of Maker's Mark whiskey. He returned and leaned in the doorway, his arms folded across his chest. "Please drop this case." He came forward and worriedly embraced me. He smelled of good bourbon and fear.

"No. I don't quit. Billy was a quitter. I'm not."

"Oh, you think I am."

No, big brother, I thought. You never try so you never have to quit. "Of course I don't think that," I lied.

"At least confront the client," Mack pressed, mollified. "It's Iris Sherwood, isn't it? Find out why she's lying to you."

I thought of scheming Iris far upfloor. I was afraid of her, more than before, but also angry at her deceptions. Anger gave me resolve. "Yes," I murmured, squeezing my elbows with my hands. "I'll chat with my lying client."

7

CHARLES BEAUFORT LEANED back, withdrew his hands from the holo, and folded his arms over his chest, covering his fingertips and thereby suspending the dactylograph. "The City Operator is engaged."

"Never mind that," I said in the warning tone that had got me past Charles's assistant's secretary, and then his assistant herself. "Call her now."

Charles smiled at me. "She is not to be disturbed."

"I'm on a personal assignment for her. She's expecting my report. She won't appreciate your blocking me."

"Miz O'Meara," said Charles easily, "I've worked for Iris Sherwood for three years, ever since I transferred over from Police Administration. You've worked for her for less than a day. Don't threaten me."

The unexpected rebuff surprised me, and I grinned. Maybe he hadn't been so misplaced working for the rods, after all. "Chuck, I'm astonished. I thought you were nothing but a pretty face."

He raised his bushy black eyebrows. "It's Charles," he said thinly. "As in Manson. And you're trying to anger me. It's unworthy of you." With a small sigh, Charles returned to the dactylograph.

His desktop holo represented, as best I could tell from my skewed-angle perspective of its 3-D fresnel image, the peppered hide of a molting Tulgut. The surface rippled as Charles's fingers moved purposefully within the ethercube.

"What's that?" I asked, hoping to draw him out.

"A dynasim of interest and arbitrage earnings from inter-departmental transfers and discounting conventions," he answered distantly, paying me no heed.

Briefly thwarted, I plucked at my lower lip and tried another tack. "I have information about Diana."

He closed his hands into fists, freezing the simulation, carefully closed his eyes to break retinal-scan command lock, and glanced my way. "Tell it to me."

"No. I tell only icicle bones herself."

He leaned back, a ghost of a smile flitting over his face. "You'll have to show me some evidence. I can hardly let you pass on your unsupported word."

I laughed at him. "You can hardly *stop* me. I work for Iris, not you, and my reports are confidential. I'm doing you a favor by giving you another chance to call her."

"Well, well," murmured Charles in what might have been appreciation. His eyes shifted to the mover door, which opened as if in response.

I started toward it.

"The knife," he said primly, clinging to his small authority. "Remove it."

I complied. "For you, anything," I murmured. "Bye, Chuck," I waved as Akktri scampered in. "Maybe I'll quit and solve your problems for you." We whisked upfloor.

On my way, I realized I had no idea where Iris's office was in relation to Charles's. With its own dedicated mover, it could be anywhere—dozens of levels in a random direction. Not even the Phneri could track her; their sense was structural, not directional. She was invincible and impregnable in her tower, impossible to pry out. I wondered how many people had tried to do that and failed, and what Iris's vengeance on them had been.

Meanwhile, Iris had hired a detective unqualified in abductions, then deceived her operative into thinking it a simple locate. No doubt she would have a plausible cover story for this self-defeating behavior. I was looking forward to dismantling her story.

"Your daughter was kidnapped," I began when the doors opened, then stopped, stupefied.

Bright yellow sunshine poured from the huge exterior window, rebounded off her smooth desk, and splashed painfully into my eyes. I put up my arm as if to block a blow and squinted into the sizzling glare.

"Remind me never to introduce you to my friends," Iris Sherwood murmured coolly. "You have no sense of propriety."

I groped toward the light. Far below, the harbor sparkled like living diamonds. Small craft zipped and darted on and over it. The bright blue sky was breathtakingly clear. The sunlight buffeted me and I staggered unevenly toward Sherwood's featureless green-black silhouette.

I shaded my eyes. "I can't see you."

"A chair is near," Sherwood instructed. "Sit. Thank you. Your partner may come up." Unperturbed, Akktri hopped onto the desk's black surface and blinked at Sherwood. That amoral traitor.

Wedging my teary eyes open even a crack was an amazonian effort that made my eyeballs ache. All shapes were streaky blurs. "I looked at the other reads of the incident. You must have too."

"And if I did?" She was utterly unfazed at having her charade exposed. "What do you conclude from this?"

"Don't waste my time," I said angrily. "This is no locate, it's a felony."

"Perhaps," she said, still unruffled. "You realize that you breached my confidence by showing the read to your brother."

"You knew where I was? Then you have a trace on the key."

To my surprise, Iris chuckled. "Miz O'Meara, you seem to

take the most elementary precautions as a personal affront. Old icicle bones knows more than you think."

So she *had* been listening in Charles's office, I thought. At least I was right about something. "And Mack's ware got fired."

She grunted. "A consequence of excessive curiosity. He was engaged in improper actions and the key took appropriate countermeasures."

"You didn't warn me not to copy it," I said, sticking up for Mack. "Do you know how much that stuff cost?"

"Oh, if *that's* all that's bothering you," said Iris. "Charles?" She addressed the air. "Miz O'Meara's brother, a datasifter named Mack O'Meara—you have him on file, I trust—had a household accident today. An unexpected power surge. Ware damage through power fluctuations is entitled to reimbursement from DPW, is it not?"

"Yes, Iris." His smooth tenor voice wafted from the ceiling. "I'll take care of it."

"Thank you, Charles," she murmured graciously.

Damn her for her wallet. "Thanks," I said in a strangled voice. I was furious at her put-down but she had just done me a favor. "I appreciate it."

"You're welcome, Miz O'Meara." Her confirming nod was brief but unequivocal. I had to give her credit. She was tough and quick, hard to knock off her feet. "What did you make of the read?"

"I just told you—it's an obvious kidnap. Where's the ransom demand?"

"I have yet to receive one," she answered. "And, to answer your original question, I chose not to display the full read because I didn't want to prejudice your investigation."

"Investigation? Of what?"

"Diana may have just run away." Iris chose her words with care. "To punish me. My daughter is shallow."

"Shallow people sometimes do deep things." Why was she

so set on biasing me against Diana? "And if you thought that, why not ignore it?"

"Fair question," she said almost mournfully after a long pause. "I couldn't take the chance. She *is* my daughter, regardless of anything else."

"Then why not call out the rods? You could get favors from Petravelli."

"I have a position of responsibility and power," Sherwood answered, offended. "To exploit that for personal gain would be an abuse of my authority. So I do what any cit can do: hire a private agent."

"You're not serious." But I knew as I said it that she was. To my surprise, I even thought I understood her a little.

"If I am not true to my principles, Miz O'Meara, I am nothing. You probably cannot understand this, because you have never wielded great power"—her tone was frozen with condescension and contempt—"but if I do not have rigid rules of conduct, I will corrupt myself. Can you understand that?"

I did, much better than she realized. I was hearing the brilliant rationalization of a squelched woman who had lived inside her armor so long she no longer realized it was a prison. Yet ragged emotion lurked under her words. In that instant of perceiving her vulnerable soul through the interlocking steel plates of logic with which she shielded it, Iris Sherwood got me, however briefly, to sympathize with her.

"I think so," I said.

Her brown eyes widened slightly, then narrowed, distrustful of understanding too glibly claimed.

I wondered cynically if she was maneuvering for an effect. "There's a more personal reason, isn't there? Asking favors would give them power over you."

"I don't know what you could possibly mean," she huffed.

"You remember the call from Ulkudge asking you to spare Vinnie Akibira? If you were dirty, even just smudged by your own white-glove standards, you'd have to play ball with them. And that would be intolerable for you, wouldn't it?"

Her glare told me I had scored.

"Iris!" Charles Beaufort's voice was agitated. "Someone here you must see."

Sherwood was momentarily distracted. "Who?"

"I don't know," he answered almost helplessly. A high-pitched voice shrieked in the background and we heard slamming and thumping.

"Impossible. You know the procedures."

"Iris," Charles entreated as if in pain. "Listen to me. See him. See him now."

"All right," Sherwood said warily. "Vet him first."

The doors opened an instant later. Murmuring soothing words, Charles led out a disheveled, bewildered nine-year-old boy.

His shirt, matted and rumpled, was covered with holographic human eyes of all shapes, colors, and sizes, appearing and disappearing randomly. The eyes blinked, shifted, stared. Their alertness mocked the boy's own features, which seemed too small for his face, his eyes and nose too close together. His teeth were set at eccentric angles as if they had been carelessly shoved into his gums before the grout had hardened.

His hair was a tangled squirrel's-nest, his face smudged with dirt and dried snot. He cowered against the mover's walls, frightened by the light. Iris immediately polarized the windows and, as the room darkened to normal, the boy's whimpering quieted.

"Come on, Butch," coaxed Charles, enfolding the child's small hand in his. "I call him that because he's got no tags and can't say his name." He breathed carefully and lightly through his mouth and kept his body well away from his charge.

The boy's head wobbled rhythmically and his lips moved as he chanted to himself. His eyes were squeezed shut so hard his cheeks were wrinkled.

Iris had retreated behind her desk. "Did you check him?"

she demanded in a grating tone, squatting down, her hands on its edge and her eyes barely above the level of its surface.

"Yes," said Charles. "No bombs, eyes, or germs. He's vetted. Harmless, if filthy," he said with distaste. "No weapons."

"You searched him?"

"Touch that?" Charles was mortified. "Of course not. But I six-way-scanned him. Clean. Well, not *clean*—but weaponless."

"What about Targive mods? Could he be a rabid wolverine?"

"Nothing but human organic material." Iris's assistant was tolerant but impeccably dispassionate. "Unmodified genetics."

"Why are you so paranoid?" I asked Iris as Butch goggled. "Can't you see the boy is miserable and scared?"

"Grow up, dearie," Iris snapped, unbending herself into a crouched standing position. "You're in the big game now. I've been given trojan horses before."

Akktri spread himself more comfortably in the sun—conversation bores him. He snorted and rolled over, indolent.

"Iris, he's safe," Charles repeated with a touch of urgency.

"He has no *business* here." Sherwood's words fired out. "I don't care about your difficulty handling him. We have whole *departments* to deal with his kind. I can't be expected to treat them one by one. What'd you bring him here for, anyhow?"

Charles quailed before her anger. "Iris, he kept repeating your name," he said. "*Your* name, Iris."

"All right." Shooting a final dagger glance at Charles, Sherwood rose and came around her desk. "What's pinned to his shirt?"

The boy shuffled forward until we could hear his words. "Goddess ee yieriss." His voice was slurred and anxious. "Goddess ee yieriss, goddess ee yieriss, goddess ee yieriss," he chanted faster, the sim-eyes on his jersey winking.

"I'm Iris, son," said Sherwood gently. The change in her manner—from towering impatient rage to solicitude in an instant—was astonishing. She squatted and extended her hand, hitching up her wool skirt. Akktri had told me it was real sheep's-hair fabric, unfashionable and itchy. "You've got to see me?"

"GODDESS EE YIERISS!" the boy abruptly shouted. He hopped furiously on both feet, his hands clenching into fists.

"Shh," Sherwood answered. Slowly she cupped the boy's neck and drew him to her. After an initial flinch, he enjoyed the contact; his voice muted and a sloppy grin flashed across his dull face. Sherwood tenderly reached her arms around the boy and hugged him to her. He stank with the profound acrid smell of months without washing. "Shh," she murmured, stroking his neck. "Shh, son."

My mother used to hold me that way when I came home in tears from being teased at elementary school. My father Billy's hands were always rough, hands to hit but not to hold. He seldom wanted to touch me and his hugs were always stiff and awkward, the embraces of an overly strong bear.

"Goddess ee yieriss," the boy whimpered into her shoulder.

"I know, I know," she said, stroking his filthy hair. "You're a good boy, son. You did what they told you. Can you remember who told you?"

The rugrat smiled tearfully at her. "Goddess ee yieriss."

If she could feel so tender to this mangled boy, she could not be indifferent to her own daughter's problems. But she had earlier refused even to hint at these emotions in my presence, as if doing so would render her mortal. As I learned more about Iris Sherwood, I comprehended her less.

"That's all he says," Charles Beaufort commented from across the office. Jesus, he was handsome, standing there. I wanted his nude holo hanging on my wall. What use had the police department put him to? Perhaps he was Roderick's special friend. "Butch kept repeating that phrase, louder and more hysterically, until I brought him to you."

"Okay, son, hold still so I can take this." Deftly Sherwood

opened the safety pin holding the note, glanced at whatever was written on it, grimaced and made to crumple it, but checked her action.

The boy's empty face transfixed me. What did his gray world look like, inside his broken head?

"Who could let the poor guy run free?" wondered Charles in disgust. "Who'd abandon their kid?"

"Your upfloor breeding is showing," murmured Iris. Her shrug told of despair. "Being poor is no moral failing, just the luck of the draw. Maybe he's the son of suicides."

"Second most common cause of death in Boston, after homicide," Charles commented to me.

"It is?" I asked. "Nice symmetry to that."

"We have all natural mortality sources under control," he went on. "Unnatural causes of death such as human and other sentient violence are the responsibility of the police. Not our department."

"It's not all Petravelli's fiefdom," added Iris, pulling the boy's clothing into some semblance of order. "We also get orphans when bankrupt parents flee town."

"How'd he ever survive on his own?"

"Ugly ways," Sherwood answered darkly. "No one starves in my rich City. Rugrats such as Butch roam in packs like renegade dogs, scavenging garbage, begging, and hiding. My eyes see them occasionally."

The boy was a brilliant choice of messenger. A child with no mind cannot describe who spoke to him. Who would use a helpless rugrat so callously? Whoever it was, I hated him. Or her.

"It's all right." Sherwood patted the boy's neck. "Charles, Butch is now officially a ward of the City. We can do that for him. Get him to Mass General. Clean him, feed him, debug him, get him new clothing."

"Who's going to pay?"

"*Boston* pays, dammit. We *owe* children like this. If Family

Welfare gives you any lip, tell them to bill the City Operator personally."

Charles grinned. "Nobody'll dare take the money."

"That's their problem." Sherwood's face was cold and determined.

"My pleasure," Charles replied with a brief bow. "The little guy's taken a shine to me. Haven't you, Butch?" He held out his hand, extended at the end of his arm as if he wished to disown it, and the boy's fingers crawled eyelessly into his palm. "Let's go." Charles started to lead his charge toward the mover, but the boy yelled and dragged his feet. "Goddess ee yieriss," he cried, legs twitching, scratching at his pants pocket with his free hand.

"What have you got?" Charles asked.

The boy groped, deep in concentration. Pen caps, bubblegum–fused paper clips, and dusty gimcrack jewelry spilled from his pocket like popcorn. Finally he pulled out a cigar-sized grayish cylinder.

Charles unfolded its wrapping newsfax, gagged, and held it out to Sherwood.

A severed finger, blue-white and sallow like a wax image, lay like a ghoulish gift.

The cut was as clean as if the finger had been frozen before amputation. Circling it tightly, milk-white flesh bulging around it, was an antique ring, finely wrought in dull gray metal, with a small crystal dome in a setting of filigree and paisley metalwork.

Akktri flashed off Iris's desk, trembling with excitement, but I signaled him to stay back. She wouldn't want an art-loving Phner to destroy the finger, no matter how rich an esfn would result.

The scratched and worn crystal was ovoid and hollow. Several thin silvery hairs were curled inside it.

"I'll take this to forensics," Charles said, breathing heavily and moving to rewrap it.

"No," Sherwood ordered, pushing it gently from side to

side as if examining a piece of sausage. "Show the Phner." She whistled.

Akktri scooted. "Show *me* ring of pewter!" my assistant piped enthusiastically. "See sk-k-in!" he exclaimed a moment later. "Skin is in Louisburg room!"

"Diana's?" I asked. "Are you sure?"

"Skin is on desk-k-k, on bald head of stone," he babbled on. "Skin is on bed, on doorknob, everywhere!"

"He's right," Sherwood tonelessly added. This grotesque discovery had shocked her back inside her professional turtle shell. "That is Diana's left ring finger. I gave her that mourning band years ago. The hair was clipped from the head of Ethel Endicott Cobb."

"The Madwoman of Hull?"

Iris nodded. "My great-aunt. The only woman who survived the Bombing of Hull and continued to live there afterward. Ethel knew Mi Nyo when Mi was a teen gang moll. Diana revered her." She gestured at the finger, whose stump Akktri was examining. I could tell that he wanted to poke the severed flesh. "The ring won't come off," Sherwood concluded.

"I'll have them verify it," said Charles.

"It's a finger," Iris muttered. "It's *Diana's* finger. I'm being set up."

The boy was delighted by the commotion he had caused. "Goddess ee yieriss," he gurgled as Charles ushered him out.

Sherwood was kneeling on the floor, one hand covering her eyes, the note still gripped in the other. "Suffer the little children to come unto me," she muttered, so low I almost couldn't hear.

"He's suffered enough," I replied.

"It means *allow* them to come," she said with a withering look. "Butch shouldn't benefit when other rugrats cannot. But once he came here"—she shrugged defensively—"I could not leave him uncared for."

"Don't perform for me, Iris. I'm the hired help, remember?

The one you tricked from the get-go. You don't need to impress me."

Sherwood blinked, as if seeing me for the first time, and walked heavily back to her desk. "Here, read this," she continued, her tone matter-of-fact.

On cheap lined paper, scraggly capital letters in red crayon said:

WE HAVE THE REST OF HER

I laid the note before Akktri. He crept forward, his small head bent, until he could examine it. "Children!" he said. "This is in the hands of many children."

"The boy didn't know what he was carrying, of course." Sherwood ruffled her gray hair, absently rebinding her bun and running her gold stickpin through it. "Whoever gave him *that* did him a favor sending him to us. Are you impressed *now?*"

My hand tightened on the note, my jaw grinding. "I'm sorry," I finally said. "That last crack of mine was unfair."

"As opposed to your previous insults, which I deserve?" She smiled with half her mouth.

"Learn how to accept an apology, ma'am," I said. "People won't hate you so much." How did this woman bring out the streetfighter in me? "Iris," I went on in a normal voice, "why do you put up with me?"

"You?" She opened her tough hands. "I don't have to suspect your motives. For better or worse, connivance and ulterior interests are beyond you. I suppose I find that refreshing. Or maybe you remind me of who I once was."

"Hm." It was an answer, if I chose to believe it.

We both stared out the window onto the gleaming blue harbor, and the image of that child's face filled my mind.

"There's a girl I know in the Basement," I said. "She can't be more than fifteen. She never goes hungry, never sleeps in the corridors. Every day she finds a sugar daddy. Or sugar momma. Or sugar wog. She's an expert at identifying sexual fetishes. The calmest person I know, never raises her voice, never cries. But she has the eyes of a widow and she cannot remember what day it is."

Iris looked briefly at me. "We have no reliable statistics on sexual sponges," she said. "Between twenty-five hundred and three thousand, we think. We give them drugs, of course."

"What?" I gaped. *You're* their supplier?"

"It's not commonly known."

"Why?"

"Only the most benign of motives." With her fingernail, she traced a design on the back of her other hand. The skin flashed white, then recolored red. "We lace the drugs with every vaccine we can. The sexual sponges are the most dangerous and prolific epidemiological vector in Boston. We simply pander to their tastes." Sherwood was indifferent to my indignation; she had probably faced similar reactions many times before. "Their kind will get satisfaction somewhere. This way they have an incentive to return to us, which permits us to contain their diseases." She wiped her mouth. "You are appalled, I see. Just remember that I did not make this city."

"And you'll do nothing for her or for Butch."

"We do what we can." The boy's name saddened her. "We'll clean him, delouse him. But he's like broken pottery. We can sweep the pieces into a bag and call it a human being, but they're just shards. You don't fix a Butch in an afternoon."

"You don't fix him in a lifetime," I said. "You live with him the way he is. This is some job you do."

"Sarcasm again? The hard-boiled cubehunter returns?"

"I hope not," I said, and I meant it. "Lord knows I've seen a hundred Butches. Each one hurts me, if only a little. That's what separates the two of us."

"Bah. You sound like Diana." She blinked at herself and drew a long breath. "But you're both wrong. If I saw them, one by one, I would never act. Can you understand that?" A cold river of pain rose to the surface of her lined, tough face. "Can you *possibly* understand that?"

In that moment of silent torment, to be Iris Sherwood—a person who had trained herself to behave like a bot, a Fate whose every choice meant life for one, death for another—seemed the worst punishment in the world.

"I think so," I said reluctantly.

Iris grew thoughtful. "That man you killed—Lemos?"

"Yes?" I was startled. "What do you know about him?"

"You said you were tormented by doubt about whether you acted rightly. My reads cannot tell you that—I've had them reviewed. The structure of that moment has been written"—she glanced over at Akktri, who was smacking his lips in his sleep—"and will never change. But, however awful it was to you, you must stop torturing yourself for it."

"You're an expert in forgiveness?" I asked, my voice uneven. I wouldn't let myself believe her. It would be like taking soiled money.

"I'm an expert in death." Iris held my gaze for a long moment, then turned away and spoke in a lower voice. "After the Siege, after I killed all those people"—she briefly put her hand to her face—"I adopted Diana. I've raised her as best I can. God knows I've tried. And she repays me with this."

She didn't want to look at me, but then the confessor never sees her priest. "What are you talking about?" I prompted. "Are you *blaming* her for being abducted?"

"I doubt that Diana's kidnapping is real." She turned to look me full in the eyes, daring me to disagree. Her face was a sandstone statue: aged, ruined, impassive.

I moved closer. "Part of your daughter's body is delivered to you and you don't *believe* it?"

"The event could have been staged," she explained with the slow stolid precision of a dull but honest witness under hectoring cross-examination.

"Why would Diana do such a thing?" The detective's reflex: whenever thwarted, always ask another question. You can think on their time. "What could she hope to accomplish?"

"She wants me to take her seriously."

"You mean you *don't?*" I was grasping at straws.

"Diana is pretending to be an adult," said Iris, still lost in herself and unaware of me.

"In what way?" Your client is your best informant, especially when she doesn't realize it.

On the window, Akktri snored and mumbled. "Diana's been kidnapped." I gestured at the wall. "We saw it occur. That is the *fact.*"

"A play acted for my benefit." Iris drew a deep breath. "And she has underestimated me," she added to herself.

"Nonsense."

"Really?" Bit by bit, Sherwood was recovering her tenacity. "Let me show you." She put the read onscreen and we watched the two dark figures bracket Diana. "Look how they move. How Diana reacts. No struggle, did you notice that? Akktri!"

"Diana does not fight," my associate agreed lazily. Stretched out on his stomach, arms and legs splayed wide like a bodysurfer, he preened in the splashing sunlight. "She is not tense."

"Stunned, maybe," I allowed. You missed this, didn't you? I thought bitterly to myself.

"Consider their movements," Sherwood continued. Taking me by the upper arm, she led us to the screen. "Gloves on their hands. Who wears gloves in Boston? Baseball caps. Black garb from head to toe. Isn't it all a little *melodramatic?* A tad stagy? Here comes the pistol shot," Sherwood narrated. "Akktri! Watch the gunman's eyes. Does he know what he's searching for?"

"Naturally." My Phner companion stretched his neck and scratched it with one hand. "He sees it in his past."

"Why didn't the kidnappers shoot my eye *before* they approached Diana?" mused Sherwood. "For that matter, why a kidnap at Old North? Why not in a less visible place?"

"They *wanted* to be seen," I realized. "Damn."

She nodded. "Seen by the City Operator."

I paced back and forth, thinking hard. "The abduction might still be real."

"How so?"

"To put pressure on you. They *know* you can search the reads. So they leave you one that's unmistakable. Simpler than a ransom note."

Iris pondered this, her head moving in short jerks. "Yes. It's conceivable. Good for you to spot it. And I shall ignore it," she finished decisively.

"You'll have to explain that one."

"They seek to pressure me? I shall send no fear signal. I hold myself ignorant, as if there had been no kidnapping. That's safest for my child."

"But we just got her *finger.*"

"But they have no means of knowing their message was delivered. Charles!"

"Yes, Iris?"

"Cancel previous orders," she said, looking upward. "Hold Butch. Return Diana's finger to his pocket, rewrapped in the fax it came in. Come collect the ransom note so we can repin it on his breast."

"Iris," I asked, "what are you saying?"

"You have that, Charles? Good. Sherwood out. Surely you see, Miz O'Meara," she said, bringing her chin and her gaze back to earth. "This is even better. Thanks for your assistance."

"What about Butch?" I was almost speechless. "You're going to send him back to his miserable existence?"

She actually snickered. "A moment ago you were chastising me for not caring about my daughter. Now you complain when I value her above a brain-damaged orphan. I suggest you examine your *own* views."

"Is Diana as obsessive as you are?"

"Diana? Sometimes I think she hates me." With a dismissive gesture, Sherwood blanked the screen. "She is certainly an enemy of the people. I was wrong about her. Now she is trying to wrest power from me. I will not allow it." With a long sigh, she let the kidnap note air-slalom onto her desk. "Allow me my skepticism, Miz O'Meara."

"Can you bet Diana's life on your judgment?"

"*Is* it at stake?" Sherwood asked. "Prove that and I might alter my view. Until then, I cannot trade Boston for my daughter, and I will not be swayed by emotion. Nor may you. You must refuse to act as if Diana is kidnapped. Only in that way can we maintain any mystery about our motives and our enemies' successes."

"Don't you care about Diana at all?" I demanded.

"Iris think-ks always," Akktri interjected approvingly. "She is a critic-k-k of art. Like us Phneri. We are all dead already," he added, curling into a toasty ball in the sun.

I ignored my assistant. "Why aren't you more emotional?"

"Because they *want* me to be," she said tightly.

"You don't really want me to find her, do you?"

Sherwood gazed at me in horror and astonishment. "You foolish woman. You know nothing of me," she whispered, spacing her words in her anger. "Find her. Pretending not to have received their threat will buy us only a few hours. They'll send another message, a worse one, and soon. Find my daughter. Find her quickly."

"And what do I do then?"

"I'll decide that," she said. "Your job is tactics. Mine is strategy."

"No."

"No? I *am* the client," she said softly.

"No longer. You're too tricky for me, and I'm over my head. I won't risk Diana's life by remaining on the case."

"Afraid, Bev?" Iris was scornful. "Frightened you'll fail?"

"Realistic." I crossed to the mover and summoned it. "I've done what you *really* hired me to do. I've unobtrusively established that it *is* a kidnap. I didn't do that, Diana's finger did, but you got the result you wanted. No one knows but us. So I'm done."

The mover door closed on her open mouth.

Back in the DPW executive offices, I bustled past Charles Beaufort. "Goodbye, dreamboat. And I'll collect my knife again."

"Wait, Bev." He put his hand on my arm and drew me around. "Why are you so upset? Why is Iris jettisoning Butch?"

"I can't tell you," I said, taking his hands and pushing them away from me. "But I did quit, just as I promised."

"You *what?*" He was not merely surprised but visibly agitated, as if my resignation was scuttling a plan of his. "You can't do that."

"What's it to you?"

"I don't mind Iris chewing me out," he rattled hastily on as if scrambling to say anything to keep me with him. "It just means she's upset. Who wouldn't be, with the burden she carries? But Butch. That poor rugrat."

"Charles, Butch has lived in the Basement for years. You're just shocked at seeing him up close."

"But giving him Diana's finger. That's insanity. It could be reattached, you know—*if* we can find her fast enough."

"Not my problem. I just quit, remember?"

He ignored me, looking into the distance as if talking to someone else.

"You don't understand how hard it is for her to unbend, even a little. That display you just witnessed"—Charles waved his arm vaguely, as if to indicate his boss's presence surrounding us—"that's unprecedented. Iris must trust you enormously. If you continue the case, I'm sure she'll forgive you."

"Save it." I didn't want Iris's forgiveness, or Charles's for that matter—he sure as hell didn't understand what went on inside me, any more than Iris did.

"Can I try to change your mind over dinner? Anywhere in Boston?"

"A bribe, Chuck?"

His blush was charming; his earlobes and neck reddened. "Will you?"

"I need sleep," I replied irritably, angry at him because he worked for that sphinx. "I'm going to bed. I'm exhausted."

8

"PARTNER, THANK GOODNESS that Indian-poker fiasco is behind us," I commented to Akktri as we stepped out of the creaky mover that serves the 70 Fed shell. "Actually, I'm glad to be rid of it. Sooner or later I'd've screwed up, and then that botbrain Iris would've fried my butt. All I want now is sleep." Saying it made me yawn so wide my jaw ached.

"Sleep is not yet," purred Akktri mischievously.

"Oh?" We turned the corner to my apt front door. "Stand back or you'll get squashed when I collapse. I'm home," I called to my recognizer.

A few paces behind me, Akktri chirped, "Sleep is not yet." He gestured with his brown head. The lock was seared black around the handle.

Fatigue instantly gone, I checked with my assistant. He held out his arms, turned down his hands as if he had thumbs, stuck out his brown tongue, and silently blew a rich raspberry in a perfect imitation of Mack.

I wish he had a better sense of the nuances of human gestures. "That bad?"

Akktri repeated the pose, oblivious to its incongruity. With a reluctant nod, I laid my palm against the door and gently pushed, dropping into a crouch as I did.

Plasticware and prock cups were strewn in the entryway. Somewhere inside the apt, my recognizer ineffectually squawked, "You can't come in! You can't come in!"

I reholstered my pistol and stood up. "Okay, buddy?"

He bolted inside without bothering to answer.

My living room had been obliterated. The easy chair's leatherette cushions were slashed, their padding strewn about. My bookshelves had been looted, the volumes scattered in heaps on the floor, some ripped in half along the spines. My main vid monitor had a gaping hole blown through its screen, as if hit with a sledgehammer. Below it, shards of glass twinkled in the pale brown carpeting.

My eye caught something, and I bent. "Oh, no," I said. "Oh, Jesus, no."

"Beverlee?"

The intruder had destroyed the holo of Billy and me. Here an arm, floating in no-space, held a string of flounder. There a bit of girl's shoulder, sunburned and peeling, with a hairy hand clamped proudly on it.

"Destroyed. Oh, Jesus." I clutched the fragments. "There was no reason for this. Just pure personal malice."

"But it is only destroyed-but-copyable," said Akktri, confused. "And you own its memories, which are esfn'ed."

A rusted round sign—a red circle with a broad white horizontal bar across its center—had been driven into my bedroom door with enough force to bend the metal at each nail point.

I slumped into my exploded chair. "Who did this?" I whispered.

"Great force," Akktri cheerfully replied, inspecting the door. "City struc-k-k-tural rivet-driver. High-compression hydraulic." He shivered with vicarious pleasure in those bolts blasted into my wall.

My maps' picture frames had been pulled off my bedroom walls and torn into kindling. The white parchmentlike paper was already curling along its ripped edges. I picked up the twisted and shattered wood, ran my finger along the crumbling paper. "My Boston maps," I muttered, sitting heavily on the bed. "Jesus, the holo wasn't enough, they had to smash my antique maps too. Why?"

As hesitantly as if it were a dying bird, I picked up Colton's

1855 Plan. A huge chunk had been torn from the center section, as if a massive fist had grabbed a handful of history. "Look at that." I tendered the broken frame to Akktri.

He peered over his reddish nose and whiffled his nostrils. "Old dust tickles," he apologized.

"Billy gave me that one. For graduation."

That gift was the first fragile thing that my father ever gave me. Everything else broke on first or second use, crunched by a thoughtless brother or father. Only durability counted in our home. Plates thrown in anger left tiny shards found months later under spring-cleaned kitchen sinks. Sofas sprung leaks from bouncing heavy sitters. Gadgetry shed tiny parts and refused to readmit them.

My father had even wrapped the map; that was how I knew, two days before Christmas when it went under the Tarmod eternal tree, that it was different. I had felt Billy's eyes on me as I unwrapped it, and then I had seen nothing through my joyful tears as, stunned, I held it.

The shreds slid to the floor. Numbly I bent and tried to reassemble the torn pages like a devil's jigsaw puzzle, but the hopelessness of it overcame me and I dropped them. "Is anything else taken?" I asked dully. "Who did this?"

Akktri skittered about the apt. My bookshelves had gouges in them, jagged wounds as if someone had sliced them with a serrated butcher knife. Most of my crockery was smashed into shrapnel in my kitchen floor. I took in the wholesale destruction, my jaw hanging limp, then tightening.

"A careful being," Akktri answered after a moment. "The k-k-cuts are made by a human arm. I am cautious but anxious. I am in a great hurry." Recreating the marauder's actions, he bounced and tap-danced about my rooms. "I must slash quick, now!" He stabbed the air as if wielding an ice pick. "I must destroy soon, fast! But I leave no sweat or spit-tle or sk-kin, because I wear mask-k-k and gloves."

"What about my bot eyes?"

"Punc-k-tured," reported Akktri after surveying. "Your

storage is taken," answered my assistant. "I am careful, I know you have eyes. I k-k-kill them, so!" He poked his claws forward with a sharp fierce movement, his teeth glinting. "I take what they see. I blind you, Beverlee!" he cried. "I blind you! Ha! Ha! Ha!" He was trembling with emotion and excitement.

"Stop," I said more firmly than I expected to be able to, and Akktri's seizure slowed. "Who was here? Who are you feeling?"

"Delight," he said, swallowing and licking his amber lips. "Ending things like a brute Sh'k-k"—Akktri's tone was contemptuous and full of hate—"not for art but to hurt you. To hurt you, Beverlee! I *enjoy* hurting you." He ran his fingers delicately along the wood's jagged scars. "Too much might, badly used," he clucked with mild reproof, as if criticizing a theater performance. "Most wasteful."

I felt my teeth grit together. "This is my *home,* not some Phneri *experience."* I pounded the doorframe. "Who did this? Where are they?"

My friend edged away from the bookshelf, jumped in the wastebasket, and squinted furtively over its rim at me. "I did not do this, Beverlee," he interrupted slowly and softly.

"Did a *Phner* destroy my apt?" I was burning with rage.

"No, no, not possible."

"Why not? Your kind blew up Boston!"

"Only the parts Iris tells us to," Akktri said righteously. "We k-k-kill the Siege good." He made the sound of surf rushing through corridors and shaftways. "We k-k-kill."

"You shouldn't be *pleased* by it, you past-blind Sh'k lover!" My anger was an avalanche. "Billy *died* in the Siege, you ghoul!"

"I know, Beverlee." Akktri was calm but his shoulders hunched and he held himself tense, ready to flee. "Your suffer does not enjoy me," he said, fracturing his grammar in his stress. "I study actions to esfn their doer, so we find him and hurt him." Claws whizzed as he slashed his small golden-brown hand across the air. "We end his art. I rip his throat out."

I clutched my head tightly with both hands as if it were a cracking eggshell. "Oh, God." Angry tears sprang to my eyes.

Akktri awkwardly patted me. "What is wrong, my Beverlee?" he solicitously asked. "All this is fleeting." He waved his hand about. "The day of its ending *is,* and is always. As it is. You know its ending is one day."

"But the Colton's was *mine."* Every time I saw it, I thought of why I loved my father, a violent, lumpy, coarse man who had selected a gift that he did not comprehend but knew his little girl would cherish.

I looked at Akktri, who wanted to understand but had never known Billy. All I said was, "It's personal," in a half-whisper as if my arm were broken. I lifted my head and tried to smile at him. My face was wet and I wiped my blotchy eyes, then gestured at the cracked frames at my feet. "Originals. Antiques." I kicked at one, which splintered. "They're ruined. And the holo of Billy and me." I picked up its fragments, cut into twisted pieces.

My father adored his daughter. Nothing in Diana's dorm room spoke to me of gifts from Iris. How could Iris have such a loveless relationship with *her* daughter?

"You care so much for leaves that fall." Akktri shook his head, his voice curious and wry. "Now they are safe. Now they are in memoree."

"Whoever destroys my things hurts me inside." I pushed my fingers into my sternum between my breasts.

"Nothing in you is break-k-ked."

"Not that you can see, but the damage is done." I shook my head and wiped my mouth again. Not even a Phner can esfn a soul. "Sorry, but I'm no Phner. I needed to have my maps here to remember them."

"You remember Billee," he reminded me, tenderly punching my shoulder the way Mack occasionally does to me, because Billy often used the same gesture with him. My brother and father could never touch each other except with punches, shoulder butts, and hip checks, contact that no one could mistake for weakness or effeminacy.

"Billee is in your mind ever," added Akktri.

My smile was wan. "Partly because of these."

"Would you like them back?" he asked uncertainly. "Your pick-k-tures of past lands? Do you love them more if they are recreated-through-esfn?"

I looked at his furry face. "Even *you* can't esfn what is no longer here."

"I esfn before," my Phner companion bashfully answered, as if confessing to peeping through the shades. "I esfn them." He tapped his head the way Mack does when he's being smug. "I know them. Esfn your maps, I think, and I might esfn more of Billee." He gave a brusque shrug of his narrow shoulders.

"Truly?" I said, unwilling to believe.

"I esfn them k-k-carefully," he answered. "I can make more. Why do more mat-ter?"

I fell back in my ravaged easy chair. "Your eyes can see a thousand years," I said, giddy with relief.

"They will not be formed-and-complete-without-copy," said Akktri hastily, as if embarrassed by my compliment and unwilling to claim undeserved praise, "but they will be re-formed-based-on-esfn-and-identical-in-gross-detail."

Phneri have no word for original. Nor can they understand why *Guernica* 1 is any more valuable than *Guernica* 624,559. Rembrandt's *Juno* meant nothing to them until it was burned and ripped in the Great Los Angeles Quake of 2019. They prefer the ruined version, for they taste its history in its char.

I knew about Phneri duplication ability, but I had never asked. Why is this, I wondered. My mind leaped to Iris refusing to ask Petravelli for help in finding her daughter. Was my caution similar to hers? Did I fear being in Akktri's debt?

I shook myself. If so, so be it. I looked at him, and said slowly, "Please re-create my map. I will owe you, partner."

"Ok-k-kay, Beverlee," my friend replied easily, as if it were of no consequence.

I had to express my relief, so I scooped him into my arms and threw him at the ceiling.

"Ow-ee-yoo!" shrieked Akktri, spinning like a propellor. "Yee-ee-ya!" He stretched out his hands to catch my shirt, then hauled himself across my back and onto my shoulders. "I make perfect maps," he babbled in relief, peering around the left side of my chin. "A hundred, two hundred! I make maps forever!"

"One will do." I reached across my neck to scratch his throat, and added, "You know, I said terrible things to you a moment ago. I'm sorry. I didn't mean them."

"You mean them," Akktri insisted, clawing at my head to keep his purchase, "but not to me. You hate he-who-is-gone. You hate us Phneri who steal South Boston but not Akktri, who is a Phner."

I started to deny it, then stopped short. *Was* I a bigot? The thought frightened me, and I found myself shivering.

Bostonians feel superior to only a few of the aliens. The spatiens do all the disgusting, dangerous, or drudgelike work, but they are so immense, so resilient, and so uncomplaining that they have become part of our urban myths: The Brave Spatien Who Saves The Troubled Child. The Phneri are so numerous and their appetites so simple, so tangible—water, fish, sleep, destruction, and the past—that most people think of them as nonsentient, and in any event clownlike. I had convinced myself I was superior to the gijos, because *I* had a Phner friend. Was I? Or did I, in truth, treat him like a pet?

Nonsense. Impossible. Akktri was too close to me, too important.

I was sure he'd notice and interpret my agitation, but my assistant was preoccupied with the map's rip patterns. To him what he had said was neither truth, accusation, nor revelation, merely a fact like any other. And that upset me almost as much as the words themselves.

For a moment I held myself, chewing my lower lip, thinking and not thinking, my mind overloaded. Then I ruffled his fur. "Partner, we can't sleep yet." I stood and kicked through the mess of debris at my feet as if to convince myself I was over the trauma. "I have to get them."

"We hunt more?" Akktri appraised me. "You know why this is done?"

"You see that sign?" I ran my fingertips over its chipped, painted surface. "Long ago, when vehicles were allowed in Boston, this warned drivers. It means Do Not Enter."

"Our human who is not-ended-but-will-end-soon sees us and is frightened." Akktri rubbed his hands eagerly together. "He tries to scare us. We hunt again now?"

"Yes." I felt a resolute pleasure in saying it. *"I'm* hiring us."

He grew coy, like Mack with a good poker hand. "We have swordfish fish when we k-k-kill him?"

"Lobster fish, buddy. The same bonus."

"Lobster fish! Lobster fish!"

I had a score to settle, a nemesis to uncover. "Let's find who did this. That person doesn't know me very well."

"That one's future has much pain," replied Akktri, gratified at the prospect. "He is evil because he hurts you. We end him," my little Phner vowed with a cheerfulness that chilled me. He held up his hands, claws flexed. "You and I, my Beverlee, we end his art."

9

"Good," said Akktri firmly. "We hunt again." He pushed debris around my floor, lowering his nose to peer at the fracture surfaces in my broken stoneware. With immense satisfaction he fingered the rip lines in a brown map fragment.

I sat cross-legged on the floor, tossing unsalvageable remnants into a wastebot. Top-heavy, it fell over, then struggled to right itself and began circling, pushing the spilled fragments that had fallen out of its head back into a liftable pile. It squatted over them and lowered itself, drawing the trash inside like a hen unlaying an egg.

"Iris tastes your hunt," Akktri added. "She eats news like flounder fish."

"Let her starve," I answered, dismembering a broken picture frame as if breaking a turkey carcass. There was a kind of toughening comfort in snapping the sticks into smaller splinters, as if I were proving my invulnerability by destroying them myself. "I'm going to take a shower."

The variable needle spray was fiercely hot on the left side, chill on the right. I swayed slowly underneath it for a long time, moving the different parts of my body from heat to cold and back again, finding the contrasts soothing and restful.

Toweling off, I checked myself in the mirror. The bags under my eyes seemed even more cadaverous than usual. I needed sleep but vengeance drove me. I scowled at the gray hairs creeping in like fifth columnists among my wavy red ones, grabbed one and yanked it out. It was thick and frizzy, as if petrified in place.

I grabbed a sandwich and stuffed it into my face while I dressed, strapping on my knife and gun. "We might as well get started on Petravelli's favor. Let's go find out where Guillermo Rey's gone."

I got Mack on the line. Delighted with the new ware Charles Beaufort had delivered, he had spent hours hunting for data. Guillermo Rey's name was missing from today's attendance rolls at his Louisburg classes, he told me, and he had not used his meals credits. "I'm pretty sure he's not at the school," my brother finished.

"Keep searching for him. He's important." Mack agreed, still gushing appreciation for Iris's prompt replacement. I thanked him and hastily signed off, then turned to my associate. "Where should we look?"

Akktri thought. "Guillermo sign is in Diana's room."

"All right. I'll need a uniform."

From my closet I selected a khaki shirt, rolled the sleeves down, picked and programmed an ID and stuck it in my breast pocket, and pulled on sensible heavy brown shoes. "Ready."

Three quick mover rides and a short walk brought us to Louisburg's main entrance.

"What business do you have at this late hour?" the lion's head knocker asked us. "Please identify yourselves."

"City of Boston Insurance Division to see Superintendent Hubert." Mack had given me the name.

An enormously tall older man, balding on top and with bright blue eyes, greeted me a moment later. "Wow," he boomed in a voice that would have roused the comatose to play volleyball. "Grant Hubert"——he pumped my hand——"I'm the super. How are you? What's the trouble? We in dutch?" With a wink, he prodded my rib.

"Nothing serious, Super." I explained that a Dep Op ohmmeter reading indicated fraying wires. "Thought we'd check it out."

"No problem," he shouted. "Never can be too careful

about fire in these old woodies. Sure am glad you scopers are on the job. Some folks think it's spying, but hey, I'd rather be spied and alive than private and crispy. Place like this, one match and it's tinderbox city. Wow!"

I assured him I could handle things, and he ambled genially back to his office.

If you're ever forced to prowl somewhere you don't belong, what you wear is less important than who you decide to be. I was a City structural engineer, confirming the building's fire safety. Akktri was my DPW assistant. I was toting a City-issue infomat, simplest model, well beat-up, and a light pen with a recalcitrant power cell. On the way I had rehearsed a list of irritating unanswerable questions to ask anyone who might come along, things like Are your circuit breakers cross-integrated? and Can you direct me to the nearest high-pressure T-junction? I was looking forward to inflicting knowledge of the permissible current wattage of secondary power recovery leads that may cut through non-load-bearing–walls, or challenging questioners with the unanswerable Do you have a building permit for that equipment? Is it registered?

Naturally, none of them even cast a second glance at us, and we reached Diana's door without incident. "Are they here now?" I asked my companion.

"Oh, no," Akktri clucked. "No, no. Here before but here not now. No, no, no."

"Pity I'm off Iris's case," I said. "The Master Key would come in handy." I pulled the thing out of my pocket and glanced regretfully at it. "But I'm sure she's inerted it after the way I told her off."

"Oh, no, Master K-key is no good here," tittered Akktri. He pointed and snickered. *"Mechanical* lock." His claws tapped a shiny brass circle above the keyhole. "Personal lock. K-k-clever seers behind the door." His gnarled small hands made tiny abrupt movements as if waving invisible cutlery. "Beverlee, I pick-k-k it for you. Give me your bones."

I scrounged in my left thigh pocket and handed him my

bones, a ten-centimeter strip of bundled metal rods. Stretching himself to his full height and standing on tiptoe, Akktri peered in the keyhole, his whiskers fluttering as he whistled several times. Head cocked, he listened to the echoes, then looked down at the bones and fiddled with them. Some bits extended, others retracted. Akktri glowered at the doorlock again, whistled and chittered. More hand manipulations, more scowling at the tool.

Finally he lowered himself onto all fours, leaving the bones in the lock. "Try it," he said diffidently.

"Will it work?"

"Hmh." Akktri blinked and whiffled his nose. "Try k-k-key."

"Sure." I slowly turned it. It engaged, smooth as silk, and the door creaked open to reveal a pitch-black room. "Fantastic," I said in quiet admiration.

My Phner companion giggled and gleefully rubbed his hands together. We entered and shut the door behind us.

"Okay, buddy," I said, turning on the light. "Where has Guillermo gone?" He scooted across the foyer into the right-hand bedroom, while I examined the room.

I headed straight for Diana's desk and began methodically going through it. Chaff: notes, scribbles, homework assignments, contraceptive patches, rare drugs. I hunted around for bills and ignored her infobox. Mack would already have scanned the electronic record; he'd find anything suspicious that might have occurred among her telephone calls, financial dealings, or public correspondence. For exactly that reason, most people with anything to hide write it down, outside the peepable electronics.

Diana's jewelry, heavy with old gold and ponderous last-century metal settings, was piled in a loose handful next to a stack of beer coasters. Among the rings and bracelets, I picked out a small gold brooch in the shape of a sparrow, a diamond winking in its eye. The delicate Asian design seemed out-of-place among the solid Yankee inheritance that comprised the remainder of the heap.

Evidently she fancied herself a sculptor, for the room was dotted with figurines—on her bureau top, mantelpiece, nightstand, and amid stacks of paper books. Most were small grotesques carved from synthivory: gnomes contorted into postures of disdain, people making love with caricatured aliens—I had to turn one sideways to determine who was doing what to whom. They were amateurish but witty—I caught myself smiling. The girl had talented hands.

Minus one finger, I thought abruptly and sadly.

"Guillermo was here soon-past," Akktri replied, returning. "He takes a bag that is heavier when he k-k-comes than when he goes. See! See!"

I followed him through the other archway. "But we found Guillermo and Hu making love here," I protested.

"Schemes and lies," disagreed Akktri. He emphatically shoved the sheets this way and that. "Anger and lust in this bed, fire and tension. Hu k-copulates here, but Diana sleeps here." He bounced up and down on the coverlet.

"Are you sure?"

"Clear sign, clear sign! See!" In two abrupt bounds, he had jumped to the closet. *"These* are k-clothes of Diana." He clambered up the moulding and then flung himself onto the closet's high rear shelf. I heard him rustling among the hatboxes and shoeboxes.

Akktri's head popped up expectantly. "Clear sign? You see clear sign? What is here that you see?"

Deduction captivates him because he cannot see it. To Akktri, the past is directly visible through the traces it leaves, but logic is a bright mysterious toy, a sparkler of the imagination, indirect and therefore unreliable and infinitely exotic.

"Not much. You'll have to rely on my knowledge of human nature," I said with teasing self-deprecation.

With a pout, Akktri crawled to the shelf's edge to peer over it at Diana's wardrobe. " 'Human nature,' " he spat. "Is stupid word, stupid like 'unique.' 'Guilty.' Tcha-k-k-a."

Hanging by his nimble feet from the doorjamb, Akktri curled his head around upside down and looked at the rack. Then he grabbed the underside of the shelf in his hands and released his feet, swinging down and flipping over so that he now hung facing me like a potbellied hairy kid trying to do a chin-up. "So how means?" Flexing his forearms, he rocked back and forth and launched himself onto my shoulders.

I grunted and sagged while he landed on me and maneuvered his bulk around until he was once again draped around my neck.

Diana's clothes were expensive but carelessly treated. Underwear was heaped into a corner atop a soiled pillowcase that apparently served as a laundry carryall.

"That jacket," I said, stepping forward. "Diana was wearing it."

"Yes," Akktri agreed, puzzled. He shifted his hands and feet as I stood back up. "Patterns should be, and patterns are." His whiskers tickled my cheek.

"Check it out." The material was dark green sool, the heavy Targive-modified silk. Soft and thick, yet light and airy, it had a draped angularity that would be striking. I lifted it from the closet and sneezed as I did so.

"Dirt is from Basement," Akktri added. "I know this dirt. I esfn this dirt." He reached his arm out and snared the sool jacket. "Strong struc-k-k-ture here." He shoved the sleeve at my nose, and I sneezed again after he removed it. "Pattern is *in* weave, not *on* weave."

The jacket had a panache that would shrivel me if *I* tried to wear it, but somehow I could imagine Diana striking artful poses within it. "It's different, anyway. When was it worn last?"

My assistant manipulated it rapidly in his hands. "Diana holds this with the finger Iris has now," he explained.

With a shudder, I thought of poor Butch producing the

severed digit, dry with brown crusty blood. He hadn't known why we became so upset.

Diana's ring finger severed. My Colton's 1855 shredded to bits. Ifraim Lemos's skull crunching on concrete.

"Guillermo holds the jacket but does not wear," Akktri continued after a brief but furious inspection. "His chin hair is in sink-k-k and in sweater. Many places here he touches. Many things he moves. Now, Beverlee, how means? What past do you see?"

"Diana was wearing this when she was kidnapped," I said.

"Yes, Diana wears this," answered Akktri, puzzled by my vehemence. "So why?"

"Well then, how did it get back here?" I asked.

"Do you steal from *every* place you visit?" demanded Chris Tolliver's raspy voice behind me.

Louisburg's headmaster stood just outside the doorway, framed by the light behind him. He switched on the room lights and we blinked.

He was wearing a heavy brown bathrobe, hastily belted. His long and bony ankles, blue veined like cold marble, stuck out of his cream-colored pajamas. His toes clung inside leatherette slippers flattened from being stepped onto as much as into.

Akktri, who was out of Tolliver's sight in the dark of my shadow, was calmly blinking, delighted to have company, but then he read the tension in my body. Tiptoeing forward, he lifted the sparrow brooch from my hands, which were meekly clasped behind my back, and silently secreted himself in the shadows. I've never learned how he does that.

Tolliver's eyes swept the room without seeing my associate. He seated himself with a sigh, an expression of distaste on his long pale face. "What have you taken? Guard," he muttered.

"Not a thing, sir." I lifted my now-empty hands away from my body.

A domestic praetorian floated in, the six silver hemispheres that were its eyes studding its vaguely round shape. Mobile security bots, they are primarily observers and reporters. Most have limited defensive weaponry and shielding that is penetrable if you know what to attack, but illegal modifications can make them nasty and it's prudent to treat them with caution and to assume that one is always looking at you.

"Scan her," he curtly instructed, and the praetorian slowly orbited me. I tried to ignore it. "Now," he went on sharply, as if calling an unruly class to attention. "Why are you here?"

"I can't say."

His brow burrowed. "Hmph. Looking into Diana's disappearance, I surmise."

I saw no benefit in correcting him, and ducked my head past the inquisitive praetorian—you can't read the other guy if you can't see his face. "I have authorization to be here."

"Not from me," he snapped, wiping sleep from his eyes. Unlike our earlier encounter, he looked frail and old.

"There are other sources of authority," I said slowly, hoping my bravado would mask the vagueness of my arm-waving claim.

He mollified slightly—evidently he deferred to distant autocracy. "If that is so," he said in a tone almost of complaint, "what was the point of deceiving Hubert as to your identity? You might have known that he would rouse me to verify your bona fides."

"Sorry." He was right, and I was abashed. "Late at night, this seemed simpler."

"Expedient morality," he sniffed, mollified. "Corner cutting." Evidently he felt more comfortable now that he had pigeonholed me. "What were you seeking?" he asked around a yawn.

Since things were going well, I let him have a morsel of truth. "At the moment, I'm trying to locate Guillermo Rey."

"Why?" Tolliver was instantly alert and hostile. "Isn't he in his room?"

"No. And he's been absent since my encounter with him this morning."

"You have no business snooping my students. Guillermo surely hasn't done anything."

"I didn't say he had," I replied smoothly, wondering what psychic heat sensor in him I was near. "What makes you think my inquiry is dangerous?"

"Miz O'Meara," he said icily, "I will not have you traipsing around my school, harassing innocent students."

"I haven't encountered any students, so I can't be harassing them."

"Pfui." He nodded to the praetorian, which floated forward. "I think I shall have you arrested after all."

"Sir, I have been given certain confidences, which I am not at liberty to reveal, that empower me to be here. This key"—I held up the Master Iris had given me and wagged it—"is evidence of my rights."

"Let me see it." He held out his long hand.

I was just about to, when I froze.

I'd just told Iris to go to hell. She'd certainly have wiped the key, maybe even spiked it against any further use. It might do to the praetorian what it did to Mack's ware, and I'd be down the vent.

"Well? Give."

"No," I said with sudden indignation, as if overcome by a fit of righteous ego. No point in playing the cards weak, I thought with stoic despair, bet them like you hold them, even when you don't. "I am enjoined by the person who gave me this key from permitting you access to it."

"Nonsense." He snapped his fingers and, with a whisk faster than I could see, his praetorian extended and nipped it away.

"Test it," ordered Tolliver.

Jesus, he'd called the bet in a flash. "Dean Tolliver," I said hurriedly, "what you're doing is robbery and electronic trespass. You have no—"

"Key is authorized," said the praetorian in a tin voice.

"What?" Tolliver asked, flabbergasted.

Keeping a poker face, I moved to exploit his confusion. "You were wrong about me," I challenged him, shoving a finger at his thin chest. "I may overlook this action if you immediately drop your hostile attitude. Now let me get on with my investigation and answer my questions."

Tolliver swallowed, goggled-eyed. "Does the key grant entrance authority?" he uncertainly asked his machine.

"Access to that information is denied us," replied the praetorian. Its arm pneumaticked out and flicked the key back into my hand.

I looked at it, wishing Akktri could decode its meaning. Iris knew that I had quit, but she had not inerted the key, and that woman never let a thing go undone. Everything she did had a selfish purpose. So she wanted me to have it. Why? For the moment, I was even more troubled than Tolliver.

I covered it with bravado. "Dean Tolliver, I'm a private detective, licensed by the City of Boston to conduct investigations," I pressed. "I have the right to be here"——I shook the key at his nose and he pulled his face back——"and you are impeding my efforts."

"I don't believe you."

"You have the evidence of the key."

"I don't trust it. I shall have you detained." He nodded and the praetorian closed in. A nasty jolt of electricity shot up my left bicep and shoulder.

I had to give him credit——he stuck to his gut feelings, even when they made him look ridiculous and exposed him to considerable risk if he was proved wrong. But that integrity was an obstacle to me now. "Dean Tolliver, you are committing assault," I said.

"Nonsense." He was so angry all trace of good humor had vanished from his voice. "No one has touched you."

"Read your law. It was already assault the instant your

praetorian blocked me. The stinging shoulder makes it battery. Order it to move aside."

"Sheer sophistry," he fumed. .

"Hah. It's the law."

"Same thing."

"I didn't invent it, I just use it."

He blinked and suppressed a smile. "You know, I find myself liking you." He sounded as if he was apologizing.

"Good." I held my hands out to him. "Let me pass."

"You misunderstand. Affection makes me terribly nervous. My life's worst decisions have been to trust people, especially young people, whom I find sympathetic." He stood and ran a worried hand over his dome.

"Is that why you're shielding Guillermo Rey?" I asked. "If so, you're not helping him. He's in big trouble. I can help him." That this might even have been true surprised and gratified me.

Tolliver struggled with himself, then his jaw clamped. "Take her away," he said to the praetorian, as if he feared hearing me say anything more.

I could take the guard, I thought as it obliquely approached, although it might do some damage to the school. Or I could armlock the dean and give the machine a tough choice.

I glanced at Tolliver and saw fear and pleading in his eyes. His authority was a paper shield. The praetorian had stopped approaching and was hanging back, waiting for my reaction.

With a shrug, I made my decision. It wasn't the time for violence. "Okay," I said, letting my breath out. "Let's go."

At Tolliver's brisk nod, the praetorian accelerated behind me, prodding me down the corridor to jail.

10

A PRAETORIAN ISN'T big—small enough, in fact, to go anywhere you can go—but its spherical shape and bulk make it imposing, especially when the thing floats just behind you, at shoulder level, and you know that if you deviate from the path it thinks you should follow, it will zap you. So I was glad when we reached Boston Police Headquarters, which sits like an appendix at the Long Wharf offramp, collecting the sludge the City spits up.

Set your wayback machine for 1915, Boston's commercial wharf district. New York is using that miracle material, structural steel, to build the world's first skyscrapers, and you don't want to be outdone. You've got a seventy-year-old Greek Revival granite structure that would make a nice skyscraper base. You tear off its Monticello dome and build a square twenty-five–story candle up through it, a big throbbing monument to civic pride with a pointed top. Put lighted clocks on each face of the pyramidal tip. Call it the Old Customs House.

Fast-forward to 2014 and drop aliens in the harbor. After two decades of explosive pop growth, you need living space in the precious downtown. Fill in all the spaces between the aging concrete-and-steel buildings with floors made of the alien miracle building material called prock—nicknamed orange come—as if you were making lasagna. To preserve the historic Customs House edifice, poke a hole in each layer, so the candle gets buried in its environment.

Brown the insides for sixty years in a brothy stew of bored law, swaggering or cringing perps, and desperate, frazzled, or grief-stricken cits. Season with the cultural juices of umpteen wog races percolating through our fair metropolis. Turn up the pressure by multiplying downtown population tenfold in fifty years. Coat the building's walls with sweaty grime rubbed off rumpled clothes and greasy hair by nervous perps awaiting whatever fraction of justice they think they can shave. Don't wash it, you'll ruin the ambience.

When you're inside it, the whole damn building seems to be nothing but stairs, mover shafts, corkboards that flake outdated faxes, and metal desks probably bought at Wehrmacht or Iraqi Army fire sales.

I was plunked into the identifier, where a mechanical arm pulled my left wrist into a dark slot.

"Dook who's here," said Ulkudge with satisfaction, stopping whatever she was doing to float gracefully over.

"Yesterday you didn't know my name," I said. "Today you chortle at my arrest. I'm moving up in the world."

Ulkudge sniffled. "Breaking add eddering. Hmph. Let's ged de read." Ulkudge thinks that law equals arrest reports. Koltsoi productivity—the more records, the better.

She directed the praetorian, which had waited behind me like a horse for its cowboy sheriff, over to a reader. It extended a jointed tendril and the screen lit up. Ulkudge viewed it, her hips and arms waving back and forth as if to invisible music, and when it was done she grumbled, disappointed, "Ged out ob here."

"What?" I said in outrage. "You're not charging Tolliver with assault and battery?"

Ulkudge's yellow nostrils quivered. "Roderick wants it quiet, meathead."

"Does he now?" said a familiar voice sarcastically.

We both jumped. Charles Beaufort was cruising down upon us, favoring us both with bright smiles.

"Where'd *you* come from?" I asked.

"Iris mentioned your key was heading down here," he said. "She thought you might need help."

"I'm not working for Iris any more," I replied. "And I don't."

"I see that," he said, replying to both statements, and escorted me to a creaky old mover out the back way. "Mover, open," Charles commanded. When nothing happened, he repeated the order.

The door was a grate woven of thick black iron. A small black button like a miniature hockey puck protruded from its side. I stepped forward and pushed it. A horrible deep groan issued from inside, like an elephant giving birth.

"Antique," I said, deadpan. "The interface is hands, not voice."

I pushed the button again, but the door didn't budge.

With a grunt, Charles reached across, wrapped his hand around a lever, and hauled the door creakingly to the right. Inside was a second wire-cage door. He shoved that open too, then turned to me. "Antique," he said. "The interface is muscles, not fingers."

We rode down, the cage shuddering now and then, the shaft dark except for the dim mottled brown light thrown by the mover's discolored ceiling bulb, until the doors opened.

In the corridor before us sat Akktri, his eyes bright with satisfaction. His forearm fur was matted down as if it had been wet. His mouth and hands smelled of cod.

"Had a bite while I was in stir, did you?" I joshed him.

"Oh, yes. Ended it by me. From tank." He made deft hand motions in the air and smacked his lips. Akktri can eat food that he doesn't personally kill, but he says that the neurochemicals emitted by a dying creature add flavor, like barbecuing. "Hi, Chuck-k-k," my assistant went on. "You are swatting Beverlee's ak-k-cusers? You rip their throats out?"

"Just a nuisance complaint from a lemon-sphinctered headmaster," laughed Charles. "Now, Beverly, may I invite you to dinner? Something small and intimate, just you and me. And you too, Akktri," he added with a glance at my expectant associate. "I make wonderful nigiri sushi. Belly of fat tuna, yellowtail snapper, mackerel. What do you say?"

"We ac-c-cept," burbled Akktri. Then he glanced at me, saw the lines in my furrowed forehead, and said without a trace of embarrassment, "we don't ac-c-cept. We're suddenly busy now. Oh, suddenly suddenly busy."

"Fresh homemade tagliatelle with garlic-marinated calamari," Charles continued, turning back to me. "Soft-shelled crabs amandine. Crisp green beans."

"No," I said, telling my mouth to stop watering. My dates usually serve onion rings and his-and-hers bowls of potato chips. I patted his cheek. "See you around."

"I'll interpret that as a rain check."

"It never rains inside the Cube."

"It does if Iris tells it to," he finished.

"Where do we go now?" asked Akktri as we set off down the corridor.

"To find Hu Nyo."

"Why her? We seek-k-k Guillermo."

"Hu Nyo is Guillermo's bed partner."

"We go to find Guillermo sign on Hu's body? Will she let us touch?"

"Nothing so direct and rude. But an interview with her may prove enlightening." I tapped the Master Key against my knuckles. Since Iris had left it active without asking me, evidently I could use it how I chose. "Let's find a phone." When we did, I shoved the key in and asked, "Where is Hu Nyo?"

Akktri's expression was skeptical. "It sees this?"

"Which one?" the phone responded after a moment's mental digestion. "Boston has four."

"Mi Nyo's great-granddaughter. Louisburg School student. Where does she live?"

"Six listed homes."

"Six?"

"Yes. Cloud Palace, 129 New Chardon 15—"

I whistled. The Nyo family estate on Level 129. More sky, people said, than any other single dwelling in Boston.

"—Louisburg School, 1 Louisburg 12. Club Benedictine Downtown, 48 Atlantic 600, now en route. Outside Boston, homes in—"

"Stop. Where's the nearest freemover that'll take us to Level 48?"

"Here are directions." The phone spat out a faxchit.

We chased down a couple of corridors and snared the mover the phone had indicated, a modern one. I ordered it to the Club Benedictine.

Akktri perched on its white slick floor. "Benedictine k-k-keeps me out," he said. "Keeps me out forever."

Even today, though Phneri are legally classified citizens, to any club they are animals. Benedictine members, aside from having long pedigrees and casually hefty bank balances, must be Terran-born genetically pure humans. No aliens need apply. No gijos either, just Bostonians.

"It's enemy territory for me too, buddy."

"They let you in," Akktri snapped. "You Irish peoples. Even the C-c-cambodians."

"After two hundred years." I squatted to look eye-to-eye with him. "They still don't like us much."

"I want to touch their walls and live for myself them being bigots," he emphatically declared.

But, as it turned out, we were both disappointed. The Benedictine easily rebuffed us.

"Hmm," I said, tapping my teeth with my fingers. "I have an idea. Have you still got Hu Nyo's jewelry we filched?"

Akktri in tow, I headed for Friendly Fred's, where I hocked the sparrow brooch. Even Fred, an extraordinarily dour old man, was able to see that the trinket was a rare antique. He gave me two hundred beans for it—probably one percent of its true value—and reluctantly entered my name and address in his antique manual box, licking his fingertips with each keystroke.

"Why did we do that?" asked Akktri when we were back outside.

"You'll see. Let's go home and be findable."

Along the way, I stopped for tortillas and a beer. Might as well give the bread a chance to rise before we checked it.

"Ha," said a soft Virginia drawl when we rounded the turn to my corridor.

"Who are you?" I asked, though I suspected I knew who had sent him.

He paused as if the question were a complete revelation. "Ah work for Nyo Trading and Shipping," he said. He was leaning back, his shoulders bracing his long body. He had a wispy light brown goatee and straight dirty-blond hair that he combed carefully over a bald spot in the shape and location of a monk's tonsure. "She's a mite interested in your recent doings."

"And she wants to see me?"

Again that strange phase delay, as if he had a mental voice buffer. Was it Tarmod or just Southern breeding? "Ye-es. If y'all'll folla me?"

"What if it's not convenient right now?" I asked, just to be ornery.

"Ah'd advise against that," he said very slowly. I couldn't tell if he was thinking or if his pause was his standard duration.

"Really?"

"Ah'd *strawngly* advise against that." The lightness had left his voice. So had the hesitation. He unlevered himself from the wall and moved toward us.

I looked him up and down. "Sure," I said, breaking the tension. "I've always wanted to see how wealth lives."

The Nyo wealth flowed from a trade monopoly. Boris Nancolm's encounter with the gray glubs established the fifteen-kilometer radius Contact Zone, the sole region through which Loophole transitors can enter or leave Earth space. For a decade after Splashdown other nations, companies, and privateers tried to transit the Loophole directly, but all such ships were either turned back or simply disappeared in a flash and sizzle of Cherenkov radiation.

The Boston trading houses were built in the early years after Splashdown—the greats like the Nyos, the Mudandes, the Abts, and the lesser such as the Martinezes, Gutfreunds, and Ili. They all rose by capturing, buying, or stealing technology, which they patented or copyrighted and then resold. Now Boston, like a dissolute younger son who has surprisingly inherited the patriarchal fortune, lords its exclusivity over the rest of the world as if born to it by divine right. And when its merchant families combine, as they rarely do now but did in the Secession of 2061, they can shake nations.

If Louisburg School was a poor faded copy of entrenched elegance, the Cloud Palace was the Platonic ideal. The hall runners—wide stairs! such luxury—were dark maroon. Brown notched mouldings covered the joins between awesomely high ceilings and walls hung with faded wool tapestries. Scattered throughout the lounge were heavy leather chairs and sofas made of sturdy wood the deep crimson and black of old coals.

Sounds were damped by large-framed paintings and lithographs darkened with age. Winslow Homer seascapes—rough, angry, blue and gray and white—fought for the eye's attention against Jan Brueghel's floral still lifes and Andrew Wyeth's early Chadds Ford winters, bleak and brown.

Cases along one wall held memorabilia. An 1842 broadsheet had been signed by Elizabeth Peabody, Nathaniel Hawthorne's radical sister-in-law and the founder of American feminism. A swatch, riddled with burn holes and stained with blood, from the shirt Nyo's late competitor Sitigar Malik was wearing when he was martyred by U.S. Customs agents just before the Secession and the Siege, was counterframed against an original countersigned fax of the Warren Amendment which granted Boston its sovereignty. I bent to see Mi Nyo's signature on behalf of the City. True to form, she had signed in ideographs.

Framed in a clear case was a water-stained baseball, the last home run hit out of Fenway Park before the rising water forced its abandonment in 2061, with a holo of the proud girl who had scooped it from the Massachusetts Turnpike Canal.

The past was a palpable presence that expressed itself in wills, codicils, limited partnership agreements, proclamations, signatures. Leather sees centuries, my sidekick says, for it absorbs sweat and secretions in layers like the rings of a giant sequoia. I wished they had allowed him to see all this, but the manservant simply said, "Mi Nyo insists," and nothing could budge him. After a hurried conference with Akktri, I had acquiesced.

A two-level–high sheer window overlooked South Fusion Station, built over the submerged ruins of the railroad terminus, and the harbor, where floated the *Beaver II,* Salton Abt's replica of the original Tea Party ship. Logan Shoals' crumbling air traffic control tower stood like a forlorn lighthouse, wisps of snow on its tubular roofs, in the center of submerged tarmac tidal flats.

Far to the right, past South Boston's Telegraph Hill and its lurking black Targive citadel, were the cobbled gray shingles of West Roxbury, where I grew up, in a small two-bedroom flat house no different from all its neighbors, until we were finally forced to move into Boston.

Billy never adapted to life in the Cube. And then, in the Siege, the Cube had finally claimed him.

For gijos or Boston's new generation, the Siege is mere docudrama history: a rebellious city in an arcane taxation dispute with its parent country. In July 2061, the United States imposed a trade embargo on Boston to enforce collection of newly authorized excise taxes on intellectual property flowing through the Loophole. Boston retaliated with economic dumping. A month's stalemate ensued. Negotiations and sound bites followed. Life went on. When it was over, Boston had its economic independence.

That's the history America and the world saw, the history

that played in the polsims. In truth, we fought and won a bitter, cutthroat, costly war. Inside Boston, the Siege was grim. Power was cut, water inflow was rationed. The hot month of August 2061 dragged on. The aliens refused to trade beyond the Contact Zone, yet they also refused to intercede on our behalf, even when we started dying of thirst, heat exhaustion, or typhoid fever from drinking foul water. Riots broke out. Murders were common. By the time it ended, none of us felt like winners.

In a fig leaf to its tattered illusions of sovereignty, the United States granted us free-city status and listed us as still part of Massachusetts. The Bostonians never cared, so long as they were free to worship their great god of money. But we citizens of Boston had our freedom, and we had learned hard lessons about our dependence on the aliens and the folly of that devil's bargain. Now I stood in the parlor of the woman who, more than any other, had given Boston its revolution. If we could keep it.

Gray fog, cold and forbidding, rolled across the view. I rubbed my arms to remove the chill.

"Miz O'Meara?"

I had expected her to be much older than she was, a wizened goddess seated on a massive throne, her raven's-wing hair elaborately pomaded and encombed with authentic tortoiseshell or mother-of-pearl. Someone who trilled her *r*'s and moved delicate, twitching fingers where the veins had taken over the bones like creeper vines over the branches of a dying tree.

But the woman who greeted me, though small and compact, looked fifty, not the ninety-five she was. Her black hair was cut in an efficient, almost boyish bob. Her skin was tan, her eyes bright and black. She wore a simple pantsuit of dark gray, impeccably cut of textured fabric similar to but probably far superior than that worn by Diana. The only touch of color was the multihued scarf she had loosely wound around her neck, her only spot of jewelry a tiny blazing fire diamond mounted as the crow's nest of an eighteenth-century sailing ship.

Mi Nyo held out her small hand, shook mine precisely and almost casually, then gestured me into a cordovan leather chair, seating herself in a matching one across the fireplace from it. Above her hung a portrait of Sitigar Malik, over the legend, FREE TRADE. She crossed one leg over the other, folded her hands in her lap, and said, "Because I cherish the uniqueness of the things I own."

I was agog. "Beg your pardon?"

"On your arrival, you asked Lubomir why I denied your partner access to my rooms. A Phner is utterly predictable. Let him in and he will esfn everything he sees. And once a Phner has esfn'ed"—she shrugged amiably—"a thing is no longer unique."

"I should think you'd be above common fears."

She smiled without parting her lips. "Fears are not always racial slurs. Pure economics. I own art whose value would plummet if it were esfn'ed. Selfish of me, I know. Un-Phner."

"Akktri would never breach a confidence." I felt myself growing angry. "He couldn't be my associate if he did."

Tiny laugh lines appeared around her eyes. "Why is it in my interest to take such a risk?"

She said it all with perfect calm and complete reasonableness. Iris might have had the same thoughts but would have expressed them more flat-footedly, more combatively.

"You might wish not to offend your guest," I answered her after a moment.

Mi Nyo inclined her head. "So I might. I judged I would not. Was I wrong?"

"That isn't why I came."

She waved her index finger at me. "Child, you reveal your youth. You come seeking my favor, so you decline to reply to my challenge. You underrate yourself. You show weakness. I acquire an advantage over you." She spread her hands. "I repeat: does my exclusion of your partner offend you?" She

leaned forward a little and the fire diamond—carbon in a
stable low-density lattice structure that can be formed only by
high-pressure weightless compression, a bit of Sh'k kiln crys-
tallography—sparkled with red and green shivers of light.

I looked her square in the eyes. "Akktri is my friend."

"Good." She sat back, as if confirming a hypothesis, and
opened her miniature left hand. The sparrow brooch I had
pawned earlier lay on her olive palm as if pecking for grain.
"Your Phner touched this before you sold it."

I had figured that the news would make its way quickly
upfloor, so her legerdemain did not surprise me. But Mi Nyo's
gambit had leaped over the first several questions I expected.
"Yes," I said.

"It is no longer unique." She made as if to throw the
beautiful thing away.

I moved my shoulders, unwilling to react. "Only if Akktri
esfn'ed it."

"Did he?" Behind her soft tone I sensed the poised laser
knife.

"I didn't tell him not to."

"I feared as much." She sighed faintly. "You put great
strain on my principles, Miz O'Meara."

"Oh?"

"Dead Phneri tell no tales."

My reply came immediately. "Touch him and I'll kill you."

She tensed ever so slightly. "A noble sentiment."

"Akktri is my friend."

Mi Nyo considered this. She was not frightened, I thought,
but respectful, reflective, serious, and utterly unintimidated. I
found myself wanting her to choose peace, not war. At the
same time, I did not wish to pay the price needed to make my
claim no bluff. I would not weaken or concede. So I waited,
unspeaking, as she thought about it.

"Can the Phner keep his word?" she asked after a moment.

I took a deep breath. Play 'em like you got 'em. "Can you
keep yours?"

At this she laughed richly. "Young woman, you are peril-
ously close to incurring my anger, the more so because your
threat is so flimsy. Still." She laid the brooch on the end table
as if closing a book of matches. "You arranged for its return
to our house, albeit by devious means, and that compels me
to extend hospitality." She looked me full in the eyes. "Please
ask your Phner friend not to share his esfn. You take my
point?"

"Certainly." I relaxed a little. My hand came up from my
shin, where it gravitates in crises. Her Virginian lever had
taken my gun and knife, but old habits die hard. I saw Mi Nyo
notice and say nothing.

She made small circles with her fingertip, as if idly weighing a question. "You work for yourself, do you not?"

"You've read my background?"

"Your posture. Why are you here? Why send me this message?"

It was time for unvarnished truth, for I had neither the
necessity nor the skill to lie. "Your great-granddaughter Hu is
in trouble. She's involved with the kidnapping of Diana Sherwood, Iris Sherwood's only child. She may even be a partici-
pant in it. I suspect she is, although I cannot see why or what
she would gain. I want to find out about it."

"Indeed." The lines in her face appeared again. "So you
suspect Hu and want her to confirm your suspicions."

"I want to talk with Hu Nyo. She is not my concern, Diana
is. If I find Diana, I have no other interest in the case. Anything
peripheral that I might learn will remain confidential."

"Yes, you would be wise to keep it so."

"Will you ask her to answer my questions?"

Mi Nyo cocked her head and resettled her scarf. "I see."
She put the tips of her fingers together in front of her lips.

I sat back in my chair and watched her think, her eyes
darting just the tiniest bit. "That's your price, isn't it?" I asked.
"Testing me?"

"Of course I test you," she replied, absently and with a

trace of asperity. I had ruffled her. Good. "You try to test *me*, do you not? It is called small talk. Conversation. Repartee. Testing gives life its spice."

"Do you test Hu?"

She recrossed her legs. "Or arrange them for her."

"Does she know?"

"Of course. It's common knowledge in our family. Awareness of the rules sharpens competition."

"Why does she put up with it?"

"You know that, of course. You just wish me to say it." She touched the brooch, inspecting it from several sides, then replaced it. "I built this Nyo merchant enterprise from nothing but the contents of a single seaworthy Boston Whaler I skippered out of burning, bombed Hull. Nyo Trading and Shipping shall survive me. When it does, it will need a wise hand. The prize is worth winning."

I pondered this strange piranha tank of a household, so unlike mine had been. Was this the relationship Iris had with Diana? "What if Hu doesn't want to compete?"

"Then she may live a rich, pampered, spoiled life, her every comfort provided for," said Mi Nyo with disdain. "She is flesh of my flesh, after all. That much is due her. Anything else she must earn. And you have cleverly persuaded me to talk about myself enough. Now I need to know about you."

"Aside from my background—which you already have read, I'm sure—what you see is what you get. I'm not a horse whose teeth you can check."

"My dear, you are as predictable as your Phner," she said without raising her voice. "You can be manipulated because you broadcast who you are. If you wish to prevail, you must become different from who you have been." Her eyes slid effortlessly past me. "Great-granddaughter, I believe you know Miz O'Meara."

I turned. Hu was standing respectfully before the matriarch. Now she turned toward me and her mouth turned downward. "Yes. She caught me fucking."

Unlike her grotesque form at Louisburg, she was dressed conventionally, in blue-red laserweave. Her hair was black and shining again, all traces of the hideous yellow glop gone.

"That is your fault for being vulnerable," replied Mi.

"I *locked* the door."

"Not well enough, evidently. When will you learn to protect your own security yourself rather than rely on surrogates?"

Hu sighed with teenage reluctant patience. "What do you want, great-grandmother?"

"Miz O'Meara has a few questions for you."

"Follow me," Hu immediately said, covering her resignation by sounding world-weary and bored. She set off without a backward glance and led me along an ornate corridor.

"How far to your apt?" I glanced briefly into the huge rooms leading off to either side.

"Apt?" She was bemused. "You think we're destitute? We own all this. My rooms are this way."

All this cubic owned by one family. The opulence of it hit me like a sackful of paper money.

We came to a door made from carved boxwood, which Hu keyed open with a flick of her eyes toward the scanners.

"After you," she said with a superior smile on her face. As the door closed behind us, I noticed that the boxwood exterior covered a flush bluesteel frame that shut with the satisfied sucking sound of a hermetic seal.

For someone as determined to be outré as Hu Nyo, her bedroom showed pure Cambodian Yankee tradition. A dongsun bronze drum served as her footstool. In ironic homage to her family's roots as both pushers and users, exquisite ivory opium pipes lay casually on the Portuguese feringhi strongboxes, of burnished ironwood and blackened steel, that served as end tables. A stoic wooden sea captain in full yellow oilskin sou'wester gazed into the distance, oblivious to the day-glo orange life preserver looped like a quoit over his oak shoulders.

Hu sat herself along a Chippendale chaise longue of faded

yellow silk, tucked her legs under her bottom, and spread her arms over the chair's curving back as if holding it together. She made a tiny gesture with her hands that invited me to speak, and in the movement I saw strong echoes of Mi Nyo's regal composure. I wished Akktri were here to esfn it.

"Where and when did you last see Diana Sherwood?" I began, declining to take apparent notice of the expensive, long-earlobed jade buddhas that squatted, grinning seraphically, from subtly lit perches about the room.

"Yesterday. She didn't come back to the room after classes. I didn't think about her."

"And you haven't seen her since?"

No, she hadn't. She had made no effort to find Diana. She wasn't concerned. It was no business of hers where Diana was.

I asked a variety of routine questions, mainly to get her into the rhythm of answering, then tried a new angle. "When did you see Guillermo Rey last?"

"You said you were looking for Diana Sherwood," Hu replied, smoothing her soft brick-red slacks.

"Let me ask the questions in my own way. When did you see him?"

"You were there the last time. Actually, I was rather glad you arrived. He was becoming sweaty and tiresome."

She was forcing the cosmopolitan air. "What is he like?"

"He has a clever cock and a stupid head."

I shoved my tongue under my lower lip to keep from saying something I'd regret. She'd talk more if she thought herself superior. "What contact do you have with him?"

"Out of bed? The occasional class." She glanced pointedly over my shoulder, then brought her eyes back to me and smiled.

I coughed and thumped my chest. "So you're not a revolutionary like he is?"

Hu laughed. "Why overthrow a system when you can run

it? Besides, it's all pap. Guillermo is just dressing up You Have And I Want in altruistic sheep's clothing."

"Chris Tolliver thinks you're a believer."

"Piffle. Chris Tolliver thinks everyone's a believer. Besides, he envies me for having Guillermo's cock. He'd like to use it himself."

"He's gay?"

"No shit, Sherlock."

My nose was becoming itchy. "Would Tolliver lie for Guillermo?"

Hu laughed. "Again, you mean?"

"Sorry, I'm stupid," I said deferentially. "You'll have to explain that."

She sighed. "Tolliver has been lying or alibiing for Guillermo Rey ever since he was admitted. Waste of money, if you ask me. Guillermo's the dumbest, most arrogant, most mule-headed person in that school."

Two out of three isn't bad, I thought, and said, "Then why does he do it?"

"He likes being abused by self-righteous Basement kids. Thinks it's invigorating. Wouldn't surprise me if he made Guillermo tie him up and whip him. They'd both like that." She snorted. "He's a fool."

"Who, Tolliver? Or Guillermo?"

"Both. Tolliver mistakes claims for wisdom, cant for philosophy."

My eyes watered. "But you attend all the rallies."

"They make the mater angry." Her shrug was esthetic and indifferent. "Besides, it turns Guillermo on and he fucks better."

My head was starting to ache and the atmosphere seemed to be thickening. Colors were less bright. "You took some clothes back to your dorm room today, didn't you?"

Hu was bored. "I suppose."

"Where'd you get them?"

"What is this, underwear undercover?"

"The bag was full when you arrived in the room, emptier when you left."

"It usually is when you're returning from the laundry."

"Including a dark green sool jacket."

"No. Doesn't sound like mine." Small puffs of hot wet dust rose from her hair as Hu shook her head.

I hawked in my throat and swallowed, blinking rapidly at her to clear the tears from my eyes. "The jacket was"—I fiercely sneezed twice—"Diana's." I wiped my eyes with my hand, but they only stung more.

"You must be mistaken. You couldn't tell decent clothing if it hit you in the nose. Anyway, I haven't seen Diana. I told you that."

I dropped my head into my hands and choked. "Don't try to duck the question." I stood up to move closer to her. My sneakers seemed glued to the floor and slurped as they came loose.

"What's to duck?" Leaning forward, Hu tugged my shirt. The sleeve separated with a loud rip. "You shouldn't wear cheap stuff. Fabric dissolves." She held up the discolored remains. "Polyesters break down in here." My belt stretched like brown mozzarella as Hu pulled it through the loops. "Or would you rather be naked?"

I moved toward her, my feet wiggling warm and wet inside my socks. "The soles of your shoes are peeling," Hu commented. "And steaming."

"What are you doing?" My throat was burning and each word hurt. "What's happening?" By now the air was thick with haze, my zaftig target a wavy-edged distant form far away.

"My room is my own," Hu's ghostly form answered. "I don't like people in it. So I got Aunt Ang to give me a Rigellian stabilizer for my sixteenth birthday."

"My eyes won't stay open." I waved my hands about, groping. "There's—something wrong—with the at—mo—ssss"

I crashed to the floor.

Hu rose from her divan, bent over me for a moment, then taffied away my remaining clothes until I was completely nude. Leaving me there, she plucked at the gooey masses on her hands, palmed a panel, and said, "Grundig, some vent you should flush. I'm going out."

She disappeared into another room. I waited.

Her footsteps approached, stopped near me, then faded as she crossed to her door and let herself out.

When it had smucked shut, I opened my eyes, my body still motionless, and scanned the room. Slowly, woozily—even with nose filters and a bloodstream full of chemical inerters, breathing soup makes you dopey—I maneuvered myself upright.

After our first encounter with Hu, Akktri had jabbered excitedly about exotic gas compounds in Hu's clothing, so I'd had Mack run her family tree. Up popped Aunt Ang, whose quest for religious truth had led her to the Targive citadel, there to have her skin flayed off and replaced with alien mudgills. Years ago Ang had emigrated from Outsol, to live in the baking sulfurous swamps of Rigel. So, for this visit to Hu, I had taken the obvious precautions.

But lord, it was hot. Sweat poured off me, making vision difficult. My nostrils were singeing from the heat, the skin on my toes burning. I hopped rapidly about the room, dancing from one foot to the other as I searched.

The feringhi boxes were too obvious—Hu would surely not hide anything there. Look for voluminous objects, Beverly, things that can disguise containers. My fingers moved rapidly, touching, probing, shaking. At the fourth buddha whose belly I rubbed, I heard a click. When I tugged on both his earlobes simultaneously, a drawer extruded from the back of his head. Inside were several sheets of rice paper, covered with Cambodian script and folded into origami figures of cranes, pigs, and frogs.

The door behind me started to suck open. Hastily I grabbed the papers and flung myself into an unconscious heap on the floor, concealing them under my prostrate right side.

Heavy footsteps approached and stopped. Strong hands reached under my armpits to haul me into the hallway, where I collapsed on the rug amid a cascade of white steam. The hermetic door slammed behind us.

I saw a brown wingtip, wool sock rising from it like a tree trunk and disappearing into tweed pants. I hauled myself up this unknown leg like a cat on a scratching post.

Two strong brown hands reached into my armpits and set me on my feet. "Hold onto my arms," said a man wearing butler's togs. "My name is Grundig. The nausea will pass in a moment."

I folded my arms over my cold breasts, using the movement to hide the papers in my armpit.

"I have a robe." Soft flannel embraced my shoulders and goosefleshed arms. "And some unguents." Firm hands rubbed something slick and cool on my cheeks, throat, and forearms. "I will guide you to a washroom," Grundig offered gently. "And bring you new clothing."

"Thank you." I swallowed and wiped my mouth. My bedraggled carrot-red hair was sopping. It *was* rough in there.

He led me along the hallway. "Perhaps a glass of water too?"

"Please," I croaked as I stumbled into the bathroom. Kneeling before the toilet, I hugged it like a lost relative and vomited in tidal waves. Finally, weak but relieved, I laid my cheek against the chill porcelain and just breathed for a while.

With a soft knock, the butler entered to hand me a green cashmere sweater and a glass.

"You're an angel, Grundig."

"A mere mortal." With a brotherly pat on my shoulder, he withdrew.

Once outside, I found a phone and called Mack.

"Where have you been?" he demanded, a half-empty beer

bottle in his right hand, then rattled on, "This new ware DPW provided is great."

"Have you checked it for fellow travelers?" I asked. It would be like Iris to make her gift into a spy device.

"You're sure paranoid," Mack said. "Everything's perfect. I'll bet it's clean. In fact, I'm certain of it."

"Uh huh." Just like you were certain that copying the key couldn't fry your box.

"Got news for you," Mack burbled. "Diana Sherwood was a Siege baby."

"I knew that. Iris told me. I'm off that case."

"Good! Found the kid already? Did you remember to get paid?"

"No. I resigned. Where's Akktri?"

The arm holding Mack's beer dropped to the desktop. "So that's what he was jabbering about," he muttered.

"Come again?"

"Your little buddy is practically having a nervous break-down. He wants you at Boston Garden right away."

"Have I got time to change? I need my gun and knife."

"No. Some character named Guillermo Rey's going to speak in fifteen minutes. Akktri says Guillermo's sign is full of big salmon fish." Mack chuckled. "I think that means your buddy's onto something."

11

Hu Nyo's CASHMERE sweater, cut for her buxom torso, was big in the bust and short in the arms. Its soft woolly hairs made my forearms and waist itch as I headed into North Station——I'm a City woman, used to garments made from genuine citcloth, not thatched whiskers brushed off the family pet.

The commuter trains had stopped running forty years ago when their tracks sank beneath the rising ocean waves, but the station itself was unchanged, protected by its historic-landmark status. Billboards still advertised fourteen daily round-trips to and from Lowell, seeking to entice people to visit that singularly drab and graceless city by the frequency with which you could escape when your boredom exceeded human tolerances. Timetable racks lining the walls were stacked with the traditional faded out-of-date brochures. A stentorian voice, boulder-dented by its passage through ancient loudspeakers, announced delays, cancellations, and fare increases, with only these words ungarbled: "May I have your attention please?" As was expected, everyone ignored it.

A few concessions to modernity had been made. In the kiosks where vendors had sold monthly passes to Billerica, Swampscott, and Amesbury, jewelry appraisers and pawnbrokers several grades lower than Friendly Fred plied their trades through the holes in the lexan windows.

Rows of green canvas awnings neatly gridded the floor. The pushcarts underneath these umbrellas were festooned with merchandise: batik scarves, "authentic Bostonian" scrimshaw in white plastic, and tiny ersatz pewter Bunker Hill

Monuments that resembled dildoes for robots. An elderly man, his back so stooped that his chin seemed to rest on his navel, shouted into his too-broad tie, advertising colored elixirs in tiny glass bottles—square, round, embossed with liquor or airline brand names. They clinked like oriental wind chimes whenever his cart was jostled.

"Pardon me, ill-fitting sweater wearer," said a popcorn alien as I merged into the crowd. Like all the other members of his kind, he was dressed in ridiculous shapeless fashion as if he had just tumbled out of a laundromat dryer. His scrunched face had a baffled eager expression. "May I buy you a wondrous object of purest grue?"

"You want to sell?" I asked. No one knows where the popcorns came from or how they manage to survive here, but they have been with us since Splashdown in 2014.

"Sell to you and sell for me! Cells of two and cells of three! Cells for yet a hundred indecisions, and for a hundred visions and revisions, before the toasting of a fake or spree. This has been dyed grue, the rarest color in the galaxy."

I turned it over to check both sides. "It's just green."

"A charming error." He waggled his hands inside his enormous gardening gloves. "The fabric appears green until you buy it, then"——he dropped his shout to a whispered roar——"it turns blue."

"Blue?"

"Yes! That's why grue is unique! It retains its grueness even after it's sold. Here, have some money." He handed me a bunch of cereal box tops. "Now use it to buy this from me."

"I haven't got time for this. I'm looking for Guillermo Rey." I shoved the box tops at him and started to move away.

"Great, great haggling! You're too good for the likes of me. I'm out of my head, over my league." He clung to my arm. "If it isn't grue, I'll give you my money back."

"Okay." Anything to be done with this. I stuffed the box tops into his hand and took the swatch which, needless to say, stayed the same color. "What happened? I thought you said this was made of grue."

"Oh, gadzooks and forsooth." The popcorn alien was crestfallen. "Oh, tongue of dog. I must have mixed in too much bleen."

"I've got to go. I'm hunting for someone."

"Why didn't you *say* so?" he asked in the manner of an exasperated waiter.

"I *did* say so. You weren't paying attention."

"You weren't charging attention! I didn't know I could buy it from you."

"Here's a holo of Guillermo Rey."

The popcorn grabbed the picture and immediately turned it upside down. "Yes, yes," he replied. "Absolutely distinctive hairline. I can certainly sell you to him."

"But you haven't got him."

"Oh, but this is a *futures* contract." He shoved his sleeves up his forearms but they slid back down again, flopping like oversize socks. "If I get him, then you buy him from me, okay? I can take that commitment *to the bank.*"

"All right, fine," I said, and escaped up the ramp into the Garden itself.

The Loophole, Boston's fountain of money, was towed into Solar orbit by the Builders, a race about whom not even the centaur, Bishop 24, admits to know much. As best we can reconstruct events, it arrived somewhere around 2013 and hung unperceived, a no-space massless and energyless anomaly, just beyond Jupiter until the First Contact. On August 22, 2014, at 5:05 P.M., the gray glubs' ship made an emergency landing in Boston Harbor, only to be greeted by Boris Nancolm. And then all gold rush broke loose.

Within a scant few years, through the Loophole flowed riches and wonders to glut even the Conquistadors: biodesign on a grand scale, micronics so small and powerful that a lint-sized chip could not only beat you at chess but insult you in Swahili all the while, truly independent servobots, artificial brain aids, field-based technology; the list went on endlessly. With them came vermin, bugs, bizarre foodstuffs, and a host of alien con artists, lunatics, political fanatics, demagogues, courtesans, smugglers, and rapscalawags. And the dread disease cities, which in the late 2030's killed a fifth of the City's population before the Targives designed a treatment and vaccine.

Among the interstellar immigrants were represented all biologies, ecologies, races, and shapes: the elephantine Tulguts, who contemplated philosophy and metaphysics while crushing any furniture not made of reinforced steel or prock; the translucent shapeshifting Hnarfil, who took up homes in the newly drowned marshes; the waldo-building Sh'k, known only by their devices; the sinister Targives with their love of bioform art; the cement-skinned spatiens who believe in Zen Buddhism, work, family, and revenge; the Phneri on their diaspora from a world that no longer exists; the rock-eating cisos; the manic-depressive psychotic gray glubs; the black aliens; the long-jointed Adjwai; the madcap popcorns.

They overran Boston. We could no more stop them than the Algonquin and Wachusett Indians could hold back the Pilgrims.

Almost overnight, the City was transformed into the economic and cultural capital of Earth, the most exotic, sensuous, rich, decadent, opulent, diverse, exciting city the world had ever seen. Even now, sixty-five years after the event, Boston remains an amalgam of Oz and Xanadu.

Physicists may claim that space-time can be bent into viable four-dimensional Loopholes only far away from Sol's distorting gravity, but I know different. I've been inside the Boston Garden.

In that sports mausoleum, space folds inward on itself in an unmappable labyrinth of passageways. I zigzagged through the third-level Ladies Loo up to the tiny, obstructed-view Gallery Gods seats, where Akktri would surely be awaiting me.

Renegade albino pigeons cooed from the shadows and fluttered away at my approach, their noises covering the faint metallic booms my footsteps made. Strange small creatures hissed as I passed, and I chose my steps with care. The Antarean mudrucker, which found a second paradise in Boston's warm crevices, marks its territory with feces laced with minute traces of nitroglycerine. If you miss its licorice smell, one step in it and instant fireworks. For a few years after the mudruckers got loose from IPOB, we had a rash of basset hounds with singed and snubbed noses, until the dogs finally wised up.

At one intersection rolls of felt banners were stacked like paper logs. Some were emerald green and what must once have been white, others yellow and sooty black. I rearranged them into an impromptu sofa, sniffing first to choose those free of mudrucker dung. Seating myself on a green one that said BOSTON CELTICS, WORLD CHAMPIONS 1999, I gazed down at the Garden's parquet floor.

The scene below was both distant and absurd. A raised podium looked over a hockey rink like the bridge of a seagoing vessel. Heads clustered in a loose waving fan before it. They bounced irregularly as their owners stretched to see over one another. Spotlights above me illuminated the podium with cones of yellow-white light that nailed sharp shadows to the speakers' feet. Anyone looking toward the roof would see only the dazzling glare of those lights, not someone hiding in the darkness beyond. I was safe here.

A blackbird cruised imperturbably around in front of my eyes. "Diana's left hand was delivered to me earlier today."

"Iris?" I was too appalled to be startled. "You're sure it was hers?"

"The left ring finger had been previously amputated."

"Jesus." I felt sick. "I'm sorry. Any note?"

"Yes. It said, NOW THERE'S LESS OF HER TO SAVE. How can I persuade you to change your decision?"

"Iris, leave me alone. I quit once already." I slapped at the blackbird, which easily ducked out of reach. "Or did that slip your memory?"

"I remember." Her sigh came from far inside the machine. "I hoped you had reconsidered."

I rubbed my forehead. "Iris, I know how to trace runaway kids or check out the backgrounds of crooked property developers. I can find sequestered assets and bust most aliases." I stared into my fingers. "That isn't even in the same league as people who are using your daughter for a cutting board."

"Your apt was ransacked," Iris said quietly. "I just saw the rod rep. That must have been my fault. Tell me how I can make that up to you."

"Forget it." I didn't want to owe her any favors. "Why me, Iris? Why not just call in the rods and get on with it?"

"Because I don't trust them." She was bitter, matter-of-fact.

"Go away."

"As you wish. But, even though you despise me, please find her," concluded Iris, raw fear in her voice. "I can't take much more of this impotence. Do whatever it takes, whatever it costs, but for God's sake, find Diana." The blackbird rose and moved away from me, fleeing into the darkness among the rafters.

I watched it go and blinked, seeing my surroundings again as if for the first time.

Boston Garden had been a luxurious sports arena when it was built a hundred and fifty years before, but now, like most of the Basement, it was cluttered with forgotten junk of bygone eras. From here I could see broken chairs in the shadowed sections, their seats collapsed or stripped bare. Out-of-the-way corners were filled with the wreckage of civilization: piles of dusty or splintered wood, twisted metal and porous cement that had once been balconies, signs, concession stands. All were swathed in fine dust, so gray and uniform it looked electroplated. All color had been leached from the scene: stolen, faded, sprinkled with gray soot, or simply swallowed by the darkness hovering outside the fierce cones of light beaming down onstage.

"Beverlee," cried a cheerful voice to my left. Short arms wrapped around my neck.

Reaching behind, I grabbed Akktri by the tight fur on his sides and hauled him over my head into my arms. He giggled and squirmed in my grasp. "Mountain creature fur!" he chattered, his nose whiffling. "Fur under outer fur. Heavy washing in tubs with strong lye, carding through thick-k-k metal combs, weavings into wool cloth."

"Oh, the sweater," I laughed.

"Of *course* the sweater, Beverlee." My assistant was nettled. "Sweater has Basement dust and dust from Diana. Hu Nyo wears it. Heh heh. Your head hairs are two colors." He changed topics abruptly as his attention wandered. "Red and gray."

"Don't remind me." I felt my thatch, a dull lifeless mop.

"Gray is bet-ter. Gray is ended, is all struck-tured. Lik-k-ke your face." His small hand came up to my cheek and traced the crow's-feet at the corner of my right eye.

Before I could reply, Akktri leaped onto the railing with no thought of his safety. His whole body shivered with anticipation and pleasure. "See, see! There!" His little right arm stabbed down toward the podium like a sherpa guide.

"What is it?" His energy was contagious. My hands grasped the railing.

With a shiver, Akktri changed his posture. He straightened his back, his gestures becoming younger and more fidgety— those of Guillermo Rey.

Transfixed by his new personality, Akktri pranced on the railing, moving and declaiming in time with the speaker as if he were a tiny puppeteer. I leaned forward on the catwalk for a better view of the podium, savoring the illicit omniscience of my perch.

The people below were posturing for each other, unaware that to me they all seemed ludicrous and petty. The sensation was a drug that chilled me, and in it I recognized something of the emaciating nourishment that bot voyeurism might provide Iris Sherwood. In my loft, seeing and unseen, I felt superior to them, a dry erotic thrill like fucking your superego.

"We were doing fine until the aliens came," Akktri chirped ponderously. Even his intonation perfectly matched Guillermo Rey's.

The crowd rumbled approval, applause rising with a sound like popcorn kernels exploding in a bag. "Boston is *our* place." My associate brought his hand sharply down and made a sound uncannily like a palm hitting wood. "Our parents took Boston back from America! Now *we* must take Boston back from the aliens, and from the startit suckers, the Nyos and Mudandes, who feed on wog garbage."

The iron beams we stood on trilled with the crowd's roar.

"The Phneri who ate our children," Akktri hissed with the venal conviction of a bigot. "The Targives who twist jellyfish into tents, snails into monstrous clivuses. The Tulguts and Hnarfil and gray glubs and spatiens. They all think Boston is theirs. But let us tell them something." My small friend leaned forward as if seeing individual faces in the crowd. The silence fell until it was deathlike and fearful. "Boston is ours," he began softly. "No aliens need apply!" His voice rose and he flung his furry arms wide. "Boston is ours!" screamed Akktri, sizzling with terrible energy.

"Boston is *ours,* Boston is *ours.*" Heads in the crowd were bobbing and buzzing like water about to boil. Their war cry echoed in the cavernous Garden and followed Guillermo off the platform, continuing for several minutes.

I wiped sweat from my forehead. No wonder Roderick Petravelli wanted me to get close to him—the guy could be dangerous. For a cellarkid like Guillermo, power gave definition, dimension, and substance: he could play out his desires through other people. A rugrat would bed wealthy Hu Nyo not for sex but for the mastery it showed, the secret it created. Working one's will upon others is a rugrat's ultimate lure.

Akktri tapped my shoulder and I jumped. "Why are they angry?" he asked anxiously, and crawled into my lap.

Does a technologically inferior culture always want to kill a superior one? I thought of the American Plains Indians, shoved aside by the cowcatcher of white man's history. At the end, their tribe reduced almost to extinction, they had pinned their final hopes on the Ghost Dance. Anointed by the Great Spirit, impervious to bullets, they had gone onto the grass battlefields of North Dakota with courage and without fear, where the white men, whose rifles didn't know the Indians were protected, methodically shot them down.

Could wishing make the bad foreigners disappear?

"We've lost," I whispered.

"Lost what?" murmured Akktri, sleepy with my body's warmth.

"Control of our lives." Even I felt their pain and emptiness inside.

"You speak-k-k such nonsense, Beverlee," my friend sighed and fell asleep. His mouth fell open and he snored, a wheezy rasp like a kazoo.

Now humanity depended on Akktri and his kind. So, for that matter, did I. My Phner friend had promised to restore my map, an object whose meaning was beyond him, because I cared about it, an emotion he could not comprehend. Our city was built of alien materials, our wealth grown from the seeds of alien inventions, alien technology. Our society aped alien fashions, lusted to see alien stars. We could banish the intruders but, like the Indians who had seen neither guns nor horses until the white men came, we could never re-create the ignorant, naive, homely society we had before Splashdown. We had tasted the alien future and it was in us.

So I sat, cross-legged and suddenly bone-tired, my companion and friend snoozing in my lap. How many hours had I gone with only stolen catnaps? Since Iris had hired me, I realized. Thirty hours ago? Thirty-two?

"Beverlee?" A hand tugged my sleeve and I sat up with a jerk. "You wish we never come?"

"What?" I was groggy. Dozing for these few minutes had made me yearn even more for a warm, horizontal rest. My mouth was gummy and tasted of ammonia and spit.

His brown and gold face was unsure. "You wish Phneri never fall from the sky? You wish we all go?" asked Akktri in a minuscule voice.

I shook myself to attention. "Never. Your enemies are my enemies. Your pain is my pain."

I meant it as I said it. But, just beyond comprehension, I felt more feelings than I could articulate. I held Akktri, and he was my friend, but he frightened me and I watched my words when he was near.

"True friend, Beverlee O'Meara?" he asked, reading my face.

Yes, I thought with powerful certainty. Yes, I will trust you. "True friend, Akk-k-ktri the Phner," I said very slowly, careful to give his name the full pronunciation.

My companion's eyes glazed and his breathing stopped. "Beverlee, I esfn this moment clear."

The way he said it made my eyes moist. I nodded slowly.

He lifted his small shoulders, then leaped to the balcony. Below us, the crowds were swirling again as the meeting broke up. "Many people on the floor know us," Akktri commented. He hung over the railing by his soft belly, arms and legs dangling casually in space like a limp washcloth over a faucet.

"You mean we know many of them, don't you?"

"That's what I said," answered Akktri, perplexed.

I chuckled. "Who do you see?"

"K-k-chris Tolliver." My associate idly scratched his ear. "He tries to tell Guillermo something, but Guillermo pushes him away. Other Louisburg students. Tuoali Aleabola. And see! See!" Akktri pointed all four hands at one spot. "Charles Beaufort is here!"

"Really?" Why was handsome Chuck mingling in this crowd? What did Iris need him for down there?

"He shouts," he went on. "He is angry of Guillermo." Akktri yanked space as if grasping someone by the bicep. "Ho ho! Guillermo defies." Akktri pulled his arm back. "Charles's face gets blood in it."

I fell silent, thinking.

"You use log-ic-k-k again?" he asked hopefully. He yawned and scratched his nose. "Guillermo leaves very soon," commented Akktri lazily. "Hurry, Beverlee." He yawned again. "I must stay here. They want no Phner." With a neat spin on the bar, Akktri flung himself onto the rolled Celtics rugs. "You chase Guillermo. I sleep more." He walked a circle on the banner and then settled comfortably into the depression his weight had made. "I follow you when crowd sees not."

"Good." I ruffled his fur and stood up, my knees creaking, and descended, thinking about the aliens some thought ruled us. Bishop 24 was the most visibly influential, through Earth Venture Capital and through his self-appointed role as guardian of humanity in its pre-sentient stage. Big, smart, fast, and insectoid, he intimidated and unsettled all who met him. But there was only one centaur, and most of the stories about him were myths. The spatiens were ubiquitous and almost indestructible, certainly indefatigable, but they were too passive, reliable, and docile to cast as rulers. They took their orders from Iris, whom they almost worshipped. In truth, if we were controlled by anyone, it must be the Targives, whose brooding presence dominated our lives. From the black batwing citadel which perched on Telegraph Hill in South Boston, their biodeformed creations infiltrated every facet of our existence. If the City was a physical organism, the Targives made it so.

Of course we humans had no claim to moral superiority, for we unquestioningly and greedily used what the Targives made, from Boston's snakeskin roof to the living tonguerugs, the roachform pill dispensers. Some said pissmops were bred from cocker spaniels, while others claimed they were born of furry caterpillars, or dromedaries, or tarantulas. Or maybe all of them together.

As far as I knew, no human being had ever, with knowledge, seen a Targive. Judging from their creations, no one much wanted to.

The speeches were over by the time I clattered down the cement steps, slippery with condensation from the cool cinder-block walls, and into the Garden. Knots of people clustered on the podium. I elbowed effectively.

"Well, if it ain't the limburger babe," said Guillermo, noticing me. His eyes gravitated toward my chest as young men's do. "The meat eye who pretends to be a lawyer."

"Not anymore," I said, remembering the sharp pain of his slap in Hu Nyo's dorm room. "I've got a proposition for you." I lowered my voice. "I have traced Diana Sherwood's biological parents back through the Siege."

"Impossible," he said, agitated. Then he realized this might be a damaging admission and added quickly, "What's this to me?"

"Nothing's impossible with Phner investigators." I spun him a tale about searching old records and checking Diana's DNA from skin samples. "Her parents died not knowing that they had inherited warrants representing twelve hundred shares in Earth Venture Capital."

"Twelve hundred?" he asked, awestruck. "But that must be worth——" He stopped in consternation, his lips moving with silent calculation, as if inside him cherished beliefs were being destroyed. I enjoyed his turmoil. After slapping me earlier today, he deserved any discomfort I could create.

"Enough money to make the two of us *extremely* wealthy," I purred, laying my hand softly along his upper arm. "I have a release for Diana to sign. We can pay her more than she can imagine and still be rich ourselves. I'll give you fifteen percent for her thumb." If she still has one, I thought suddenly.

Money always hooks cellarkids. His mouth came open and his tongue touched and lingered on his lips as if wealth had a taste he wanted to savor.

"What do I need *you* for?" Guillermo asked.

You come to the bait like a mop to the piss, I thought. Like a Phner to an explosion. "Without me," I reminded him, "you don't know where the claim originates."

He chewed on that. "Wait here. I'll be right back." Bolting away from me, he trotted off the platform and strode down a long downsloping tunnel toward the B & M Train Station ruins.

12

Running isn't the fastest way through a crowd: the spectacle you make of yourself causes people to stop what they're doing and get in your way. You're liable to trip over a dachshund and dribble your nose on the pavement. Or some muscle-brained adolescent will work off his testosterone by trying heroically to tackle you.

Guillermo camouflaged his haste with the officious and impatient walk of a junior accountant, late for a crucial audit conference, trying not to sweat into his fashionable mood-color suit. He skitter-danced through the quick-changing interstices opening between the bodies, pushing people aside only where absolutely necessary.

He had told me to wait. So of course I followed him.

Boston Garden's curving exit ramp splayed like a river delta into the B & M Station's main floor, covered with the flea market through which I had entered an hour ago. Guillermo vanished into the crowd and I paused, above the fray, hunting for him in the festival.

Foodwagons concocted greased or charred delicacies: broiled schrod, souvlaki, lobsters with soft Targive-modified shells and no digestive tracts (so you could eat them antenna to tail), popovers, and Parker House rolls. The smoke from a dozen braziers rose like rival Indian signals, braiding into a thick smog that settled fatly near the ceiling. Iris's air scrubbers were working overtime.

The noise of conversations—wily haggling, emphatic disputes, passionate embraces, and the laughters of surprise and delight—reverberated through the hall. The world's worst folksinger wailed off key, accompanying himself on a mistuned Hnarfil water guitar, while a few meters away, his accomplice sold deafhoods.

A barbershop quartet on a small plywood platform to my left wore identical maroon-and-white striped summer jackets and extravagant handlebar mustaches. Arms looped around each others' waists, they sang "Bicycle Built For Two" in intricate four-part harmony and swayed with their music, left-right, right-left, rising to their tiptoes with each beat. When passersby dropped coins in the straw hats upturned at their feet, they briefly dipped their heads in perfect cadence. I wondered if they were human.

Kids, dogs, and cats chased each other through the crowd, yelling and fighting and giggling, a society within a society.

"Need a Guillermo?" asked a ridiculous voice.

My popcorn grue-seller was back. "You know where he is?"

"We specialize in finding people! We find integrity for politicians, no easy task let me tell you. Look at all the people we've found already." The little creature gestured avidly at the crowd around us. "You just pick out the one you want and I'll find him for you. For instance, I can sell you the Chief of Police. I sold his past to Mi Nyo the other day, who said he was poaching on her territory. I didn't know it was an egg. She also bought some common sense for Hu Nyo, but Hu lost it."

"Guillermo Rey," I repeated slowly. "Do you know where he's gone?"

"Ghee-*zher*-mo," the popcorn corrected me. "I bought his accent, and stole some of his charisma when he wasn't looking. *He* won't miss it, he's got plenty. I even sold some of *his* past to Petravelli." He postured extravagantly, the garden gloves drooping off his hands.

The popcorn must have encountered Guillermo to know so much about him. "Is he here? Point him out."

"Okay, no problem. I'll name any guy here Guillermo Rey

and sell him to you. No? All right. For cheapskates, I can sell the name without the person. It's also easier to carry."

"No, no." I was starting to get mad. "I need the person, not the name."

"If he's changed his name, how can I tell you who he is?"

"You don't know what he looks like." I craned my neck to see farther into the crowd.

"By jingo, damn straight I do, egad! He's tall, young, well built, a hypnotic public speaker, and he ran down the Boston Garden ramp a little while ago. I should have been a pair of mumbling maws," the creature ranted on, "bounding on the busts of brahmin bimbos."

I was amazed despite myself. "How did you know that?"

"All Guillermo Reys look the same," the popcorn alien replied matter-of-factly. "It's a characteristic of the species. You can't be much of a detective if you don't know these things. I sold him a brilliant disguise, but I'll sell you how to recognize him."

"Disguise?" I cursed under my breath. "What kind?"

"It lets him impersonate"——he leaned forward conspiratorially but kept shouting at the top of his lungs——"anyone who looks just like him." The popcorn alien clapped his canvas gloves together. "He was so pleased he put it on right away. You can't see where the disguise ends and his real face begins. Now he looks completely the same as himself."

"Regardless of his appearance," I said, enunciating very slowly and calmly, "I've got to find him."

"He went out that door over there." The popcorn pointed at the exit leading into the remains of the subway.

"Are you sure?"

"I *ought* to be able to recognize him. I sold him the disguise. You don't listen to me."

I grabbed and shook him. It was like choking a mop. "Why didn't you tell me sooner?"

"Hey, leggo!" He made an elaborate show of straightening his clothes. "I couldn't sell you where he'd gone because he was right here all along, and I couldn't take your money under false pretenses, now could I?"

I pushed through the doors just in time to see Guillermo start down a long flight of steps into the old Haymarket T stop. The corridor opened into a long arched passage wider and much louder than the Sumner Tunnel. I heard a steady thunder ahead. The air was thick with grease and fumes. I coughed and remembered the miasma of Hu Nyo's rooms.

If hell has a transportation system, its model will be Boston's Central Artery. The ocean rising around our sinking City returned the City to its original narrow-necked peninsula. Most of what we import or export passes through this channel, six speed-graded lanes each way on each of three levels. Like the bloodstream from which it takes its name, the Artery never stops, never slows. Bot-controlled vehicles blast by in gatling-gun precision, neither swerving nor slowing. They peel away down exits or merge from entrances like fast-shuffled cards with magnificent disregard for anything that might impede their progress.

As a kid, I ran the Artery with other rugrats. Each of us roadrunners tried to be the most daring, until the day when Henry Frusino stumbled. The first truck——a windowless gray and black bullet on pneumatic wheels——smashed him flat with a sick soggy thud. A second ground his bones. As we watched, helpless, a dozen more pulped him.

So I stopped running and stayed away from the Artery.

Guillermo was a ways ahead, striding alongside the highway, nonchalantly turning his back on the computer-slaved mayhem streaking past. Dust and soot surged at us in waves. Airborne grit and oil dirtied my cheeks as, without a backward glance, he walked into the traffic.

He'll never make it, I thought. He's too old.

With brilliantly timed sorties, Guillermo crossed the first two lanes and paused, graceful as a Koltsoi, in the narrow gap. His clothing whipcracked in the buffeting winds. Sizing up the flow of oncoming cars, he darted through a space to the next lull between lanes and stood, breathing heavily, his body tensed. Pause, dart. Pause, dart. In seconds he had gained the median strip. Then he disappeared.

"Beverlee?" asked the most familiar voice in the world.

"Hi, buddy. Can you follow him?"

"Ak-k-cross?" Akktri asked. He scooted to the edge, bouncing with excitement. "I follow for you! The gaps are big like rivers, big as clouds." He zipped across the lanes and in a twinkling reached the median. "Hee, hee!" His high voice reached me faintly. "The cars hunt like barracuda fish but cannot bite me!"

"Without letting him know?" I called, searching between the vehicles.

"Yes, Beverlee?" My assistant perched at my side and scratched his nose. "Dirt smells burned. I k-k-cannot hear you over there, so I come back-k-k across. Why follow? Why not go where he exists-before-and-future?"

"What do you mean?"

"His dirts-s. On his k-clothes. I can go where dirts are and meet him coming back-k-k."

"But we don't know if he'll return to where he's been. It's better to follow where he goes."

"That is dumb, is human." Akktri chittered impatiently. "You do not see in Phneri way," he added with a trace of disappointment. "You still see like a human. Go to Targives and they fik-k-ks you and you see like me."

"Scoop brains from my skull like ice cream from a bowl? No, thank you." That was too frightening. What would be left if my mind was tampered with? Would I still be myself?

"Ok-k-kay," shrugged Akktri indifferently, and I was grateful that he chose not to comment on my reactions. "I follow Guillermo human way. You let me rip his throat out?" he finished hopefully.

"No. Let him think he's escaped. See where he goes, who he talks to. You can't do *that* by seeing in Phneri way. And keep hidden until I can meet up with you."

"Ok-k-kay." He ran two lanes into the mayhem, then turned and ran back to me. "This is lobster fish good times!" And he was gone.

I headed back the way I had come. The rumble faded behind me until it was merely as loud as a waterfall.

I found a telephone, stuck in my Master Key, and said, "Get me the City Operator."

Iris's craggy face bloomed on the screen, replacing the grid map of my location. "Sherwood."

"Answering your own phone, Iris? Where's Chuck when you need him?"

"I haven't seen or spoken with him for twelve hours," she groused. "Since you so flamboyantly resigned, in fact. My employees *are* occasionally allowed to sleep. And in any case, that key is coded personally for me, no one else."

"Right." I withdrew the Master Key from the phoneslot and stuck in my reader. "Track this ID. I slapped it on Guillermo back at Boston Garden. He just ran across the Central Artery, so he thinks he's shaken any pursuit. By now he's probably in one of the movers."

"Why are you requesting my assistance? You are no longer in my service."

I hauled in a deep breath, and quietly said, "I'm willing to be." I braced for her sarcastic superiority. "If you still want me, that is. If you haven't hired someone else."

"No," she said, "I haven't engaged another investigator. Thank you," she abruptly added. "What made you do it? No, don't answer." She held up her hand. "I'm just relieved to be working with you again. But what is the benefit of following Rey?"

"He should lead us to Diana. I put a bee in his ear."

"I see." She was grim. "He's the kidnapper?"

I nodded. "One of them, anyhow."

"How do you know?"

"When I searched Diana's dorm room the second time, the sool jacket she was wearing when she was abducted had been returned. That could only have been done by someone with access to Louisburg. And when Akktri and I encountered Guillermo and Hu Nyo in Diana's dorm room, they were packing a suitcase. They finished as we left. Among the things they took were some papers, which Akktri had earlier had a chance to esfn."

Iris leaned forward, an eyebrow cocked. "And?"

"One of them was the wrapper Diana's finger came in."

She shuddered, then recovered and wiped her mouth. "Interesting," she said with an effort at bravado, "and shrewd on your part. Guillermo Rey sounds like a young man who thinks he's clever." Her laugh was a harsh, cruel sound. "He can't imagine that anyone else can be cleverer than he. If he lives long enough, he'll learn that nobody is easier to manipulate than a young man who thinks he's smart."

"Maybe. And I have a score to settle with him. I'm pretty sure he was the person in my apt."

"Ah." Iris acknowledged this with the barest flicker of her eyes. "That explains certain matters. Meanwhile, I've got two blackbirds surveilling him. You can pursue. Your nearest mover is two corridors left." She gave me the directions.

"It'll be a few minutes," she resumed once I was in and moving. Her tough face lit up the mover's viewplate.

I leaned tiredly against the mover's walls. "What level is he on?"

"Ninety-five."

"What?" I stood and rubbed my eyes. *"Up*floor? What's he doing there? How could he get in?"

"And rising. I'm trying to trace his key."

"He must have influential friends, that's for sure, to have that kind of access." I thought furiously. "Maybe this is where he's keeping Diana."

"How could that be?" asked Iris. "My eyes are everywhere."

"Not in private spaces," I countered. "Even *you* can't see

into Cloud Palace or any other upfloor cit's cube. Come to think of it, upfloor'd be a brilliant hiding area."

"But Diana was taken from the Revere House, Level 1," my client protested. "All Guillermo's movements have been in the Basement. And he used a rugrat as his messenger."

I shook my head slowly. "That could all be a deception to send us searching the wrong place."

"That's too subtle for Guillermo. He's too callow to think so."

"But Guillermo isn't working alone. He can't be."

"Hm," said Iris, unconvinced. "It's too shrewd for him. Too much like a dodge I'd try myself. Nevertheless, I'll check my eyes and review the logs for the period after Diana's disappearance. This will take some time."

For several moments the only sounds were the beating of my heart and the whooshing rattles as my mover shifted between vertical and horizontal movement.

"His mover is slowing," Iris said a moment later, swallowing to make her words clear. "We've got him, Bev."

I saw her face, lined and weary, and thought of how near panic she had sounded moments ago in Boston Garden. My quitting had in some obscure way hurt her badly. She had probably never been rejected. Except by Diana. "I'm sorry for what I said in your office," I told her.

"Never apologize for speaking the truth," she replied with ragged determination. "Diana despises me, you know. I would give everything I have to earn my daughter's love."

"Iris, you don't have to tell me this."

"That finger they sent me." She stepped on my words as if to prevent hearing them. "Of all her fingers, they cut off the one with the ring *I* gave her. They send children to deliver their messages, children that Boston has failed. Behind this crime lies cruelty, cruelty to those children and cruelty directed at me." She stopped suddenly, aimlessly shuffled papers before her, and straightened her back. "I'm sorry. I shouldn't burden you with this."

"It's okay, Iris. Welcome back to the human race."

Her face lightened a little. If she smiled, she might even be approachable. "That's the first conciliatory thing you've ever said to me. What made you dislike me so?" she asked as if it were the most casual, unthreatening question in the world, of no more significance than the way I parted my hair.

"Because you tried to kill me," I said after an agony of silence.

"Did I?" she asked curiously. "When?"

"Back in the Siege," I went on with a gulp. "You flooded the Basement. God, I still remember that message, over and over." My hands involuntarily went up to clutch my head and cover my ears. I pulled them down. " 'GET TO LEVEL 11. GET TO LEVEL 11.' I ran. I ran." I remembered the horrific pain in my chest and my side as I fled up the endless stairs, ran and ran, gasping air, sure each breath was my last. Then the roar from below as the world shook and I huddled, a tiny package with my knees against my lips, waiting to drown.

"I watched many people die," said Iris. "Too many."

"So when you called," I finished slowly, "I couldn't say no. You were death itself." And you murdered my father and I don't even know where he died.

But I was too frightened to say it.

"I'm glad you're just a human being like the rest of us," I finished lamely.

"Of course I am," she snapped. "I'm so human I shot a man in the Siege."

"Only one?" I asked without thinking.

"I killed many people, you're right about that." She laughed bitterly, with a hint of the impenetrable prock exterior her political enemies confronted. "But there was only one I looked in the eyes and shot and was glad of. Lem Snow."

"Him? Why were you glad?" I asked, thinking of Ifraim Lemos, his eyes suddenly full of shock and reproof, as if by firing I had let him down.

"He was trying to kill me," Iris said with half a chuckle.

"He climbed a hundred and fifty levels of mover shafts and walked into my office. Just to assassinate *me*. To *kill* me." She laughed again, a wolf's bark. "So I shot him. Ironic. I had already judged myself and was ready to execute my own sentence. Guilty of destroying Boston in order to save it. Thoughtful Teddy had left extra cartridges in the pistol. Yet, when Lem Snow's blood soaked my legs, I decided I'd done enough penance for my sins. So I lived, and mothered Diana." She sighed, an empty sound. "Hold on. You're coming out in the last main lobby at Level 108. After here it's restricted access, limited to residents or City officials only."

"Where's Guillermo?"

"Round the corner to your right."

Bursting from the mover, I ran and got him in sight. The corridor he was walking down was a dead end but for a single door emblazoned WARNING—NO ACCESS. He wouldn't be able to get through that one. I slowed, making no effort to conceal my presence. I'd enjoy evening the score.

"Hey, coward," I taunted, hoping he'd resist.

Hearing my footsteps, he turned. "The bad penny returns." He seemed triumphant and cocky. He walked toward me, his arms loose at his sides.

I stopped. "You vandalized my apt, didn't you?" I asked hungrily. I wanted a confession, not a denial.

He chuckled. "Redecorated, I'd've called it. You have bourgeois tastes."

I ground my jaw, wishing for my knife and gun, left behind at Mi Nyo's in my haste to reach the Garden. Unlike the encounter with Lemos, I felt no guilt, only a pure and righteous vengeance. I was going to take him. I was going to beat him. I flexed my fingers and toes in anticipation, felt the pleasant warmth and bounce in my legs, set myself, and crouched. "Stay where you are."

"Why?" He was nervous, animated. Good. He'd overplay it. "I feel a burning desire to get close to you." He clutched his hands to his chest. "Just like I got close to your partner before I killed him."

The world shook and roared. "What?" I could barely croak the word.

"The little Phner was following me. I trapped him." He made an abrupt twisting movement with his hands as he moved close to me. "Now he's ended."

"Liar!" I screamed, and cut his knees out with a round-house swing of my right leg.

He fell, twisting his body in the air, and hooked my ankle. I went down hard and he kicked at my head. Rolling away, I took the blow on my bad left shoulder, still sore from Chris Tolliver's praetorian, and howled with pain. Guillermo tried to dash past but I flung my arm out, catching his ankle and jerking him off balance. He landed hard and cracked his head against the floor. As he staggered to his feet I swung another spin kick at his head, but he slipped it quickly and chopped me in the jaw. My teeth snapped down hard on my tongue.

Guillermo's punch had knocked me toward the movers, blocking his own escape. Instead of attacking me, he fled down the cul-de-sac toward the NO ACCESS door.

I spat out blood and pulled myself to my feet. Two black-birds floated into the corridor. "The rods are on their way," Iris Sherwood's voice said.

"They'll be too late." I brushed dust from my palms and headed slowly toward him, dabbing blood off my lips onto Hu's expensive sweater. "Guillermo, you made a mistake when you touched Akktri. You're a dead man. Your key won't do you any good."

"Won't, eh?" He stuck it in the slot with the triumphant relief of a man who'd just filled an inside straight. "Bye bye, dumb cheese." The door opened. He vanished.

13

Astonished, I ran furiously to the door. Iris was shouting something about danger but I didn't care.

I rammed my Master Key into the slot and leaned hard.

"Bev," Iris shouted, "he wasn't telling——"

The door yielded and I charged through.

——And onto the roof of the world.

I burst outside of Boston. The door opened on empty air. I had a moment's glimpse of a narrow walkway and guardrail, the city and harbor spread out far below, then the agoraphobia and brightness hit and I clutched my hands to my eyes, staggering woozily.

Powerful hands shoved me and I hit the rail smack across the hips, spilled forward, pivoting around my middle, and somersaulted head over heels off the balcony. I lunged for the steel support pipe and got my fingers on it, but my left arm, still recovering from the stun of Chris Tolliver's praetorian and Guillermo's kick on the deltoid, wouldn't flex. I slipped and skidded down the roof like an out-of-control tobogganer.

Bostonians think their roof is a uniform right-angle surface but, to weatherproof it from wind and rain, the whole structure is covered with a spongy, impermeable sealant, as if the city were an ice cream bar dipped in chocolate. This covering, Targive-modified snakeskin, is durable, self-repairing—up close, I could see individual scales—and fiendishly slick, so vermin will just slide off.

Vermin like Irish meat eyes. I bounced over hard lumpy

moguls for several stories, too terrified to panic, desperately trying to keep contact with the surface, every movement directed to grabbing anything that might keep me from falling. Arms, legs, fingers, and toes extended and straining, I spread-eagled myself as wide as I could.

My passage plowed up old crusty snow that stung my eyelashes and forehead, wind slicing through my sweater. Near the final ledge, an upright pipe as thick as my arm washboarded into my vision, somewhere far below my feet. I twisted toward it without thinking and impaled myself on it with a resounding clang.

Pain exploded throughout my side but my stubborn hands remained firmly wrapped around the pole, the only thing keeping me from sliding the last ten meters and off the roof.

My feet scrabbled ineffectually on the frozen roof, unable to gain any grip. Gritting my teeth and gasping, I hauled myself up and draped my belly over the pole, where I hung, breathing spastically, trying to get my fears under control.

I was facing west and south. The swollen Charles River meandered toward me like a scintillating raised highway, black dikes holding it up. To my right, Cambridge's rows of long and frumpy interconnected red-brick buildings squatted in the lee of the Harvard and MIT Walls. Gray bristly carnations dotted the roads among the buildings—trees, bare of leaves. They looked impossibly tiny and my plight clubbed my psyche again. For a moment I clung in sheer terror at the thought of falling from such a height, but then I forced my eyes back open.

Down in Cambridge, people lived in the open. They could bake or freeze. Rain or snow could pelt them. Airplanes or ships could fall on their heads at any moment. How did anyone exist like that?

My cashmere sweater ballooned around me, funneling frigid wind against my bare torso. Was this winter? We were in January, I thought. I'd forgotten how cold winter was. My breasts felt as shriveled as dried apricots, and the hair on my arms fluffed in a pathetic attempt to keep me warm. A yellow-white sun, brighter than I had remembered, gleamed high in the sky. The cold winds stole its warmth before the rosy glow could penetrate.

A big open maw, probably an air vent, belched thin wet steam that wafted intermittently over me when the breezes shifted. No other exit or entry ports were visible, and in any case, if I were foolish enough to release my tenuous hold, I'd simply tumble over the edge. I craned my neck, searching for other entrances or even Saint Bernards with barrels on their throats, but the roof was empty.

I was cold, and alone, and hanging half a kilometer above the harbor. I tried to concentrate on the scenery to keep myself from panicking.

To my left, the nearly abandoned wooden triple-deckers of South Boston stuck up from the water in decimated rows like a burned-out forest. Scavenger boats puttered in the canals and alleyways between the buildings. A hundred years ago, when the water first started rising, some of Southie's Irish—my ancestors and relatives—had pretended it could be ignored, like they'd tried to ignore blacks and integration. Then the Phneri came, and we Irish fled to West Roxbury. Now those triple-deckers, warrened full of Akktri's kind, fell one by one. Watery graves, their sandstone brick foundations dissolved back into the muck and marsh from which they had arisen two hundred years before, when the Dorchester Shoals were filled.

The industrial enclave along the South Boston harborfront was a submerged maze of walk-up warehouses, waterproofed by their rich criminal denizens, their windows polarized with see-no-evils. Behind and above them, the Targive citadel crouched, ebony, angular, and gleaming, atop Telegraph Hill. Only the Targives' clients entered that place, to have their brains scooped and packed, their bodies and souls transmogrified, emerging without ever seeing their hosts.

The hole beneath my feet burped steam that condensed

instantly on contact with the chill winds, creating a white sock that trailed away until chopped to bits. Its rumble vibrated this whole section of the roof.

Thermals rising up the City's flanks blew my frizzy red hair straight over my head. My teeth were clacking uncontrollably, making my jaw ache, and my hands, so numb they could hardly flex, were shaking and cramping.

Hurry, Iris, I thought, trying to cheer myself up with false bravado. People get killed doing stunts like this.

Far below my free-swinging feet, the Old City Ring Wall was a squiggly line girdling Boston. When I fell, I'd probably hit concrete or prock, but at this height the ocean would be just as hard and fatal.

Hearing a whine from the exit far above me, I twisted my neck to glimpse the balcony I had fallen over, many levels above. A narrow walkway ran horizontally around and out of sight. So that was where Guillermo had gone—out, around, and back in. Several blackbirds popped into view, bouncing like ping-pong balls. They made for me and managed to get within shouting distance.

"How are . . . doing?" called Iris's voice. Gusts of wind bit holes in her speech.

"F-f-f-freezing!" My breath plumed and dispersed. Cold air stung my eyes and made my nose run.

"Bev . . . problem," said the nearer blackbird, struggling closer. ". . . explain." Swirling winds shoved it over the hot exhale vent and it was instantly blown sky-high.

Backwash from the air vent was knocking me around. Hanging on intently, I shifted elbows and stuck my liberated right hand under my sweater, hoping that the icy pain crawling up my arm would go away.

"When will you rescue me?" I asked, glancing sideways at a second blackbird, which huddled close to the surface in the lee created by my body.

"You're very awkwardly located," replied Iris in a gusty shout. "You've fallen fifteen stories. We've got spatiens with ropes on their way. It'll take them eighteen to twenty-one minutes to arrive." Iris sounded regretful.

"What's wrong with th-th-th-that?"

"Your lips are purple. You appear to be entering the preliminary stages of hypothermia. If we don't get you into warmth within seven to eleven minutes, you'll lose consciousness." She paused. "And fall ninety levels to the ground."

"Oh." Ice had formed on the river where it met the Cambridge Walls, I noted. Drifts of snow tufted it. I slapped my cheek with my free left hand and was alarmed that I couldn't feel either. "What about that big hole?"

"Which one?"

"The one right under my f-f-f-fucking feet!" I shouted.

"It's a secondary air vent. Very old. Outdated technology."

"I don't care about that! Where does it *go?*"

"It serves double duty as clivus exhale and oubliette intake."

"What if I j-j-j-jump into it?" My jaw ached from the shivers.

"It's very dangerous."

I wanted to kill her. *"What are my chances?"*

"A moment . . . well, I'll be," she said with something like appreciation. "Our sims say you've got a sixty percent chance of not missing. The odds diminish the longer you wait, because your reactions will keep slowing."

"What else, for Chrissakes!" I couldn't feel my fingers at all. I was holding on with insensate clubs. Time was running out.

"Hmm. . . . That esophagus serves multiple uses, as most of them do. Digestion is controlled by screens and valves. We're reprogramming them to give you the maximum chance of surviving the bounces." She was again the competent administrator analyzing a novel but minor problem. "At a minimum, you'll probably break some bones, and of course you'll come out—"

"Iris, I haven't got the *time*. I'm going to do it," I said resolutely. "But the outflow will try to shove me away from the hole."

"We can assist you on that. I don't want your life on my conscience on top of my daughter's. You've got forty seconds."

"Why wait?"

"So we can clear your route. Or would you rather be vacuum-compacted and mineral-stripped?"

"Oh. All right." Sure, I thought in daft amazement as the implications of my damn fool scheme hit me. I can fall into a hole. No problem at all.

"I'll count backwards," Iris instructed, her words crisp now that we had moved beyond decision-making into implementation. "When the count reaches zero, let go and dive in."

I had committed myself. My fears seemed to be on their coffee break. "Head or feet first?"

"Whichever way you can get in. Twenty seconds."

"Then what?" I unhooked my elbow from the bar and shifted my grip. The steel was painfully cold on my hands, almost burning the palms.

"My blackbirds will follow you as long as they avoid being smashed. Keep your body loose and wrap your arms around your head. Ten seconds. You can do it, Bev. Five. Four. Three."

Suddenly the roof stopped heaving. The steam pouring from the vent slowed to a trickle, a few last tendrils drifting upward.

"Two."

The air seemed almost respectful in its whispering silence. Time was infinitely slow, Iris's voice far away. I looked into the straw-yellow sun. Thin clouds caressed its face ever so gracefully. Did Phneri time-rush feel this peaceful?

"One."

With a roar like an awakening dragon, the system restarted itself in reverse. A powerful suction collected the remaining wisps of cloud, the noise building and building, louder than before.

"Zero. *Go!*"

"Oh oh oh oh oh *ohhhhh*—" I cried, releasing my grip and sliding forward.

Instantly the hole seized me. My torso threw itself into the abyss, arms flailing loose and banging against the prock cylindrical shaft. The blue sky above shrank in an eyeblink to a round circle. The vent took a sudden angle-bend and slammed my right side against the incurving wall, peppering my ribs with fierce small explosions of hurt, then I tumbled out of control.

The shaft, about three meters wide, was colored the burnt orange of unpainted prock. Other smaller shafts joined it now and then. Its lower curves were silted with grit—sand, dirt, soot, garbage—that scraped my arms and palms raw. I splayed my feet out wide, using my heels in a vain attempt to brake, but though my skin was flayed from the abrasive prock, the drop was too steep and I pitched free. Each carom belted my side—I gasped and my eyes teared—then a huge screen loomed. The suction, unbearably strong here, flung me headlong into it with a crash.

I was swatted like a fly against the coarse-grid wire mesh. Though the screen was almost vertical, I was pinned helplessly against it, my frostbitten left cheek gouging into the grid. Just centimeters away from my face, a huge rotating fan slurped continuously, its noise a cascade of sound that rattled my teeth and made my arms vibrate. My headlight band was sucked up and off my skull with the sharp pain of a few red hairs torn from their roots. Partial vacuum made breathing a struggle, but at least the air down here was lukewarm. My heart pounded insistently against my chest.

All the airborne crap of Boston—newsprint, pebbles, glubs of partially biodegraded plastic, chicken bones, bottle caps, apple cores—was thrown against my back and face like hail. A guava melon splattered against the screen as if being strained into juice. Another of Iris's blackbirds, faithful as bloodhounds, bashed the mesh just next to my immobilized right hand, denting a support strut and careening brokenly off.

"Iris!" I cried. "For God's sake, help!"

"I'm trying. Get ready, the flow's going to reverse again." Another blackbird dove in my direction, but a flow shift knocked it into the wall, where it cracked like a heavy eggshell, blue-green flashes sparking inside as its circuitry died. Its fan blades crumpled and fell away with the corkscrew motion of maple seedlings.

Already the demons clutching me were easing. My neck uncricked painfully when I was finally able to roll it away from the grill, my cheek waffled from the pressure. Several ribs were badly bruised, if not broken, my face bruised, and hands scraped bleeding raw. My right ankle ached. Crying made the pain endurable.

"One last fall," she coaxed as the final wisps of air died.

Below I saw only another black tube. "I don't want to go," I moaned, digging my fingernails into the screen, but gravity took over and I plummeted.

My ankles rammed something, then my body slammed sideways with renewed pain in my ribs. Had some just splintered? Each breath, whether gulped or sipped, was pure boiling hell. Below me, winches groaned ponderously as I fell and metal shrieked, scraped against itself as valves opened and closed.

Something flat and hard belted my spine. I closed my eyes, beyond caring, beyond fighting. Huddling my arms over my head, I let Boston's innards pound me from every direction, falling so quickly now that up and down had no meaning. Blow after blow struck, some glancing and casual, others brutally hard. I was merely one of many inert discarded objects cartwheeling toward an unknown destination. All the metal—cans, flatware, obscure machine parts—abruptly leaped sideways like a school of fish, cutting and stinging my exposed skin in a hundred places. Tinny pings echoed as they attached themselves to electromagnets.

I was tumbling along a V-shaped sieve. Shards of broken glass and sand tinkled through the slots below.

"Almost there," said Iris.

Several moldy pizza slices launched themselves at me like antiaircraft fighters and I jammed my eyes shut as the stale crusts splattered off my forehead.

Then the tom-toms stopped beating on my elbows and knees, the crap fell away, and I sailed serenely through an open space. We must be near the bottom. A horrible sweet smell like the earth belching drifted up. Surely death would be my friend and claim me now. No one could survive such a free-fall unless she landed in something giving, something absorbent, something extremely soft and wet like—

Oh no, I thought. Garbage.

14

I HIT THE black, scummy water with an enormous splash and plummeted into its depths. My ears rang as my body was churned helplessly by the froth, then the world quieted and I drifted, disoriented and lost in the murk. Could I find the surface in time to breathe again?

With a light-headed rush, I broke through just as the pain threatened to spike my heart and frantically gulped breath, flinging guck off my hair with a quick head toss.

Water and mud shooshed around me with an abrupt gurgle as a slow grinding rumbled ahead like heavy metal being winched upward. The sudden undertow threw me back into the mire. I splashed over a rapids and, before I could regain my balance or refocus my eyes, I was thrown headfirst into a mountain of blubber.

Not the slugs, I thought crazily just as the slick softness enfolded my face and body.

The slime pressed me all over with the moist skin of an overweight uncle. In sheer terror I flailed and beat at the gooey mass as the gargantuan mouth closed over me, but the spongy hide didn't break. Its smooth malleable surface squeezed on my eyelids and nostrils, jamming my head with pressure. I inhaled a last, desperate gasp as the lips sealed.

Force was useless. If I didn't think my way out of this before my single lungful of air ran out, I'd be dead. What did I know about slugs?

The thing swallowing me was a clivus, one of the Tarmod beasties Boston uses to purify its outflow. When injected into the anus twelve kilometers from shore, little clivuses are scarcely different from the sedate messy night visitor who leaves white trails in poorly lit corridors. But the babies are endowed with two special features: they swim into the current and they eat continuously, burping gases and dribbling out water. They grow without limit until they are larger than elephants, consuming so much that eventually, in a final spectacular orgy triggered by proximity to the inflow point, their skin disintegrates and they explode, draining their cleansed nutrients into other tanks for eventual recycling.

All this flashed through my mind in an instant. The goody bag was my only hope, I realized as green fog crept into the edges of my vision. Where the hell was it?

Instead of fighting the thing's gullet, I reversed direction into the flow, my arms questing before me. A slippery rope hit my fingers and I seized it, hauling it in like a docked rowboat's painter until my hands encountered the slithering, lumpy appendix. I tried to use my fingernails to tear it but they just slid off. In desperation I jammed a blob of the bag into my mouth, bit, and tore, retching.

It was like chewing a pig's intestines. I chomped and spat like a rabid wolf until my straining arms ripped the thing open.

Out fell the slug's undigestibles and I groped blindly among them, identifying each by feel before discarding it—a rusty pair of scissors frozen open like the jaws of an angry alligator, a ring, the double-curving handle from a dresser drawer, a light switch, and miscellaneous screws, nuts, and washers. Something sharp and scimitar-shaped cut my hand and I squeezed it. Oblivious to the pain scoring my palm, I reached above myself and grabbed a hunk of slug innard with my left hand, slashing at it with the unknown blade held firmly in my right.

The skin sluggishly parted like cut bread dough and water gushed out. I pushed it aside and reached higher, pulling down another roll of flab. Yank, slash, reach up. Yank, slash, reach up. I don't know how many times I did this, fear charging my muscles with maniacal strength, until my left hand groped nothing. I pulled myself through the slit and popped my head out.

Air. Blessed air.

I gasped and spat, my head and shoulders the only parts of my body free, until my heaving lungs had settled down, then slowly opened my right hand. There amidst the bloody crosshatched cuts lay a piece of leaded crystal glass from a champagne flute. Holding it gingerly so as not to cut myself any further, I scored neat lines in the slug's body and clawed my way fully out. Even as its back deflated, the creature was still snuffling forward and eating things, oblivious to my surgery.

More oversize, eager-to-burst clivuses were slouching to join their comrade. By now my eyes had dark-adjusted enough so that I could make them out, even in this ghostly arena lit only by low phosphorescence from decaying vegetable matter. I splashed my way to a dung island safe from the slugs, where I beached myself.

Iris's blackbird approached, its casing cracked and dull even in the gloom. It wobbled as if having difficulty maintaining its balance. A dead fish drooped over its dome like a rotten beret.

We stared at one another for awhile like blind dates disappointed by each other's appearance, then I spat sand and dirt off my lips and weakly asked, "Why garbage?"

"We had limited options." Iris wouldn't give me even a whiff of apology. "Metal and structural material, the burn bin, or broken glass."

"Glass?" I echoed.

"Green, brown, or clear," she said, the sound scratchy and intermittent. The blackbird wheezed and lost altitude. "All equally fatal."

Maybe garbage wasn't such a bad landing place after all. "Okay." I stiffly sat up, my bruised and cracked ribs protesting, and scraped stringy fibers from my arms.

"What happened to you moments ago?" demanded Iris. "The light's too low to make anything out." She said this as if I had deliberately arranged it to conceal some mischief.

"It's not important." I wasn't going to satisfy her voyeuristic curiosity and had no use for her condescending sympathy. "Where do I go from here?"

The battered blackbird made as if to answer but sparked and fell with a plop on the dungheap.

"Iris?" I asked as softly as if I were addressing a terminally ill relative. "What do I do now?"

No response.

I crawled gingerly over and checked the blackbird. Goop had clogged the mechanisms. Pitying the poor dead bowling ball that had become my friend, I gently rolled it into the slimy brown water. Burial at sea.

The thing bobbed. How could that be? It rose, filmy seaweed at its sides, until the dome had become a bald skull with tufted eyebrows, a thick broken nose, and a lumpy cragged face.

"Find the body," my father said to me, rising from the green-black water.

"Dad?" I croaked, crawling forward.

He was wearing the torn-elbowed flannel shirt that had been his favorite. His knuckles were cracked as they always were, and his belly hung a little over his broad leather belt. Everything about him was olive and emerald and dark gray. His eyes, set too close together and slightly crossed, were worried with the concern that filled them when, too late at night, I tiptoed back into the apt and he roused from his uncomfortable sofa dozing.

"Find who, Dad? Find Akktri?"

"You never looked for me."

"What are you talking about? You were on a bender. We knew you'd come home eventually. You weren't our responsibility."

"You never said good-bye," Billy replied, not answering.

"Me? *You* died!" I stood, my arms flapping in frustration. "I looked for you in the Plaza!" The bodies had been hideous, brown and red and swollen with decay, putrid gases making their eyesockets and nostrils hiss with escaping pressure. I had rolled them over one by one, hoping and fearing that they would be Billy's, so that I could know he was dead and not have to see these other corpses who were not the ones I wanted to grieve for. "Where *were* you?"

"You have never called on me to say good-bye," he said.

"You bastard!" I threw a clod of mud at him and sank to the ground. *"Where were you?"*

"Ask Akktri," he finished, retreating beneath the inky surface.

"He's dead too! Just like you are!" My sobs bounced back from the prock walls and the glycerine coal-black water, then my body's need for rest took over. For a long time I lay motionless, aching and spent, blinking crappy water from my eyelashes and feeling spongy mulch under my back and legs. I breathed lightly, savoring the precious relief of not being dead. My tears were like cold rain, chilling but cleansing, and I wept for Billy. I shook with anger, grief, cold, and fear.

I thought of Akktri, spontaneously reliving a gangland murder in a North End alley. If he could reach a hundred years into the past, he could also have gone back twenty years and discovered where Billy died. Maybe he had always known. All I'd have had to do was ask him.

I was shaking all over, my teeth chattering against each other.

Now I couldn't ask him, for Akktri was dead. Another loved one gone before I was ready.

After a long time I stood, keeping my weight off my twisted right ankle. My jammed left shoulder throbbed painfully so I took off Hu Nyo's sweater, now an unrecognizable soggy sheet of sludge. Tying the two ends together, I hung it around my neck and laid my left arm in it. The shard of glass I tucked in my slacks pocket as a good-luck charm.

Instead of fright, I now felt possessed of an enormous placid light-headedness, as if these travails had happened to a casual and slightly dim acquaintance whose fate was of little concern.

I would find Guillermo. And I would kill him. That was written in Akktri's blood.

The effluvium seeped out of a mud-encrusted tunnel ahead. I followed, staying near the channel's sides where enough crud had piled to allow me to breast through chest-deep water, which kept weight off my overstrained joints. I moved deliberately and rested whenever my right ankle needed relief.

The tunnel, I remembered, began under Long Wharf and ended far in Boston Harbor. Its length was periodically bulk-headed and baffled. As the waste flowed through its chambers and tanks, bacteria dismantled the complicated man-made molecules of pollutants into ammonia, water, nitrogen, carbon dioxide. The smell was surprisingly tolerable, sweet and uncommon more than repulsive.

Somewhere in the Boston Cube, Akktri lay dead. Would I ever hold his body in my arms again? Had his Phneri brethren already found him and returned him to their aqueous warren for a proper funeral? Humans never got into the warren——not that many of my gene pool would willingly journey into those dismal water-filled tunnels.

Esfn is forever, Akktri always said. Human memory is fickle, failing us even in our most cherished thoughts. The lines in my father's face were already vague and blurring, my nightmare moments before no longer so terrifying.

I won't forget you, partner. I'll find you.

I never found Billy. But I'll find *you*.

And your killer will suffer. That I promise you.

I walked along in a zombie mode somewhere beyond exhaustion. My body felt as if it was consuming itself to keep me ambulatory, but I was unbothered. Too much had already happened. I'd see this hand through to the showdown, when everyone's hole cards were exposed.

I sloshed through another half-full chicane into a big brick-over lagoon, where a gorgeous sight brought tears to my tired, mud-caked eyes.

A wall ladder. Made for a person. Leading up.

I climbed.

Grasping its pitted bars in my hands, I took two steps for every rung, using only my left leg and dragging the right behind.

The ladder ended at a platform where I stepped onto solid floor. Dim orange lights and brighter red EXIT signs glowed overhead. I giggled hysterically, reaching out my filthy fingertips as if to touch the marvelous runic shapes of the letters. My overwrought nerves let loose in a cascade of chuckles that were also sobs and moans.

I was safe. In the Basement somewhere. Now to find my way out. I rose, wiped my face and eyes, and pushed through the emergency door.

Guillermo Ray stood before me. A stunner rested familiarly in his hand like a favorite pet.

"Hello, dirty cheese," he said.

15

I AWOKE FLAT on my back, staring at a gigantic waffle iron.

I blinked. Huge squares of concrete far overhead were filled with the circular divots of dead light sockets.

A ceiling. An ancient ceiling.

I was in the Basement. The *real* Basement that hid Diana Sherwood. And Guillermo Rey, whom I owed pain.

I brought my hands to my face to rub my eyes and found my fingers and wrists encased in deprivers. Round balls of solidified foam, they were warm and dry, spongy and comfortable. I pounded my hands against the floor, the material sighing in disappointment, then scrubbed them back and forth, hoping to abrade the sponge against the rough brick. No success, so I stuck my right hand under my left armpit and pulled with all my might. My right shoulder ached with the strain but the depriver's grip remained snug around my fingers.

Even in the deprivers, I was chortling with a giddy cockiness. My clothes were stiff with dried muck, my body beaten, bruised and foul. I'd fallen through the belly of the whale, been reborn in filth and freedom, pounded and possibly broken some ribs, probably torn ligaments in my shoulder, and been swallowed by a hungry slug. To top it all off, I'd been hog-tied by the man I'd been chasing.

But I wasn't dead, and I wanted to laugh and dance a jig. I could get out of the deprivers whenever I wanted to. Now seemed a good time to loosen them.

Depriver polymer expands when wet, so exertions that

produce sweat simply tighten the deprivers painfully on your wrists. But apolar solvents like carbon tetrachloride will dissolve them. Clumsily I used the depriver to shove up my right trouser leg, bent, and after some contortions licked clean a spot on my calf. Then with my teeth I slowly pulled away from above my right ankle a small rectangular patch of pseudoskin. It came free with a ripping sound and a lot of pain as the small hairs underneath it were torn out by the roots, but I continued to pull slowly, lest the packet shred.

Maneuvering cautiously and suppressing my gag reflex at the dirt, I got the lozenge between my teeth, bent over so my deprived right wrist was hanging directly below my mouth, and bit. The packet squirted carbon tet onto the join and I gently wriggled my wrist, letting the noxious liquid seep into the crevices. I'd be free in a minute.

Except that I wasn't. The carbon tet had no effect except to make me nauseated and woozy. When the fumes had dispersed, I checked the ridge around my wrist. Unchanged. Damn. He must have sealed it. My respect went up a further notch. Not many people outside the rods knew this trick.

I was lying on a small square platform in a vast concrete arena. Small animals scurried in its dark corners. On two sides, ranks of steps led upward, framing the stage with L-shaped stone bleachers. Descending stairs on the other two sides led down to the amphitheater floor.

The far walls were huge narrow vertical rectangular panels with black graphite mullions that suggested prison bars. Originally glass, they now shimmered with pointillist movement. Revolving doors in each wall led to more bricked plazas beyond.

This building was pre-Cube, constructed of naked unfinished concrete complete with grain imprints from its plywood pouring moulds. A strange panel of segmented squares hung on the wall nearby. "From the Mayor of Jerusalem to the Mayor of Boston on the occasion of its 350th anniversary, 9 September 1980. 'God be with us as He was with our fathers.'

I Kings 8:57." Aside from its quaint, hundred-year-old sexism, I appreciated the thought. Let there be somebody with me, God or anyone else.

I was in Old New City Hall. The dark plaza beyond those sealed revolving doors must be the remains of Government Center, where Iris had adopted Diana after the Siege. A few years later the plaza had been overfloored and compartmentalized into a vast foundation honeycombed with massive prock columns.

An atrium shaft stretched above me ten levels or more. Originally this must have let in what our ancestors naively called natural light. Now it was a high black funnel where nested bats, pigeons, shedflies, and things that went bump in the night. Every city, even Boston, has a few enclaves for its outcasts, left unused by humanity because unpleasant creatures have taken up residence.

Ahead of me, a vast picture window would have overlooked Faneuil Hall and Quincy Market if not for the swarming carpet of shedflies buzzing all over it. They pulsed like a living video grid over their no-see-um host, a lily pad Targive-modified to attach itself to vertical surfaces and grow to fill any light-receiving space.

I hobbled to it and shoved my deprivers against the mass of shedflies, trying to scrape them away so I could peel the lily pad off the glass.

"Help!" I shouted, hoping my voice would carry through the spongy brown surface to the tourists a few levels below. Flies buzzed into my mouth—I coughed and spat them out—up my nostrils, and underneath my filthy clothing. Thousands of tiny legs tickled me as the shedflies ate the garbage that still clung to my skin and clothes. Eyes narrowed to slits lest the shedflies land on them, I tried to pry up the lily pad's edge, but the deprivers were too slippery and I gave up, retreating hurriedly and twisting like a dervish to rid myself of the winged parasites.

In the silence I heard human whimpering behind and to my right.

She was crumpled behind a counter labeled INFORMATION BOOTH. "Diana?" I asked, steadying myself against it. "Are you Diana Sherwood?"

Her eyes moved diffidently, and she licked her cracked lips. "*I* don't know who I am," she answered crossly. "Do you know who *you* are?"

The woman I now confronted was vastly different from the chill pastel figurine Akktri and I had watched on Iris's viewscreens. Filthy, bruised, and sullen, she was struggling to right herself. Her ankles were tied together and her hands bound in front of her.

Hand. Her left forearm ended in a bandaged stump. The right was encased in a depriver like mine.

The hair on my neck and scalp stood on end as elation surged in me, so pure it was erotic. There she was, my subject, still alive. Fearing observation, I limited myself to a tiny sigh. "I've been looking for you," I said, keeping my voice neutral.

Diana's face was streaked with red lines and tear tracks through grimy dirt. She'd been sleeping curled into a ball in her booth. Her fine stylish clothing was soiled and rumpled. She looked miserable, resentful, and angry.

In my mind I heard a tiny voice chirp, Be most careful, little Beverlee. Akktri could have deciphered how long Diana had been bound and whether her suffering was real or self-inflicted. But my partner was dead at Guillermo's hands.

Diana's closed, sullen face glared as if I were the embodiment of evil. "Who're you?"

I left her question unanswered. "Are you all right?"

"Compared to what?" She laughed bitterly. "Where's my mother?"

She had a peremptory manner for someone captured and tortured. "She sent me to find you."

"Typical. Won't leave her haven, will she?"

"How long have you been here?"

"I knew she wouldn't come." Diana's long blond hair, matted with dirt and grease, was coming unbound from its ponytail. Her thin delicate face was hard with anger.

"Why don't you ask her about Venture Capital?" said Guillermo Rey behind me.

I sprang out of the information booth and tripped over my bound feet, my elbow smacking against the brick tiles.

"There are no unclaimed warrants," Guillermo went on. He was perched confidently on a ledge, his calves hanging over, swinging his feet like a malevolent Humpty-Dumpty. His chin was sunk in one hand, a stunner held comfortably in the other. "I checked. You were lying. Why?"

I shifted myself into a more or less seated position, canting my torso to relieve the stress on my hurt ribs, and struggled to my feet. He enjoyed not helping me.

"I *told* you that you need me," I said curtly, or as much so as could be managed given my condition. "It's nothing so simple as finding unclaimed shares. They're depository receipts held in a blind anonymous trust. You have to trace through several layers." I reeled all this out with the tired negligence of a woman too tired and beaten to lie, all the better to keep him off balance. Even if he doubted me, he could not be certain. That uncertainty would give me maneuvering room.

"Hmph." The answer did not satisfy him. "You know, you could be attractive if you wanted to." He pulled a tendril of dried kelp from the ruins of Hu Nyo's cashmere sweater, then hefted my right breast. I stiffened but didn't move.

He abruptly dropped my breast and, with an expression of disgust, used my cheeks to wipe the guck off his hand. "At least you'll be a better messenger than a brain-dead rugrat."

You venthole, I thought savagely. Eat it up. Be merry. Tomorrow you die. I managed to hold myself back and croaked, "Messenger for what?"

He raked the stunner lightly across my head.

Face frozen in impassivity—the stunner jams your nerves,

so you are as expressionless as a mannequin——I fell against the pavement, ineffectually trying to protect my damaged ribs. I lay there and let the pain possess me, breathing as shallowly as I could.

Guillermo strolled over and squatted, watching me suffer. "Speak only when you're spoken to," he said mildly. He shoved the stunner under my chin and moved my face around. "Do you understand?"

Play the game, Beverlee. Coil like a snak-k-ke. Ending is forever.

Eyes squeezed shut to keep out the blood, I nodded. The paving brick felt cool beneath my cheek; its pebbly grit comforted me.

"Iris Sherwood wants her daughter back." Guillermo stood and walked over to Diana, ticking off points on his fingers.

"The Butcher of Boston?"

"Shut up. You find her."

"Nobody can get to her."

"Do it! You'll figure it out. When you get to her, tell her that if she wants Diana, she stops wiring the Basement. She delivers nullifiers and smudgers to us. She stops sending scurrybots to put in new eyes when we punch them out. Got that?"

"Permission to ask a question," I asked meekly, rolling my body as suggestively as I could.

My helpless subservience seemed to intrigue and perhaps to arouse him. He hooked his thumbs into his belt. "One," he allowed.

"How do I know that's her daughter?"

Guillermo grabbed Diana's left arm and brandished the bandaged stump. "This. And this." He twirled his finger around a lock of Diana's long blond hair, and with a sharp jerk yanked it free. "Let her Phneri check *this.*"

"Okay, but once Iris Sherwood agrees, what's to stop her rewiring as soon as she's got her daughter safe?"

Diana gasped, but Guillermo was unruffled. "Because *she*

has to come here. Bring the nullifiers and smudgers herself, Iris does. And code it from here. We'll tape it and spread the reads to safe places." He jumped butt-first onto his perch and crossed his legs at the ankles.

Neat, I thought. If Mayor Mike Juarez or the media saw the City Operator violating her charter, she'd be finished. Guillermo was transmuting a kidnap into a blackmail. Conservation of manipulation.

"So what?" I asked. "Iris just steps down. And then you have nothing."

"She'll never do that," said Guillermo. "The Butcher of Boston loves her job too much."

"My, my, amateur psychologist." I snickered as best I could through my thawing lips. "Who told you this? You're too dumb to have figured this out on your own." I waved my deprivered hand. "You have an upfloor key. You must have had one to elude me upfloor and then to find me in the Basement. Someone gave it to you. You knew about that access door and what lay behind it. Someone must have told you about that. You knew where I'd come out after I fell through the City. Someone told you that too. So who's pulling your strings? And how long is your leash?"

He swung the stunner hard and broke my left forearm.

I clutched myself into a ball, gasping desperately. Gray pain flooded my arm and shoulder. Jesus, Mary, and Joseph, it hurt. I gritted my teeth, wishing I could faint.

Guillermo stood astride me, his feet triumphantly planted, brandishing the stunner. "You persuade her, cubehunter."

I barely heard him. Drowning in my own pain, I concentrated my thoughts into a bore of light down a dark tunnel, to hold the agony away from me.

I hated him, I realized with a warm contentment. I hated myself for sucking up to his vanity, for baiting him to show Diana what a fiend he was. I hated him for what he was doing to people around him. I hated what I was allowing him to do to me. Lying on the floor of Old New City Hall, I wrapped my body around that glowing core and let my hate fill me. My emotions floated away from my body like clouds, blood throbbing through my left arm like the pulses of distant thunder.

Diana was fascinated, her eyes alight, relishing her mother's minion suffering. She looked admiringly at Guillermo. I wanted to grab her and shake some sense into her. I had to show Diana that Guillermo would kill her in an instant, no matter what had gone between them before, and I knew how to do it.

"Iris won't—pay ransom because—she knows you're—a coward," I hissed to Guillermo in between pants for breath. Challenging him was risky to me, but keeping silent was riskier to Diana. "You'd never—really hurt Diana."

"I wouldn't?" He leaped off me and crossed to where Diana stood. She didn't cringe as he moved close. He tapped the stunner lightly against her jaw. "I wouldn't?"

"No, you wouldn't."

He brought the stunner down on Diana's right elbow and broke it with one sharp blow.

She fell to the floor with an inhuman shriek born of pain, humiliation, and outrage, trying to clutch her broken elbow with her amputated hand. "Oh, God!" she screamed, rolling around on the floor, kicking her feet against the bricks.

"Why'd you do that?" she moaned to Guillermo in a hurt voice. Her face was a tragic clown mask of betrayal and shock.

"Shut up." He turned away from her.

"I'm sorry," Diana replied in a childish voice as if she deserved this punishment, and my eyes narrowed. This man had balled her, lied to her, cut her hand off, broken her arm, and she was accepting it all as her responsibility. "Iris will come for me. She'll have to!"

Her behavior was weirdly symbiotic with her mother. Iris tried valiantly to earn love and Diana punished her for this. Then, when Diana was punished in turn, she reacted by asking her tormenter for affection. Diana and Iris were counterweights on either end of a seesaw, each approach causing a retreat, doomed forever to remain fixed at a distance from one another, each hurting the other without trying to, each unable to break the cycle.

Now I was part of their mesh, for it was I who had really fractured Diana's arm. Guillermo had just been my instrument. "Your mother loves you," I said, kneeling and trying to help her up with my unbroken right arm.

Diana struggled to her knees, her elbow swollen like a small red balloon. "You bitch," she snarled at me, bracing her left arm against her body to reduce the pain. "You like seeing me brought down to your filthy level, don't you?" She spat in my face. I rolled away but it hit my throat.

"Make her a sling, for Jesus' sake," I muttered to Guillermo, rubbing my neck against my shoulder to get as much spittle off as I could. "You've made your point."

Iris had spent years building her walls so that she could always act no matter how horrible the situation. Those barriers were formidable, but they were cracking. When she emerged from the wreckage, would she hate herself?

"Bring the Butcher here, cheesee," Guillermo said flatly. He too seemed drained. "Old New City Hall. Alone. In six hours."

We were far beyond charades. "I'll do as you say," I said.

"Excellent." He pointed the stunner at me and everything went mercifully black.

16

A BAYONET POKED my side. "Up, ye witless sot."

I groaned and opened my eyes. The words 1737 BOSTON had been carved into an aged flaking sandstone sphere just above my head. The rock and its hexagonal pedestal formed the cornerstone of a brick building whose walls rippled and canted. My head ached, my left arm was numb and cold with shock, and my ribs were a forest of needles.

The Boston Stone, against which I was resting, is an old paint mill and grinder. A tavernkeeper found it in his backyard, engraved the date of his discovery on its weathered surface, and set it into the walls of his house as a conversation piece.

A rod wearing clothing from Boston's Colonial period stared down at me. He held his antique brass flintlock like a pike, using his bayonet as a prod. "Give me a second," I muttered, and stiffly crawled my hands up the wall until I was standing.

The Colonial disney is a small cluster of carefully preserved buildings cheek by jowl in cobblestone streets just north of Faneuil Hall Marketplace. Guillermo had been clever to dump me here, an untraceable location despite being only a few hundred meters from Old New City Hall. Ordinarily a man toting a dirty, unconscious woman over his shoulder would attract attention. Here the honest cits would take it for an authentic reenactment of some sordid episode in Boston's long history.

In the disneys, anyone not a tourist must dress, speak, and

behave in period fashion, from the Union Oyster House to the periwigged and black-robed barristers of Swartz and Swartz. So private security rods, who lived in the Cube like everyone else, donned breeches, long hose, buckled shoes, blue and white morning coats, and tricornes, and practiced archaic English, mock-arresting offplanet Tulguts or Adjawi for their podmates' vids or clopping up and down the streets intoning, "Ten o'clock and all's well."

"Public drunkenness and lewd behavior," the rod concluded, reaching toward my eyelids, which kept fluttering shut despite my explicit orders to remain open. His swallowed *r*'s and flattened *a*'s were pure salt-marsh Yankee. He was tall and gaunt, his bowed chest overhanging his torso like a vulture sitting on a stump. "I'm takin' ye in charge," he said, bending to clamp a strong sinewy hand under my armpit. "Coom along with ye."

I howled with renewed agony. "My arm's broken, for Jesus' sake."

"Truly?" He examined the swollen purple flesh with knowledgeable tender fingers. "So 'tis," he drawled. "Methinks I've a potion'll ease yer sufferin'."

I felt the bite of a frozen bee and my arm went dead. The cessation of ache was so ineffably refreshing I almost fainted. "Thank you," I gasped.

"Ye're a tough one, mistress." He held me up by my good arm. "We'll just splint yer wounds here." From another pocket he produced a large clear capsule and slapped it around my arm, puncturing its membrane. The Targive-modified amoeba colony, stimulated to action by the whiffs of oxygen it now sensed, oozed itself into a thin cylinder up and down my forearm, then stiffened into a rigid, impermeable sleeve that covered me from armpit to wrist.

The patrolman touched my arm and clacked his fingernails along the amoeba's hardening sides. "That'll hold ye until a sawbones can repair ye better," he said with satisfaction. "Who be ye, goodwoman?"

"My name is Beverly O'Meara. I'm a private detective." The world wouldn't hold still long enough to let me stand. My shoulders and chest were numb from Guillermo's stunner and the bee's feelgoods were wafting me toward dreamland. I fell against the tall white-haired rod and he gently reoriented me.

"Ye've got no moniker," he said. "Nor pockets, neither," he added, glancing at my bedraggled skirt. The shredded remains of Hu Nyo's sweater had left me largely uncovered above the waist. "Ye'd be indecent if ye were clean." His manner became more solicitous. "Goody O'Meara, ye're not fit to wander aboot in pooblic, neither for yer state nor yer appearance. And yer arm wants better tendin'."

He unbuttoned his bright blue morning coat and draped it over my shoulders, where its bifurcated ends dangled almost to my feet like a devil's forked tail. The comforting serge, still warm from the rod's body, made me realize how cold I was. With my good hand I drew the lapels closed around me. "I'm working for the Chief of Police. Take me to him."

"Good to see you," Roderick Petravelli said a few moments later. The officer had announced himself to Ulkudge and the big dour Koltsoi, her droopy nostrils whiffling with extreme irritation, had ushered us into the Presence. Half a dozen animated screens were open on his desk, feeding him crime and arrest reports. With a serene swipe of his hand, he cleared them, restoring its rectangular crystalline perfection, and settled himself in his chair, fitting his spine ramrod-straight against its uncompromising right angle.

"You are dismissed," he added to my escort.

The Colonial straightened up, resettled his tricorne, and saluted. "I shall have someone fetch my topcoat when ye no longer need it," he added with a bow to me as he left. In character to the last.

"I was sad to hear the news of your partner's death," said Roderick as soon as the door had closed on the rod's long dour back. He ran his open hand, palm down and flat like a metal detector, across his immaculate desk surface. "What happened?"

I told him the whole story, beginning with my attempt to bribe Guillermo at Boston Garden. Eyes half-lidded, he listened passively but intently, like a veteran music critic at a recital.

"All right then." Petravelli ground his knuckles against his palm, then leaned forward to tap a pattern on his crystal desk. A window of digitized light opened under his hands and a grizzled black face appeared. "Srinavaca, I want the anti-grab squad mobilized in ten minutes. We're going bottom-fishing."

"You can't do that." I laid my right hand over the comm window and the image disappeared.

Roderick's big mitt encircled my wrist and squeezed it hard enough to bulge his biceps through his darted shirt. "Your job's done. Go home." He tried to lift my wrist but I leaned my weight on it and held firm. The hell with him and his prissy intimidations.

"Guillermo has too many places to hide," I said smoothly, as if no effort were required to maintain my position. This wasn't the time to invoke Iris, or the person to do it in front of. Persuasion, not leverage, was called for. "You'll never surprise him. He's bought himself a link into your department."

I expected this revelation to call forth a burst of anger, but Petravelli merely raised his eyebrows. "Mm." He released my wrist and resettled himself in his glass throne. This time he wasn't so careful to maintain his military-school posture. "Any idea who?" He rubbed his close-shaven cheek, then stroked his gray sideburns.

"You don't seem very upset to learn about this."

He made a sound midway between a chuckle and a snort. "Wood rots. Garbage draws flies. So I use these foibles rather than curse them." Petravelli knitted his fingers together on his desk and leaned forward over them. "Have you told anyone else?" he brusquely demanded.

"No," I said. "I haven't had a chance."

"Then don't," he instructed. I must have looked questioning, because he added, "A turned rod is especially useful if we can keep it quiet."

"What?"

He grinned at my outrage. "You're nowhere near as urb as you pretend to be. Turned rods make excellent volunteers for dangerous or unpopular duties." His smile was feline. "They find it hard to refuse once they know I know. Have you identified the link?"

I kept my voice extra soft. "You let me return to the Basement and maybe I can find out."

"There are laws. Procedures." He smiled coldly. "Iris Sherwood's rules."

"You know as well as I do that the victim's safety is paramount. The kidnapper has instructed me what to do. Any variation runs needless risk. Let me have a shot first."

Petravelli considered this. Then he moved his shoulders. "Justice can wait a little longer." He picked up a chromium dumbbell and absently did curls with it. "You have four hours left on Rey's deadline." He grimaced. "And get Ulkudge in here to polish my desk."

Outside headquarters, I found an anonymous pay phone and, via laborious digit dialing, reported in to Iris. "She's alive," I said when her gray lined face came on the screen. "Guillermo has her."

Iris held herself still, but her torso shivered. "What does he want?" she asked softly, almost a whisper.

I rubbed clotted mud from my eye socket. "The two of us. In the Basement. In four hours."

Her pale eyes were vacant. "If we do as he says," she said with difficulty, "will he give her back to me?"

"Iris——" I began. I wanted to shield her with a comforting white lie, but she was my client, and Diana's mother. She had earned the right to chilling, blunt truth. "I don't know," I said finally. "Maybe not."

"It doesn't matter," she answered after a pause. "Of course I'll go."

"All right. I'll come to you in a few hours."

"Why not now?" she asked with a trace of impatience that verged on panic.

I shook my head. "I have to prepare."

Iris looked at me, and for the first time her eyes actually saw me as I was. Sympathy lightened them. "You're injured," she said.

"Yes," I said heavily. Compassion could wait. I had things to do. "O'Meara out."

I went home to restore myself. When I turned the corner from my creaky old mover, my front door was slightly ajar. I pushed it open.

Charles Beaufort was bent over, snapping wooden map frames into kindling and stacking them in my circling waste-bot. He was wearing denimweave jeans, the seat intriguingly tightened by his posture, and a rough shirt. His black hair, combed straight back, was full of paper dust. He straightened when he heard me enter. "Hello," he said uncertainly.

"What?" I stood stupidly in the doorway, aware that I reeked from head to toe. "Why——?" I licked my lips. My throat was dry. "Why are you here?"

"Iris told me to bring you a replacement Master Key. Yours is heading out to sea somewhere. Arriving, I used it to enter. And saw this chaos." He indicated the ruins. "I thought you'd appreciate some cleaning." He laid his hand on my back, warm and comforting, and rubbed large gentle circles. Then he tapped the flowcast on my left arm. "You're injured."

"Busted arm. No fracture, thank goodness."

"Who did this to you?"

"It goes with the territory." My mind elsewhere, I shrugged listlessly with my good shoulder. My injuries bored me. They'd been inflicted on somebody else, in another country, and besides, the wench was dead.

Charles slapped his palms against his thighs. "You need a shower."

"Yeah." With a nod, I started to rise. The world rolled under my feet and I covered my eyes before everything tilted too far.

"Come on." Charles curled his arm around my good shoulder and squeezed. "I'll help you." His low baritone was soothing and commanding. I clung to him as he led me to my bathroom, where he lifted the absurd Colonial morning coat from my shoulders. He placed me on the toilet and inspected my wounds—arm, shoulder, and ribs—his hands as careful and impersonal as a doctor's.

"Chuck, I haven't got any clothes on," I protested weakly.

"You are swaddled in mud," he replied grandly with a smile, peeling away my disintegrating plumber's pants. He lifted my heels, hooked his thumbs under the waistband of my mud-caked panties, and drew them down and off my legs.

"You sure know how to flatter a girl."

"That's the spirit." Chuckling, he stood and led me to the shower. "In you go." As he lifted me over the sill, I put my arm round his neck for support and laid my sleepy head against his neck. He was strong and very solicitous, and I was so tired. I took a deep breath of contentment and snuggled against my handsome, charming teddy bear.

"Stand upright," Charles barked, snapping me back to consciousness. "Hold the bars."

The hot spray hit me like an enveloping blanket and I leaned against it, enjoying the warm rivulets sliding around my jaw, down my throat, and between my breasts. Charles's hands caught me round the waist and steadied me. His fingers tickled my stomach and abdomen.

I blinked and spluttered through the spray of water and giggled at him. "You're getting soaked."

He didn't laugh. "I'll dry." He repositioned me under the water. "Turn around." When I complied, he washed my back. "Sit." He scrubbed my legs, then handed me a washcloth and pointed to my groin. He looked away as I diligently cleaned myself.

"Now your hair." He positioned my head under the water and borrowed shampoo from my rack to massage my scalp. I swayed under his expert hands, enjoying the warmth sliding down my kneepits and calves, between my toes, drifting aimlessly between sleep and wakefulness.

"Time to dry." He shut off the shower and turned on the ultrasonic and infrared. My skin buzzed pleasantly as hot dry air whisked away the remaining water. "Here's your bathrobe," Charles said.

With the dirt gone, my allover freckles were orange sparkles on my pink skin. I drew my thick white terrycloth robe around myself and sat on the bed, using my uninjured right arm to brush my hair with strokes slow enough not to hurt too much.

Charles stood before me. Black ringlets of soaked hair curled around his ears to muss his perfection. His pale blue eyes were questioning. I looked into them.

Leaning slowly forward, he took my face in his hands, bent his head, and kissed me.

It was slow and delicate, like his bathing had been. I tilted back my neck and opened my mouth, fitting my lips to his. They were cool and firm. His breath was cinnamony, his tongue warm and intriguing.

Still kissing me, he sat beside me on the bed and drew me toward him. I put out my healthy arm and pressed my right hand against his back. His hand rose to my neck and cupped my head. The kiss went on——he knew how to breathe without disrupting the sweet, tender closeness—until finally our lips withdrew politely from one another, like emissaries who have concluded their business and may now turn matters over to their principals.

"I couldn't do that while you were naked," he whispered softly into my ear. "It would have been exploiting you."

I rested my head on his salty neck and shoulder. "Thank you." I sighed with contentment.

"Does your arm hurt?"

"Totally numb now." I shook my head, then smiled sleepily at him. "That was lovely."

"The shower or the kiss?" he asked disingenuously.

"Both." I lifted my head, found his lips, and kissed him again. My hand grasped the velcro of his shirt and slid downward, opening it with a soft rip. His chest was ridged with sensuous muscular undulations. His heartbeat was a rhythmic knock against my tingling palm.

His hands explored my torso, sliding open my bathrobe to cup my breasts, which rose to his warm caresses. He undid the bathrobe's belt and slid his hand over my stomach. I gasped with pleasure and anticipation and fiery lances shot into my side. My cry was a whimper muffled against his cheek.

"No," he said firmly. "You're badly hurt. I would be taking advantage of you."

"Of course you aren't." Tears of frustration sprang unbidden into my eyes, and I covered his hand where it still lay against my bare belly. "You're wonderful and I want you. But I have things to do." Akktri was dead and Diana's time was running out. I drew my bathrobe together and belted it shut. "And I changed my mind. Iris can keep her toy."

"You need it."

"It's addictive and immoral."

Charles had started to lay the Master Key on my night table, then at my words drew it sharply back. He weighed the resolution in my tone, as if he rather than Iris had been the one to make the offer. "If you say so," he said reluctantly.

Reaching up, I patted his cheek. "I can handle myself."

"Woman, look at yourself. You're disintegrating." His voice dropped. "If you return to the Basement, I will feel responsible for whatever befalls you."

I laughed, dizzy with fatigue. "You're a romantic fool, Chuck. Tell your boss I'll see her in four hours."

*   *   *

Spray from the bow flicked chill ice against my forehead as the robot water taxi trundled its fat-bottomed way across the drowned South Boston Shoals. Ahead lay the half-empty husks of nineteenth-century industrial buildings and beyond loomed the Targive cathedral on Telegraph Hill.

Alone with my thoughts and my grief, I called aloud, "Should I do this?" but the seagulls merely swooped around me, cawing to one another over the ripples of my wake. I blew on the frigid fingers of my right hand, but they just got wetter and colder in the winter wind.

My friend and companion was dead. My client was a shambles, her daughter still a captive. If I was going to avenge Akktri and rescue Diana, I needed my partner's skills. I needed to esfn like a Phner. The Targives would give me that, and extract their price.

Tarmods were paid in kind—the surgeons took some of each body in trade. Genetic material and biological systems were their raw materials. True collectors, the Targives sought the rare, the unique. When they rummaged in my open skull, they would choose what they wished. That was the condition upon which a person entered their fortress.

Until now, I had been too fearful to contemplate that. With Akktri gone, I had motive. Perhaps, I consoled myself, they will in mercy take from me the memory of what I now feel.

"Akktri is not ended-and-completed," whistled a voice to my left, using the Phner word that means a dozen things, including dead.

My hair blew sideways across my face, obscuring my vision, as another Phner echoed behind me, "Akktri is not dead-d-d. Akktri is changing-and-not-yet-art."

"Taxi, stop," I instructed; then waited until the backwash rocked through and the boat was once again stable. Around me were several score Phneri, their heads bobbing over and under the surface like lobster buoys. "Akktri is not dead, Akktri is not d-d-dead," they chittered, as if this were a great joke.

Of course not, I thought. I am not dead, you are not dead. "We are all dead," I answered, wondering where and why the Phneri had come to me. The cold turned my breath into white mist.

"We are all dead," a dozen small voices repeated, diving with quick flips that left only an impression of rounded backs and sleek stubby legs. "Akktri is not dead." They dove and disappeared.

The harbor's apparent emptiness is deceptive: it's a place of dangers above and below the waterline. The restarted taxi gave a wide berth to the industrial buildings covered with lily-pad no-see-ums, their windowsills sprinkled with fractal-patterned frost. It guided into a half pier and I alighted on the soggy tar-paper roof of a nearly submerged triple-decker, my steps crunching through the thin ice puddles. The boat nuzzled itself into the leeward side, hidden from the slapping waves.

The citadel loomed before and above me, black upon black, squatting on its South Boston High School foundation. Neither snow nor ice marred its molasses-liquid blackness. Huge tentacular beams reached through windows of brick that had been scorched the color and texture of glistening oily charcoal. Long sweeps of raven roofline merged into tight wrinkled folds.

The cathedral is always changing, extruding or retracting parts of itself. No one knows how much of it is alive, or what grotesque alien creature it was modified from, or even if it is a gargantuan scarab beetle.

The hillside was devoid of the sounds of humanity. Only the gulls, the ocean, and the small noises of shore creatures broke at the edges of the immense quiet.

The high school's old front doors had long since vanished, overgrown and enwrapped with more of the slick black Tar-mod surface. The aperture was irregular, very hard for me to squeeze into, and twisted just inside so that it was impossible to see far. I stood at the entrance and called out, but my voice brought no reply, not even a ghost of an echo.

To the door's left hung down a glistening tarpitch corkscrew baton about the length of my arm. I reached for it, my fingers sliding on the slimy surface, and the thing stiffened. A loan groan echoed from the interior and the doorway seemed to widen slightly, its outline becoming vaguely more rectangular. Inside, the gloom seemed to lighten, if only a little.

I could walk in there, I thought. It is ready to accept me. My knees started to shake. I sagged to the ground.

The penislike knocker was drooping. The sun, setting to the west, dropped behind a cloud, making me pull my clothing tighter about myself.

If I do this, I can avenge Akktri.

What if they take my memories? I suddenly thought. Can I give up Billy? Mack? Can I risk the Targives taking my feelings for Akktri? My memories of him?

I shivered with sudden cold. My knees were damp from the freezing mud. The door awaited.

"No," I said finally, my eyes dry.

I was too old to pawn my soul. Too set in my ways. I should have done this when I was younger, before I had accumulated a life.

"No," I said more firmly. For better or worse, I would play the cards the Fates had dealt me.

Turning away, I set off down the hill, amid the rubble of melted auto tires, stacked asphalt shingles, and charred wood splits. I climbed into the boat and ordered it slowly back to Boston.

The city rose before me, massive and convex, its towers jostling one another under the blanket of its Targive snakeskin roof. Long horizontal shadows stained its sides. At its crown, steam rose from the outflow vents like the smoke signals of an occupying army. Windows sparkled beneath. The shadows rose as the sun set, starting at sea level and crawling up the building's sides, spots of light appearing in the umbra like the amber lights that hillside campfires make.

I twisted in my thwart, looking back at the Targive citadel. Its dark surface absorbed all the sunlight except for cold curled lines of bluish reflection.

They resemble each other, I realized. We look out from our Cube and see the hideous shape the aliens have made, yet we are never able to look from the outside at our own City of Boston and see objectively what we have used the aliens to make it become.

A Phner floated in the water taxi's path, energetically waving its short arms. I slowed.

"I am not dead, Beverlee," the little creature said, clambering into the boat.

"Partner?" I said, not believing.

"I am Akktri. I am not dead." The Phner giggled.

"Am I nuts? What are you doing here?" My voice was ragged and angry. "Guillermo killed you."

"He lies, Beverlee. He lies to mad-den you." He scrabbled toward me, perceiving my fatigue and injuries with rapid diagnostic whistles.

Slowly, so things would hurt the least, I crouched to bring myself to Akktri's level. That stressed my ribs and I laid myself across the thwarts, sighing with relief.

"Beverlee." Akktri's voice was soft. His wet whiskers brushed my cheek. His fur was silky in my fingers. "Beverlee is not ended," he murmured.

"I thought Guillermo had killed you, partner." I stroked his small bony head as Akktri wriggled his neck under my hand, rivulets of cold salt water squishing into my clothing.

Akktri chittered with nervous laughter. "Silly Beverlee." All the while we were touching one another. Akktri was running his claws along my throat, neck, and shoulders, sensing my structure, discovering injuries and tired muscles, reading the past in the crevices of my skin. I just wanted my doubting hands to feel his wiry living body underneath his glistening fur. "You touch dumb," my partner said. "You learn nothing by this."

"Never mind." Relieved, exhausted, overjoyed, I laughed and cried and pulled him to me, oblivious of the freezing water, savoring the feel of his slick fur against my collarbones and throat, remembering with gratitude his wet, fishy smell.

"You fall from great height, Beverlee," Akktri admonished in my ear after I had held him for several minutes. His breath was warm and tickled. "I warn you but you do not listen. You fall in dead fish."

"I know, partner," I replied, my eyes sleepily shut. "Don't rub it in."

"Rub what in? Why rub it in? Why you are laughing at Akktri? Ugh." He pulled out a tiny lump of gray pumice from my ear and held it before his whiskered nose like a jeweler squinting at a setting. "Beverlee, you meet Diana." My partner licked it with his long pebbly tongue. Extending his neck, he rolled his face around before me, blocking my vision. "Why is hurt Diana?"

I had to cross my eyes to keep his black triangular nose in focus. "Guillermo Rey."

"Ah." Akktri blinked and nodded. "We end his art, Beverlee, then you give me lobster fish." He felt my side and I winced, though his carefully modulated touches were almost imperceptible. "You have four crack-k-ked ribs, with many tiny tiny pieces of frac-k-k-tured bones in you. They hurts," he informed me.

"Yes," I whispered. "They hurts."

"Ok-k-kay." He pressed his clawed fingers against my neck and felt my pulse. "We go to Guillermo, aren't we?" I nodded, rolling my head to see his squat furry face. "We go to rescue Diana." Another nod. "Must fix you first," concluded my partner. "My people fik-k-ks you," Akktri offered stoutly.

"Are you serious? Are you sure you want to ask them to put me back together?"

"Of course warren heals you!" Akktri was indignant. His

fingers worked furiously, assessing damage. "I ask-k-k. Glue ribs and set arm proper. But Beverlee"—he laid his hand flat against my cheek, his claws retracted—"you find warren strange. You are never there before. Warren is for us. Not for you. You think strange okay?"

Compared with the Targive hill, this would be like visiting old friends. "Phneri strange is okay, partner." I rubbed his neck and belly and Akktri giggled. "I'll manage."

17

In the wet dark cold, the tiny drips were staccato and random, their echoes overloud like rustles in dreams. They fell from arched brick ceilings with continuous plip-plops.

I was up to my knees in water, and I was afraid.

My headlight shone on surfaces made glistening and silvery with moisture. The stones twinkled with a thousand tiny lights that rebounded from my beacon like a frieze of galaxies.

I carried, balanced on my head like an African woman, a waterproof box containing the ruins of Hu Nyo's bedraggled sweater. Akktri had insisted that I bring the material to the warren. "Others see better," he apologized.

The Phneri slum lay below the City's Level 0—sea level. Foundation leaks trickled into puddles, rivers, even lagoons of salty brown water. The ocean tang mingled with the sweet aromas of decay. People had abandoned these soggy tunnels as Boston sank, leaving them to the amphibious Phneri.

Cracking plaster walls and water-stippled wallpaper peeled away from ill-formed bricks and haphazard stone mosaics. Mildew and moss grew on faded billboard ads for Lucky Strike cigarettes and Corvairs. The tunnels, much darker than a Bostonian likes, were echoing, cold, and forbidding. The water made a too-cool ring around my calves. The thighs and seat of my thick twill trousers were damp.

Beside me, Akktri squirted over and under the surface, frolicking with the contented exuberance of a returning prodigal. He stuck his bullet head out of the water and sprayed me as he shook it. "Beverlee, this is our place, made for us. We live here all. Why are you fearful?"

"You know why, partner." Every Bostonian, no matter how high-leveled, fears drowning in a tunnel of rushing water, black and cold. Every one of us who lived through the Siege starts when we hear a low, floor-shaking rumble. To be in rising water, even if only thigh-deep, with an immovable tunnel roof overhead, gave me tremors that were not from the cold.

"Pfui." Mimicking Chris Tolliver, Akktri snorted water from his nostrils. "Even big furless ones see better when farther in the warren." And he dove again. I felt his hands and feet as he paddled swiftly around my legs, chasing fish and small crabs for snacks.

As I sloshed on, struggling to appear lighthearted, I shivered, as much from the spooky quiet as the chill. By now the water was up to my chest, each step cooling another ribbon of my skin. Around, above, and below me, the Phneri had constructed an elaborate honeycomb of passageways, walls, and bars. Like beavers, whose talents they shared in an example of interplanetary parallel evolution, they had scavenged lost materials—deformed and rusted concrete structural rods, lost refrigerator doors, frayed mover cables—and built them into a tightly compacted palace where thousands of them could live.

This was their promised land.

And, I realized as I moved among the lumpy buildings of their adobe city, they had cleaned it all. Somewhere along the route, I had passed a line of demarcation. How they had done it I did not know, but not a mosquito buzzed in here, nor shedfly, nor scuffler, nor any other Boston pests. The water that slipped through my fingers when I raised my free hand was clear and, I was certain, drinkable. The Phneri had taken the spaces in Boston that we humans had discarded and made an empire in them, and I was humbled.

The water ahead of me roiled and bubbled. I approached, wondering where the inflow was coming from.

The pool was full of shimmering aquatic creatures who

tumbled over one another in a scintillating frenzy. The cavern rang with their high keening noises, whistles, chitters, and exotic clacks.

Hundreds of Phneri were crammed into a close wet space, talking and laughing and singing to each other. Tails and slippery back feet rose like short flags as the Phneri stood on their heads to dive to the bottom. Paws slapped wet furry flanks. Whiskers waved at other whiskers in a constant sea of movement and splashes.

I was terrified yet fascinated. These were the monsters of my childhood's bedtime stories, demons who loved death and ate human babies. Their fur glowed with a dark wet sheen. Their small teeth flashed as they chittered in their own language.

As I followed my partner into the churn, the aliens copied my movements, hunching their shoulders together, shuffling awkwardly on their bruised right ankles, holding their broken left arms stiff. It was eerie and unnerving.

"Beverlee!" Akktri poked his head up in front of me. "Beverlee, come and be among us."

"What?" I looked at the turbulent swimming mass. "Where?"

"Lay yourself in the water."

I'll drown, I thought with a child's fear, but I said, "I'll freeze." Memories of the Siege returned—fleeing up the stairwell, huddling as the world roared and I waited for the tidal wave to overwhelm me.

Akktri clambered, sopping and happy, up my good side. "Warren will warm you." He leaped off my shoulders and belly flopped before me, splashing my chest. "In the water." He flipped onto his back, his hands and feet held above the surface, and propelled himself with beats of his short tail. "We clean you."

"All right." Reluctantly I sank down, my wavy red hair floating around me like a doily as it touched the surface.

"And your light." Akktri touched my forehead, lifting free my new headlamp without tangling it in my soggy hair.

As the band slid off, I experienced an anxiety greater than any I had felt before. To be unclothed is merely embarrassing, but to be without light is to be blind and helpless. I willed myself not to cringe, not to bolt, not to strike out in panic.

Dozens of Phneri swam and probed me. My shoes were deftly lifted off to vanish unseen. My socks slid down off my toes with a tickling sensation. Small clever fingers undid my belt—I tried to swat them away but Akktri reassured me. My sweater ballooned around me, the Phneri pushing my arms up until they could stretch it off. In a moment I was nude, the icy water numbing my body like a punch, hard all over. My teeth rattled in my head.

"C-c-cold," I muttered. "I don't like this."

"Is necessary. You are future-warm," explained Akktri as he carried away part of my clothing. Other Phneri were cleaning me with precise fingers, scouring around and in my ears, between my toes. I barely felt them. "Is great honor to you. We need to hear your shape so we can esfn it."

"Esfn? Thanks for the compliment, but I need to be fixed." A distant soft warmth was replacing the numbness in my extremities.

My partner returned. "Esfn *is* fik-k-ks," he hissed as if embarrassed by my ignorance. "Words mean the same. Be still." He pushed my head to the left like an impersonal barber and held it while another Phner, deeper brown and smaller, swam up and slapped my neck. I felt a small prick.

"What was that?" I asked. My skin, though tight with cold, felt energized from the Phneri washing.

"Feel-g-g-good," said the newcomer, whose English needed work. "Relack-k-k-sant-t-t." Another prick in the shoulder and my whole left arm went dead.

As he spoke, the cold diminished except for a ring of ice around my neck. I dimly sensed many small hands touching me. Tiny fingers shoved themselves between my ribs, one after the other, each pressure bringing me to the edge of pain in a virtuoso display of anatomical perception.

There was no humanity in these touches; the Phneri were no more interested in my nest than my armpits. They wanted to know my structure without the complications of my personality—content without meaning, process without objective. Other claws zipped along my Targive flowcast, delicately slicing it open. Many fingers and claws caught my limb and held it, tender as a butterfly, while others poked the wounds, centimeter by precise centimeter.

Now the cylindrical tunnel was alive with sounds: rapid, chopped, and animated, the Phneri words far too fast for me to follow. The vocabulary they were using was huge, a whole lexicon of structure that humans can never know because we have no means of perceiving reality as they do.

I looked over at Akktri splashing around. He was home and in his place, but his partner Beverly was adrift and confused by recent events. I very much wanted to go to bed with Charles. Thinking of him, I wanted him to give me pleasure. I wanted him to embrace me. I wanted to explore his body, to make him gasp with delight.

I wanted to esfn him. I wanted to be able to esfn him.

The pool was dark. The water had become pleasantly warm, almost a toasty blanket, and the gentle susurrus of Phneri swimming was lulling me into a comfortable drowsiness. Their delicate hands cared for my body. Who'd protect my frazzled psyche?

So I floated in the water, almost dreaming, and lost my fear of the unknown. By now all the Phneri must know that it had been my bullet, my hand on the trigger, that had murdered Ekkikka.

Ifraim Lemos had deserved to die. I watched in my mind as my gun fired, watched Ifraim seize his chest and convulse as his guts collapsed, and I no longer grieved, no longer berated myself for that death. As Akktri would say, his end was artful, and I was pleased with my hand that had crafted it. I watched it again, critically, admiring the accuracy and effectiveness of my shot.

But Ekkikka's ending—that was artless. I saw this clearly. It stung my soul like a ragged, infected knife cut, tormenting me. In ending Ekkikka, I had made not art but desecration. Now the Phneri would repair Ekkikka's killer. In so doing, *they* would make art from his death and, if they were merciful and I was honest, they might absolve my crime.

"I am Ksak-k-ksos," a voice chirped in my ear.

A small brown Phner paddled beside my head. Her darker color in the shoulders and upper throat marked her as a female. "Your past bright, Ksaksos," I said awkwardly in her own language. I always mash Phner verbs. Makes me feel like a dolt.

She sternly slapped the water with her paws. "Your left radius has fractured sclat-t-t-iwah and we have ik-ksa-k-klow-dah to make it better." I'd never heard the words she used. As she spoke, two other Phneri straightened my arm and held it in place while new flowcasts were put on it. It was as sense-less and inert as a piece of wood. "Its future-state heals and is broken-and-reformed-better when you do not too soon kee-k-ka-t-t-so or ok-k-k-t-tee-tasa with it."

"I'm sorry, what do those mean?"

Ksaksos scowled, disappointed in my ignorance, and lifted her hand out of the water. *"Kee-k-ka-t-t-so."* She made a motion like turning a doorknob. "Pronate. *Ok-k-k-t-tee-tasa."* She grabbed an imaginary bar and tugged it toward her. "Flek-k-ksion."

I mimicked her movements with my right hand. "Turn and pull," I said.

She nodded. "Out of the water now." Ksaksos tugged me to a cement ledge on which the Phneri had laid an old wood-frame oak door as a pallet. They maneuvered me onto it, the chill air pinking my skin as the water evaporated. "You dry in future-near-and-likely-to-exist-always."

"How?" I asked, curious what clever means they would use. Ultrasonics?

Ksaksos handed me a towel.

I laughed at my own absurdity but she glowered, and I covered my mouth with my good hand. "You are our guest, Beverlee O'Meara," she snapped in quick Phner. "Now kneel," she said in English as I sheepishly nodded.

Ksaksos touched my ribs. They were red and purple, and she tsked. Another Phner came around to my right and hefted my wrist. "Abduct your limb," she said.

I managed to comply without cracking a smile, my torso now exposed on both sides.

More Phneri brought a roll of black material about ten centimeters wide. Ksaksos laid a strip of it against my damaged side and with a flick of her claws sliced it off. She patted it carefully into place, scowling at her handiwork.

"What's she doing?" I asked Akktri, who was perched in the background.

"Hush, Beverlee," my partner answered. "K-k-sak-k-sos moves your bones to be cong-g-gruent."

Ksaksos brought out a pot of a clear gel and began applying it over the black. "Hardener," Akktri explained. "Bends at your movement but absorbs blows away from your ribs."

"Blows?" I asked.

"You suffer many blows," answered Ksaksos, not taking her attention away from her chore. "You need much protec-k-k-tion."

Akktri hurried up to me and hissed in my ear, "Ksaksos is very great surgeon. Be respec-k-ktful."

"Trying, partner," I whispered back in English, feeling uneasily that the Phner doctor understood every word we two said.

A dozen more Phneri stood in a ring behind Ksaksos, hands-up attentive, watching and muttering very quietly to avoid disturbing her. The little Phner surgeon was extraordinarily intent, moving the gel in her paws as if it were alive.

Structural ridges and arches fanned out across my stomach and back, even as Ksaksos made space for my breasts. What architects the Phneri would make, I thought as I watched. What cathedrals they could have built.

Finally Ksaksos nodded, dissatisfied with something but evidently done, and the other Phneri rolled more black material around my gut and snicked it off. Ksaksos pushed the edges together and they sealed. From navel to armpits, I was girded in a protective tubetop. The alien surgeon had even carved room in the left side so that I could swing my similarly protected left arm.

"Arms down," Ksaksos ordered. Her manner had taken on a great dignity. "Rotate and revolve." She demonstrated and I copied her movements. "Body needs rest." She glared at me.

"Not just the body," I agreed wearily. "But there is no time. I must save Diana."

"Diana dies," Ksaksos said with slow emphasis. "Beverlee dies. Akktri dies. Ksaksos dies." She took her time with each name, as if examining each life trail and speaking only when she reached its end and confirmed the death. "You k-k-kill Ekkik-k-ka Phner."

The small creatures brought forward the bleached white skull of a large rodent. The cranial cavity was small, the jaw elongated. Incisors canted forward to tear flesh. "Ek-k-kik-k-ka dies."

Ksaksos's left shoulder lifted and twisted in a movement that I well remembered as that of Ekkikka's body, seizing when my bullet struck. Her arms flung backward. Her spine arched. Each movement precisely mirrored the way Ekkikka had fallen. "You k-k-kill me," she moaned.

All around the chamber, every Phner copied Ksaksos.

I was shocked, distraught. Ksaksos's neck twitched as if in a death rattle. Her body collapsed in a small heap and the life seemed to drain from it. Instinctively I reached for her, to lift the corpse and check for signs of life, but I stopped myself.

"We die," chittered Ksaksos and the Phneri all around

cried, We die, the sound echoing to and fro in the tunnels, an endless dirge, We die, we die, we die, die-die-die, fading into silence.

Ksaksos's body stirred as if blown by a breath of wind. She raised her head and confronted me. "We live," she continued, and the walls resounded, *We live, we live, we live-live-live*.

She drew herself up and waddled toward me. "Now Ek-k-kik-k-ka lives," she said.

To a Phner, this phrase signals absolution. Moved by her formality and command, I sat up straighter and laid my good right hand over my chest. It thudded dully, the force deflected across my seamless black shield. "You change me," I said in Phner, using the word that means improve-and-strengthen. "You honor me."

"You are wise," Ksaksos answered in the same language. She jerked her head at my partner. "Akktri owes us."

"No." I put out my hand, palm forward. "Akktri does this for Beverlee. Beverlee owes, not Ak-k-ktri." I tapped myself on the black tube, which clacked.

Ksaksos glanced from me to my partner. "As it is," he said. The Phner reply for everything. "Stand," she ordered.

My clothes were brought, clean and dry.

"You belong to our warren now," said Ksaksos when I had dressed. "We feel your death. Stand."

I obeyed her instructions and Akktri moved away, for the deceased must die alone.

Ksaksos looked at me for a long time. "Now we mourn you."

Hundreds of Phneri emerged from the shadows, brown and orange and gold.

I stood, my arms at my sides.

They gathered around me, each pressed against the other. Small hands came forward to touch my feet, ankles, calves. Silent as mimes, they worked their way up my body until they were standing around me, touching everywhere from hip down. All I heard was the steady drip-drip-drip of water in distant corners.

The Phneri trilled.

The sound began as a high-pitched buzzing like a thousand mosquitoes. It strengthened and broadened into deeper ranges. My skin tingled from the vibrations.

"We fall forever," Ksaksos said softly in her own language, and my hair stood on end. "We are close and high and we explode." The Phneri around her shuddered.

Very soon after the Boston Loophole opened, the Phneri lost an offplanet war with the Sh'k, a waldo-building supercilious race. The victorious Sh'k built a huge combination ark and rabbit warren, stuffed it to the gunwales with Phneri, and sent it through the Loophole into Solspace. Once here, the spherical crewless robot ship oriented itself, made a course for Earth, took up orbit over the Contact Zone in Boston Harbor . . . and blew itself to pieces.

"We are falling," chanted Ksaksos. "Our hands and feet reach but we cannot climb the ladders of the airs."

As one, several million Phneri fell almost five kilometers, down through the high atmosphere.

"We die," Ksaksos whispered. "We all die."

With their exquisite esfn sense, they could *see* their deaths coming as the Earth rose like a giant blue fist. Because they have a strong race consciousness and a diminished sense of individuality, they *all* felt like they *all* were dying. They mourned each other's deaths as they fell, a huge symphony of trilling and clicking voices like a squadron of bees, until they hit the water.

Although they can accelerate their time-sense at moments of stress, their terminal velocity was so great that most of them—the old, the infirm, the babies, the unlucky—died on impact. Several hundred thousand brown and gold creatures half-mad with pain and fear survived impact. Those lucky few immediately started swimming for the nearest shore—South Boston.

The night sky, gray and orange from mist and streetlights, became black with glistening hairy bodies. To my grandmother Sweeney, looking out the window of her L Street triple-decker, they fell so fast and so heavily that she couldn't distinguish individuals, just shapes crashing into the harbor with a sound like the pounding of tom-toms. Some hit the streets in a staccato rhythm of splats and thuds. She looked up but could see no stars, only small animals in a steady torrent that poured for several minutes. People gathered along the shoreline, hushed, watching.

"We are dead and we drown," the Phneri said together.

The splashes from so many bodies landing created a small tidal wave that flooded many houses. Children sleeping on first floors drowned in their beds.

The Phneri swam closer and emerged, ratlike, from the water. People panicked. Some got rifles and tried to kill the invaders. The Phneri fought desperately back. Both people and Phneri died—many more of them than us. Some people fled, among them my grandfather and grandmother. They moved to the safe high ground of Irish, blue-collar West Roxbury, where my mother grew up and met Billy O'Meara, my father.

"We come to our land," murmured Ksaksos, gently now, and around her the warren crooned. "We come to our water."

Desperate to find a place to recover, the amphibious Phneri moved into the vacated, waterlogged houses of South Boston, dozens to a room.

"You are dead," said Ksaksos in Phner, squatting in front of me.

"I am dead," I responded.

To the Phneri, grief is more meaningful before death, shared with soon-to-be-deceased, when all the things left undone by death can be said and remembered.

"We know you now," Ksaksos continued. She held up her paws in blessing. I held up my hands and she wagged her head so her whiskers brushed both my cheeks.

Wordlessly she dove into the water.

One by one, the other Phneri passed before me, held up their hands, rubbed whiskers, and then submerged. Deftly and with no splash, they swam into the gloomy tunnels, until it was just Akktri and me. He touched whiskers with me and dove, like the others, his face compressed and alien.

I knelt, my bottom on my heels and my hands on my knees. When a funeral ends, the soon-to-be-deceased is alone. The Phneri have no afterlife, only a void with neither time nor structure. The tunnel was dark and quiet. My hands were unnaturally sensitive from touching several hundred Phneri. The water no longer felt cold.

I wept for my father, who died unmourned in the Flood. And I wept for Ekkikka, whom I had killed.

I was a Phner, my body small but quick. The bullet, faster than I had imagined, smashed into my ribs even as I tried desperately to dodge. They shattered with the impact and a shock wave blew through my body, instantly bursting cells everywhere. A fire burned in my heart as the arteries ruptured. My body was lifted backwards and slammed into a wall, stifling the cry which formed in my pulped lungs. I crumpled and died.

Huddled into my own ball, trapped in my own black infinity of dying, I cried softly, and felt relief.

Eventually the pain memories faded and my senses again reported the half-submerged tunnel that surrounded me.

I breathed gently, at peace, and unknotted my right arm, which I had clenched about my armored torso. My fingers flexed and relaxed.

Billy never had a funeral, I thought. I owe him one.

Akktri surfaced and tapped my arm. "Live," he said. My funeral was over.

"We are sorry that you die," my partner commented as he led me back out the tunnel. I was refreshed, purified, invigorated. Ready for battle.

When we arrived at Iris's office a few minutes later, Charles

Beaufort was out. "Even assistants get some hours off," my client said in a halfhearted attempt at humor.

"Have you slept at all?" I asked, approaching her desk.

Iris shrugged. "Put my head down on the desk a couple of times and nodded off." She closed her eyes. "Slept badly. Nightmares. I had monitors, hundreds of monitors, and Diana on each one. But I could not read their locations." She sat back in her chair and rested her head against its cushion.

"I've got some bright-eyes to keep you going." I hauled the pills out of my pocket. "Here. I've already taken mine."

She frowned at them. "What side effects do they have?"

"As you'd expect, for Chrissakes," I snapped, exasperated. Charm school personified. "They speed up your reactions, pump you full of adrenalin, suppress fatigue responses, and generally wire you to the gills." I grinned heartlessly. "It'll be good for you."

"All right." She looked with distaste at the things in her hand, then made up her mind and swallowed them. "I'm trusting you."

In her own arrogant way, she wanted me to cradle her head and tell the frightened little girl she denied inside herself that it would be all right, but she was still too proud to ask comfort from a mere untutored rugrat. "I've changed my mind," I said. "You're not coming. I go alone."

"Nonsense. Of course I'm accompanying you."

"It's dangerous. Foolhardy, even."

"She's *my* daughter. I have to come."

We glared at one another. "There is no reason to believe that Guillermo will release you, even if you do everything he demands," I said.

"He ordered you to bring me. He has proven he will torture and kill to achieve his ends. I will take my chances. Now I must arrange the eyes."

"No, you won't." I put my hand against her shoulder. "Bad enough that you insist on coming, which needlessly puts you at risk. You have already lost Diana's hand. Are you willing to bet the rest of her that you can outsmart him?" I hiked my butt up and sat on Iris's desk. "We do it my way or you go alone."

She glared. "Without you, I won't find him."

"Right. If you accompany me, we go with no support, no bot eyes, nothing."

"Why? I'm the client, remember?"

I tapped my Phneri cast. "In case it hasn't registered on your infomat, Guillermo broke my arm earlier today. Just to make a point. *I* decide what risks we take."

She glowered at me with a gaze obviously intended to weaken my resolve. "Can I take my own gear?" she asked, breaking off the eye wrestling before she lost.

I shrugged. "Sure, cloak yourself in any little gadgets your heart desires. Guillermo expects *some* tricks. He'll strip them from you long before you ever see Diana. That'll make him confident. Maybe even cocky—if we're lucky."

"I see." She chewed on this, then nodded oddly at me. "You're turning into a hard woman."

"A broken arm and thirty-six hours without proper sleep will do that to you."

"You'll indulge me, then?" she asked sarcastically. "I'll need a few minutes to rig up." She began to tap commands into her infomat.

"Take all the time you want. Diana's *your* daughter."

"I see." Her eyes narrowing, she shoved back her chair and stood. "Let's go."

18

"THIS ISN'T SO hard," said Iris with a hint of challenge as we emerged from the mover. She nervously rebound her hair, aggressively shoving in her gold stickpin and patting her bun tightly down.

Her oversize public works department coverall bulged in odd places. Its carpenter's bib stretched down to meet loose canvas painter's pants festooned with pockets of every shape and size: long and thin for small hand tools, big and rectangular for minibots. Suzy Society on city safari.

"Don't waste your bravado on me," I replied. Lumps covering her gadgetry grew randomly about her torso and arms like boils. "And you won't get any of that peanut brittle past them."

I led her across the plaza, maneuvering around piles of urbjunk including broken wooden boxes and twisted aluminum suspension-ceiling frameworks like the webbing from some rectangular spider. Meanwhile strange people and grubby aliens moved about us, carrying on their mysterious business. Smudgers gave their faces a blurred quality as if seen in the rain. We paid scant attention to them—in the Basement, curiosity is dangerous. You mind your own business.

In seconds we had lost the mover in the maze around us. Fluorescent lights above us flickered on and off, casting weird flashes of light and shadow.

More people passed in different directions, their eyes averted. We did the same, moving swiftly through the corridors.

A few minutes later, we heard moaning and came upon a heavy man, his back bent and tight. "Get up," he slurred at his feet. "If you keep doin' this the rods'll be here."

The woman he was berating sat on the ground, her legs slightly spread, her forehead in her hands. She was crying.

"Get up," the man growled as if whipping a mule. He was squat, his wide trousers sagging against his hips to reveal the crack of his buttocks, tufted with thick black hair. The cuffs were matted with dirt and dust.

The woman whimpered and buried her head in her arms.

"All right." He stood, bent, and swept up a canvas carryall by her side. "I'm leavin'."

"No, Bernie," she moaned, lurching to her knees and holding out her hands.

"Well, then," said the man. "Are you comin'?"

Shaking her head, she sniffled and sank back on her haunches.

In disgust he threw the bag to the ground and she flinched. But he stayed where he was.

Footsteps sounded: uniformed rods heading our way. The couple heard them too, the woman scrambling to her feet. They began to shuffle away, but the rods reached and corralled them. We melted into the darkness.

After a few moments the black windows of Old New City Hall loomed before us. I peered through its sooty glass panes into the darker interior. Iris drew level with my shoulder. "In there?" she whispered.

"It's where Guillermo told me to bring you. And don't bother to keep your voice down. We're not sneaking up on anybody."

The revolving door creaked from dust and crystallized rubber gaskets as we pushed into the foyer.

"Well, howdy-do!" said a merry female voice.

A roly-poly woman sat on a wood stool in the amphitheater's center, her buttocks and thighs overhanging its seat like warm candle wax. She had curly hair and huge fat cheeks splotched pink by burst capillaries. "Guillermo said you'd arrive about now. Turn off all your eyes."

"Eyes?" asked Iris too blankly.

"The little flying ones." The fat woman waggled her fingers up by her temples. "And the crawly ones you have on yourself somewhere." She held up a peeper and waved it at Iris and me as if offering us joints from a pack. It squealed. "Strip," Calpurnia ordered, shoving her hams off the stool and moving close to Iris. Her huge barrel chest seemed to expand over us.

"No," replied Iris, points of color appearing on her cheeks.

Calpurnia's big fleshy hand slapped Iris's cheek with a sound like a baseball bat hitting a slab of meat. As Iris recoiled, Calpurnia grabbed the coverall's front and tore it from neck to crotch with two sharp yanks. Grasping the flaps in her hands, she ripped outward, leaving Iris in only a functional beige bra and sensible above-navel panties. "Strip," she repeated.

With a gulp, Iris complied. When she was finished, she crouched over a pile of her things, her knees crossed and her arms held protectively over her bosom. Her skin sagged a little and her frame was bony. "I need shoes," Iris demanded sullenly. "And covering." Her gray hair, tight-wound to her head, made her resemble a penitent flagellant.

Calpurnia gathered Iris's destroyed costume and threw it in an open oildrum where a garbage fire smoldered, throwing smoke in a ball near the ceiling scrubbers. "Over here." She nodded toward a box full of discarded clothes. "Your wardrobe."

Nothing fit. Everything stank. I found a mismatched pair of sneakers, a flannel shirt someone had used as a grease and oil wiper, and a pair of size 900 trousers that I managed to belt around my waist with a couple of loops of wire. I tossed back the underwear, most of which had bluish mildewed patches and a slimy, mossy feel.

"What's this?" demanded Calpurnia, whacking my torso vest and arm flowcast with her mitt.

234 § DAVID ALEXANDER SMITH

"Phneri. Your boss beat me up. It won't come off. Scan it if you like."

"Hmph." She waved her device. "How can you stand to have beaverwork next to you?"

I let myself not be drawn into anger; for all I knew, she was simply provoking me to test my limits. "It's better than pain."

Iris crawled into an enormous earth-mother bibbed dirndl—the bosom alone could have held a clivus—and stinking loafers with enormous toeholes. She had to shuffle to keep them on her feet.

"Follow me, bimbo," Calpurnia said, slapping Iris in the stomach. She led us onto what remained of State Street. "Over here." Pointing to a large grate in the pavement, she rummaged in the debris and brought forth a huge crowbar, stuck one end into the thumbhole, and wrenched it upward with a creak of rusted metal crumbling. "Into the subway."

The blue enamel steps we descended were wet-velvet smooth with green and gray slime. Iris slipped but caught herself on the rail. "Where are we?"

"Hold on." I ran my headlamp along the walls until I found a blue-tiled rectangle. Using an extra yard of my shirt sleeve, I wiped grime and dirt away. "Court Street. The Blue Line of the old subway." I nodded down the tunnel and my light played across the bobbing white lozenge of Calpurnia's broad back.

"Down." Our guide perched at the platform lip like a fat gargoyle. Daintily she pushed herself off and dropped a couple of meters into the blackness, then turned and beckoned. I was impressed with her agility. "Follow me."

I crouched and lowered myself over the side, my bruised but girded stomach scraping against the edge, until my questing left foot felt the wooden eight-by-eights that held the rails.

The subway tunnels arched black overhead, splintering and decayed, dry and decrepit. My light cast a bright cone into the dusty air, reflecting the inky surface behind it. Water trickled along the gutters beside the rusted tracks. The platform, now at our eye level, was ragged and pitted like corrugated cardboard sawn apart by a giant knife. Rats, pissmops, mudruckers, and other scurriers whispered about our feet and ankles.

We had walked several hundred meters along the tracks when Calpurnia stared into the darkness. "Okay, over here!" she chortled, directing her light on a segment of rail. "Step on this." Her glitzy voice was nevertheless a sharp command.

As I started forward, the big woman clutched my good arm in her meaty paw. "Not you. Her."

"Me?" asked Iris. "What's the point?"

Calpurnia giggled. "We wired it into your central peeping system. Big transformer too, switched in through South Fusion. So if you've got any eyes lit anywhere around here, the volts'll zip through you. Be a whole lotta shakin' goin' on." Her eyes widened like moons.

"That's impossible." Iris's eyes darted between the band of steel and Calpurnia's doughy face. "It's an exposed, grounded rail."

"Just one itsy-bitsy step and we'll all see." The big woman was enjoying herself. "Or you could just squat and pee onto it. Urine conducts electricity too."

"You're lying," Iris said.

Calpurnia's shrug set off small aftershocks in her jiggling arms and chest. "So what's the risk?"

After a brief struggle between Iris's intellect and her nervous system, logic won, as I knew it always would for her: defiantly she planted her foot on the rail—no sizzle, no sparks, no scream of agony—and walked a half-dozen paces along it. "You *couldn't* have wired it," Iris said, angry but also triumphant.

Calpurnia gestured at the darkness ahead. "Down that tunnel. Stay straight. I'm right behind you."

Iris marched obediently ahead, turning frequently to glare at me over her shoulder as if dragging a reluctant puppy. The darkness descended more thoroughly around us and the sounds dampened into the tiny still scrabblings of insects, bats, and rodents.

Calpurnia's wheezes puffed behind us like a bellows. The beams of her headlamp threw bouncing shadows like wraiths onto our path.

"That man and woman," Iris began after we had moved out of Calpurnia's sight. "Back in the plaza." She jerked her head.

I kept my eyes on my path; a sprained ankle was all too likely. "What about them?"

"Who were they?" Iris was troubled. "Why were they fighting?"

"It'll go on a rod rep as a domestic disturbance," I replied.

"And then what?"

"A night in jail each, a meal or two, a disinfect and a drug flush, then release. Tomorrow night they'll be doing the same thing. You're probably their pusher."

"How can you suggest——"

I cut her off. "Aren't you the woman who told me about sexual sponges? 'Their kind will get satisfaction somewhere,' you said." I echoed the tough cynical tone she had used. " 'I simply pander to their tastes,' you said. Weren't those your words?"

"I'm not responsible for how their lives turn out," Iris said. I had never seen her so angry.

"No, Iris." I matched her bluntness. She had no exemption from morality's shadows. "You just make their wretched lives easier."

"I see. So that's how you see it." Iris's jaw set. She walked several score paces, her face granite, and then said, "That woman—why didn't she want the rods?"

"She's afraid of them."

"Why didn't she call to us?"

"She's afraid of us." I tried to keep my voice unemotional, unprovocative.

Iris was growing exasperated. "Why doesn't she leave him?"

"She's afraid of living without him."

"Why didn't *you* help her?" she demanded, grasping my Phneri-cast arm above the elbow.

"That hurts." I looked at her. With a small jerk, she let go. "How?" I asked softly. "How would I help her?"

"Talk to her." Iris made energetic gestures with her hands. "Take her away from him."

"As if I could."

"You could try."

"If I did, would you provide her with food, clothing, shelter?"

"Yes, of course. The City will. Until she gets on her feet again."

"She's afraid of the City."

"All right, then, we'll—"

"Can you get her a job?" I interrupted impatiently. "Can you shove an education into her? Can you undo a lifetime of living on other people's handouts? Following other people's orders? Will *you* tell her what to do? *That's* what he gives her."

Iris walked in angry silence. "And in exchange he beats her," she muttered.

"Or humiliates her," I said. "When he thinks she deserves it."

"And she *accepts* it?"

"Yes. She too thinks she deserves it."

"I see." Iris was boiling but speechless.

"You have no idea how people *feel*, do you? You don't understand how anyone can be trapped by his or her past. Emotions that lead to illogical decisions are a mystery to you. You don't even have the slightest idea how I felt when my father died."

She barely glanced over her shoulder. "Beverly, you think you're the only person I've encountered in nineteen years who had a relative die in the Siege?" Her tread didn't waver. "I've been barricaded in my office by screaming lunatics revenging themselves for the deaths of their children. People have broken into my apt waving stunners to discuss the matter with me. It was nineteen years ago. Grow up, Bev. You're too young to understand the Siege."

"Understand it?" I was incredulous. "I *lived* through it."

"Being a victim is easy, the moral highroad," Iris replied bitterly. Her voice was laced with payback satisfaction for my entrapping her a few moments earlier. "Try being the executioner."

"You're a hypocrite," I said. "You don't give a damn about my dad. You have no conception."

"What are you talking about?" Iris demanded. She stopped and turned, confronting me. "You think I don't know what grief is? I had a father once too, you know. And what about Diana?" She spat into the darkness. "You still don't understand what the Siege did to me, do you?" She looked up at me. "It wasn't one man, one child I grieved for, it was multitudes. I watched babies screaming in their cribs, their hair on fire. Grandmothers died of typhoid fever caught when they drank from the river, mucus streaming from their nostrils and mouths. Pregnant women drowned when I flooded the Basement. My Phneri showed me the bodies. All my fault. Their faces blur now." She drew a long breath and rubbed her jaw. "Would you believe me if I said I was sorry for your father's death? Sorry for hundreds and thousands of deaths which I caused?" She shrugged and seated herself on the greasy stones and railroad ties of the subway tracks. "I can't apologize to your generation anymore. Every new person I meet is a potential time bomb of grief and hate and blame. As if their loved ones' own actions had nothing whatsoever to do with their deaths. As if *my* action absolved their lives, canonized them saints and damned me as their Judas. Well, I have no more feelings to give."

I squatted down on my haunches, moving stiffly to avoid scraping or stretching my ribs. "How could you kill them all?"

She gazed far down the black tunnel into her past, where Calpurnia's light slowly approached. "The normal rules didn't apply. We—performed—tasks. We made—decisions." Her words came slow and distant as if dredged. "Iris Sherwood was just one more cog." For a moment she was silent, rubbing her hands into her palms as if to wear away the skin. "Is the trigger more guilty than the bullet? More guilty than the pistol barrel or the explosive charge?" She rubbed her forehead.

"And then?" I prompted, as softly as a thought.

"Then it was over and my hand hurt from the recoil. Lem Snow lay dead in his own blood. He had climbed a hundred and fifty levels' worth of mover shafts to reach me." She stared into the dark and her hand idly gathered dirty pebbles and tossed them, one by one, to bounce in the dark. "We burned and buried the bodies. We drained the mud and cleaned the flooded Basement. My Phneri restored the Golden Dome."

"My father died," I said. "I don't understand any more than that."

"When it ended," Iris resumed, her voice stronger and more rapid, "I went to Center Plaza. I was delirious from fatigue and dehydration. The lost survivors were all there— the abandoned, the orphans, the unclaimed, like the Day of Judgment when the earth opens and the naked dead rise to heaven. I walked among them like Christ weighing their souls. Heaven or hell?" She held out her hand, palm up, the fingers spread, and wiggled them as if sand were falling through the gaps.

"And you adopted Diana. Then and there."

"Yes."

"Why? Why *her?*"

"I've never told her," Iris said after a long silence.

I leaned forward, though my ribs ached from the movement. "Why did you choose *Diana?*"

She looked at me for a long time and the desire to confess rose within her, filling her gray eyes until I thought she would weep. "Because she was not crying," Iris whispered. "A tiny child, sallow and underfed like everyone in the City. Lying flat on her back. Her arms moved weakly. I walked along the row of lost children"—she closed her eyes and tilted back her head—"and they were all crying. All the babies, crying for their parents whom I had killed. Except Diana. She was *watching*. Those *eyes.*" She closed hers, remembering, and wiped her cheekbones with the dirty heel of her hand. "I passed her by. I was moved by her silence and proud of this stoic child. I passed her by, and as I did, she whimpered."

"For you?"

She brusquely shook her head. "It couldn't possibly have been for me. She was less than a week old. They can't really focus at that age." Iris seemed determined to deny any uniqueness for herself. "But I took that step and she cried and I thought, 'I have turned away from too much suffering.' " She held up her hand, the wrinkled fingers curled as if to hold her words. "I thought, 'I must take this child to save myself.' It was fair. I thought, 'She is mine. Boston wants me to take her. Of all of them. To take *her.*' " Iris's eyes locked on mine and she opened her hand, dismissing the memory. "So I did."

"Diana doesn't know this."

"No. How could I tell her, 'Darling, sweetie, you were chosen on a whim'?"

"Was it a whim?" I asked, not to challenge her but because I did not know.

"It was a long time ago," replied Iris. "All I know is that I love her now. I love her more than my happiness or my life."

A thought came to me. "You probably killed her parents."

"It's possible." She rubbed her face with a dirty hand. "I hope not. I have often hoped that they fled. And just as often I hoped that they were dead, so that they could never return and take my daughter from me." I heard her sigh, her face a gray silhouette against a black background. She bent her head so her lamp lit an ellipse of ground. "I have tried so hard to make it up to her."

"And you failed, didn't you?"

Calpurnia was nearing and I could tell Iris wanted to keep distance between herself and her jailer. She reached up and adjusted her light, then held out her hand. "Help me up." I grasped it and leaned backwards as she stood. She was emotionally exhausted, beyond outrage. Aimlessly she brushed dirt from her filthy dirndl. "Diana had an alcove in my office. She called it Biana's besk. She always had trouble with *b*'s and *d*'s. It had an infomat, videoscreen, everything. All on small scale. I had a tiny desk built for her."

I imagined a four-year-old with a desk. Did she have a tiny secretary? What's a four-year-old's billing rate?

"Bev, you and I are more alike than you want to admit," Iris went on. "You can't say no to need either. Otherwise you'd have dumped me long ago." Straightening her headlamp, she set off down the tracks.

I followed, walking at her shoulder. "Iris, we are responsible for everything we do. Adults own their pasts."

"But not everything that happens. I'm responsible for how I raised my daughter, but not for how she turned out."

"Why didn't you want her to be like you?" I asked after a few more paces.

She snorted. "Why? What's to love about me?"

"Lose the martyrdom, Iris. Answer the question."

"You're right. I deserved that." She sighed. "Power changes a person. I despised what power had done to me. I was afraid of what emulating me might do to Diana."

I thought of Mi Nyo setting hurdles and traps for her grand-niece Hu. "But you're still in your job."

"It's a drug," Iris tartly replied. "You don't give it up just because you despise it and yourself."

Just ahead was a lit station area. "Everybody out of the pool," burbled Calpurnia, mincing along the platform edge ahead of us. She pointed at a pillared, downsloping corridor perpendicular to our previous path. "Through the turnstiles at the end. I'm right behind you."

We passed into a broad plaza with an asphalt floor and a

low cement ceiling. At an ancient control panel, Calpurnia flipped an oversize lever with a red plastic handle. A hideous creaking sounded and a caged wire-mesh box groaned toward us, suspended between four huge steel poles. Winches and gears cranked, lowering the cab toward us.

"Step into Mohammed's Coffin." Calpurnia shoved the lever to vertical, unlatching the gate, and dragged it open. The floor was made of gray tongue-and-grooved wood, uneven with wear and scarred from heavy use. Pigeon and mudrucker stool littered its corners gray and white. The right-hand wall held a time clock and dusty pink punch cards.

"What the vent is *this?*" I asked.

"A manually controlled car mover from the pre-Cube days," Iris answered distantly. She craned her neck to left and right. "We must be in the old Batterymarch Parking Garage." Five more identical floors loomed above us, each divided into horizontal bays about the size of our mover cage.

"In," Calpurnia ordered impatiently. She stepped out of the mover, hauled its gate shut, and pulled a couple of levers. We rose and shifted as the shuttle moved into darkness like a constipated dragon. Then it stopped. In the silence, the ropes that held us rubbed against one another like corduroy trousers.

"We're probably being scanned," Iris commented after a pause. "Neat."

Moments later the cage started up with a rumble and a shriek. I twined my fingers through its mesh as we lurched and rocked upward.

A tall, well-built young man unhinged the far gate and swung it open.

"Hello, Interim Director Sherwood," said a voice I wished I didn't recognize.

Iris was staring at Guillermo with an expression of rage and horrified recognition. "You!" she hissed.

19

GUILLERMO REY——*WAS* it Guillermo?——sat on a makeshift throne of stacked fruit crates. His cheekbones rose higher than I remembered and the dark skin around them was pulled more taut, flattening his eyes. They were green now, instead of dark brown, and his hair was lighter. He smiled stiffly. Faceclamping rapidly and radically changes your appearance, right down to the bone structure; it's extreme, permanent, and excruciating. His ability to endure that torture and smile as he was now shocked me to the core. Beside him, Calpurnia giggled like an overweight Virgin Mary.

Diana sat miserably at their feet, a sadist's plaything. She held her left arm in a crude sling, swaddled in a dirty white swirl of cloth. The weight dragged her neck and torso to the left. Her eyes were pale loose dots in a wounded face, all its lines vertical as if centrifuged. Her cheeks were gray and collapsed. She looked dead.

The garage bay was illuminated with antique sodium lights that cast a smoky tiger-orange pall over everything. Many were burned out, dividing the space into bars of light and darkness. Small critters rustled in the shadows.

"You knew Lem Snow?" Iris went on. She moved tentatively toward Guillermo as if arguing with a ghost. "No, you couldn't have. You're too young."

"Wrong." His cold green eyes were locked on hers. The faceclamped skin, stretched and hormoned for quick recovery, was burnt umber and glossy. I winced at the ground-glass shivers it must be sending through his face. Guillermo's lips were pulled back in a skull's permanent grin, his jaw reset. He was radiating bloodlust.

"Lem Snow," breathed Iris. "You've made yourself into him. Why? What is he to you?"

"You murdered him." He crossed his ankles and tapped his heel against the crates.

"Of course I did," Iris answered perfunctorily. "I shot the damn gijo in the chest and he died at my feet." She stopped and looked at Guillermo as a person, not a nightmare from her past. "I didn't know he had a family."

"You can be a father without having a family," he answered with bitterness and pride. "He was an American. Not a tool of Boston's money. You murdered him."

Balling Hu Nyo, I thought as my mind clicked, of course. How can a rugrat express his rage? By fucking the daughter of the Siege's biggest winner, Boston's richest merchant family.

"Tut, tut," Iris interrupted briskly, silencing Guillermo. "If I hadn't fired first, he'd've killed me."

I was amazed as ever at her claim of prerogative. Where did it come from? Was it just the parlor trick of her colossal oblivion to anything other than her own authority? Was authority no more than arrogance's self-fulfilling prophecy?

Guillermo leaped down from his perch. "Shut up," he said flatly. "Now." He flicked the stunner at her.

Iris fell like a log, her head cracking on the flooring. "Truth isn't what you say it is," he hissed down at her. "You understand?"

"No." Iris pulled out a tooth fragment, examined it with distaste, and flicked it away.

"The moral high ground?" he added with reflective sarcasm.

So he had listened, I thought. He had sent us into that black tunnel to give us the illusion of freedom, just so he could hear what we had to say. He had been playing with us the whole time. He'd probably arranged the third-rail bluff to make Iris overconfident.

As he stepped back, evidently to stun her again, I dove for him. It was foolish and contrary to my plans, but I had had enough of his tortures and posturings. Catching Calpurnia by surprise, I managed to get my shoulder into Guillermo's body, knocking him off-balance and away from Iris. As we fell apart stunners fired, a sound like air sizzling, and I shrieked.

My whole right side below Ksaksos's body cast flared, then went numb. With a wordless cry, I landed partially on top of Iris, my fingers and arm twitching with involuntary muscle spasms. They had the cheap, illegal stunners that feed back your own nerve reactions, so the more you move, the more it hurts. Each breath was a double-handled saw against my ribs. My fingers burned as if slit with paper cuts and then dipped in battery acid.

Diana hauled herself to her feet. "How does *that* feel, mother?" she asked.

Struggling out from under me, Iris shoved her stringy gray hair away from her eyes and peered at her daughter. Her eyelids were twitching spasmodically from the stunner. "It hurts, Diana," she said with a suppressed shudder. "You know that."

"Does it feel guilty?" pressed the girl. She moved to Guillermo, curled her good arm around him, and snuggled against his chest, her right hand dipping toward his belt to caress him. But her eyes were on her mother as she did.

"You fondle his nuts," said Iris. "So he cuts your hand off. I see."

Diana jerked away as if zapped. "I *had* to! You don't care about me!"

"If you thought that," Iris commented coolly, recovering her poker face, "why did you think I'd come?"

"Because you thought you ought to!" She pounced as if this was an old argument. "Because a *mother* would. You aren't my mother, you're a demonstration prototype. Was it good for you, mother dear? Guillermo's good for me. We're using you," Diana finished, her voice ragged. "How does it feel to be used?"

For a long moment Iris looked at her child, just the two of them locked in their private war. Even Guillermo was fascinated rather than scornful.

And then Iris laughed, wounded and cynical.

"To be used? It feels like life!" Tears ran down her cheeks as she lay on her back, clutching her sides, laughing until she coughed. Gasping for breath, she wiped blood from her mouth and pushed herself into a sitting position. "I'm used like everyone else is."

"Mother," Diana snarled, "you're a whore."

"I'd've thought that was *your* title, my darling."

"Where do you get the right to play God?"

"Someone has to." Iris's voice was flint. "Power exists whether we like it or not. Did we have a choice when the gray glubs fell out of our sky? Did we have a choice in the Siege? Power rules our world, you foolish child, and we are used by it." She drew a deep breath. "It's life," she continued in a mother's voice, not an executive's. "The City uses me and I'm glad of it. My poor miserable foolish Biana." She reached up as if to touch her daughter's cheek.

Diana recoiled. "Don't give me that self-pitying-tough-dame crap," she answered bluntly. "I've heard it so many years I'm finally immune. Climb up on the cross if you want to but don't give me the goddamn nails to pound into your hands and feet."

"All right, I won't pity you." Iris rubbed her jaw where Guillermo had struck her. Blood trickled from her mouth.

"I'll never forgive you," Diana snarled.

"I've never asked forgiveness for doing my duty," Iris shot back, unrepentant.

The girl pushed herself away from her mother and put her free arm out like a woman feeling for the walls in a dark room. "You said you knew my real parents," she said to Guillermo, rising and advancing toward him. "Where are they?"

Leaning against the fruit crates, Guillermo looked steadily at her as she jerked toward him like a broken marionette. "How should I know?" he finally drawled when they were close enough to touch.

With a demented shriek, Diana flung herself at him, clawing at his face with her single hand. He smacked her wounded stump with the stunner and Diana moaned, a whistle of agony that rose into a hiss until her breath was gone. She fell to the floor.

Blood welled like red rubies from the jagged line of half-moon gouges Diana's nails had torn in Guillermo's left cheek. He rubbed his fingertips across the scratches, looked at them, then thoughtfully sucked the blood. "I always said you were a coward," he commented to her crumpled body.

"Mama?" Diana was groping in Iris's direction, her arms shuddering uncontrollably. "Mama, help me."

Iris crawled forward and caught Diana's head, then drew it into her bosom. "Oh, my Biana," she crooned, stroking the matted blond hair. "You're my only girl, and I love you."

"But why me, mother? I'm not good enough. Why *me?*"

They clung together, arms wrapped tightly about each other, heads resting on each other's shoulders.

Guillermo came up and knocked the two women apart. "Move away from her," he said in a low voice. Diana's head spun around and she flinched. "Move," Guillermo repeated softly. "Whether you love me or hate me, get away from her." He slapped the stunner's head against his palm as if weighing it. "Turn off your Basement eyes," he ordered Iris. "And keep them off."

"No." Iris was crisp, decisive, sure.

He raised the stunner slowly over his head like a hatchet.

"Don't you dare hurt my mother," Diana ordered, as if she were discovering the words. Guillermo flicked the stunner lightly at her and she cried and fell away.

"Here's the coder." Guillermo held a hand controller out to Iris. "Turn off the Basement. Or you die." He shoved it under her chin and lifted her face with it. His hand moved and Iris's chin shot up, her teeth clacking together. I smelled burned skin.

He wanted to degrade her. Pain was secondary. Pain was temporary. Enduring pain stoically was brave. Humiliation, debasement, abject groveling—these were permanent.

I shifted my weight forward but Calpurnia saw the action and leveled her stunner at me. "Nah-*uhh,*" she warbled.

"Iris!" I shouted desperately. "Do it! What difference does it make?" Just a few moments, I thought desperately at her, placate him for just a few more moments.

Guillermo's head swung toward me in astonishment and satisfaction. Iris saw the movement, saw Guillermo swell.

Her hands came up to her jaw. She half-stood. Still clutching her head in agony, she stumbled blindly forward.

Guillermo relaxed, leaning away from her.

Iris leaped for him, her big gold stickpin flashing, clutched in her fist like a brass knuckles. Of course, I thought, that large sensible unattractive fastener. She *did* realize what it could be used for.

"Jesus Chr-aah!" shouted Guillermo. Iris's pick caught the side of his throat, gouged deep into the soft skin near his larynx. He fell, madly waving his stunner, as Calpurnia crashed onto Iris.

Guillermo was rolling away, his hands at his throat. Behind him I heard three massive thuds as Calpurnia's fists descended. As I moved, he staggered to his feet, the stunner bearing on me. A jagged wound flowed bright red blood between his fingers as he coughed and gagged, Iris's stickpin clutched in his left hand. Slowly he recovered his balance and stumbled over to where Calpurnia had wrenched Iris into an awkward kneeling position. Both of her arms were pulled almost out of their sockets behind her.

"You didn't search her, you bitch," Guillermo hissed at Calpurnia.

"I stripped her and scanned for electronics, but—"

"Shut up." Dropping the pin, Guillermo lifted the vocontroller and shoved it with a clack into Iris's teeth. "Talk," he ordered, his voice a wet rasp from swallowing blood. "Now. Or she dies."

Iris looked at Diana, at Guillermo, at me, her torso quaking and heaving with indecision. She sagged in Calpurnia's grasp as if crucified.

She's beaten, I thought. He's torched her soul. She'll never be the same again.

"This . . . Sherwood," she said, panting. Her eyes and lips were the only things that moved in her ruined and tortured face. She choked and stopped.

Guillermo curled over her as if shielding her. She feebly tried to push the controller away but he guided it roughly back to her mouth.

Iris looked over it at Diana and mumbled words.

Bot eyes poured from the ceiling like clattering hail, their lenses cracking. Guillermo half-stood and swung rapidly around, his arms rising like a drought farmer who has just felt the first few drops of rain.

Beside him, Iris collapsed.

"Mother!" Diana lurched for her.

She tilted sideways, her body totally flaccid. The controller skittered loose as more bot paraphernalia pelted us from above.

"What's happening?" shouted Guillermo in confusion. He wheeled on Diana. "What's she done to herself?" He grabbed Iris's armpit and shook her, her head bobbing on a loose neck. "She's dead!" He pushed Iris away and she flopped like a broken doll. "She's dead! Why is the Butcher dead?"

Diana gazed in total shock at her mother. "She told me the Targives had fixed her," she whispered. "I forgot."

A deathbomb. Iris built a deathbomb into herself. Yet, even knowing what would detonate it, she had ordered her eyes to fall. With her final act she had humanized herself, become the mother she had tried so hard to be. She had put her duty to her daughter ahead of her duty to the City. Now both were betrayed. Who had Iris sacrificed herself for? For me? For Diana? For herself?

Guillermo straightened and thoughtfully adjusted the setting on his stunner. "You forgot." He brought it to bear on Diana. "You're no longer of use," he said almost to himself.

My feet seemed anchored in molasses, my muscles made of putty. The stunner was impossibly far away, Guillermo's hand tightening all too quickly on it. As I sprang for him, screaming like a kamikaze, I knew for certain that I would not reach him before he burned her.

His fire caught me across the abdomen and my legs turned to jelly as the beam blew out cells and capillaries, but as my torso fell, the force was diffused by whatever mysterious substance Ksaksos had added to the cast. My heart clutched and I crashed to the ground, paralyzed but alive.

Guillermo swaggered over. "Here it comes," he said, handling the stunner.

A brown blur dropped from the ceiling onto his neck.

Blood spouted like a garden hose, splattering Guillermo's cheeks and chest. He fell to the floor, rolling on his back trying to squash the thing behind him, but then his eyes bulged and rolled up. Dozens more brown and gold blurs attacked.

The stunner rolled free and I crawled stiffly toward it as it skidded across the floor.

Calpurnia's stunner was wildly blasting at full disruption in every direction, splattering Phneri into explosions of fur and blood, but the small toothy creatures kept coming from all sides, heedless of the toll she was taking on them. They had a job to do.

I reached Guillermo's discarded weapon and rolled clumsily, came to a sitting position, and swung the beam around, looking for a target.

Guillermo, Calpurnia, and Iris were totally still. Dead Phneri littered the floor. Other Phneri sat next to each human corpse, their hands up, blinking cheerfully.

Diana was motionless, aghast, even her eyes immobile.

The Phneri whistled to one another, then turned away from us. Some spirited off their fallen warrenmates; others clustered animatedly around each human body. Whistles and chitters sounded as they flexed the limbs with quick decisive movements.

I hauled myself over to Diana. "Are you all right?"

Her jaw was vibrating and her mouth was full of red foam. "Who—What—?"

I slapped her face, once, twice. "Are you all right?"

She swallowed and nodded. "Why did mother die?"

"To save you," I replied, not knowing if it was the truth.

After a moment the Phneri pulled away from the bodies, surrounding each in a ring of small servants, their hands perched together.

Calpurnia's head was shredded as if by hundreds of fish hooks. Her eyelids were punctured, her hands—drawn up in a futile effort to cover her face—drilled and pitted, the skin hanging in irregular strips that exposed whitish gristle. Her big body had collapsed like punctured bread dough.

My partner wriggled from underneath Guillermo's corpse, where blood still flowed into widening sticky puddles, and scampered over to me. His eyes were bright. "I rip his throat out!" he shouted, raising both bloodsoaked arms in delight. "Whee!"

"Akktri!" I called fearfully.

"Good k-k-kill!" he jabbered, berserk. "Good k-k-kill!"

I picked him up and shook him. "Akktri!"

"Beverlee?" My partner sneezed and blinked. "Beverlee. Put me down."

I released him and he hunched his shoulders and hands into his normal attentive posture.

"I could not wait more," he said. His teeth and muzzle were soaked with dark brown blood. It had sopped into his fur. "Diana was dead in her future. Guillermo ends her. I rip his throat out." He slashed his claws. Flecks of blood hit my

252 ■ DAVID ALEXANDER SMITH

lips. "I wait until Guillermo is k-k-complete. He is a stupid hurtful man who does his most stupidest thing. Ending him is artful."

So that was what had wrecked my plan. The Phneri had taken my sweater, rich with Diana's esfn, and found the soil that matched it. They had tracked back to that soil, defeating Guillermo's precautions by coming their own way, seeing in a Phneri way. All was as I had planned, as I had hoped. Against my better judgment, I had brought Iris into the Basement, believing that we could stall Guillermo until the Phneri closed in. But Akktri and his mates had stopped, judging the art of his life, and had executed him only when he had defined himself properly enough to satisfy their incomprehensible Phneri esthetic sense.

There was no point arguing about it now. Akktri would never understand. Besides, he had just saved my life. "What about Iris?" I asked finally.

"Iris?" My partner was approving. "Iris ends herself with art."

"I don't understand."

"Iris hurts herself to feel good." Akktri's whiskers whiffled. "Hurts herself to prove she is honorable. Iris can love Diana by hurts herself to end. Is good end. We k-k-kill her if she does not."

"You *wanted* her to die," I said, appalled.

"She wants to die, Beverlee. We lik-k-ke her die."

"Akktri! You'd have *murdered* her?"

"Beverlee, she ends good," said my partner, puzzled. "Good ends is ok-k-kay?"

I gazed at the scientific, knowledgeable carnage the Phneri had wrought, the precision with which they had attacked. The claws of Akktri's left hand had caught Guillermo in the side of the neck, tearing out the carotid artery. Then, as centrifugal force had swung him around, he had expertly punctured the neck to slice the spinal column right between two vertebrae. As Guillermo's corpse fell, Akktri had released and reoriented himself to land lightly on the floor, dodging the body that collapsed over him.

All in the blink of an eye.

"It's okay, partner," I said dully, retreating in confusion.

Diana had limped over to her mother. "I was never good enough," she sobbed. "Oh, Mama, I'm sorry." She sank to her knees, lifted Iris's torso, and cradled her mother to her chest. The gray bony head was intact, the eyes open but blank.

"The hairpin," I said, pointing to the gold glinting on the floor. Guillermo's blood caked it. "Take it. She wanted you to have it."

"She did?" whispered Diana as if reluctant to move.

I bent and lifted it. Putting it into Diana's hand, I closed her fingers over it. "Yes." I put my hand gently on her shoulder and she let me guide her away. "She tried. She did everything she could. Honor her for that."

"It's *disgusting*." Diana threw the pin away from her.

I almost hit her, but instead limped slowly over to it and picked it from the dirt into which it had fallen. I felt the rage a Phner feels when the art of death is wasted, savored the rightness of my anger. "Take this," I ordered, bringing it to her and holding it close to her eyes. "I want it for myself, but it belongs to you. Take it in your mother's memory. *Take it.*"

Cowering, she complied. I do not know what I would have done to her if she had refused.

"Guillermo," she said, pulling herself free from my grasp. "I have to see him."

The Phneri had slit the skin of his face into a checkerboard, half the squares untouched, the other half flayed red. They were examining loose limp rectangles of skin like holoslides.

They had taken Guillermo and cut him apart as if for an anatomy lesson. All the tendons in his forearms had been carefully separated from the muscles and spread in a fan, each the same angle from the others. Two Phneri had removed his shoes and were cutting open his left foot, unpeeling ligaments, lifting out the tarsal bones and laying them in a grid graded by size and color.

"He tried to kill me," Diana said.

"Yes."

"He never cared about me at all." She began to weep.

"No."

"He just hated my mother."

I nodded.

Weeping, she kicked his head, which snapped to the side. Diana's foot smashed him again. Bones, newly bent into unfamiliar shapes, cracked with loud pops. The skin tore and curled back. The Phneri, agitated but enthralled, drew closer in appreciation.

Akktri examined the scene with immense satisfaction. His warrenmates clustered around, jabbering in Phner and pointing out features of their massacre. A pair of them had wedged Calpurnia's mouth open and were prying at the fillings in her teeth. They had already cut away the lips and cheeks, the better to study the mandibles.

On a misty night sixty years ago, Akktri's ancestors had landed in my grandmother's neighborhood. I'd scoffed at tales of dismembered children, dismissed them as hysterical boogeyman bedtime stories. I was a fool.

Akktri knew what had happened that night. All Phneri remember the Endless Fall. They were all Guillermo's killers. Every one of them.

And my saviors, I thought, troubled. Every one of them.

As I was the murderer of Ekkikka Phner. And they all remembered and felt it. Every one of them.

Several more Phneri were fashioning a death mask for Iris from Basement mud. Next to it was a detailed model of the Boston Cube. Beyond lay a reconstruction of my face and arm, a pistol in my hand as I fired at Ifraim Lemos.

And Billy's face. My weapon was pointed at my father. His eyes were rolled up. His mouth was open as if to scream. His hands, rising from the floor, clawed space.

Akktri saw me see Billy. He watched me sink to my knees before the sculpture. He said nothing, but his brown eyes observed, and I felt uncomfortably as if he could read my mind. The past's truths lay behind those unreadable eyes, but I knew he would never tell me. He had allowed me to treat him as a cuddly pet, despite what he or his warren or his warren's warren had done.

They had done all of this, and Akktri had approved.

Would I let him sleep on my bed curled in a ball near my feet? Could I?

"You had no trouble finding us from the mud on Diana's sweater," I said when it was artful to cut the rope of silence between us.

"Beverlee brings us!" cackled Akktri. "We hunt through Cube, all through Basement"—he spread his short arms and happily waved them—"and find mud close. We know all mud in City. As it is. We remember where Diana's sweater is been." He shrugged in perfect imitation of the smug gesture Iris had used on us hours before. "We find you." He rubbed his hands rapidly together like a squirrel. "Easy, easy."

Diana swiveled her head toward me like death denied. Her eyes, set far into her skull, were rimmed with dark circles. "Your friend," she slurred, though whether it was a compliment or a curse I dared not ask.

"My partner," I answered uncertainly.

Ksaksos hustled over, her paws and face covered with blood. Her eyes were those of an avenging killer. I wondered if Saint Michael's eyes had held such ferocity as he confronted the defeated Lucifer. "You owe us more now, Beverlee O'Meara," she said, pronouncing my name exactly as Akktri does.

Behind her the other Phneri were disappearing into the crevices, vanishing like water down a drain, their work done, returning to the warren to remember this good kill and enjoy it over and over.

"You owe us more," Ksaksos repeated, glaring at me as she waited for acknowledgment.

I doubted I could ever satisfy her. What would she demand in payment? When? If ever in my lifetime. Race memory is forever. Esfn is forever.

I bowed formally and said, "I owe you more. As it is."

Diana watched all this with wise dead eyes that had seen too much and burned out their sockets. "Please," she said slowly, "take me to a hospital."

We struggled to our feet and left.

20

I KNEW THE way back to the mover. The walk was short.

"She chose me," said Diana, shell-shocked. "She's dead. She was fallible and cold." Each sentence was paced, a separate revelation, doubted even now. "But she died to protect me." She lifted her hand and examined the bloody stickpin. "She *was* my mother."

God applauded when Abraham was willing to sacrifice Isaac for his faith. Iris had sacrificed duty and herself for her daughter, and I was proud of her.

"That was my fault," Diana went on.

"Yes, it was," I replied shortly. My well of sympathy for her was drained.

Diana's jaw tightened. "You're too quick with your mouth. *You* didn't have her for a mother. You didn't feel driven to do *this.*" She waved her stump under my nose.

I started to argue, then swallowed it. Why bicker over the dead? Iris and I had each done what we thought was right, and we had suffered.

The two of us limped, our legs still rubbery from the stunners. We breathed heavily but kept moving. If we sat down we'd both pass out.

Akktri scampered ahead, frequently looking back or waiting. When he reached the mover, he summoned it and we fell gratefully inside.

"Mass Gen—" I croaked, my voice scratchy and phlegmy. I stopped, cleared my throat, and spat in the corner. "Mass General. Emergency."

When the mover doors shucked open a few moments later into the frenetic bustle of an emergency room, the white coats took one look at us and galvanized into adroit motion. Once the mechanical gurney was wheeling Diana away, the doctor, a short dark-eyed woman with curly black hair, squinted skeptically at me, as if clucking to herself. "What about you?" she asked.

My head hurt. My ribs ached. Sweat had worked cribbles of grunge under my armpits. "I'm all right," I said.

"No, you're not." She shook her head, as if my presence were an embarrassment to us both. "You tore cartilage around those cracked ribs under your armor. You've got fifteen percent cutaneous capillary rupture from a series of stunner hits. Must sting like blue blazes. And you're——"

I protested weakly with my hands. "I'd rather be home in bed."

The doctor raised her shoulders and let them fall. "You're crazy, but I won't admit you if you don't want me to. Adios."

Akktri led me away. "Diana should be die too," he said reflectively. "We think-k-k of her end before we go. Diana's end is art-f-ful because she is a child. We want to end her. But"——he lifted his shoulders and dropped them exactly as the doctor had done——"she changes herself. So we live her."

"You'd have killed *her* too?" I asked slowly, convinced that I had misunderstood my partner.

Akktri saw my posture. "No, Beverlee," he answered meekly. "Of k-k-course not."

I had heard Akktri use that tone a hundred times before and always missed its implications. This time I stopped and squatted, bringing myself eye-to-eye with him. "You and your warren made a sculpture of my father. Was that from life?"

"Yes, Beverlee."

"From an esfnai? What moment were you esfn'ing?"

"When he ends," my partner answered as if this were self-evident. The moment when life becomes art.

"All you Phneri remember when he ends?"

"Yes, Beverlee," he said bashfully.

"You know how he died? Where he died?"

Akktri was strangely reluctant. "Yes."

"Can you take me there?"

"Yes-s-s."

There was only one more question to ask, and I knew what its answer would be: the same answer there had always been, if I had ever had the courage to ask Akktri before. My partner waited, watching me, esfn'ing me.

I licked my lips and asked, "Will you show me the place?"

In a Level 9 corridor like any other, a crash door led into a rising stairwell. "Here, Beverlee." Akktri pointed to a landing where the stairway turned a right angle. An olive-green steel balustrade rose counterclockwise into higher levels.

"This is where my father died?" When Akktri nodded, I said grimly, "Show me how."

Akktri's body seized. His head wobbled. His hands began to describe aimless arcs in space. He hauled himself upright and lurched from side to side, his feet shuffling awkwardly against the stairs, banging the steps or slipping off them. He was stinking drunk, falling-down drunk, comatose drunk.

From his throat issued a sound like water rising. Akktri started, his feet recoiling as if shocked from the cold seeping into unseen socks. He splashed, blinked his eyes, and then hacked out a sneeze that turned into spasms of harsh coughs. Clutching his chest, he bent over, groping for the balustrade, sinking back into a lumpy seated position on the landing.

He lolled on his back, the risers bracing him, sniffling and crying, muttering unintelligible imprecations.

"No," I said faintly, taking a hesitant step toward him. "Not like this. This can't be right."

Akktri swung his head back and forth, snorting to clear it of the water that must have been flooding up it. Grunting formless groans and mumbles, he struggled onto his hands and knees, gagging and spitting, trying to claw his way up above the surface of the water. He rose, fell back, rose again, his arms and legs flailing spasmodically all the while. Now he was turning his face upward as if away from the fast-rising flood, his neck twisting as his head pressed against an overhang where the stairs turned left and up.

He gasped and choked.

His mouth opened to scream.

His hands rose, scraping against the concrete ledge.

His face contorted into Billy's agony. It was the same face the Phneri had sculpted from the Basement mud, the face they had fashioned next to their image of myself. He had tried to crawl, riser by riser, but had been caught under a landing and been too drunk and brain-addled to save himself as the water lifted him, up and up, until his face was jammed against the airless cement. If he'd been clearheaded then, he would still be alive. It had not been Iris's fault he died. *It had been his own.* "Oh, Jesus," I whispered.

Akktri froze, then sagged away, his body collapsing, limp, inert, motionless.

Kneeling before him, I cried.

I put my head into my hands and I wept, calling my father's name over and over, the tears running through my fingers onto my trembling lips. Time ceased, the stairway vanished, and I was alone with my hideous memories, my father dying because there was no one to help him, my father to whom I had never said good-bye.

"Come, my Beverlee," said Akktri in his own voice. A small hand touched mine. It drew my right hand away from my face. "I tak-k-ke you home."

I didn't recover until we were passing those putrid green columns in my corridor at 15 Fed 70. I stepped into my apt and stopped.

It was clean, neat. My furniture seemed familiar yet new. This is a wooden swivel chair? What a clever invention. I collapsed in it before my desk.

Home. Fatigue hit me in the head like a bag of cement and I grasped the desk's knurled oak moulding to steady myself. The divots under my fingers were familiar, comfortable. How long had I gone without proper sleep? Thirty hours? Forty? I crossed my arms over the closed, ribbed rolltop and rested my head on them, nuzzling my cheek into my forearm. Just for a minute.

Akktri leaped onto the desk to my left, settling himself like a mophead. "Open desk," he chirped, and tapped the wood with his claws. "Open desk-k-k."

"Why?" I slid the cover back into its recess and lifted an oversize sheet of thick creamy paper. "Oh, sweet baby Jesus."

The paper's edges and borders were fresh and new, but inside them someone had fashioned a prematurely aged rectangle on which was engraved a delicate tracing of lines.

Streets, wards, buildings, bridges, and piers.

My 1855 map was coming to life. Akktri had completed all the lineaments, even to the filigree border and the ornate serifed captions, and was starting the coloration. A few polygons of pale green had bloomed among the natural buff yellow: East Boston, the Charlestown Navy Yard, the South Boston Lunatic Asylum and House of Reformation. Nearby stood small bottles of pink, yellow, and blue tinctures.

I held the precious thing in my hands like a newborn baby, treasuring Akktri. How could I ever be worthy of such a friend?

Using my fingertips to hold the reconstituted map by its edges, I sat lightly on my bed. "You did this for me," I murmured in awe.

South Boston Bay was shaded with drawn-in concentric lines like isobars. I touched the Mill Dam and Western Avenue across Back Bay's vanished waters, saw the prong of the Rope Walk, the inlet curve of Roxbury Canal. Pieces of Boston's history now buried under our relentless infill.

"It's beautiful, partner," I said thickly, and ran my finger along the narrow grooved slats. "This frame was just a cheap relic I picked up at an estate auction on Level 7. You didn't need to duplicate that."

"Frame is part of map," Akktri insisted. He crept up to it like a ferret at a burrow, his hands before him as his whiskers waved, caressing the edges. "Body is part of soul. Frame holds map. Rug holds pattern."

I reached for him to draw him close. Then I remembered Guillermo Rey's blood flying from his body and Calpurnia's ravaged corpse. My partner, purring and giggling, had rolled onto his back so his hands and feet stuck up at me. They were crusted with brown dried blood. His teeth had pink slivers between them. Human skin. I tried hard to forget that.

"You lift me away from you," said Akktri uncertainly, opening his eyes and craning his neck.

"You're dirty. You need a bath." I shoved my chair back, stood, and headed into the bathroom.

But he stayed behind. "Leave my art on," he peeped.

I returned to him and squatted. "Partner," I said gently, "it hurts me to see the blood."

"You do not lik-k-ke killing Guillermo?" asked Akktri uncertainly. "Should Guillermo not end?"

I cupped my hands over my mouth and nose and breathed several times. "I only want to end—my upset," I said finally. "I want to forget what we saw. What we did."

"Death is forever," he said. "Forgetting does not change it."

"You're right. I know you're right." I wiped my mouth, distraught. "But—as my friend—will you wash?"

"Humans is goofy. But I am your friend," Akktri said. "I mak-k-ke this art for Beverlee. I end this art for Beverlee. I wash. I wash with Beverlee."

"Thank you, partner."

I laid Akktri in the tub, turned on the water, stripped, and got in with him. A dark misty streamer of blood and dirt like a comet's tail flowed from his fur down the drain as I scrubbed. I took out my frustrations in soaping him thoroughly, digging in his ears, even picking him up and thrusting his face right under the shower head so the spray hit his bloody teeth.

"Hee hee." Akktri snickered, his small black nose alert, whiffling and snorting breath through the steamy rainstorm. His arms and legs were splayed in indolent childlike relaxation. He dandled in my grip, watching the pattern of colors run off his fur, dance in the rivulets of water, and spiral down the drain.

"You want to k-k-keep the shedflies?" Akktri plucked one of the loathsome creatures off my body and held it too close to my nose.

"Why would I want to do that?"

Akktri precisely replaced the creature in my armpit. "Flies and lice are part of ek-k-xperience. I keep them after we end If-f-fraim but you tak-k-ke them off me before, so——?" He shrugged with a Mack gesture of indifference.

"Remove them," I said weakly. Akktri tries so hard to understand human squeamishness. "End them. I want to be clean."

When he was done, I scoured myself. Off came the blood, the dirt, the clivus slime. My thighs and calves were splotched carnelian and lavender from the stunner shots. Akktri watched me and I was pleased he did, for we two understood the meaning of that dirt, that blood, that grime. They were our vestments. I squatted and cleaned crud from between my toes, thinking of Charles Beaufort bathing me in this shower only a few hours before. The thought warmed me and my spirits rose as I gradually cleansed and rehumanized myself.

Setting Akktri down, I tossed a towel at him. He instantly flipped onto his back and caught it by all four corners, one in each hand and foot, stretching the sides taut like a trampoline. He chittered, rocking and arching his back, and then, with a pirouette quicker than my eyes could follow, spun and wrapped himself in it, mimicking my after-bath posture.

Wearing the towel like a fluffy bathrobe, he sashayed

toward me the way I do when I'm feeling pretty and no one is around.

I tried to smile but it was tight.

Akktri slowed, his shoulders drooping, and regarded me. With a shiver, he drew his body into a different shape and became Ksaksos, the Phneri warren leader. The towel draped around his shoulders like a priest's cowl. "You fear me, Beverlee. You fear all Phneri."

"Yes." He deserved the truth. I squatted, then sat cross-legged.

Akktri drew the lapels of his towel closer to his small receding chin. "Because of how we k-k-kill Guillermo?"

I nodded.

"Because I rip his throat out." He gestured, the claws slick and fast as cracking glass.

"Yes."

He looked me up and down, considering, his whiskers bobbing like antennae. "You owe us now. Ksak-k-ksos says and you agree."

"Yes." There was no denying my commitment.

"Is our future same?" he asked in his own voice, not Ksaksos's. "Akktri's and Beverlee's?"

I looked at his anxious dark eyes. No whites cushioned them against his thick furry eyelids. "Partner, I don't want to be afraid of you."

"Lik-k-ke now you are afraid?"

I nodded somberly. "Like now."

His body seemed to retreat down a long tunnel except for his unreadable small eyes, flat and black as buttons. I checked my desire to speak. We had to deal with this. As Akktri says, now is always.

Finally my partner shrugged. "As it is. Chuck-k-k is here."

"What?" I blinked. "I don't understand."

Akktri whipped off the towel and twirled it above his head like a lasso. "Chuck-k-k Beaufort comes." He nodded at the door. "His footsteps come." He drew the towel around his shoulders like a shawl against the cold as I crossed to the door and opened it.

Charles stood like a dream in the doorway, clean and strong. "You're alive," he breathed with relief.

"Sort of." I swayed at the sight of him and he stepped forward, grasping my tired biceps in his hands. I laid my head against his chest. All the fatigue and pain that I had experienced suddenly transformed itself into a desperate desire. "I want you," I murmured as his arms enfolded me. "Now. This minute." I reached behind his neck and drew his mouth down, silencing him with a long, deep kiss.

"Where's the bed?" he asked huskily when I let his lips go.

"I'll point. You carry."

I lay on my back, every muscle relaxed, feeling the tangy chill of sweat drying on my arms, bare belly, and legs. For the first time I regretted my chest brace, which had prevented Charles from massaging my breasts. My toes tingled pleasantly. "Mmmm," I said, hugging myself and running my hands along my flanks below my torso armor. My eyes were heavy as if weighted with flannel blankets. "That was a great fuck . . . Charles."

He rolled onto his back and laughed, his hands gripping his taut muscular abdomen. Naked but for his watch, which somehow he'd not found time to remove, he was angular and strong with muscles like ropes. He propped his head on his hand and thumped my Phneri-built chest protector, my only clothing. "Next time I'll want this off," he said with drowsy contentment.

"It has to stay on six weeks." I stretched, the brace squeezing my armpits as I breathed deeply.

"I can't wait that long."

"We'll manage." I leaned forward to kiss his nose. It had been a wonderful romp and a blissful nap afterward, but it was time for some home truths. I groped around on the floor for my discarded clothing and struggled into my underwear and shirt. Looking appreciatively at his indolent long body as if taking the last bite of a delicious dessert, I strapped on my sheath, withdrew the knife, and laid it in my palm where he could not see it. "Who's paying you?" I asked, my throat dry.

"Paying?" He yawned. "To do what?"

"This. Seducing me." I gestured at his stretched-out nudity. "Guillermo was hired to seduce Diana. Who hired *you*, Chuck? The same person? Why?"

He sat up, angry. "Is your self-opinion so low that you automatically assume no one will sleep with you? That's twisted." Charles stood and began hunting for his trousers.

"Stay where you are. Move away from your clothing."

"Bev, you're making—" He saw the knife then, and licked his lips. "What are you doing with that?"

"You were a spy in Iris's office."

"A spy?" He was attempting sarcasm but I could hear the apprehension. "What makes you think so?" He could not withdraw his eyes from the knife blade. I moved it lazily to and fro.

"After I fell through the City, Guillermo Rey was waiting for me. He knew *exactly* where I'd emerge. That wasn't top net news. How'd he know it?"

Charles held his shirt at arm's length, shook it to show that nothing was concealed within, then without taking his eyes from mine slid his arms into it, and ran its seams together. I did not like these movements; they were too knowledgeable, too careful. "Anyone could have known."

"No," I said flatly. "Iris had reprogrammed a fall route for me. I had no idea where I was."

"Your Master Key gave your location," he responded immediately.

"Sure. And it was *Iris's* key. Only two people were in a position to know where that key was. Iris Sherwood, the bot lady. And her faithful assistant, Charles Beaufort." I looked at him, my heart melting, but kept my face closed.

"Well, then," he said, trying to rally, "Iris must have told someone."

"Miz Secrecy herself spill the beans about her daughter? Impossible. And there's much more evidence. You went to Boston Garden. You confronted Guillermo Rey and argued with him."

"On Iris's instructions. She told me that—"

"Charles, stop lying," I said with a snap. "Iris hadn't seen you in hours. She told me so later. Even earlier, at my first encounter with Guillermo, way back in Louisburg School, he said, 'Tell your client Iris.' He *knew* who I was working for."

His hands were flapping in agitation. "You must have told him."

"No. At the time I was pretending to be someone else. How could he know so quickly who was employing me? Chris Tolliver never had a chance to tell him. Who else but you?"

"There *must* have been somebody else."

"The coincidences kept piling up," I rolled on. "When I got arrested, *you* conveniently showed up, claiming Iris's authorization. Your boss didn't know about that. After I got out of the Basement, you thoughtfully brought me a second Master Key. She didn't authorize that either. *You* did it, because you had orders to keep me traceable. That was why you wanted me to have it; it was my beeper. You were my guardian angel. Disgusting." I ran my hand through my rumpled red hair. "Charles, it's bad enough that you've tricked and betrayed Iris. Don't lie to me now."

He held his wadded clothing over his groin. "Have you told these suspicions to anyone?"

"I only put it together as Diana and I were walking out of the Basement." I made a tired gesture with the knife. "Iris is dead. Diana's safe. Charles, Charles," I said in despair, "how could you use me that way? I should have suspected you. Pretending to find me attractive." I hated myself for my gullibility. I had been so blind. "You've lied to me from the first moment we met. Why?"

I waited an eternity. Then he rolled his hand over, a small gesture that held in it more confession and plea for mercy than any words. I bled inside to see my suspicions confirmed. "I reported what you did," he said in a low voice, his lips twisted. "Where you went." He sat on the bed. "But I wasn't ordered to sleep with you. That I did on my own initiative." He tried his boyish grin but it was shallow and trivial and after a moment he had the good sense to refold it and put it away.

"How can I believe that?"

"I wanted to tell you eventually." Still clinging to his trousers, he stood, trying to confront me, but his face was filled with shame. "Spying on Iris—that made no difference, just a bureaucratic power struggle like knights jousting. A symbolic winner and a loser but no real hurt. But then it got mean." His face darkened and his brows drew together. "That boy Butch. Diana's severed finger." His handsome mouth summoned up an expression of grief. He closed his eyes and his breath shuddered. "What Guillermo did to you." The expressions moved, one into the other, with integrated-circuit precision.

Despite myself, I wanted to believe him. I feared that. "Some of what you claim to have felt may be genuine. So what? What did you do about these tortured emotions of yours?" My tone was heavy with sarcasm.

"I *had* to follow through," he said in a rush, eager now to confess. "I'm glad you've found me out."

"You're culpable in Iris's death and Diana's mutilation," I said bluntly. "You're an accessory before the fact. Who could make you do that? Who owns you?"

He was cowed into answering. "An—important individual," he said in a pathetic attempt at evasion.

"You had personal contact?"

"Yes." He wriggled uncomfortably but kept his place.

"You met face-to-face?"

He nodded.

"Good," I said with satisfaction. "I know who it is."

His head came up and he blinked. "You do? How?"

"That person made a huge mistake." For the first time I smiled, then frowned. "But I've got no proof. *You're* my proof. You will do as I say. And of course"——I paused and looked significantly at him—"judges and pols are kinder to small fry who help land the big fish."

He colored, evidently disliking my characterization, but had the prudence not to challenge me. "I'll be humiliated," he said in a tone that suggested manful containment of self-pity.

His vanity made me chuckle. "That's the *least* of your problems, Chuck. Right now you're a favorite for a long jail term."

That sobered him. "And if I don't?" he asked with a misera-ble pleading tone of voice that I recognized as one I used to use. "What will you do?"

It was on the tip of my tongue to bludgeon him. It would have been so easy. My artillery had softened his morale, de-stroyed his defenses. He was weak, ready to fold. One more threat, suitably rough and callous, and he would topple. It was right there for me.

"Nothing," I said after a moment, sliding my knife back into its sheath, but leaving my trouser leg rolled up. I had had enough of deception and manipulation. Down that slippery slope I would not go. "Nothing at all, Charles. You'd just have to live with yourself afterward." But I stayed well beyond even his lunging reach.

"You'd let me go?" He was disbelieving.

I shrugged. There was no way to explain. "Call me a romantic."

Charles looked for a long time at his hands. "All right."

"Tell me again what you did *right* in this case," Roderick Petravelli said after I'd related what had happened in the Basement. He rolled his chromium dumbbells up and down his wrists. "It seems to have slipped my mind." He recited my alleged incompetences. I let him talk without interrupting.

"Still." Petravelli placed the two dumbbells together on his

gleaming crystal desk and neatly aligned their ends. He scruti-
nized them, admiring his silver-headed reflection in their pol-
ished convex surfaces. "Despite all your efforts, we have a
satisfactory resolution. Guillermo Rey is discredited as a taw-
dry kidnapper, torturer, and hoodlum. Who wants to follow a
dead nut who made hot dogs out of people's fingers?"

"That's damn crude."

"Too bad about the daughter," Petravelli went on, unruffled. "Still, the Targives can fix anything. Yes, it's all tidy now."
He nodded curtly. It was a dismissal.

I got up, then paused at the door. "Guillermo Rey claimed
he knew you."

Petravelli chuckled. *"Highly* reliable testimony."

"You had no contact with him? None at all?"

He tapped his infomat. "No, nothing." He stuck out his
lower lip, reading over his nose. "A record of juvenile proba-
tionary offenses. I have never seen Guillermo Rey before."
Though I'd been deliberately pronouncing the name wrong,
Roderick said it right.

"That's funny. You gave him an award."

He was uninterested. "I did?"

"There's a holo of the event on Chris Tolliver's office wall.
Akktri says the figures in it know one another well."

"Phneri testimony on motivation and intent is completely
inadmissible and given no credence."

"Can you deny you know him?"

"Spare me the histrionics. A man in my position shakes
thousands of hands, grants hundreds of indulgences. You
can't expect me to remember them all."

"You're right. I'm wasting my time. But where'd Guillermo
get his key?" I asked, turning back into the room.

"What key?"

"Guillermo fled from the Artery up above Level 150. That's
limited access. He opened an emergency exterior door and
vanished through it onto the roof. I was too busy trying not to
die to think about it then, but later I asked myself, where'd he

get that key? Only city officials can issue them. What does your data base say about it?" I crossed behind his right shoulder, inside his circle of defense, so I could watch his actions.

Too distracted to order me away, Petravelli tapped his infomat. "The key that opened that door is unknown," he read off the screen. "The authorization and identification fields are blank."

"Isn't that interesting?" I strolled in front of his desk and leaned against it. "Why did you think Akktri was dead?"

Petravelli stilled just a touch. "I beg your pardon?"

"When I got out of the Basement, I reported in to you." I bit my thumbnail as if in thought. "Do you remember the first thing you said? You offered condolences about Akktri. You said he was dead. But he was alive."

Petravelli let exasperation show. "Hell, you thought so too."

"That was just Guillermo's lie to provoke me. It worked, too." I moved closer until I stood leaning over his desk, my good right hand on its immaculate surface. "I charged over the balcony. Iris knew he was lying. She tried to tell me so but I didn't hear her. If Iris knows something, it's because her eyes told her. The only person who'd claim Akktri was dead was Guillermo. So why did *you* think so? Guillermo always was fond of his lies," I went on over his beginning interruption. "His little fantasies. He enjoyed this one so much he must have repeated it to you. And you repeated it to me. So you obviously talked with him in between. When and how?"

I've never seen a human being hold himself as tightly in check as Petravelli then did, conscious as he was of the eyes that might even now be feeding this conversation to Ulkudge. He must have been a brilliant poker player. His brown face was still and immobile as if carved from ironwood. Only his fingers moved, curling and uncurling as if they still held the chrome dumbbells. His eyes were unfocused.

"This interview is over," he said. "You're making no sense. And stop smearing my desk."

"I'm not finished yet," I said. "To make your plan work, you needed someone close to Diana. And so you searched for Guillermo." I ran my fingertips along the clear crystal surface. Retaliation for spooking Akktri. "Was he already a student at Louisburg, or did you swing that too?" His eyelids flickered at that and I knew I'd scored. "Chris Tolliver can probably draw that link for us. You see, you *knew* the only lever to Iris was her daughter." I looked at his chiseled, tanned Roman face. "So you set Guillermo on Diana."

"What nonsense. Why would I do all this?" demanded Petravelli. "Why would I care about freeing the Basement?"

"That's what stymied me for a while," I replied, seating myself comfortably. "But when Iris gave those idiotic orders Guillermo demanded, I realized it was all a giant con." I remembered my client stammering desperately into the mike, her eyes fixed on her brutalized daughter. Like a forced confession beaten from a prisoner. "Someone just wanted Iris to betray her duty on tape. When all was said and done, that's what it came down to. All the way back to the mover, I asked myself, 'Who stood to gain from that?' You do."

"You haven't proved a thing," he said with finality. "Your criteria could apply to hundreds of people in the City. You've become as paranoid as that bitch was." He stood, sucked in his stomach, and smartly pulled his vest down, smoothing the fabric over it.

"Okay, we'll let the nets decide," I said, deliberately smug to taunt and infuriate him further. "I'm going public with this."

He guffawed. "I'll break you like dry twigs." For the first time he was feeling expansive and superior. "Punch out your license. Bankrupt you. Hound you from Boston."

"I can embarrass you," I continued without ruffling.

"Cubehunter, I'm a man of principle." He sensed he had me on the run and loudly cracked his knuckles. "When people try to shake me down, I destroy them, no matter how much nuisance is involved."

"So do I, Chief. That's why I turned Charles Beaufort."

"Who?" Another flicker of eyelids—his tell. "Iris's dogs-body?"

"Your paid ear," I corrected him. "We've got his full affidavit on read. Want a copy?" Plucking the cube from my pocket, I tossed it at his lap.

He caught it awkwardly and slapped it into the reader square, then paused, refusing to activate the read, glaring at it.

"Diana said that Iris would never take anything *she* did seriously," I went on. "To destroy Iris, her antagonist had to force her out of her tower. Iris would only come for someone she loved. You couldn't hurt the administrator, so you got to the mother. Your strategic plan was brilliant, Roderick." I shook my head in reluctant admiration.

"If so, why'd I involve you at all?"

"Validation. Iris would come only if she *believed* Diana to be in danger. And she was a tough skeptic. She would accept this conclusion only from someone *she* had chosen. And that's exactly what defined my role in your production. Guillermo was just your lever to move me, as I was your lever to move Iris. Once she had picked me, no matter how randomly, I became crucial to your plan. You needed to convince *me* that the threats to Diana were real. Guillermo broke my arm simply to make a point with Iris. You were stuck with me. That's why when I quit the case, my apt was trashed within minutes."

"It was a warning to get out. You said so yourself."

"That was how it looked," I agreed. "But I had already resigned. And you knew that because Charles Beaufort had already reported. So why was it done? *To get me back in.*"

"Pretty tricky double reasoning," noted Petravelli absently. "Your vandal would have had to know what would move you."

"Oh, I've been predictable in my life," I replied sourly, grimacing. "You knew that from the start. You didn't trust me to find Guillermo for myself, so you sicced me directly onto him. Bit obvious, but I fell right for it. I'm less readable now. You and Iris have taught me deceit."

Idly, his fingers moving as if by themselves, Roderick slid the datacube into the reader. Charles Beaufort's face lit up and his mouth began to move.

"That moron," muttered Petravelli. "He'll get life for the stuff I've got on him." He watched a moment more, his jaw working, then asked, "How'd you suborn Chuck?" His eyes flicked to the screen below his hands. "Bribery? Blackmail? No, that you'd never find. Or sex?" He glanced sidways at me. "That must be it. Chuck always was guided by his warhead. You screwed him, didn't you?"

"Yeah, I fucked him silly," I said after a second.

"I was thinking poorly," he said almost to himself. "I used his libido to gain a hold on him. I should have figured some-one else might try the same thing."

"By the way," I went on, "Mayor Juarez has the whole story now."

"You told Mike?" whispered Petravelli as if to his god.

"A few minutes ago he accepted your resignation."

"My what?"

"You tendered it so that you can 'clear your name during this investigation.' Mike gives great theater. It'll be on the nets now."

If a man can die while still breathing, I saw it happen then. Petravelli aged a dozen years in the space of a breath. His cheeks paled. His eyes shrank in his head and his jaw slack-ened like a derelict's. His hands went limp as if he had been knocked unconscious. "Fired?"

"Don't look surprised, Roderick," I murmured, shrugging a little. "His polsims say he must, and Mike's always bent with the winds." I chuckled again. "He expressed 110 percent con-fidence in you and is sure that your trial will result in your complete vindication from these odious charges. And Charles has been granted immunity in return for becoming the City's star witness. Your hold over him is useless now."

"I've got rights," he spluttered, emerging from his trance into indignation. "Seniority. It'll never stick."

"Maybe. It'll make great vids, especially Baka's close-ups of your nostril hairs. But Mike shucked you once he saw the cubes and cubes that Iris left about you. Names, people, places, dates, evidence. They all downloaded when she died. You aren't the only one who built laundry files as insurance. A twenty-year trail, all captured on vid. Her bot eyes won." After all we had said and done, I found this postmortem victory comforting. "You've lost, Roderick. Lost everything."

Petravelli was in shock. He touched the datacube absently while his nearby infomat spewed out the charges in computer-crafted legalese. His right hand came up and rubbed his chin, where gray whiskers protruded, making him appear an old man whose skull had shriveled inside his skin. His left hand squeezed his right bicep.

"Why'd you do it?"

"Why?" Petravelli's mind was elsewhere. "Do what?"

I spread my hands. "Hire Guillermo. Develop this obsessed plan. What for?"

"Why?" His blue eyes focused like targeting lasers. "You pathetic moronic rugrat, you don't *know* why?"

"No, Roderick, I don't," I said softly. "Tell me."

"Iris Sherwood was everything that I hate about the Cube," he said softly. "Soulless, indifferent, automated, perverse, twisted, dehumanized, half-blind and self-fucking-righteous, no better than those sloshfoot alien spatiens she was so fond of. A startit sucker who protected rugscum and then tore apart good officers like Vinnie Akibira." Petravelli swung his arm through the air like a club, his lips pulled fiercely back, breathing rapidly as if stoking a fire. "So I brought her down," he growled, gathering himself. "I subverted her." His eyes flicked to me. "Do you know how hard it was to find the right rugrat to cultivate? Then I discovered Lem Snow's bastard son." The devil's grin is kinder than the evil leer Roderick flashed in my direction. "He was moved into position." He drew his hands together and gestured as if pushing a stack of poker chips. "I coaxed him," Roderick cooed. "I tempted him. I played him on my lead. He thought it was all his idea, all his control. That seed of ego was fed, nurtured, harvested." He was gloating now, full of himself, everything forgotten but his revenge. "And I pulled the ice queen out of her sanitized box. Turned her into something lower than those rugrats she so ostentatiously and earnestly loved. And *I* saw it. I watched her whole groveling, sniveling degradation, right here on this screen. On one of *these*." He grabbed up the datacube of Charles Beaufort's confession.

"You and Iris fought the ultimate war, Roderick," I said bleakly, standing and moving toward the door. "You both risked everything you had. And you both lost." I sighed, looked down at my hands, and then up. "Take him away."

Ulkudge, ever alert to changes in the power structure, glided in, collared her former boss, and, with a succulent sniff, gracefully hauled him from the room.

21

THE FOLDED RICE papers, still covered with dried mud and dust, rested cool in my hands, clasped behind my back as I looked onto Boston Harbor twinkling in the sunlight far below. Yesterday I had hung on the roof, naked to the elements, terrified and freezing. Now I was safely behind the Cloud Palace's floor-to-ceiling windows, the City once again perfect and unreal.

I waited, my offering concealed.

"Yes?"

Mi Nyo walked crisply across the room. As before, she was dark, compact, and patient, her manner somehow conveying that although completely ignorant of my purpose, she trusted that it was important.

"I came to return this," I said, taking my hands from behind my back and opening my palm to reveal the origami: crane, pig, frog, executed in three sheets of rice paper folded with razor-crisp edges, now dulled by water and sweat.

Mi Nyo craned her wizened brown neck slightly without moving her feet, her glance giving no indication whatsoever that the papers were familiar. "May I?" she asked, holding up one small hand. I nodded and she took the crane, lifting it by one wing, still delicate and beautiful despite crumpling and mildew.

"It's unique," I went on. Dried mud cracked and fell as she unfolded it gingerly, her careful slow movements calling forth memories of Akktri unveiling the flounder which Mack had given him. "The handwriting is your great-granddaughter's, I'm sure. Particles of her skin will also surely be on it."

She scraped off a flake of mud with her short fingernail, then glanced as if for guidance at the portrait of mustachioed bandito Sitigar Malik. The old buccaneer grinned raffishly at us. "Are you selling them?" Mi Nyo asked.

I admired the compactness of her question. She was letting me know that she had acknowledged her vulnerability, and was asking me to state my blackmail price.

"No. It's too dangerous for me to have them."

"Are there only these three?" she asked. Wise woman.

I made a noncommittal gesture with my hand. No sense revealing that just yet. "I didn't need them, of course. Even before I found these, I knew Hu was involved. The jacket Diana wore when she was abducted later turned up in her dorm room. Akktri saw Hu's recent-skin, as he calls it, on the material. Let's not fence, Mi Nyo. That's not my objective. I have no recorders on me—"

"I know," she interjected.

"—and the case is closed," I continued, nodding acknowledgment of her comment. "You are holding evidence of your great-granddaughter's involvement—notes she had written which I removed from her Cloud Palace rooms. The younger generation has learned that valuable private information is safest written down rather than stored in corruptible electronics. But Hu did not consider that her rooms, like bot reads, can be searched."

"Indeed she did not." Mi Nyo cocked her head. "Have you deciphered the writing?"

"It's in Cambodian. I have not shown them to anyone, nor even opened them. But let me guess what you have just read: a chronicle of Hu's involvement with Guillermo, probably a listing of his other felonies and how to obtain conclusive evidence, all prepared in anticipation of eventual blackmail. She wouldn't bother with misdemeanors. Your great-granddaughter is too shrewd to have had any questionable dealings with him without a deadman's lever. And what safer place to store her doomsday than her own secure, climate-protected lair?"

"Not as safe as she thought, evidently," the old woman replied, turning away from me to contemplate the glittering cold sky outside. "You realize, of course, that these small bits of Japanese art are evidence only if *you* testify where and how you obtained them and only if your testimony is believed." She tilted her neck to watch the iceboats zipping along the shoreline.

"I know that. I have no plans to become a celebrity." I grimaced and shook my head, dismissing the option.

"Then why show them to me? What do you wish?"

"Miz Nyo, your great-granddaughter was a conspirator. I don't expect you to be shocked or outraged. I don't expect you to take any action. But *why?* May I ask that, if only to satisfy my curiosity? What for?"

Mi Nyo crossed to her ornate carved rosewood desk and sat. "If you were a great nation and a civil war broke out in a neighboring country," she said, placing the three little foldings on the maroon leather blotter before her, "would you send a reporter to investigate?"

I followed her and sat in the high-backed guest chair. "Iris and Roderick?"

"They are important people." Mi Nyo nimbly refolded the crane into its former shape, the paper snuggling back among its original creases like wayward hair combed into place. She aligned it with the other two figures, then sat back and placed her fingertips together before her mouth. "You should appreciate that that is enough motivation."

"No longer," I said. "Iris is dead, Roderick disgraced and indicted."

The popcorn alien had claimed he had sold Guillermo's past to Petravelli, and Petravelli's past to Mi Nyo. Had the little maniac told the truth after all? With the popcorns, one never knows. I laid my arm on the desk and leaned over it. "You could have prevented this."

"You overestimate me." She slid her chair back, conceding no visual advantage. "When demigods battle, heaven shakes with thunder. Mortals who intervene are inevitably destroyed or maimed. As were Guillermo and Diana."

"Mi Nyo, we're talking about people's *lives,* not Olympian ritual combat." I slammed my palm flat on the desk.

"Don't do that again," she said, utterly furious but level voiced.

I felt my cheeks grow hot. "You're right. I apologize." I sat down.

"You're young," she went on, her voice lightening to microscopic friendliness. "Boston is a vast machine of several million interactive components. You see flawed output and want direct change. Natural enough. Commendable in its way. I have tried that, with results similar to your disaster. As I grow older, I am reluctant to pull the levers for fear of causing more harm. I observe more and act less."

"And the Lord said, 'What have you done? The voice of your brother's blood is crying to me from the ground.' "

Mi Nyo merely smiled at my quotation. "Fortunately I am not my sister's keeper. I had no part in Iris's death." But her eyes went to the cubist paper animals that lay between us, her hand touched her chin in thought, and the smile turned to a soft frown.

"Did Hu pass your test?" I asked after letting her reflect on this for a moment.

Mi Nyo knitted her fingers together, her hands flat on her desk, and leaned forward on her elbows, scrutinizing the origami like a chess player studying the board. "My great-granddaughter avoided detection, but left evidence that allowed a particular observer"—she flicked her glance briefly to me—"to deduce her involvement. I should call it an Incomplete."

She continued watching the paper crane closely, as if it were merely shamming and might rouse itself whenever it thought no one was looking. I tried to imagine living in a family where scheming and duplicity were daily vitamins.

"Perhaps my great-granddaughter was using these to send me a message," mused Mi Nyo. "After all, why should she so conveniently allow you to find them?"

"She didn't *allow* me. I did that on my own."

"Perhaps Hu was testing me," Mi Nyo went on without acknowledgment.

Manipulation was taken for granted in this household, love and filial duty merely coins of exchange. Iris had used Diana, but without intent or malice, and was victimized in turn by her. Mi used Hu consciously and with callous disregard for the risks, and was repaid in kind.

"Or perhaps she was testing *you*, Miz O'Meara," finished Mi Nyo, the smile in her lips unkind. "In which case it was *you* who passed. Are these all there are?"

"Yes, ma'am. I brought all three."

"You have my thanks. And you have displayed your talents before me, as you intended. Do you need anything from me?" she asked as I tried to shake the chill her words had laid on my arms.

I shook my head. "As long as I have this evidence, I feel exposed. Vulnerable. The things felt hot in my palm, as if they were sending danger signals to you. I found myself preoccupied with their whereabouts. Please. Take them back."

Mi Nyo laughed, a tinking sound like wind chimes. "Here." She lifted the crane by its long straight neck. "Give this one to your Phner partner. Let him destroy it in a clever way. He will enjoy that."

"As you wish. He *will* enjoy it." I stood and held out my hand to her. "I came simply for the satisfaction of having my guesses confirmed. What I know goes no further. On that you have my word."

"I appreciate your discretion." She came around the desk and escorted me to the door. "You know I am aware of you now," she added as the butler arrived.

Two days ago, the idea that merchant queen Mi Nyo knew my name would have rattled and floored me, as I had been intimidated by Iris's peremptory summons and Roderick Petravelli's extorted favor.

"I'll take that as a compliment," I said with a short, formal bow.

Back home, I gave the origami bird to Akktri and then moved in a dream, my mind vacant as an eviction. Sleep was impossible. My mental engines, so long overstoked, had to cool down at their own pace. I wandered among my small rooms, touching my remade 1855 Boston map, my rolltop oak desk, my white bathrobe, still in its careless, Charles Beaufort-flung heap.

I sat next to the 1855 map. The original, the one Billy had given me, was broken. I had cracked its frame myself and thrown the pieces in the wastebot. Akktri had made it anew. The holo of Billy and me would be recreated with only a slight fuzziness. Things are destroyed, things are remade. No one who looked at the map would ever know the difference. Its difference lay in my memory, because I had experienced it. For a moment I felt as if my emotions touched that state of grace which the Phneri achieved, that embracing ecstatic awareness of the transience of all things tangible, the permanence only of memory.

Akktri had shown me how my father had died. Even memories had to be broken and remade.

I took down from my bookshelves the old Aviator red diamond-back cards. Guillermo hadn't known that my dad and I'd played poker with this deck or he'd probably have shredded it.

I had memorized every dog-ear and wrinkle and could read Billy's hand from the backs of the cards. It was the way I first learned the game.

I riffled the deck and found the king of hearts, the suicide king, whose somber goateed profile always reminded me of

Billy. Then I riffled again until I found the queen of spades, the black widow, for Iris Sherwood. And the queen of clubs, the sad virgin, for myself.

Even after all this time, the loss of my father still clutched my throat with pain and grief. But his death had not been Iris's fault, as I had believed, or my fault, or even no one's fault. He had died of his own failures. I had sought knowledge of his passing and been given this. I had to learn to live with it. I did not wish to, but I had to. So, somehow, I would.

Billy was dead, Iris was dead. Had I risked my life for Iris, a woman I had grudgingly learned to respect? For Diana, a child-woman not yet formed? Of course not. Yet I still felt enormously bound to the two of them, their lives handcuffed together by that happenstance of Iris's weakness and humanity after Boston's Siege. Is all connection just coincidence and proximity?

Is all love?

I microed a brick of something red and gooey and ate it in silence, feeling selfish and miserable.

Akktri perched in ecstasy over his whole lobster, playing. Some limbs he extracted slowly, flexing the shells in all directions. Others he speedily devoured as if in a race with himself. Tragedy sluffs off a Phner's back like water off its fur.

"Partner."

Akktri read my seriousness and came to attention.

"You saved my life but . . . things between us." I stopped and wiped my mouth. "They aren't what they should be."

Akktri sucked impassively at a leg claw.

Stymied by his incomprehension, I lumbered onward. "Are things all right with you? Are we okay?"

"As it is, Beverlee. Why aren't we okay?"

How do you tell your friend that you're bigoted against his species? "I thought you were different from—other Phneri," I stammered, wincing at my own words. I thought you were a good nigger. How feeble, how shameful, to realize my own beliefs.

"I'm a Phner," Akktri answered. "We is all Phneri."

"Then I killed one of your warren. One of your race. You all esfn'ed me killing you. Akktri, you know inside your body what my bullet felt like. I can't understand that."

"Yes, Beverlee. Bad k-k-kill, no art." He shrugged. "But it is. You kill better in future."

"Then you let Iris die for the sake of your art," I staggered on. "Perhaps the two deaths are balanced. And you showed me Billy's death. I'm grateful for that." By now I was crying again, but these were sobless tears and my face was calm.

I told him all about Billy, everything I remembered as far back as my child's mind would reach. How I grew up without a mother. I recalled my adulation, hopes and fears, my elation at praise, the pits of gloom Billy's criticism exiled me to. Suddenly I was telling Akktri things forgotten for decades, stories and incidents and impressions, and the shape of the fat dimpled hands of my favorite baby doll.

I said all this and Akktri listened. He slowed, then stopped his eating. He watched me dab my eyes, blow my nose. When I had finished and was quiet, he picked up the lobster tail and sucked between its joints.

"Is it okay?" I asked desperately.

Akktri blinked. "Sure, Beverlee," he said with a tiny shrug that echoed one of mine. "Why isn't it okay?"

"Never mind," I said, aware of the huge relief inside myself. He had no idea of what was consuming me. He just wanted me to be at peace with him. As I watched him with his lobster, I realized that my loyalty to Akktri transcended all others. He deserved that and more.

I thought about calling Mack to tell him about my journey to Billy's death spot, but didn't want to hear my brother smoke-screening his pain with superficialities. I wanted to grieve.

So I ate guck and mourned.

"I'm only good for hurting people," I said to Akktri after a few tasteless bites.

"No," he said immediately, the lobster's big hand claw in his hands. "You fix Iris. You fix Akk-k-k-tri."

"I do?"

"Sure you do." Akktri bent the thumb claw back until it cracked free, his quick tongue scooping out the meat. "Iris is art now. I have lobster. Things is okay. Maybe we together fix Diana."

"Thank you, partner," I said from my heart.

"For what, Beverlee?" asked Akktri.

I'd burned my bridges with Charles who, though great for pleasure and restoring the ego, was young, callow, and a criminal. I was suddenly, profoundly scared.

Perched on my kitchen counter, my oddly cheerful partner watched me eat. "All is finished," he said. "Except Diana. She is balanced if she is dead."

I swallowed cold coffee. "What do you mean?"

"Diana's life begins years past." He held up his left hand. "She fights Iris. She moves to Guillermo." His hand slid across air. "Guillermo ends." Akktri grinned toothily, proudly. "Diana is not fighting Iris." He lifted his right hand, held it apart from his left as if holding Diana's soul in the space between. "If Diana ends then"——he brought his hands together, fitting finger to finger, claw to claw——"her life completes its pattern. Now"——he shrugged——"now rug reweaves itself. Now she must make art in her life again."

"She's a palimpsest." I set down my coffee cup and moved to the couch. "Written on, now erased, and rewritten."

"Past never erases," clucked Akktri. He made waves with his hands. "You never erase Billy. You never erase Chuck-k-k. You never erase little Akktri."

Hours before, we had returned from the Basement, and I had been afraid of my Phner companion. It came to me now that the idea of not trusting him was absurd. I might as well doubt my left hand. I flexed the fingers, wondering if Diana would make the journey that I had made across Boston Harbor, whether she would stand before the Targive portal and ask them to restore what had been cut from her. What price would the Targives demand? And was she prepared to pay it?

"It's okay, buddy," I said after a moment. "You and me, that is. We're okay again."

"I know it's okay," Akktri replied affectionately. "You and me is us. We is us."

"A while ago," I said, almost stuttering, "I doubted that we was us." Shame wrenched the words from me. "I'm sorry for that."

Akktri's whiskers twitched. "Beverlee, we is *always* us."

"Truly, Akktri the Phner?"

"Truly, Beverlee O'Meara. We is *always* okay."

I was overwhelmed with gratitude. Who was I to hold the responsibility of being so completely trusted? What angel had arranged this luck for me?

I was joyful and contented. And very tired.

I yawned, leaden with fatigue. My eyes were heavy and I laid myself down, tucking my hands under my head. "Finally," I sighed in peaceful satisfaction.

And the last thing I remembered was my thick woolen blanket being gently drawn over my shoulder and a chipmunk voice saying, "Go to sleep, my Beverlee."